I0533923

NEW ROME RISES

# DUX IMPERATORIUS
# BY
# BRIAN BAILIE, JR.

**WOLF PAW MEDIA**

Boulder, Colorado - Orlando, Florida

Wolf Paw Media
3415 W. Lake Mary Blvd. #950879
Lake Mary, Florida 32795, USA
wolfpawmedia.com

The characters and events in this book, living and dead, are works of fiction. Any similarity to real persons, living or dead, is not intended by the author and is coincidence.

Cover art based upon concept by the author.

ISBN: 978-0-9835952-0-5

# PROLOGUE

In the mid 21$^{st}$ century, Europe had become wrought with turmoil; by design, a new empire rose from the unrest, one fueled by hatred and greed. The Vasekts, who began as a terrorist organization in Turkey, had flourished to the point they were building a new empire, based in their own ultra-strict law. The Vasekts had a grip on the bulk of the Middle East, and craved more. They were relentless and spread across the map with such rapidity, that by the time the world realized what was happening, they were too formidable to stop.

Because of Vasekt suicide bombings, economic stability and national security had collapsed in several European nations, of which Italy bore the brunt of the assaults. Italy was targeted because it was teetering on the edge of the abyss due to a banking crisis bail out by the government that had ruined their credit rating. Austerity measures were put in place, which were rejected by the Italian public, resulting in strikes and riots. A general state of confusion and near anarchy made the invasion of Italy relatively easy for the Vasekts. The troops used Tunisia as a launching point to invade Europe, flowing into Italy with brutal effect. The southern part of the peninsula, from Naples to Ragusa, had fallen under Vasekts control. Next they set their sights on the other half of Italy. The Vasekts main weapon of choice was rudimentary and almost impossible to guard against: fire. Homes, businesses, churches, and forest were all easy targets for pyro-terrorism. They used gas bombs, torches, and even stolen forestry trucks designed to ignite controlled burns.

The arid climate of southern Italy provided perfect conditions for the fires. The blazes flashed across the landscape, devouring everything they could consume. Onlookers were horrified, fifty foot tongues of crimson flames leapt from cypress trees onto rooftops and spilled onto to the dry brush below. It appeared to those who observed it as if the end-times had come. Voices could be heard crying out in agony, certain of their own impending death. Children who survived wandered the streets shrieking for their parents, while parents sobbed over lost children. Giant walls were constructed to place pictures of the dead, so the countless bodies could be identified. Entire towns were destroyed, leaving those who survived homeless and downtrodden. Thousands who fled were incinerated in their cars, unable to outrun the inferno behind them. Daily life in Italy began to change by attrition, the mood ranged from anger to depression, and most Italians had developed a complete lack of faith in their government; the nation began to descend into anarchy.

The final collapse took place after the President, Prime Minister, and members comprising the Council of Ministries were all killed in a mass suicide bombing. Vasekt agents infiltrated the Carabinieri, the Law Enforcement branch responsible for guarding the government, using stolen uniforms and forged identification. When parliament had assembled in the Palazzo Montecitorio, a stolen truck from a parcel service was allowed to park outside the hallowed Old-World building. Another pulled within a block of the Palazzo del Quirinale, where the President was meeting with the Prime Minister. Another was allowed to park next to the Palazzo Madama, with most of the Senate gathered inside. A fourth and final truck parked behind the Palazzo Chigi. Inside each of the trucks were boxes filled with over three hundred pounds of C-4, triggered to detonate remotely by cell phone. The buildings, which had stood since the fourteenth and fifteenth centuries, were instantly disintegrated and most of those inside the buildings were vaporized. The Vasekts had created a pivotal moment- chaos, which they believed, would allow them to seize control of Italy. The Vasekts could not have known their plans would be thwarted in a way they never conceived; by their own actions, they had created the instrument of their demise.

The vacuum left by the loss of a central government and articulate leadership was quickly filled by a young charismatic general, Giovanni Caprera. His magnetism was undeniable; it was said those in a room with him felt as if they were drawn to him. His rugged good looks were capped by a shock of raven hair. He was an imposing figure at 6'3 and his dark eyes burned with ambition. Caprera could be both disarming and terrifying in the same moment, a quality that garnered him both respect and fear. He had become the highest remaining government official by default. Days before the attacks, Caprera had been a Colonel who was critical of the government's treatment of the attacks as a criminal action and not a military one. Caprera's history was intertwined with the Vasekts. Caprera's father had been the Italian Ambassador to Turkey, and assassinated by the Vasekts. Caprera received the news while he was attending the Virginia Military Institute. His younger brother, Roberto, living with his Mother and Father in Turkey at the time, was abducted by the Vasekts. After Roberto was released, he shocked his brother and willingly chose to stay behind and become a Vasekt. He had been brainwashed while in captivity, groomed to be a propaganda tool.

Caprera's hatred for the Vasekts was deeply ingrained in his soul due to the killing of his father. He hated his brother more than the Vasekts for joining those who murdered his father. When he returned to Italy he enrolled in the army and became a member of the elite Alpini. He displayed courage and honor repeatedly, while his knowledge of military tactics facilitated his rise to power. He became admired among both his peers and superiors due to his record, which elaborated on his neutralization of Vasekt high value targets.

Caprera was a tactical warfare genius, who mobilized the military quickly into action; martial law was declared and order was restored. Forces from the North were ordered to engage the enemy head on in the South. None remained behind. Bloody Skirmishes took place with the Vasekt forces that were flowing into Italy at the rate of ten thousand troops a day. The enemy numbers continued to rise until there were nearly eight-hundred thousand Vasekt forces in Italy. Caprera knew they were badly outnumbered, and reached out to a mercenary army, Credential Bond, to bolster his numbers. They were mostly made up of South African, Russian and Ukrainian forces. A promise of billions of dollars was given to them, plus Roman citizenship to the generals who were victorious in battle. Next

Caprera recruited anyone who could fight women, teenagers, and even senior citizens.

Caprera knew they were perilously low on supplies, so he improvised; guerilla warfare would be utilized, the cities and countryside were scavenged in the march south, and makeshift weapons fashioned. He also knew that he needed more, his numbers were not large enough to defeat the Vasekts alone; so fear would become a weapon as well. The rallying point to launch the attack was just north of Aprilia. Caprera spoke to the gathered troops about the glory of their homeland; he spoke of the Battle of Agrigentum, where the Romans first rose to a world power. His zeal for the story roused his troops' appetite for battle to feverish levels.

The Italian army had risen to its full force under Caprera in South Italy. They were transformed; the assault was swift and deadly, with vicious success, leaving no enemy survivors. Torture was used to both gain information and intimidate the Vasekts. Small Vasekt patrols when captured would be subjected to the same treatment, leaving one or two survivors to return and spread the word about the Italians.

Caprera was as ruthless with his own troops. Deserters in the Italian forces were shot on sight, no trial, no second chances. Soldiers who were afraid to advance against the enemy were made an example of by being beaten with a wood cane in front of their comrades. Through his actions, Caprera had managed to hold a fractured and precarious military together, turning them into a force that filled the Vasekts with dread. The Italians propelled forward, leaving a trail of carnage and anxiety behind them.

The Italian Forces gained the upper hand in the battle of Salerno. The city was a mix of buildings from the Roman Empire, Byzantine, Medieval, and Renaissance. It had stood since the Etruscans ruled the area, and had seen battles before, but none like this. The docile town was transformed into a hot zone. Vasekts bodies piled waist high and blocked doorways preventing the escape of the citizens trapped in their homes and businesses. General Caprera was a student of ancient warfare, be it Roman, Macedonian or Viking; it was this knowledge that made him a formidable foe. He used that knowledge to the bewilderment of the Vasekts by creating his version of boiling oil. There had been some modern construction in the town, but for the most part the streets were old and cramped. The Vasekts were drawn into the narrow, steep, thousand-year-old roadways. Caprera exploited the Vasekts position by using vats of Napalm B. The giant vats made from dumpsters were poured from rooftops into the streets, quickly inflicting damage on the enemy. Clusters of Vasekts troops dropped to the ground shrieking in agony as the napalm rushed against them, and clung to their skin at a searing fourteen-hundred seventy-two degrees Fahrenheit. Upon seeing the effect of the unorthodox weapon, the Italian troops roared jubilantly and engaged their enemy. In a little over five hours the Vasekt army had been driven into the Mediterranean Sea, many had jumped in and drown in a vain attempt to get the Napalm off their skin. When the battle was done the Vasekt Crescent-Sword flags were pulled down and burned along with their dead, it was in that moment a world power was reborn.

Italy was criticized by the United Nations for the use of an outlawed substance in warfare; Caprera ignored the critics, and instead basked in the declarations of his genius. His international acclaim was outpacing the concerns over his methods; he had become the toast of Europe. His people looked upon him as a savior.

Caprera next turned his focus to reconstructing the nation, as he was its undisputed leader. He had been a great admirer of the Roman Empire since childhood. He had dreamed of a new Roman Empire, restoring its glory and of being its emperor. The chance to become Emperor was no longer a phantom, but a tangible reality for Caprera. The gods, he believed, had chosen him to restore the glory of Rome. At only thirty-two years old, he had unlimited power.

The people of Italy were poor, frightened and weary; they were ready to accept any leader who could quell the bedlam of the past year. They blindly threw themselves at Caprera's feet, accepting his totalitarian rule; it brought a serenity that allowed people to sleep soundly at night, without fear of awaking to chaos the next morning. The price for peace was certainly worth losing some of their personal freedoms. There was some resistance from certain segments of society. They were quickly imprisoned or executed.

Among the international intelligence agencies, rumors began to circulate that Caprera was building a government modeled after the Roman Empire. Highly secretive "transition teams" toiled for weeks on the new government, orchestrated by Charles Fletcher, the US ambassador to Italy and one of the few surviving government officials in Rome after the bombing. Caprera had sought out Fletcher because of his genius to help craft the new government. Fletcher agreed, resigning his post as ambassador.

Caprera began only making statements through a press secretary; he was not seen in public for weeks. Speculation grew as to what Caprera was planning and the adoring citizens began to gather outside his home, holding a vigil until he gave them more instruction. The press secretary soon announced a press conference regarding the future of the nation was soon to be held by Caprera. Finally, the announcement was made at the Roman Forum, hundreds of representatives from the press had gathered as if the word was coming directly from Heaven. Caprera came out of a bus parked not far away and strolled to the podium wearing a full Roman military uniform including an ornate gold breastplate. He stood there and announced that Italy would be disbanded, and the Roman Empire resurrected. He was to be given the title Dux Imperatorius. The Roman Troops marched out in their new dress uniforms, which were inspired by those of Rome's past. With a fanfare from trumpeters a giant flag was unfurled across the giant ionic columns of the Temple of Antonius and Faustina. The flag was crimson with a depiction of Romulus and Remus nursing from a she-wolf in black, underneath were the letters SPQR in gold. The citizens of the New Roman Empire erupted with applause of approval at their new flag.

Charles Fletcher, who had accepted the title Praetorian Prefecture, came to the podium after the debut of the new flag and proceeded to disseminate to the press how the new government was to be structured. There would two branches that would encompass the central government, Emperor and Senate. There would also be an "elite" class based on each citizen's individual accomplishments for the glory of Rome, referred to as the Equestrian Class; the rest would be Plebeians.

The gathered press was stunned, they had heard rumors from various sources, but no one believed them to be true. The President of the United States was woken by the Secret Service to be briefed. As international television audiences watched they called, emailed, or sent text messages, temporarily bogging down the world's communication systems. The British Prime-Minister was whisked to Buckingham Palace for a meeting with the King. The U.N. called an emergency meeting of the Security Council to determine if a member could become a new nation and institute a new system of government. The Roman Empire had returned, and whether the international community liked it or not, Rome sought no approval to do so.

On January 9th, one year after his ascension to power, Caprera was crowned Emperor in front of the Column of Marcus Aurelius and presented to the world as "Giovanni Caprera Augustus". The date was to re-establish the Festival of Janus, and to be used for all new emperors to be crowned with a golden laurel wreath.

Caprera's first official order as Emperor was to have all Vasekt prisoners crucified on reusable titanium crosses, and left to hang for fourteen days in public as an example to Rome's enemies that to confront Rome was to court destruction. Caprera took breakfast in front of thirty Vasekts who were slowly dying from crucifixion. He sat coolly, eating prima colazione and sipping cappuccino. Horrified members of the press were allowed to cover the abomination. The world found the crucifixions to be an atrocity, but the Roman people loved Caprera for exacting revenge.

New economic stimulus packages were enacted; incentives were put forward for foreign investment in Rome. Unemployment dropped from a high of 39% to just 5%. Caprera's solution for poverty and debt was simple; plebeians that were in debt could have it relieved by entering into "servitude", the politically correct name for slavery. The concept of servitude was that a wealthy family or company could buy a person's "debt" and based on a formula for years to Lira. Some "servants" were bought with no hope of working enough years to have their freedom again. With cheap labor available, and a military buildup underway, Rome became the fourth strongest economy in the world within eighteen months of its rebirth.

Rome also became a cultural giant, designers in Rome, were "asked" to produce fashions that were inspired by Roman antiquity. Updated versions of the stola and palla, and the toga were seen adorning models on the catwalks all over Europe. Caprera's own design was a hit, a combination of the suit and the toga, which bore his name. The top consisted of a jacket and tie and the bottom from the toga. A sash from the toga was draped across the chest, and worn with sandals. Classic Roman architecture was the rage not only in Rome, but also across Europe.

Caprera believed the fall of the first empire was due to Christianity and believed a national religion should be established. The new religion would be simple and honor the gods of antiquity whom he worshiped. Churches around the city were turned into temples honoring Jupiter, Juno, Venus, Mars, Bacchus, Diana, and others. The Vatican protested, to no avail, they were warned to be silent if they wished to remain in existence. Caprera knew that world opinion would be against Rome if the Pope was expelled or harmed, so he let the Vatican continue to stand.

Rome next turned its sights to her neighbors. France, Spain and the United Kingdom were all under assault by the Vasekts and, like Italy, all were on the verge of collapse. Rome offered its neighbors assistance, if a "Governor" would be appointed to the country, giving Rome de-facto rule over the government. France and Spain agreed almost immediately, Great Britain declined; the King issued a statement that "One boot on the throat of England is not more appealing than another just because it is offered in the guise of friendship." The British Prime Minster went to Rome to meet with Caprera; he told him that England would seek to oppose Rome at the U.N. if they continued to pressure them. Caprera was furious at the United Kingdom's refusal of his offer; he believed he could save England, if they would just bow to him.

The Vasekts were driven from France in six months and from Spain in ten, the defeated suffered the same fate as their predecessors did in Rome. In Paris and Barcelona the streets were lined with crosses, decomposing bodies dangling from them.

Financial markets surged with Europe's new stability, the Dax, F.T. 100 and Dow all hit new highs. Investment Bankers were all too eager to fund new technological projects in Rome. However, some warned that the stability was frail, and the newfound peace even weaker.

Rome also returned to its former glory with new feats of Vitruvian like engineering, buildings with the familiar Doric columns and new lighter stronger materials, Venice was saved from sinking with new floating foundations placed under the originals. Caprera also had a vision Rome would be the world's top tourist destination, and it needed a symbol, like the Eiffel Tower or the Statue of Liberty. A giant palace was constructed on the former sight of Nero's Circus; it was eight stories, complete with a throne room and underground bunker, with reinforced four foot thick concrete walls. He contracted great artists from around the world to create frescos and sculptures for the palace. The outside was adorned with a giant frieze on each floor portraying a great moment from Rome's history. The inside was just as breathtaking as the outside. From the Louvre he had plundered great works of art : a sculpture of Aphrodite ("Venus Genitrix"), Diana of Versailles, Apollo of the Kassel, Borghese Gladiator, sculptures of Emperor Hadrian and his wife Sabina as Mars and Venus . A sixty-foot marble statue portraying Caprera as Jupiter was erected next to the temple honoring the Roman god of the same name.

Despite Rome's many accomplishments, there was great concern among many in the world. The United States, United Kingdom, and Germany were the vanguard of the opposition to Rome's practices. Diplomats were recalled in protest to the new Roman paradigm. Human rights violations, suppression of a free press, and invasion of weaker nations for their "protection" were the main complaints of the Allied countries. The complaints fell on deaf ears at the United Nations and the European Union; Europe's economic boom ensured no sanctions would be leveled against them.

When the United Kingdom suffered a new rash of Vasekt attacks, Caprera seized on the opportunity. Rome invaded the United Kingdom claiming it had to "rescue" it from its attackers. British troops clashed with Roman troops, both clashed with Vasekts. In the end, the British were no match for the advanced Roman technology. The Romans had ornate tanks called "Gilded Screamers" fitted with altered Long Range Acoustic Devices (or LRAD) and Light Emitting Diodes (LED) incapacitator weapons to be deadly and devastating. Gilded Screamers were designed to be intimidating; ornate patterns adorned the heavily armored vehicles; which each were equipped with a 30mm machine gun. A fifteen-foot hydraulic arm would rise out of the screamers, on the end was a bronze sculpture of Mars's face with the LED set in the eyes and the LRAD in the mouth. Soldiers that were in the device's path would become deaf and suffer severe palpitations from the LRAD weapon while the LED would cause temporarily blindness and vomiting. The next wave of Romans would swoop in with stacked projectile rifles (SPR) and slaughter scores of helpless soldiers, still dazed from the screamers.

Emperor Caprera sent his own elite Praetorian Guard Units to aide in the overthrow of the British government. Vasekt troops from London to Glasgow were rounded up, and as before, crucified. When all the members of the Royal Family were killed in "Vasekt attacks" he placed his sister, Julia, on the throne as a "gesture of goodwill". Those who were in the line of succession to the throne continued dying in mysterious accidents, or "suicides". Parliament was disbanded and some members imprisoned. No Governor was to be appointed to the United Kingdom since Caprera had control through Julia.

With the majority of Europe under its control, Rome focused on the Middle East and North Africa, laying waste to the Vasekts and destroying everything in their wake. Rome was stopped only when they reached Israel, who drove back the Romans and gave them their first defeat. It was a blow to Roman prestige and its perception of invincibility. Their reputation was further damaged by United States forces in Germany. Rome had amassed troops at the French border with Germany for an invasion. The United States sent troops to support the German forces and thwart the assault.

Caprera, in response, had used a chemical attack on U.S. troops killing tens of thousands. A young Colonel, George Vernon, abruptly found himself in charge of all forces in the region when communications were severed with the Pentagon due to Roman attacks on communication satellites. Vernon was loved by his troops, and he was known for being virtuous and fair. He had already lead "Operation Aqueduct", an assault that claimed several Roman divisions and two of their generals, so he was not without experience. Vernon, in accordance with orders should he assume command, was given free rein to "act with impunity" and took back part of France, before both sarin gas and anthrax were used on the U.S. forces. The losses were staggering - twenty thousand American troops killed, another nine thousand wounded. Alex Wright, a Major in the U.S. Army, foresaw the uncharacteristic Roman retreat into France as a warning sign and ordered his troops to retreat. With severed communications his warning to Colonel Vernon arrived too late to save the other troops.

In the months that followed the atrocity in France, Americans grew weary of conflict. The theme of the Presidential election the following year was peace with Rome. The concept of aggressive diplomacy was ultimately the deciding issue in who took the Oval Office. A new administration was elected and troops were rapidly removed from Europe. Vernon resigned from the Army in protest of the new policy after pleading with the President to reconsider his position.

Caprera saw the change in Washington as an opportunity, and a sign of weakness. During the campaign the President had stated that he would speak without pre-conditions to Caprera and would "pursue a peaceful resolution to our differences". One year after the battle in France, the United States drafted and signed a non-aggression pact with Rome. The signing took place in Oslo. During the press conference with the President, Caprera smiled like a jackal that had found wounded prey. His thirst for conquest had grown with each new day; the U.S was still the biggest threat to Rome. He would neutralize that threat. While the President received Nobel Peace Prize nominations, the Romans readied their forces for a full-scale invasion.

CIA operations had been scaled back in the Mediterranean in fear of violating the pact, so very little intelligence made its way to Washington. America had been lulled to sleep by hollow promises of newfound friendship with Rome, and was about to be awakened by the repercussions of their naiveté.

On the night of May 5th, using a technique copied from the Vasekts, Roman agents lit massive fires in California, Oregon, Utah, and Colorado. National Guard units from surrounding states were deployed to assist in suppression of the raging forest fires. The Romans were confident the Americans were oblivious to their plans, so they launched the offensive.

On the night of May 12th, the Romans launched an invasion of North Mexico, Arizona, New Mexico, and Western Texas. They came in stealth air transports, invisible to N.O.R.A.D. The Mexicans fell almost immediately, giving the Romans a base of operations to stream into the Southwest. The National Guard units that remained in the accosted states were too thin to push back the Roman's massive assault. Simultaneously on the opposite side of the country they seized Charleston, South Carolina and Wilmington, North Carolina by submarine attack, giving them a foothold in the east. The Pentagon had not constructed any contingency plans to deal with a Roman invasion, having employed the administration's new philosophy. Disjointed attempts to repel Roman advances were futile and tragic.

The administration was disgraced, and quickly lost the support of the American people. With the realization that new leadership was needed, the President, Vice President, Secretary of State and Secretary of Defense all resigned in shame. In his last act, the president appointed the leading candidate in the upcoming presidential election, Senator John Braintree, as Vice-President. Congress convened at 2:00am the following morning in an emergency session to swear in the new resident. Bleary-eyed, the members of the House and Senate watched as Braintree was sworn in as the new President of the United States; the atmosphere of desperation in the room was palpable and had manifested itself in the person of Senator Harold Reynolds from Nevada, who had a complete breakdown during the ceremony and alternated between hysterical laughter and panicked screams. Calm was only restored when the President invoked the name of George Vernon in defense of the nation. Vernon was offered the position of five Star General if he would return. Vernon agreed and recruited Alex Wright as his first general. There were some in Congress who had been in contact with Rome and had been promised prominent positions if Rome defeated the United States, while intentionally delaying what was to have been fast-tracked approval of essential cabinet nominees.

The invasion of the U.S. had not broken the American spirit, as Emperor Caprera had predicted; it had done the opposite. The American people had proven that their legendary pluck was still intact. The creativity, ingenuity and generosity they exhibited on a daily basis had enraged the Emperor. The American pastimes continued as a signal to the world. They would not submit. Teams located in occupied territory from all professional sports continued to play in host cities. Coaches and players, who had risked their lives to escape, did so that fabric of American life would not unravel. Refugees were taken into stranger's homes as if they were family members. Those displaced by the invasion did not sit and wait for the war to end to return home; they were determined to contribute. Record numbers of sign-ups for the military were recorded; aid organizations happily had more applicants than they could process. Before the invasion, Americans were splintered on the war with the Romans, but afterwards they forged a unity against a common enemy not seen since the Second World War.

# CHAPTER I

August 27ᵗʰ, four years before the Romans invade the United States….

The night air was cool for New Mexico, just before sundown it had been ninety degrees and four hours later it had dropped to sixty-five, as it was not apt to do in late August. An army of crickets kept up their relentless serenade, at times becoming, almost ear splitting. In the distance, a thunderstorm flashed an incandescent bolt, revealing rain streaming from the base of the cloud, appearing like a giant gray jellyfish dragging its tentacles across the desert horizon. The sound of thunder reverberated through the mesas, announcing the storm's looming arrival.

Two riders sat silently, hidden in the dark, their horses restless and wanting to run. The radiant lights from the refinery shone in the distance, while the full moon above faintly lit the orange rocks of the mesa where the two figures were positioned. It was an unusual night, but one the two riders had been waiting for patiently. Despite the storm, there was more than enough light to pull off the job.

One of the two jumped from his horse and walked to the edge of the rocky hill. He crouched down and looked closely at the ground making sure that there was a clear path for the horses to run. His eyes followed the path to the bottom of the mesa where a set of railroad tracks ran next to an old service road. The service road, which had not been used in over a decade, had fallen into a state of acute disrepair. The road was over-run with jagged cracks, filled with sagebrush that had pushed through to the surface. Large portions of the road were so cracked that it was nothing more than a collection of asphalt chunks and red dirt. Never was a road less fit for use than the old service road was, yet it remained central to the two rider's plans.

The mastermind behind the scheme was William West, number four on the FBI's most wanted list for his numerous and spectacular heists. William had proven his genius again and again, never having been caught in any robbery he orchestrated. His fame grew with each of his exploits, something he did not shy away from, but gleefully encouraged. His reputation with a gun made him seem dangerous, yet he never took another's life during a job. He had become a folk hero at a young age.

William was dressed- as one would expect a cowboy to dress- black Stetson hat, denim shirt, and a brown barn jacket with a wool collar. His features and demeanor were less of a cowboy and looked more like that of a surfer. William had a mop of sandy blond hair, wide, light blue eyes, and a lanky frame. No matter what the situation, William always maintained a laid-back attitude no matter if the circumstances were pleasant or dire. Although he always remained cool, his skill for planning a robbery was second to none.

The robbery William had planned was undoubtedly his biggest. The Roman Empire's grip on Europe had created an energy shortage across the globe and was sharply felt in the United States. Dozens of companies were all too willing to pay above the market rate to obtain crude oil, and not ask where or how it was obtained. Stealing crude oil was the goal of William's plan, and as usual, he wanted to do it in his signature style. William's accomplices were no strangers to his sensational heists, having had been with him on prior jobs, they were his partner Roost Roberts, his wife Cassidy, and their "Boulder" Gang. They were dubbed the Boulder Gang by the media after they pulled a bold hold up of a bank, receiving an armored car delivery in Downtown Boulder during broad daylight. Not one shot was fired by the gang through the entirety of the robbery. They repeated the same feat in Denver and in Phoenix. They also had stolen priceless works of art from some of the biggest mansions and galleries in the West.

It was an arduous task William had undertaken, to bring the plan to fruition. William had taken weeks to prepare for each step of the way. He grew a beard to hide his identity, all the while studying everything he could on refineries so that he could produce the proper resume. While working as a pump system operator he had learned the intricacies of the refinery, including the train schedules. The plan was clear once he was working among the steel pipes and smokestacks of the refinery: rob a tanker car full of oil and sell it to the highest bidder. William had spent countless hours studying and building train couplings, and after months of practice he could disconnect one with ease. As was the case with all of the jobs he had pulled, William was as thorough as he was daring. He left nothing to chance; every possible scenario had a contingency plan. There were no radio frequency identification readers for five miles, so the train dispatch would never miss a car. In less than five minutes, a train hauling light sweet crude would be heading to the Socorro Refinery, six miles down the tracks. When the train reached an exact point, the two riders would descend upon it. It was William's meticulous planning that allowed him to remain at large, never having been in danger of being caught. Even if there was an ambush, he knew exactly where the escape routes were, and when to use them.

Like William, Roost was a planner; he also shared the same desire to never fire a weapon during a heist. Roost felt that William was a kindred spirit the way he pulled off a job with precision, never having to fire a weapon; that was the way Roost wanted to do things. The thrill was the driving force for both of them. At the age of sixteen Roost had found himself involved in a liquor store hold up. His partner on the job shot the helpless owner, who was just a little old man trying to protect his business. After that, Roost decided he would never take part in a heist where someone would get hurt. He would be more than just a common criminal robbing convenience stores at three in the morning.

William was impressed that Roost had successfully tracked him down, when the FBI, ATF and numerous state law enforcement agencies had failed to find him. Even though Roost was two years older than William, the respect was completely mutual. They became the best of friends and along with Cassidy, a very successful trio. Roost was level headed, resourceful, and held a degree in criminology from the University of Wyoming. He had used the knowledge he gained to become a great thief. Roost, like William, also loved the challenge of stealing things that were considered unobtainable. A heist like the one they were about to undertake was the reason Roost chose to be an outlaw. Roost kept a rugged cowboy exterior, having been called a pretty-boy enough times growing up. He tried to hide his high cheekbones with a thick blonde mustache to detract from them. He had dark blue eyes and thick blonde hair that he wore parted to the side. He was told he could have been a model if he wanted to, but Roost despised the idea of such things.

A growing pinpoint of light in the distance signaled that the freight train was on its way. Roost gave a sharp whistle to alert William of the approaching train. William reached into his coat pocket and fished out the pre-paid cell phone he had purchased a few hours earlier. William never purchased a phone too far in advance, using cash so the phone would be untraceable. He quickly called Cassidy, and then his gang who were awaiting his arrival. He spoke in a quick hushed voice, "It's a go Cass, see you soon honey."

The black insulated tanker cars connected to the train were made by the Tomex Corporation. Each one of the tanker cars could hold up to thirty-three thousand gallons of crude. The ramshackle truck and dented tanker trailer obtained by William had a fifteen-thousand gallon capacity. William knew the exact specifications on every vehicle, tanker and instrument involved in the job.

If the Boulder Gang was successful, this would be the first train robbery of any kind pulled off in the United States in well over one-hundred years. William went back and remounted his chestnut mustang that had a small white star on his forehead. He glanced over to Roost and nodded with a wry smile, cocksure of his plan. The two then took off their Stetsons and put on a pair of night vision glasses. They swung their horses around and perched on the side of the mesa, leaning forward like jockeys in the starting gate at a racetrack. The train lumbered down the tracks, rolling ever forward, shaking the ground as it went. The horn grew louder each time it blew, until it finally came into view.

The duo turned their heads away from the train's headlamp as it passed, so as not to be blinded with the night vision glasses on. Once the engine had gone by, William spun around to see if they had been sighted by the engineer. The engineer, a husky man with a long grey beard hung out the window, focused on where he was going. He had not seen William or Roost.

"Let's rob a train!" William shouted gleefully as Roost let out an exuberant "Yah!" and the two horses broke into full gallop and raced down the hill towards the steel tanker cars glinting under the moonlight.

The two riders raced along side of the train, matching their speed with that of the last tanker car. It was black and the sides were covered with graffiti. Two of the rungs on the ladder towards the top were bent down to a point, like something sizeable had fallen against them. William was disoriented by the night vision, but still could make out all the points on the car he had so thoroughly studied. The heavy breathing of the mustangs, and the thundering of the hooves mixed with the clacking of the wheels on the track, made it problematic for William and Roost to hear each other, even when they shouted. William signaled his intent to board the train to Roost. William let go of the reigns and his horse, who continued to run at the same pace. William jumped from his horse to the ladder on the tanker car. William's horse continued to run alongside the train.

"Get! Go home Slingshot!" he yelled at the mustang. The horse obeyed and veered away from the train.

William quickly waved his hand signaling Roost to throw him his tool bag. Roost moved in as close as he could without colliding with the train, and with a wide wind up motion flung the worn canvas duffle bag to William. Seeing the bag hurtling towards him, William stretched as far as he could off the ladder so that only one foot and one hand were touching. He caught the bag with one hand, and immediately had trouble grasping the handle; he felt it start to slip off the end of his fingertips. He yanked up as hard as he could, tossing the bag into the air in front of him. It hung motionless for a fraction of a second, at which time he swiped it with his hand grasping it tightly he pulled against his torso and exhaled a sigh of relief.

William reached into his bag and pulled out a screwdriver and a socket wrench. He then proceeded up the ladder, tying off the bag to its top. He then shimmied on his stomach, his arms and legs prostrate on either side for balance, to the front of the car; he steadied himself and sat up, bringing both legs together, outstretched in front of him. He waited a moment, knowing there was not much time and then summoned the courage to slide down the rounded front of the car, his feat landing on the narrow platform at the bottom.

Quickly, he laid flat on the platform and dangled over the edge where he could reach the coupling. Because the release pin on the coupling would not unlock under tension, William had to disassemble it. He glanced down at the tracks passing underneath for a moment, almost mesmerized by the constant pattern and repetitive clacking of wheels on the tracks. William refocused and began working on separating the car from the rest of the train. Because of his obsessive practicing, he was able to disassemble the coupling in less than a minute. He chuckled at how well events had gone to that point; he hoped the rest of the plan would be as uneventful.

There was a violent clunking noise as the coupling ricocheted against the train and disappeared, skipping underneath the car. William pulled himself upright and prepared for the next phase of the plan. The car began to slow to a coast, as the rest of the train pulled away.

"Now Cass!" William shouted into his cell phone. Seconds later, Cassidy swung the tractor-trailer onto the old service road. The truck roared as she gunned the engine and downshifted to pull even with the tanker car. The semi and tanker car had been painted flat black and camouflaged perfectly with the darkness. Cassidy jumped out of the truck and removed her night vision glasses to reveal her electric green eyes. She had driven with the truck headlights off so they would be invisible to the police helicopters that were sure to come. Roost was amazed at how someone five feet tall, one-hundred and ten pounds, could drive an eighteen-wheeler with such skill. He also could not figure out how she managed to stay so together, and not look disheveled, even in job like the one they were undertaking. Cassidy's short blonde hair reached the back of her neck; just below her hairline was tattooed in cursive "Let the World Slip" a phrase from The Taming of the Shrew. On her left forearm extending from her elbow to her hand was tattooed "Sentence first, verdict afterwards". a quote taken from Alice in Wonderland. On her right arm just above the elbow was a small butterfly, yet the tattoos did not make her seem coarse. She seemed frail and dainty despite her confident demeanor.

"Howdy Cowboy!" she said to William giving him a quick peck before getting to work. When she smiled at Roost and winked he thought to himself how lucky William was to have her. Roost dismounted and ran to help her unload six fuel transfer pumps. Cassidy scampered up the side of the tanker car and caught the hoses that Roost tossed up to her and she quickly slid them into the tank. She was wearing black jeans and a black t-shirt and it seemed to Roost as if she disappeared against the black tanker trailer. He then looked over to William who nodded to signal his readiness. He cranked open the lid of the tank car with an ear splitting creak, and caught the hoses Roost tossed which were connected to the intake valves. The pumps started with a harmonious hum as Roost cranked them to life and the transfer of oil from one car to the other began.

William looked up to see the train still moving in the distance. He knew the missing car would not be discovered until the train reached the refinery, which would not be long. Cassidy put on her glasses to see how much oil had been transferred; she peered into the tank to see the shimmering liquid was nearly to the top.

"It's close enough to the top guys," she yelled. Roost waived his understanding and shut off the pump. He quickly ran to his horse, leaving the four pumps sitting in the dirt next to the road. He did not like leaving that much evidence, but he and Cassidy were wearing gloves and it would be hard to pull DNA evidence in the desert with a storm approaching. William, however, did not wear gloves since he never had been fingerprinted, but it was well known by law enforcement that they belonged to him. He had stolen the four fuel transfer pumps at a store some five hundred miles away. He had chosen the store's distant location so that no suspicion would arise from transfer pumps being stolen near a refinery.

Roost glanced back at William who was now getting into the passenger side of the truck with Cassidy.

"See you in Albuquerque. Will, don't do anything reckless," Roost shouted as he waved. He was not sure he would see his partners again; this was easily the biggest chance they had ever dared to take. Roost gave his horse a nudge and they galloped back up the mesa.

William looked up, the train had made it to the refinery; he estimated they had about a seven minute lead before the police would come for them, but that was not a certainty since just up the road the rain had begun to fall. The rain had been accounted for and was part of the contingency plan, four miles up the service road was a cut-off that followed a dirt road leading to a cave. Before they could reach the cave, they would have to cross an exceptionally deep and expansive ravine that was prone to flash flooding in a downpour. As daunting as a flash flood was, it was a welcome asset; it would wash away the tire tracks left by the truck, leaving authorities without any way to track them. They would only have moments to cross the ravine without getting stuck or washed away, and that was the unpredictable part that worried William.

Cassidy gunned the engine and then thrust the gear-shift forward. The truck growled and quickly rolled ahead, gaining momentum with every inch. Sagebrush whipped against the tires and grill of the truck as they sped down the road. William looked over at Cassidy, who gave him a smile. He was not as confident as she was in the situation. The cab seemed as if it was going to shake apart, and the tan headliner dangling in front of him did not do anything to make him feel better. He looked up at the discolored foam, which was revealed, struggling to remember if the truck was built in the Teens or the Nineties. William had managed to find the dilapidated old semi, and rebuild it at almost no cost, but at that moment he wished he'd spent more time tightening screws and bolts. Perhaps the plan was not thought through as well as it should have been, William thought to himself, and at that moment he was sure- it was manufactured in the 1990's.

Cassidy hit a pothole, jarring her and William. The jolt was so intense; William thought they might have been weightless for a moment, before gravity pulled them back down against the worn seats with scarce padding. There was another equally hard jolt, which caused the broken CB radio to drop off the ceiling. William wondered if they would even have a chance to get to the ravine. The road may blow their tires, or, he thought, the cab may simply shake apart before they get there.

William leaned out the window and looked behind them; he could now see two distant but distinct silver lights above the horizon. He recognized them right away as helicopters, and from experience he knew they had less than ten minutes to hide the truck. They were out of sensor range, but with each minute that passed, they were getting closer to being caught.

The condition of the road continued to deteriorate the closer they got to the ravine. The potholes were more frequent and deep where the road had been repeatedly washed out. Cassidy wrestled with the wheel in order to keep the big rig on the road, at the same time swerving from side to side trying to avoid potholes. Suddenly William gasped; they were hurtling toward a chained and padlocked chain link gate. Just the day before he and Roost had picked the lock and pulled the gate back in preparation for the heist.

"Slow down, Cass, I am going to have to pick the lock!" William yelled over the roaring engine. Cassidy glanced over at him with an impetuous grin, which William immediately interpreted, "OH NO, NO, NO!" he pleaded as he braced for impact. They lurched forward in their seats as they smashed into the gate. In a fraction of a second the gate flew out in front of them, bouncing end over end and then before Cassidy could swerve, the big rig ran over it. Cassidy looked at William.

"It's pulling to the right!"

William heard the unmistakable sound of metal scraping on asphalt; he looked in the side mirror to see a shower of sparks flying out from under the tank car. The gate had become ensnared on valves underneath the tanker car, dragging the gate with it.

"Well that's just great!" William shouted, slamming his hand into the dashboard.

William took off his Stetson and set it in front of him.

"Don't go anywhere," he said to Cassidy as he carefully opened the door to the cab and slowly leaned out reaching for the ladder mounted to the back of the tank.

William felt with his fingertips as he stretched out, not quite able to see around the cab. He grabbed the ladder with one hand and held his breath as he carefully let go of the side of the cab to bring the other hand around. As he did so the truck hit an immense pothole, everything was jarred again, including William. His feet slipped off the floorboard and he was sent careening around to the back of the cab; he grasped the ladder with his left arm. William quickly reached up with his right arm and grasped the wrung. He looked down at the road streaking by below his feet, his legs getting whipped by the razor sharp sagebrush as the truck hurtled down the road. Each time he was hit, his concentration was broken. William finally managed to pull himself up; he rested for just a moment, trying to let the adrenaline surging through his torso subside. He knew that if he did not remain calm, he would not think clearly. He also knew that if he failed to loosen the gate, the sparks showering the dry sagebrush would ignite it and the fumes from the oil, causing an explosion. The gate was caught on a valve at the bottom of the tank. Tumbleweeds and sagebrush became so thick on the fence it was almost camouflaged.  He climbed up the ladder and clinched the top of the tank. He edged his way out, hand over hand until he was over the gate.

William took quick glances, alternating between his hands and the fence. Suddenly, he saw that his fears were correct- the smoke rising from the brush on the fence indicated it was starting to burn. Although it was about to rain, there had not been any precipitation for nearly a month, and the brush was dead and dry. He lowered himself over the edge and, dangling from the side, kicked at the gate to no avail. He tightened his grip and redoubled his effort kicking harder, with no success. William looked down he could now see flames with the smoke, and knew that it would not take long for the flames to spread to the valves.

William hung there, trying to think as his fingers started to slip from the top of the tank. Suddenly, William realized what needed to be done; he took a deep breath and prepared himself for the next move. William lowered himself by letting one hand go from the tank, and then dipping his foot into an opening in the chain link, pulling upwards. He strained to move the fence, feeling his quadriceps going numb, his fingers burning as they slowly began to slide. There was barbed wire attached to the top of the gate, which became caught on the cuff of his jeans, and slowly started sawing into the top of his ankle. William realized he was trapped; suddenly, he became aware of a sharp popping noise and the gate slid loose.  The barbed wire sliced even deeper, taking William's shoe with it. He yelped in pain and pulled himself back on top of the tanker just in time to see the truck turning off the service road, onto the dirt path that lead to the ravine. The rain began to fall in a blinding downpour.  The drops stung William's exposed skin like thousands of bullets. He scurried across the slippery top to the front of the tanker and climbed down the ladder. He knocked on the back of the cab so that Cassidy could let him in. The door handle was too far for her to reach so she rolled down the window. "You have to go through the window!" Cassidy yelled at the top of her lungs. William crawled through the window, thankful not to be dangling off the tank car. He pivoted so that his feet hung out of the window, and his back was on the seat. He brought in one leg at a time, and sat up in the seat. He took a deep breath and shook his head in disbelief at what he had just done. Cassidy glanced over and let out a victorious "WHOOOOHOOOO!" and began to laugh. William gave a wry smile and joined his wife in laughing.

The laughter was short-lived because they soon came to the ravine that was beginning to fill with water. The sandstone walls on either side acted as giant reservoir, allowing the muddy water to rise quickly. The depth seemed to be only a few inches, but depth could be deceiving. William knew that Cassidy's instinct would be to plunge the truck headlong into the water, and emerge at full speed on the other side.

"Cass, you are going to have to take it slow this time. We don't know how deep that water is- we may get stuck if it is too deep."

"Come on Will! We can go right through that puddle!" William looked at `Cassidy with an unyielding stare that conveyed the gravity of the situation. Cassidy reluctantly slowed down and eased it into the murky pool of water.

"Turn the headlights on and take off the glasses." William instructed.

The lights flashed on and lit the surprisingly calm puddle in front of them. There was a slight swirling motion to the reddish brown water, almost serene in its appearance. William leaned halfway out the window to get a look over the hood.

"Looks passable; ease it in so we can back up if it's too deep!"

The engine roared and gears grinded as Cassidy pushed the truck forward. The water was deceptively deep and rushed against the passenger side of the cab. The water rose quickly, enveloping the tires of the truck. William pulled himself back in, water pouring through the window from the current below. He was shocked; he had made a critical miscalculation in how fast the water would rise. There had been a drought, and the hard ground was not absorbing the rainwater, transforming the ravine into a giant cistern. William watched the murky water rise above the headlights, suffocating the beam in front of them, and making it alarmingly dark.

"Punch it Cass!" William blurted out, realizing they only had seconds to get out of the stream. Cassidy turned slightly into the current, with some difficulty, feeling the tires start to drift behind her. She gunned the engine and pushed through the vast ravine. The water around the truck had become so deep, that William's passenger window had become completely obscured by the water rushing against it. The engine coughed and sputtered from the invading water, threatening to stall and trap them in the flash flood. Cassidy gunned the engine once again and they lurched forward, hauling the massive tank they were towing back in line with the truck. They finally emerged on the other side of the ravine, the water still rising behind them. If it had taken just a minute more, the truck would have been swallowed whole. There was no laughter from William and Cassidy this time, just relief.

In front of them was the rest of the narrow dirt road that ran uphill, water cascading downhill under their tires. Cassidy shut off the headlights and placed the night vision glasses back over her eyes. She shifted to a lower gear and the truck let out a long, deep growl as they climbed upwards towards the base of another mesa. The road now became a path that William, Roost and the rest of the gang had cleared of rocks and debris the previous day. The path snaked around the back of the mesa, between two large truncated red rocks. At the end of the path was a cave with a large, arch-shaped mouth, large enough to drive a semi into without complications. Cassidy zipped the truck through the opening and quickly turned off the engine. The waiting members of the gang unrolled camouflage netting to cover the entrance of the cave and then ran to the bottom and secured it. They threw dirt over the edges with some tumbleweed and slipped behind the netting. A few minutes later they could hear the helicopters searching the area, but the large cave hid them from the sensors the authorities were searching with. William slid out of the cab into the cave that was lit by several old gasoline generator-powered halogen lamps like those that used to be used in road repair. He looked down at his blood soaked pants leg, he knew his ankle would need stitches, and there was no anesthetic to numb it with. Cassidy had done it for him more than once, and it hurt, but William thought to himself that it was worth it; once again pulling off another great heist.

After four days of hiding out in the cave, Cassidy backed the semi out and down to the base of the Mesa. Her grandfather had been a truck driver and taught her how to handle a big rig when she was a girl. The black plastic strips that had covered the truck had been removed and left inside the cave. The cab was now covered with a shiny new coat of white paint,

"Leaning Rock Oil Co." was written in candy apple red with a bold black outline, the namesake of the company that was buying the oil William had procured. The tanker trailer was also transformed; it was shiny metal, along with the same logo as the cab. The metamorphosis was a stunning one, which made it an onerous task for law enforcement to identify it as the truck involved in the train job.

Cassidy maneuvered the truck down old dirt road, which eventually brought them to I-85, and they continued to I-40 until they reached their destination, a rest stop. They pulled in next to a brand new black SUV, complete with tinted windows. William and Cassidy got out and walked over to the driver side of the SUV. A stocky man wearing a Leaning Rock uniform stepped out and nodded to William and Cassidy. The two parties exchanged keys, and proceed to the other vehicle. William got in and immediately reached behind the driver seat and pulled out a large black duffle bag. He unzipped the top to reveal it was stuffed with bundles of cash in denominations of twenty, fifty, and one hundred-dollar bills.
Cassidy got in the driver's side and quickly grabbed a bundle of one hundred dollar bills from the bag, running her thumb across the top.

"I think this sound says celebration" she then looked down at her soiled and torn clothes "and a new outfit!"

"You know Cass, you're right! When we meet Roost and the boys in Albuquerque let's do it. We will get you fixed up too, you deserve it."
"We can stay somewhere really nice!"
"Yeah, that's a good idea, I know just the place," William said smirking.

William, Cassidy and Roost sat in a hotel room at the Frontier Inn, located in Albuquerque; it was an old Route Sixty-Six stop from the highway's heyday. The hotel had recently become a luxury resort after its restoration, part of the city's renaissance. William stared out the room window at the motel sign next to the entrance; it was pure art deco, a wedge shape, the bottom half being comprised of tan stucco and the top half of red brick. On top sat an illuminated white square plastic sign with a picture of a horse's head, an authentic recreation of when the motel was first opened. He looked further past the sign, to the orange and white self-storage facility across the street that now contained a large part of the cash they received for stealing the oil. William had cash and supplies stashed in other storage facilities from Phoenix to Topeka. He was always careful not to place too much in one location in case the authorities finally figured out where he had hidden the gang's money.

Cassidy came over and gave him a long, intense kiss that broke his concentration.

"Come on, baby, let's party!" Cassidy said before taking a long swig from a half empty bottle of tequila and handing it to William who did the same. William then threw Cassidy over his shoulder and spun her around, before tossing her onto the bed.

"Cass" Roost said in an earnest voice, "I don' think you are tall enough to get on that ride!" he said finally breaking into a laugh. Cassidy threw a pillow across the room at Roost, knocking his black Stetson off his head.

"Alright, we are going to get tossed out of here if we don't all settle down," William said as he eased back into a red velvet chair in the corner. "Remember what happened the last time we were thrown out? The owner called the FBI because he was angry and knew who I was; I don't want a repeat of that anytime soon."

There was a candle on the cherry wood end table next to him; he slid the drawer open to see if there were any matches provided by the motel. William instead saw a bible; he stared for a moment, thinking of his father, who was a Baptist Minister, and how many times he had sat in church reading along in the Bible as his father preached a sermon. He quickly shut the drawer and tried to push the image from his mind. Cassidy noticed that William was suddenly pale, and against the dark red walls, and black furniture, his pallid complexion was even more noticeably pronounced. Cassidy, sensing something was troubling William, bounced across the room and hopped onto his lap.

"Come on, let's go get something to eat at the restaurant here, it will cheer you up!" She said with her characteristic cheer. She then reached across him to her small black bag sitting on the floor next to him, and produced a small zip-lock bag filled with cocaine, "How about a pick me up?" she purred. William shook his head no.

"Not right now, Cass." She smiled and swung the bag back and forth in the air in front of him

"That's more for me then! I know Roost does not partake."

"I don't think they are going to let you in barefoot wearing jean shorts and a white t-shirt." William kidded, trying to downplay the spell he just had. Cassidy patted him on the head.

"Good idea!" and she disappeared into the bathroom to change.

"So, Will, what's next?" Roost said leaning back in his chair with his boots on the table next to him.

"We have enough for now, we need to lay low for a while."

"Don't give me that. You've always got something up your sleeve."

"I don't know what's next."

"Are you serious? Right after we pulled the armored car job; you were talking about stealing oil." Roost leaned forward examining William's eyes, "You wouldn't shut up about it. You were almost giddy. What's wrong Will?"

"Roost, do you ever think about getting out, doing something else?"

Roost leaned back in his chair; he was shocked at what William was saying.

"Of course I think about doing something else, but hell Will, you're only twenty and I'm only twenty-two! We have at least a few years left in us before we are put out to pasture." William glanced over at the bathroom to see if Cassidy had come out yet. Seeing she had not, he continued.

"I love the thrill of pulling jobs no one else could, or would even think of doing. I like living in different places and experiencing new things, but sometimes I get tired. Sometimes I just want to be normal. I want to go to the movies or a football game. I want to have kids. I love doing this, but how long can we really do it?"

"You are the most famous thief in the world, and you want to settle down? Maybe Cassidy or I could, but you can't. Most of America knows your face, and, sure, millions of people think you are some kind of folk hero, but the government will never stop coming as long as you are alive. The only way you can settle down is if you are dead. Besides, Cassidy loves this lifestyle more than you and I combined. She would kill you if you quit!"

William laughed at the truth in what Roost said, before being distracted once again by the emergence of Cassidy. She popped out from behind the bathroom door wearing a small red dress and open-toed gold shoes, which accentuated the tattoo of a daisy on her right foot.

"How do I look?" she said while standing as if she were waiting for a bevy of photographers to snap her picture

"Like you are too gorgeous for me to take out in public. It's hard to be low key when your wife is unbelievably hot!" William responded. The remark actually caused Cassidy to blush. She turned to Roost.

"Come on handsome, you are too good looking not to have a woman. We are going to find someone for you tonight."

Roost stood up and shot Cassidy a wry smile, "It's kind of hard to find a steady girl when you only live in a town for two months at a time."

The trio stood up and headed for the door. William glanced back at the table once more still trying to forget what he saw, and turned off the lights.

# CHAPTER II

Ten months after the Roman invasion of the United States....

The pre-dawn fog sat thick on Fairfax County, Virginia; the unseasonably cold fall temperatures made the air bitingly sharp. Only a few cars were on the roads, as was normal for a Saturday morning. A few farmers were up feeding their livestock, and joggers were bundled, struggling to take the frigid air into their lungs. The entire scene was so placid that it could have made almost anyone forget that part of the country had been seized by Roman forces. The truth was that no one had forgotten about the invasion and the havoc it had unleashed on the nation. A secret gathering of several high-level government officials was about to take place with the singular purpose of driving the Romans out. It was not without risk. Many within the highest reaches of the government were being openly courted by the Romans with promises of positions with clout if they assisted in the United States' surrender to Rome. The members of Congress who advocated surrender to Rome were dubbed by the media as "Marble Heads". The situation created an atmosphere of acrimony and distrust that the gathering group had been operating in, trying to find and root out all the Marble Heads. The small band consisted of the few trusted allies of president Braintree and of each other. They knew that if they succeeded they would change the course of history and write a redefined chapter; if they failed, it would be death of the United States of America.

The meeting place was unusual, but it was the only place where they felt surreptitious electronic surveillance would not be present. They chose General George Vernon's family farm, as it sat squarely in the unincorporated part of the Fairfax County, less likely to be in the sights of Roman spy satellites. The old farm house had safely survived two-hundred and fifty years of progress, being handed down from one family member to another. The old building had fallen into disrepair when General Vernon had inherited it. It had lost some of its luster, but the structure was mostly still intact. Vernon had it lovingly restored, and over time found it was a sanctuary, allowing his thoughts to turn from the horrors he had seen in battle.

Senator Ted Bulloch had switched cars three times in route to the meeting, one of many cloak and dagger maneuvers to avoid Roman spies. Bulloch was the most visible and vocal opponent of the Marble Heads, and next to the President, he was the most likely to draw Roman surveillance, which made the extra precautions a necessity. The car he was driving was rented by a staffer's mother in law, so that no one from his office would be connected to it, and therefore it would not register on a surreptitious Roman surveillance program. Bulloch hurtled down the road in the darkness and fog- better camouflage could not have been produced by the defense industry. He slowed as he approached the unmarked turn off that lead to Vernon's farm. The unpaved private road snaked through a thicket made up of oaks and poplars before opening into an expansive field. The tires of the car produced a crunching sound as they rolled over the gravel underneath them. Finally, the headlights of the car shone through the fog and rested on the farmhouse. The stately old white building was topped by a hip-shingled roof, underneath were neat rows rounded dormers, each containing double hug windows with green plantation shutters on either side. Four red brick chimneys ascended from the east and west sides, three were for fireplaces, and one for a brick oven. There were covered front, side, and back farmer's porches. Surrounding it was an old post fence put up in 1925, a replica of the original fence that was flattened by a civil war skirmish.

The farm had been listed on the National Register of Historic Places for as long as the register had existed. General Vernon's great-great-great-great grandfather had invented the keyless letter lock, and President James K. Polk had once stayed there; thus giving the house its historic value, aside from its pristine condition. The home had seen ten wars, a man on the moon and, later, a woman on the moon. During the first decade of the nineteenth-century it had also served as an inn and stagecoach station for travelers on their way from Pennsylvania to Washington. None of the farm's lengthy history carried as much weight as what was about to transpire; it was doubtlessly the most significant event it was ever to hold. Bulloch pulled his car in next to several other nondescript sedans parked in the circular drive in front of the house. Ted Bulloch had made a name for himself as senator from New York, perhaps the most popular politician in the United States. He had been the Mayor of White Plains, New York before being elected to the Senate. He had accomplished all of this by the age of thirty-four. Bulloch was in his third year of his senate term when Rome invaded. He had been quoted as saying "I will never sit idly by when something of great magnitude is occurring to the country I love. If a bully attacks you, punch him in the mouth". He had a thirst to be part of history, and more so, to make history. Bulloch also possessed an engrained sense of duty and honor; it was something he learned from the books he read as a sick child. He had long-since been transformed into a stocky adult; his constitution was that of a pioneer who crossed the width of the U.S by wagon train. His oblong head sat on top of a thickset neck and broad shoulders. His brown hair was closely cropped to his head, a thick, but well-groomed mustache hung over his mouth. When he smiled seemed to have too many teeth for his head. He was of average height, but his charisma made him seem a more imposing figure. Bulloch had an iron will that made his enemies detest, but respect, him and his colleagues admire him.

Shortly after the invasion occurred, Bulloch was studying a map of the occupied states, and it occurred to him that the majority under Roman control were western states. He spent much of his childhood in the West, and had come to love it as much as his home state of New York. It was with his first hand knowledge of the West that Bulloch had pitched an idea to the President; a regimen on horseback to traverse canyons and gullies, through thick pine forests and back alleyways in urban combat. The Cavalry would fight the Romans in an unorthodox fashion. The soldiers who made up its ranks would be required to have experience with horses, and some other type of specialized skills. The idea was radical, there had been no soldier on horseback for well over one-hundred years, and nevertheless the terrain the Romans had taken dictated that type of warfare, even if the Romans had not realized it in their hunger for power. A mounted cavalry was not a new idea; it was very old, and it was a gamble, but it had possibilities that the Romans might not have realized. Bulloch had expressed the idea to the president, unaware of the plan to make George Vernon a five star general. The President, skeptical at first, came to see the merit in the plan and agreed. The idea was incorporated into the overall strategy to defeat the Romans; that strategy that was to be discussed at the meeting Bulloch had taken such lengthy measures to get to undetected. He walked up to the old pastoral mansion, its windows lit; looking much like it did as an inn. Bulloch approached the door, surprised at the lack of security systems for someone in General Vernon's position. Bulloch was unaware of the hidden cameras trained on him, but it became obvious when Vernon himself opened the front door before he had a chance to ring the doorbell.

"Thank you for coming, Senator," Vernon said in his usual calm manner, his soft voice a contrast to his sinewy six-foot three-inch frame.

His slate blue eyes fixed on Bulloch with a friendly but steady gaze. His demeanor was always calm and considerate, but underneath was the raging spirit of a warrior. His long, distinguished nose combined with his other features reminded Bulloch of a bird of prey. Bulloch was also unaccustomed to seeing the General out of uniform. He was wearing a white wool turtleneck sweater and khaki slacks. He swung the door open and gestured for Bulloch to enter. Bulloch grasped his hand and shook it with the fervor of a campaign stop.

"I am damned glad you are with us General." he said in his boisterous but high, shrill voice.

An aid in uniform closed the door behind them as they made their way into the foyer, past the great stairway made of varnished hickory, through a neo-classical doorway topped with a white pediment, and into the library. Sitting in the middle of the room, amidst the mahogany bookshelves filled with antique books, in a semi-circle of old colonial straight back chairs, were Alex Wright, Henry Hardin and Helga Kleist. The group was as brilliant as it was distinguished. Alex Wright had been Vernon's right hand, and an unequaled military tactician. He was an intellectual virtuoso who not only understood military strategy but could see with equal clarity the financial, political and social implications of any plan. During the first war with Rome, Wright was promoted repeatedly from captain all the way to Lieutenant Colonel. He had come at the behest of the President to convince Vernon that he should lead the fight against Rome.

General Henry Hardin was also an advisor to Vernon during the first war with Rome. Hardin met Vernon who came into his antique bookstore on a trip to Boston. Vernon and Henry sat for hours discussing military history from antiquity to the twentieth century. Hardin was an army reservist whose wife ran the store when he was gone on duty. Vernon would speak to Hardin over the next few months, asking him about strategy in past battles, never finding Hardin at a loss. Vernon was impressed with Hardin's vast knowledge of military strategy and offered him a job as an advisor. Like Wright, Hardin had also been promoted to Colonel from advisor. Under the President's plan, he and Wright would be promoted to General, just as Vernon was made a five star general with command over all the armed forces, only answering to the president. Hardin's appearance was not quite what one would expect. Like Bulloch, he was dressed in a suit, but he was portly, his complexion pallid, and his hairline receding badly. It was his determination, organization and dogged attention to detail, which made him invaluable.

Helga Kleist was the New Secretary of State who had just gone through a blistering confirmation hearing with the Marbleheads, in the Senate, unable to block her confirmation. Her undeniable charm combined with her confidence usually made her the smartest person in the room, allowing for a skillful deflection of scathing attacks hurled in her direction during the meeting. She was tall, blonde-haired and blue-eyed, and some had suggested she was too attractive for her station, a barb that was one of the few things that bothered her. In response, she always dressed conservatively in suits with her hair up or pulled back. They gray suit she was wearing with high heel black boots was one such outfit. She wore little makeup, but even with those pains taken, she was still striking.

Vernon and Bulloch walked across the room, and took a seat with the others. Bulloch noticed his host's hands were clinched in his lap as they sat. Vernon felt the weight of the nation's hopes on his shoulders. It would be his duty to drive the Romans out, and if the Romans were not defeated, the responsibility, he believed, would be his. President Braintree had personally asked for Vernon to come back, there would be a sea change at the Pentagon, purging the brass from the previous pacifist leaning administration. Vernon had been among those who warned the previous President that diplomacy with Rome was tantamount to surrender, but those warnings fell on deaf ears. Vernon looked at the two trusted confidants, then Bulloch, a man he admired but never met, and finally at Secretary Kleist, who he believed to be an endless well of knowledge. The meeting that was taking place in his library, he realized, would determine if the United States would cease to exist or if they would strike back against Rome, driving them from the continent. He also knew everything would have to move swiftly in order to keep the Romans from reacting. He took a deep breath and stood up to address his guests.

"I would first like to express my sincere gratitude to everyone for holding me in such high esteem, I only hope that I can live up to the faith you have placed in me. I feel that I cannot ignore the wishes of the President, the American people and my good friends."

He took a few more steps to look out the old frame window onto the sloping grass hill, on top of which the farm stood.

"I accepted the President's offer, not only to justify the trust placed in me, but to help save America as not just a place, but as a principle, as an ideal. We could build a wall and contain the areas Rome has taken from us, but that would be saying to the world that when pushed, democracy will crumble."

Vernon turned back around to face the group, the resolve evident on his face.

"No, we must drive out the Romans not only for ourselves, but for all the people they have enslaved and killed. We must do it for all those who came before us, who fought and died to protect the Constitution."

A hush fell over the room for a moment; the reverence for the Vernon was apparent. After hearing Vernon's discourse, there was a sense among the group that a historic moment had just transpired. Bulloch broke the silence with his piercing voice:

"General, I have to say that I believe you are what this country needs to drive the Romans off the continent and send them scurrying home in utter and complete defeat!" He turned and faced Alexander Wright, "I would also like to hear from the esteemed General Wright. I don't think there is a better mind in the world for this sort of work."

Wright stood up; he wore the dress uniform of a Colonel, not yet having been officially given the promotion yet. The blue coat dropped down to the hips and had red trim on the cuffs of the sleeves and on the lapels. The shoulders were covered with two straps containing an eagle behind a shield, grasping arrows in its left talon and wheat in its right. The trousers were blue with a red stripe down the side and tucked into his boots. He was of average height and a slight athletic build. His largish forehead gave some indication of his superior brain behind it. It was topped by salt and pepper hair, cut into a standard military part to the side. His thick eyebrows and sharp dark eyes made anyone he spoke to feel his gaze was aimed at them. His square jaw was the only indication he was not the type of genius who sat in a room all day staring at a computer screen. In fact, he had been somewhat of a ladies' man earlier in his life. Wright waited a moment before he spoke, making eye contact with everyone in the room to gauge their attention. Wright commanded respect; there was no dispute from those gathered that of all their intellects, his was chief among them. Vernon had promoted him to Colonel faster than anyone in the history of the army, often to the protests of career soldiers with more experience. All of the complaints stopped when Wright proved his genius time and again. Now he was being looked upon once again to help save America.

"I know that you may feel the same trepidation as I do; there is no doubt we are in uncertain, dangerous times. Now it's up to us to bear the burden of saving this country from being Balkanized or being conquered altogether. I am sure since we are in a transitional phase with the new administration, Rome will mount an offensive to capture more territory. No doubt you are all thinking the same thing." Wright walked around the room with a swagger that was in stark contrast to Vernon's placid demeanor. "Rome will test our preparedness. We will not only be ready, we are going to take back ground from them."

The words had weight coming from Wright, and they shored up the confidence of those listening. He was like an actor giving a soliloquy, the way he could describe something and hold the rapt attention of those who were listening.

"We have the fate of the nation in our hands; we will deliver it from our enemies. I will not attempt to placate you with platitudes on the greatness of our forces; we face a nation that has a greater military than our own, lead by a military genius. Their weapons technology is superior to ours due to the last administration and Congress, defunding the defense budget. If we are to win this war, we must begin to develop technology on par with the Romans, or find a way to level the playing field. We must use any advantage we have, and the only clear advantage is our air power. The other means will be guerilla campaigns and obtaining and using Roman technology. This war can be won if we anticipate Rome's plans and calculate the appropriate responses." Wright sat back down and turned to Secretary Kleist.

"Madame Secretary, I believe you have insight on the Emperor."

She leaned back in her chair and gave a smirk to the response.

"Anyone who has studied the Emperor can tell you he is vain," she said in a thick German accent "that is apparent. What is less visible my dear General, is fear of failure. That is what drives him."

Wright stood up and began pacing.

"Let me get this straight, you're saying that the man who single handedly commanded the Italian army against a Vasekt force ten times their size and beat them is a coward?"

Secretary Kleist gave a small snicker at the suggestion.

"Not at all. I am suggesting he is afraid of not being the best. He is afraid he will not have a place in history alongside Julius Cesar, or Alexander the Great."

"Is he really that wrapped up in himself?" Wright said, doubting that Caprera was so self-absorbed.

She smiled politely again, "Yes, but he does have some positive attributes, otherwise his popularity would not be as high. Caprera has a deep sense of honor and duty. He sincerely believes what he is doing is for the betterment of mankind. He does care about his people, and will crush anyone who gets in his way."

Wright walked over to Secretary Kleist and gave a polite smile of his own.     "Is he over confident?"

"It would be hard not to after his successive victories, wouldn't you agree?"

"You're the expert on Caprera"

She smiled again, "Come now general, you're being modest."

Wright laughed "Didn't you say in that Wall Street Journal piece that I was, what was the phrase you used?" Wright stopped for a moment, sarcastically scratching his chin, "Oh yeah, I did not possess a modest bone in my body. Let me ask you, Madame Secretary, when did I develop modesty? Maybe three ghosts came to visit me?"

Bulloch stood up and interrupted. "Well clearly there are two other people in the world with egos as big as the Emperor's. I suggest we focus on the task at hand rather than practice verbal one-upmanship."

Wright nodded his head in agreement. "You're right. I apologize, Senator, and to you Madame Secretary. We have much to accomplish in a short time."

Secretary Kleist had a sour look on her face, but still forced a smile. "I apologize as well.  The answer to the previous question is yes, he is overconfident, and that has cost him the only losses he has ever had."

"That will be what we use to defeat him. He will underestimate us, and we will take full advantage of his mistakes as they present themselves." Wright stopped for a moment and changed his tone.

"The economy has nearly collapsed and industry is anemic at best. If we convert industry used to produce cars, air conditioners, refrigerators, and other durable goods, to produce goods for the war effort, it will achieve two things we desperately need: reviving commerce and strengthening our armed forces."

Wright walked over to Bulloch and placed his hand on his shoulder.

"Senator Bulloch's plan for a mounted force will be a key component to gathering intelligence and sabotaging Roman positions. We need to start compiling a list of those qualified to be part of that force immediately. Some in this country may see the situation as bleak and hopeless, but it's not. They think we should accept the inevitable and surrender, but they're wrong. We have a sacred duty to uphold our promise to protect the men, women and children of this country. It is a promise we cannot break. I don't believe I need to expound on that point; you are all aware of what must be done. We must capture or kill the so-called Pax-Americana Yakiv Kravchenko at all costs. That will be the symbol to both the United States and Rome that the invasion of our nation has ended."

There was a sense of optimism that filled the room; for the first time since the invasion, there was a sense that it was possible for Rome to be defeated. Wright sat down and sank back into his chair, now seeming more like a detached observer rather than a participant. Vernon knew that what his old emissary had said was the truth. He felt that he had to grasp hold of Wright's words and add his vision to them.

"We will restore discipline to our forces; it will make our smaller numbers more formidable." His face looked both resigned and determined, he knew that the fate of the free world was about to be decided before the sun rose.

"I know we all understand what is at stake; if we fail, democracy may vanish from the Earth forever. The chance of defeating Rome becomes more fleeting with each passing moment we delay. We have many enemies inside our own government, but we must, and will, find a way to defeat them. I am honored to undertake this daunting task with all of you. With God's help, we will win." Bulloch leaned forward, "One more thing, keep this quiet until we have everything in place on Monday. I can't begin to tell you how bad it would be if our enemies were to get wind of this." A silent nod of agreement was given by all present.

Bulloch, anticipating the battle over the sweeping reforms the President was about to impart on Congress, had summoned his staff to an impromptu meeting in order to prepare. He knew that, being in the minority, it was going to be difficult to convince a majority of the Senate that confirming the President's candidates for the new Joint Chiefs of Staff was the right decision. Bulloch had received a call on his way back from President Braintree's Chief of Staff. He informed Bulloch that the President had sent letters to the current Joint Chiefs of Staff requesting their immediate resignations.

Bulloch was in deep concentration as he walked up Constitution Avenue to the Dirksen building where his office was. The building was typical of Washington, built in 1958, it was in the neoclassical style; as Bulloch looked up at it, he was struck that the Romans wanted the entire country to look like Washington. He was so absorbed in his thoughts that he did not notice the figure approaching him. A homeless man, with a long, scraggly, brown beard and face smudged with what appeared to be some black-oily substance, stumbled on the sidewalk in front of him. As Bulloch walked toward him, he finally noticed the man struggling to get to his feet. He could smell the unsavory combination of wine and body odor. Bulloch's nature was such that he could not ignore the pitiful scene in front of him.

"Easy old fellow!" he said as he grasped the man's dirty trench coat just below the shoulders and lifted him to his feet.

The homeless man pulled down a tattered Yankees cap over his forehead trying in vain to make a better appearance. He smiled, revealing teeth that were caked with the remnants of various foodstuffs. He extended his dirty hand to shake Bulloch's. When Bulloch reluctantly returned the man's gesture, the man missed his hand and bumped into Bulloch, sending both of them careening to the ground. Bulloch again lifted him off the ground.

"Be careful friend. There is a shelter a few blocks to the south, they can help you," he said as he returned to his intended course.

As he approached the door to the building he heard a cell phone ring, he turned to see where it had come from, but he could see no one, even the homeless man had stumbled away. Bulloch realized it was not coming from someone else, but the inside pocket of his jacket. He reached in to the pocket and produced not only the phone, but a memory dot as well. Bulloch flipped the phone open.

"Who is this and what kind of game are you playing?"

# CHAPTER III

Thirty-five Green Berets from the Tenth Special Forces Battalion sat in the belly of an aging C-17 cruising at thirty-five thousand feet. Prior to the Roman invasion they had been based out of Fort Collins in Colorado, but they had lifted off from Scott Air Force Base in Illinois, which was, for the time being, their interim home. Those on the plane were veterans of previous high-risk missions. They possessed both the skills and demeanor needed in extreme pressure situations where life and death scenarios were commonplace. They had been tasked with intercepting a Roman column that had broken through the front lines, and were racing towards Kansas City, only eighteen miles from the front lines. They adjusted their black jump suits as they watched a Holo-Def screen at the front of the plane. CENTCOM (Central Command) was providing a final briefing before their jump. A three-dimensional map hovered in front of the screen showing where the Romans were expected to strike. General Wright's voice described in an even, steady tone what they were seeing: "The Romans are sending a heavily armored column up Interstate 71 and are advancing at a rapid pace. They already overwhelmed our blockade at that location, and we can't spare any more resources. Because we cannot stop them with a blockade, we are feigning resistance and letting them pass. They are most likely searching for components to construct a weapon located at an aerospace company in the city that was developing the part for us. We are sending you in on a high altitude drop; when you are on the ground you will break into four groups to track, paint the target with a laser, and hold the Romans in a target area. A word of advice gentlemen, vacate the area and be at least half a klick away, five minutes after painting the target. We are striking with scramjet missiles armed with high explosives. These warheads are just a step down from tactical nukes, so you do not want to be anywhere near when they hit. That is all gentlemen, Godspeed. Major Morrison, put on your com-link for additional data." After General Wright finished speaking the screen went black. Major Morrison Claret Lions was considered a war hero for the numerous missions he had been on; he already had four purple hearts. The war had been perhaps more personal to him than most. His father was the head of the Department of African American Studies at a local college when he was growing up in White Plains, New York. The taking of slaves by the Romans was deeply disturbing because of

~ 39 ~

everything he had learned from his father. Morrison had also lost his fiancée when she was killed visiting her parents in New Mexico. He had been crushed by her death and, in his grief, he threw himself into being a more efficient and deadly soldier. His father had died when he was fifteen and his mother died of cancer just six months before the tragic death of his fiancée. He was alone in the world, a fact that made him attack the Romans with abandon. He knew that no one would grieve for him if he died. His appearance outside of his uniform and his physique did not relay the air of a soldier. He had bright twinkling eyes while his head was an oval shape. He frequently smiled masking the turmoil that filled him. There was no doubt though, he was a soldier's soldier.

Morrison walked away from his troops, "Go ahead General" he said putting the com-link in his ear.

"Major, this is for your ears only", Wrights voice crackled with inference, "The component we believe the Romans are trying to acquire is for a devastating weapon that is still in the experimental stage. Its name is *The Variable Specific Impulse Magnetoplasma Canon*, VASMIC for short. The VASMIC is based on the same technology as the VASMIR rocket, and is the most devastating weapon DARPA is developing. The plasma shell burns at one-million degrees Fahrenheit and has a range of up to five klicks. In order for the Canon to work it requires several Helicon Radio Frequency Antennas to turn gas into plasma. These VASMIC cannons were just about to be put into production before the Romans made Kansas City a priority. We believe it is no coincidence that their interest in the town peaked at the same time a classified communication was sent, stating the project was a go. We also believe that the Romans have begun construction of ten VASMIC along the front, but need components only found at the top-secret DARPA facility in Kansas City. We know at least one antenna was left behind during the evacuation of the facility. You are to track them and let them gather at the target area. Whatever happens, do not let them escape the city with the components, when there are five pieces of armor there, call in the strike. We are attacking with the Privateer Missiles, because they are scramjets, again you will have less than five minutes to evacuate the area once you paint the target area. Your secondary mission will be to capture and deliver a Roman officer for interrogation if possible. We have downloaded this to your field tablet."

Morrison checked his field tablet to confirm that the data had been sent. "Understood General, I have received the data."

"One more thing, Major, there are variables that can't be accounted for in this mission. This could go south quickly, but the mission cannot be aborted, It must be completed at all costs, no matter how hard the choices are to make." Wrights voice conveyed an almost apologetic tone.

"Understood," Morrison said flatly he knew of the inherent danger of the mission.

The com-link went dead, leaving only the sound of rushing wind washing across the fuselage and the high pitched whine of the engines. Morrison turned to gathered units and signaled to put on their oxygen masks, the soldiers then strapped on their Personal Flying Wings (PFW's) and moved in position to jump. They would head some 30 miles to the south and hit the target drop zone of Arrowhead stadium in Kansas City. It was a rare daylight mission for the Green Berets, but there was no other option, the Romans were on their way.

The hydraulics made a loud whirring sound as the mammoth cargo ramp slowly opened to reveal the landscape below. Cold air rushed in against them, cutting through their insulated jump suits and causing their muscles to tense and contract. Morrison's second in command, Captain Reynolds, a young enthusiastic soldier from Georgia, walked over to his commander

"Now I know how Jonah felt coming out of the whale!" he chuckled and managed to draw a smile from Morrison.

"Yeah, well, you be careful out there Rey! When this is all over we will go see a football game in the stadium," Morrison said.

He and Reynolds had grown close over the course of the war. Both of them were hesitant to make friends with anyone else because they were less likely to survive. Both of them had seen too many friends die.

Three soldiers at a time hurtled out and ignited their PFW's. The half-light of the sinking sun obscured their target, so they followed the GPS heads up display in their visors that descended from their black helmets to just above the tip of their noses. They flew together in a cluster in case a change of course had to be made, so none would be left behind. Anyone who was on the ground looking up would have mistaken them for a flock of large black birds.

Major Morrison stood and watched until all the Green Berets had taken flight. He took one last look around the cargo hold, as if he had left some detail undone. He checked his field tablet one more time, but it slipped from his hand, tumbling end over end down the ramp. He dove for it, sliding on his stomach and slapping it flat against the ramp with his hand. He walked back up the ramp and checked to see that it was working. He was relieved when it powered up and displayed the mission data. His com-link crackled to life in his ear.

"Better Jump now Major, we are about to exit the drop zone." the pilot implored.

"Roger that." Morrison said before finally pulling his visor down and jumping out of the plane.

The rest of his units were nearly half a mile in front of him. It would only take about seven minutes for the group to reach their target area. Morrison could see the two stadiums in the distance, Kaufman to the right and Arrowhead to the left. He watched the group in front of him as their engines cut off, and they glided silently down for the remainder of the drop. Morrison's engine finally cut off as well, and he began his decent. He looked downward at the stadium parking lot. As the pavement around the two stadiums rushed up, deserted cars from the evacuation attempt became visible. As the stadium continued to grow larger, it was evident the grass in the stadium had grown quite tall due to its lack of use. Most of the city had evacuated nineteen months earlier, leaving only a few die-hard residents who reluctantly left in the last evacuation. Morrison watched his men began their descent into the stadium one by one. They would circle as each soldier broke off from the whole and landed, until only Morrison was left behind them.

Morrison swooped in close over the scoreboard when he saw what the rest of his troops had not: an ambush. Elite Roman Soldiers known as the Praetorian Guard came surging out of the tunnels and onto the field, spraying the Green Berets with their SPR's. Unlike the other Roman Soldiers, they were dressed completely in black, still having the molded chest plates and helmets with crests, albeit ebony crests. The rest of their armor was segmented for a wide range of motion. The ammunition being fed through a tube from a pack on their backs, made the gunfire seemed endless. Morrison, realizing he only had seconds to act, quickly unstrapped himself from his wing in an attempt to keep from suffering the same fate as the others. A Praetorian who had just left the tunnel turned up to see him simultaneously opened fire. Morrison was struck as he plummeted, bullets ripping through his thigh, left shoulder, and grazing his left side. He plunged into the grass that had grown nearly four feet high, and upon slamming into the ground he heard a loud pop from his right side. He clinched his teeth together to suppress a scream as he felt a sharp pinch on his right side. As he lurched to reach for his weapon he felt a clicking from the same side; he knew from experience at least two ribs had been broken. As he pulled his pistol from its holster, he realized his breathing had become labored. Morrison knew as badly as he was injured, if he did not act quickly his injuries would no longer concern him. He tentatively and quite painfully raised himself up to peer above the grass, becoming lightheaded as he sat up. He did not see any of his troops, nor did he hear any return fire. The Romans waded into the grass, shooting each American Soldier they found in the head to ensure they were dead. Morrison had braced for the inevitable, when he saw it through bleary eyes. What looked like a soldier rose up behind one of the Praetorians and jabbed a knife into his throat while simultaneously covering his victim's mouth. The Roman slumped over and fell backward into the grass in the mysterious soldier's embrace. A few seconds later the soldier re-emerged and repeated the same maneuver with another Roman five feet in front of where the last one lay. Morrison looked to his left and saw another soldier on the other side of the field executing the identical maneuver with the same lethal results. He was so mesmerized by the incredible scene he was witnessing that he momentarily forgot about his pain; he was soon reminded when he struggled to sit back up and felt concurrent waves of pain and extreme weakness. When he managed to rise up again he saw a Praetorian standing over him with a pistol aimed at his head. The soldiers face suddenly contorted into an expression of agony and shock, falling in front of Morrison, his eyes still locked in a gaze him. He looked up at the soldier who saved him. He was tall with dark eyes and hair, his frame was sturdy, like you would expect a Green Beret to be, Morrison thought to himself upon seeing him. His features were strong, square chin, high cheek-bones and thick eyebrows, making him look utterly the part of a hero. Morrison realized at once it was not one of his men; his rescuer, who was holding a titanium sword with a black handle, looked at him.

"Are you all quite alright?" The man spoke with a British accent that was aristocratic, yet caring.

"British? They're British?" Morrison muttered barely aware of what was happening.

He looked over again as a Praetorian came charging at them firing his weapon as he went. The dark figure of the British soldier dove headlong into the grass and reemerged with the lifeless body of the Roman he had just run through. The advancing assailant raised his gun again and pulled the trigger, but it failed to fire. He shook it, as if there were some loose pin or screw that had caused the problem, before realizing to his horror the weapon was not faulty. The British soldier very slowly re-sheathed his sword on his back. He as equally slow and deliberately took aim with a pistol, shooting the solder in the throat. The Praetorian looked more confused than afraid of his impending death as he grasped and pushed against the gushing wound in a vain attempt to stop the bleeding. Morrison sat up and came to the realization the other British soldiers were walking and holding live Praetorians in front of them while shooting the others, who had frantically begun to retreat into the tunnels. Morrison could only count four soldiers running away when he suddenly felt the faintness overtake him. He fought against slipping away and stood up, in doing so felt a blinding pain coming from his left leg. He looked down to see his fibula had broken and was protruding from a hole in his jump suit. At the same time he became aware that his left boot was nearly filled with blood. His breaths were beginning to come in short bursts, his heart was racing just as quickly, and he had an unimaginable thirst. He tumbled over, unable to hold himself up. The British soldier knelt down to him and cradled his head on his forearm.

"Lay still, we are going to get you away from here."

"How did you do that?" Morrison gasped, his amazement momentarily overriding concern for his own well being.

"Are you referring to the SPR's failing to shoot? We discovered the Roman's have restrictor chips embedded in them, to keep them from shooting each other. Now try and lie still" The British soldier said as he checked Morrison's wounds.

"Who are you? How did you know?"

"We have been tracking the Praetorians for days; they set up here last night. We knew something was afoot, entered, hid, and waited. They must have been aware you were coming, they arrived twenty four hours before you did."

"You have to complete our mission!" Morrison said in an audible wheeze.

"What was your mission?"

"Roman convoy, heading into town, must paint it with a laser, report it on my com. Tell them what killed me and my troops."

"Now you *listen* to me!" the soldier said sternly, leaning over and glaring into Morrison's eyes, "*Nothing* is going to happen to you, we are getting you help. Am I clear?"

"You have to get the target first! They are in route. We softened our defenses to let them in, I don't matter, complete the mission!" Morrison gasped before blacking out.

When Morrison awoke he felt the sensation of being on wet grass growing from the cold hard ground. Confused, he looked around until he saw in front of him a granite cross with an inscription that read: "THE HOURS THAT PART US BRING US TOGETHER AGAIN". He looked around to see other granite markers and plastic flowers and his mind finally was able to decipher where he was, a cemetery. He thought he was dead and being readied for interment, until the pain in his ribs reconfirmed he was among the living. He struggled to move his head to see what was happening, why he was there. He glanced at his shoulder and leg, and could see where his uniform had been torn back, and his wounds cauterized. He had no recollection of the wounds being treated.

"How long was I out?" he gasped, although no one was near him.

He lifted his head slightly and gazed past his shoulder where he saw two of the British soldiers, their backs flat against a granite crypt. Morrison struggled to focus; he recognized the armor they were wearing, modular tactical vests, which were standard issue for British Special Forces. One of the solders with light brown hair and a pallid complexion, who also appeared to be very young, leaned around the side of the crypt and held up a detached gun scope. He closed one eye and squinted with the other as he scanned the area. He raised his hand and held up two fingers signaling the soldier beside him that there were two targets. He then held out the same hand and opened and shut it several times, while never breaking his gaze through the scope. The hulking soldier next to him interpreted the signal and handed him what Morrison recognized as an Israeli made pistol with a silencer on the end. The soldier took the pistol and slowly wrapped his arm around the side of the crypt, taking careful aim, and said under his breath "cheers". Morrison could hear two small pops, he could tell by the satisfied expression on the soldier's face that he had been successful. He looked over at Morrison and winked, before walking over and kneeling down.

"Don't fret; we are going to get you patched right up."

He reached under Morrison's arm to lift him; suddenly, the soldier who had saved him in the stadium appeared and was lifting him up from the other side. He could see the two Roman Legionnaires who had been eliminated by a single shot to each of their heads.

Morrison realized his feet had become numb as they scraped the ground, as was the lower half of his body. He could see that he was being taken to a flat, black, heavily-armored Roman transport known as Runner. They all piled in, aware that the two Legionnaires lying on the ground were probably only sentinels left to guard the vehicle, as it seated seventeen, the rest were probably Praetorians, Morrison thought. The burly British soldier jumped behind the wheel and pulled at some memory boards trying to bypass the security system. He threw his backpack on the seat next to his, opened it with a speedy zip and pulled out another board clicking it in where another board had been. He pressed a button on the steering column and the huge armored beast roared to life. A smug expression on his face he turned around.

"The telematics have been compromised! I believe this may belong to the lot we sent belly-up. Should be a med-kit in here, we can patch our boy up a little more."

Morrison sat listening to what was being said, barely aware as his vision began to tunnel. He fought against it, but once again everything went slowly black. He awoke once again, much less alert this time, as he strained to hear the soldier who rescued him speak the words "DARPA contractor, Bennu Aerospace." as he read from the field tablet. Morrison strained and in between fits of coughing managed to explain their objective.

"That's where they are going, must paint the convoy with laser. They will be hit with scramjet missiles. Five minutes to clear after!" he said before again passing out.

Morrison awoke again, jarred by a blast that struck the left side of the Runner, followed seconds later by an equally loud blast on the same side. There was a third impact that came crashing against the side sending the armored transport careening down the street. The burly British soldier struggled to regain control of the vehicle and cut the steering wheel hard to the right. There was an ear-splitting groan of metal straining from underneath the vehicle before it tipped and landed on its side sending it skidding down the street. The sparks sprayed from its side and made a horrible shrieking sound of metal scraping asphalt before unceremoniously smashing into a streetlight. Morrison was aware of shouting and the smell of smoke.  He strained to hold himself up by his elbows and was able to look out through the windshield and see the green street sign above them read 14$^{th}$ Street. Morrison's training for the mission overrode the fog in his mind. He turned to see the art-deco red drum of the President Hotel's "Drum Room". The hotel was near the target location.  He instinctively started pulling himself up. Morrison knew that undoubtedly the explosions had come from a shoulder-fired missile, most likely fired by the missing Praetorians from the Runner. The trajectory had come from the old Art Deco hotel that had been constructed in the 1920's and Morrison found himself thinking of how strange and out of place it seemed for a firefight. Its red bricks and ornate fixtures seemed like something from an old movie; it did not belong in a modern battle, he thought. Morrison refocused and fought passing out again, aware that his life was slipping away and he may not regain consciousness if he sipped under one more time. The sun had just set, making the cracking flames and smoke perfect camouflage for the Romans to pick them off one by one.  The British soldiers were stunned, wounded or dead. Although Morrison could barely breathe, and passed out if he sat up too fast, he reached over and grabbed a HK 416 Assault Rifle that had been dropped by one of the British soldiers killed in the crash. He calculated where the gunfire peppering the vehicle was originating from and pointed his weapon. Knowing the bulletproof glass in the windshield was one way, Morrison fired through it. He could just barely make out the form of a sniper plunging out a fourth story window of the hotel.

Another burst of gunfire came from two floors below where the first sniper had been. Morrison could not see where it was coming from, but he could hear the distinctive sound of a SPR firing at them. He aimed at the sound and pulled the trigger on the grenade launcher. There was a flash and concussion form the grenade exploding in the room. Morrison waited; he suppressed the pain, thirst and lightheadedness to see if any more gunfire would be returned. More SPR's peppered the vehicle sounding like hail on a tin roof.  Morrison was able to crawl next to the British soldier that rescued him and whisper "two and seven o'clock." The soldier shook his head in an effort to clear it; then he nodded in acknowledgement and took the weapon out of Morrison hands.  He quickly scampered out through the shattered windshield and disappeared. Morrison reached over and grabbed a bottle of water that had been dislodged from storage when they were hit. He drank the whole bottle in a matter of seconds with the dual purpose to stop his overpowering thirst and to stay alive.  Morrison wondered despite his efforts if he would survive, if he ever would have the chance to get married and have children. Morrison's thoughts were quickly brought back to the present when he heard two short bursts of gunfire. A few moments later the British soldier appeared as quickly as he had vanished.

"Got both of them," he said as he held up two fingers while he looked around at his men who were alive, "Come with me, we don't have time for a bounding maneuver, this will be us, running up the street. Be very aware of snipers on rooftops or in windows."

He motioned for them to exit. He stopped for a moment looking at the three dead soldiers in the vehicle and shook his head in grief. He handed Morrison a pistol and looked him in the eyes.

"We have got to get to Bennu on foot. We will come back for you." He said to Morrison in a resolute but reassuring manner.

"Two blocks over. Paint targets, press COM, give code: Delta, Sierra, Zulu 134." Morrison gasped, with a gurgling sound the British soldier took to be a death rattle.

"I promise, we will not abandon you. I give you my word."

The large British soldier stuck his face into the runner and gave Morrison a wink.

"Give us a smile!" he said in an attempt to bolster Morrison's spirits. The soldier who rescued Morrison, clearly in charge, barked at the sturdy soldier.

"Sir Kenneth! We have a mission to complete!"

The larger soldier turned and bowed before they both sprinted off with the remaining three other soldiers. Morrison was left alone to contemplate his fate. He did not want to die, but he was not afraid of death, and if he was to die he wanted the mission to be a success. Though his own mortality did not frighten him, his survival instincts and his years of training overpowered any urges to give in and stop clinging to life. His eyes scanned the scattered contents of the vehicle to see if there were any medical supplies. A box labeled "morphine" lay on top of one of the dead soldiers. Morrison was in pain but wanted to stay alert, if he was going to survive the whole ordeal, he had to remain lucid. Morrison chuckled to himself when he thought of lucidity; he was not sure after being shot if everything he had witnessed hadn't been a vivid hallucination. As he struggled to stay awake, he was also aware of becoming disoriented. He knew that if the British soldiers were successful, the missiles would be launched from MacDill Air Force Base in Florida and they would have five minutes to evacuate the area.

The scramjet missiles could very easily vaporize a city block. Morrison heard the sound of a vehicle approaching and pulling up next to the runner. He checked the recoil nine-millimeter pistol to ensure that it was loaded and aimed it at the front of the Runner. As the sound of footsteps grew closer, he readied himself to shoot. The large British soldier he heard called Kenneth climbed into the front of the vehicle and held up his hands at the sight of a gun being pointed at him.

"How am I supposed to rescue you whilst you have that very large pistol pointed at me?"

Morrison dropped the gun in relief and tried to crawl to the front of the runner. Kenneth and the younger British soldier Morrison had seen earlier came in and grabbed him. He was carefully but quickly lifted by his shoulders and feet and carried out to an SUV that had been hot-wired by Kenneth. They gingerly loaded Morrison in the back before climbing in themselves. The engine was gunned and the SUV tore away from the scene. Everyone held on as they barreled down the street at full speed, fleeing from the target.

"We called it in, now let's see if they believed us," the leader of the British soldiers said from the front passenger seat.

Morrison again propped himself up on his elbows and lifted his head. He could see in the fading sunset three brilliant orange dots streaking across the sky. The leader of the British soldiers also saw them.

"There are the Scramjets!"

The missiles were traveling at such a high velocity that they had begun to glow from friction with the air. Kenneth floored the SUV again when he saw them, wanting to get more distance between them and the target. Morrison, realizing the mission had been accomplished, let himself pass out one final time.

The British soldiers pulled over in an open field next to a children's hospital and stepped out to watch the impact behind them. The scramjet missiles came in faster than the speed of sound, and were almost undetectable to the human eye. They heard and felt the thump of the missiles impacting followed by the sound of the missiles themselves. The ground shook and a huge crimson fireball emerged from behind a high-rise hotel as the missiles hit the secret research facility and the Roman Armor. The hotel, constructed in 1998, was solid, it's exterior walls were brown granite; the whole construction of the hotel looked as if it was cut from a mountain and placed there in the middle of downtown Kansas City. Yet for all its strength, the building began to lean, and let out a deafening crack, before collapsing and sending up a cloud of dust, raining debris over the whole area. The impact from the missiles had eradicated the Roman column, but at a high cost. There were only twenty scramjet missiles left in the U.S. arsenal, and the Romans were developing their own version of the scramjet.

Morrison slowly opened his eyes, blurry from a deep sleep. He was aware of a beeping noise, which came from a heart monitor next to him. He felt his chest, running his fingers over the two wireless diodes affixed to it. He looked down at his arm that had an I.V. catheter fed into it from a plastic bag hanging off of an old hat rack. He was in a hospital bed that would commonly be found in any hospital, although it was clearly older and had been used frequently. Morrison felt for a button to call a nurse, but he could not find one. This was not the first time he had awoken in hospital after a mission, so he was not alarmed. He strained to sit up and look around. When he did, the realization came that he was not in a hospital room, but in a house. It was an older house that by its design Morrison estimated was built in the 1950's. He sat up and looked around the room- he was sore and realized everything that happened was not a dream.

An assortment of old furniture from the 1950's through the twenty-teens filled the room. He turned his head quickly at the sound of footsteps and saw the silhouette of a figure filling the doorway; Morrison realized who it was right away even though midday fall sun flooded the doorway with light from behind, obscuring the strangers' face. It was the soldier that rescued him in Arrowhead Stadium. The soldier read the confusion on Morrison's face and answered unsolicited.

"We found the owners of this house dead. They had been done in by Legionnaires doing a house-to-house search. Our intelligence tells us the door-to-door searches were not even strategic. Apparently, General Kravchenko has a taste for blonde teenage girls and sent a unit of Praetorians to find one. Anyone who answered the door and did not fit the bill was shot, as were many people in their sleep." The soldier looked around the room, imagining the quaint life the former occupants must have lived. "It is such a waste of life, I found an old scrap book, the couple were in their 80's and had just celebrated their 60th wedding anniversary; this had been their home for that long. We took over the house as a base of operations. It is a large house so it could accommodate all of us. These ranch-style homes were laid out long, so we have positions set up around the entire perimeter. We buried the couple in coffins in their back yard. We will make sure that they have the proper respect when all this is over. No one knows we are here, we are all supposed to be dead."

Morrison sat up and gave an intense stare to the soldier.

"Funny you should mention that. Who are you people?"

The soldier walked into the room and sat in a dented old brown metal folding chair that had been placed next to Morrison's bed.

"My name is Owen Badon, and I am the last surviving member of The House of Badon, I am the legitimate King of England."

Morrison gave out a quick laugh, "How do I know that's true?"

King Owen gave a slight polite smile in response, "You don't. I was eighth in succession to the throne. Caprera killed my entire family, and anyone who could be remotely considered in succession to the throne in order to legitimize making his sister Queen of England. It was the last formal act of Parliament before it was disbanded. "

"King…." Morrison paused for a moment, "…Owen was it? You have to understand just how crazy this all sounds. My team drops in to Arrowhead, we get ambushed by Roman Special Forces, and then I am saved by the King of England? That is just a little surreal. Besides, I thought Royalty did not use last names."

King Owen nodded in agreement, "I never thought I would be King, I suppose I have to learn not to use it."

Morrison looked at the bandages on his side, "Who patched me up?"

"We have a physician who came from Canada; he's an expert in battlefield medicine. Fortunately, we have five type O's here, their blood is what kept you alive. Our doctor is also an accomplished surgeon and he was able to repair the internal injuries and stop the hemorrhaging."

Morrison forgot about his weakness and pain, and sat bolt upright, still in disbelief that he was actually speaking to the King of England.

"What was your title before your family was killed?" He said quickly and forcefully using a reverse interrogation technique in hopes of catching his host off guard.

King Owen smiled and calmly leaned back in his chair.

"Ah yes, my vaunted title. I did not want a title, but my Uncle felt the need to bestow one upon me. On my eighteenth birthday, I was named the *Duke of Sussex*, much to the dismay two of my cousins who were upset their father gave me the title instead of one of them. They were first and second in line for the throne, and they both wanted that title, I assured them that it was not something I solicited. It caused a little friction, but I was not going to be spending a lot of time at Buckingham Palace since I was going into the army, so I was not troubled by it."

Still performing a reverse interrogation, Morrison latched on another detail that stood out.

"Look, I have to ask you, what is up with the sword?"

King Owen had heard the question more than once.

"I am very proficient with it" he said in a non-boastful tone "when I was nine years old I was given the choice between horseback riding, archery and fencing. I chose fencing, at which I excelled. I became fascinated with different types of swords and sword fighting. I studied Kendo, Musool and the German, Spanish and Italian schools of fencing. It has been quite a handy tool. The sword can be thrust between joints in Roman armor to kill them."

Morrison was still skeptical, but the story King Owen told about his life had a level of detail he had not expected to hear. Conversely, Morrison knew that an insane person could not easily make up a story as intricate as the one he was just told, and give no external signs of lying.

He again snapped at King Owen.

"Why are you in the United States, and how the hell did you get here?"

King Owen's patience had not run short, he knew if he was in Morrison's position he would be as equally leery of anything he was told.

"As I said, I was eighth in line to be on the throne, so I was not likely to be King. I wanted to serve my country so I joined the Army. I became a member of the S.A.S. three years after joining, on my nineteenth birthday. It was then on my 22$^{nd}$ birthday that the invasion of my country occurred. I was on a mission to destroy a Roman satellite relay station on the French side of Burgundy when the invasion happened. My uncle, King Harold the third, was advised by the Prime Minister that the entire royal family was likely to be targeted for assassination, and a member of the Caprera family placed on the throne. My uncle had my family's entire fortune, six-billion pounds, wired to a Swiss bank account just a few days before he was killed. I tried to make my way back to England when the rest of my family was killed in what was supposed to be Vasekt terrorist attacks, but everyone knew it was Caprera's doing. I lost both of my parents, my brothers, my grandparents, my cousins, my aunt and uncle".

King Owen stopped for a moment, he looked straight ahead, like he was staring past Morrison, his eyes did not seem sad, but angry which relayed what had been taken from him. King Owen gathered himself and continued.

"The members in my unit and other S.A.S. units met at the rally point, Villa Kennedy in Frankfurt. The Special Forces units that were there pledged their loyalty to me as the new King, and were knighted. It was a moment I shall never forget, my friends and people I did not know, blindly trusting me to be their leader. A month later, the United States was invaded, and it was clear that we had to get to America and attack the Romans. A plan was devised and the best from each unit joined me. We acquired a cargo freighter and sailed to Jacksonville, Florida, from there, making our way to the battle zone. The U.S. security was so lax when we arrived we were never stopped, even though we were loaded down with military grade weapons."

Morrison's doubt in King Owen's story was fading and his curiosity grew.

"Why here, why not go back to England? If you're King, isn't that where you should be?"

King Owen leaned forward with the same burning look Morrison had noticed in his eyes earlier.

"The United Kingdom cannot be freed from the shackles of Rome without its greatest friend and ally; the United States must be whole for that to happen. We will only take England back with U.S. military intervention." King Owen then stood, turned, and paced several times before turning back to Morrison. "I have been called brave by many, and a great warrior by some of my fellow soldiers, which may or may not be true. What is true is that I don't know if I could have continued to fight if the life was bleeding out of me. I spoke to the doctor about it, you were in circulatory shock. I don't know of anyone who could fight the way you fought in that condition, save not dying from it. I have no doubt that you are the greatest soldier that I or any of us has ever seen. I think you could be a great asset in fighting the Romans, one that gives us a greater chance of success."

Morrison was woozy, and he was not sure of what he was hearing.

"Just what is your unit? You want me to join the SAS?" he said in a sharp tone.

King Owen walked over and tore a Velcro flap back on the left shoulder of his black uniform to reveal a coat of arms.

"We are all supposed to be dead, it gives us an advantage. We operate on our own, as a group of knights. We have no authority to answer to but my authority. I weigh each knight's opinions as equal to mine. There is a code that we adhere to but it is basically this: defend the weak, display honor at all times, and keep no secrets from your fellow knights. Yes, we are the resurrection of a long dead ideal, but with new purpose. You are now dead in the eyes of your government. Our blood now flows through you veins. Now that I have lost several good knights, I ask, will you join us?"

Morrison was silent, caught off guard and uncharacteristically speechless. He thought about loyalty to his country, joining a group of British Knights could be considered treason, or at the very least desertion. He also realized that spies had infiltrated the Pentagon, Arrowhead was proof enough of that, and that there could be no covert missions as long as that was true.

"I will join you, but I won't give up my citizenship," Morrison said with conviction.

"I understand your loyalty, nor would I require that of you. But it has to be understood I am in command."

Morrison laughed out loud and grabbed his side in pain.

"Why would I dispute your authority after you saved me, smacked down the Romans and completed my mission? I would follow you anywhere; you are a great commander and tactician from what I've seen so far."

King Owen did not acknowledge the compliment as if he were uncomfortable with that much praise.

"We train almost every day, we live in the shadows while we grow our ranks. Are you sure you want to be a part of our order."

"Look, with all due respect your highness, I am, ...was, a Green Beret. I am used to training and working behind enemy lines. I am going to trust you, even though this sounds insane."

King Owen was a perfectionist and had deep conviction when it came to his group of knights.

"I was in the S.A.S. and that, nor the Green Berets, is not enough on their own. We have to be better than the Praetorian Guard if we are to win. They have better technology, more support and greater numbers. What we possess, that the Praetorian lacks is virtue, conviction and providence. We train harder than they do because we have to, and because that is what it means to be a knight. We defend the weak; we don't prey on them as do the Romans. We don't expect to be trusted or respected by anyone, we must earn those privileges. We constantly strive to learn so we have an edge in intelligence and knowledge. We never give up, even in the face of death, which is what we saw in you. The threat of impending death did not keep you from completing your mission. "

"So, what's the name of your order?" Morrison said still somewhat suspicious.

"I swore that Big Ben would ring again when I return as King. One of the knights, Kenneth, dubbed us the Knights of the Clock Tower. He is the overly muscular one who looks like a rhinoceros. Kenneth was the one who carried you most of the way when you were shot. "

King Owen turned his head and looked out the window at the trees whose leaves were turning gold and amber; it reminded him of the way autumn looked in Sandringham Forest. Suddenly, he remembered the feeling he had when his home was invaded. He turned back and looked at Morrison with a piercing stare.

"The Praetorians knew you were coming, you don't need me to tell you that. What you don't realize is that the Romans were panicked. We know from chatter that someone infiltrated their forward command post, and downloaded information about their systems, hardware, and plans. We don't know who did it, and I assume it was not the CIA or your unit would not have been here. Whoever did it was not only brave, but also brilliant. We would do well to recruit whoever it was to our ranks, but until then we must fight. We will stay put until you are well enough to travel, and then we strike the Romans."

# CHAPTER IV

Emperor Caprera was dressed in the hybrid toga-suit combination named after him, seated outdoors at a long mahogany table eating breakfast, as was his custom. The table was situated in the middle of the courtyard and surrounded by a colonnade at his newly constructed country Villa. As was the case with all new construction since Caprera became Emperor, it looked as if it could have been transported from Roman antiquity. The surrounding interior walls were adorned with freezes made from cultured marble, one depicting the birth of Venus, the next wall had a depiction of Castor and Pollux abducting the daughters of King Leucippus, and two other marble walls had depictions of Caprera's defeat of the Vasekts. The landscaping was equally impeccable; a small garden containing chamomile, oleanders and violets were planted in clusters in front of Date palms. A reflecting pool stretched out from the garden to the table where Caprera sat. The whole scene was idyllic and tranquil, which stood in contrast to Caprera's love of battle and conquest.

Standing just behind the emperor on either side were two striking slave girls. Both were dressed in white tunics that came up six inches above the knee, and both were barefoot. One was a trophy, the youngest daughter of the Vasekt Sultan, a slender dark haired dark eyed beauty, used to being treated as property, and whose life had actually improved from the constant beatings and fear of being sold to a husband as her older sister had been. The other, an auburn haired waif with pale skin was indentured to remove her family's debt. She was to remain the emperor's personal slave for five years; the betrayal of her parents had crushed her spirit. Both slaves stood at the ready, for whatever the Emperor needed.

Caprera always attended to some official matter while he ate breakfast, he found it productive to do both at the same time. From the far side of the courtyard four young soldiers in formal attire strolled in front of him and lined up shoulder to shoulder, saluting him by beating their fists over their hearts. Caprera stood up and returned the salute to the four young men in front of him.

"You are to be congratulated; you each have completed seven months of training to be a candidate for the Praetorian Guard. You can shoot with the precision of a sniper, you can fight with the ferocity of a lion, and you can sneak up on your enemy without being detected. You are the best of the Roman Legion. You can kill more efficiently and with less effort than your brothers in arms, yet that is not enough. Anyone can learn to kill; it is the nature of man to kill to save himself. Killing comes as natural to us as breathing if we find our life is in danger. Killing is easy; that is not what makes you a Praetorian. Sacrifice for the glory of Rome is what separates a Praetorian from a lesser man. You must not only be willing to kill, but be gladly willing to die if it means that Rome will continue to bring order to the other lands of the earth." Caprera smiled, truly proud of the group in front of him.

"There are three tasks that you can choose from to complete your training. Your first choice is to ascend to the summit of Mount Everest unaided and return in five days. Your next choice is to swim across Trasimeno Lake while wearing a diver's belt. Your third choice is to be dropped into Greenland with no equipment and find your way to our base thirty miles away. Death is the consequence of failure in all of these tasks, but it is better to die in the pursuit of glory, than to live with the bitter taste of failure. Know that when you have completed this, other men will look at you and know that you are superior to them; they will step aside to let you pass. Wives will look at their husbands and wish they were a Praetorian, like you. Children will look at you and see what they want to become when they grow up. I will choose my successor from the ranks of the Praetorian Guard one day. If you decide that you do not want to choose one of these three tasks, there will be no punishment. The shame of being a coward will be punishment enough." Caprera saluted them and sat back in his char. They quickly saluted again, turned, and strode for the exit.

Another figure passed them on the garden path, he was a tall and slightly chubby figure dressed in a gray Armani suit. His face was clean shaven and his dark brown hair parted and slicked back, he walked with a confidence that showed he was of some importance. He stood in front of the table and gave a tepid salute "Emperor" he said with an assured smile his eyebrows slightly raised in a waggish expression. He took the chair next to Caprera, and began to gather mounds of biscotti and colazione on a china plate. He was Charles Fletcher, former child genus, Rhode Scholar, playwright, Broadway director and U.S. ambassador to Italy. He was young by anyone's standards. At age twenty-eight he was dispatched to Italy by the White House after working in the state department. He had been in Italy for six months when the Vasekts brought about the collapse of the Italian government. Caprera, after conquering the Vasekts, sought out Charles to help him restore the government. It was the two together that devised the idea of a new Roman Empire. Charles accepted the position of Praetorian Prefect, the highest ranking official next to the Emperor. Together he and Caprera planned and molded the new Empire. Both Charles and Caprera agreed a benevolent dictator would be needed to bring order to Rome and the surrounding European countries that were also descending into anarchy after Vasekt attacks. Charles had become one of the most powerful and feared men in the world in a very short time.

"Well Giovanni, that looked to be a promising group of fine young men." Charles said as one of the slaves poured coffee into his cup, he turned and smiled at the sultan's daughter, "Thank you dear" he had a weakness for attractive women and could not resist flirting, even in that setting.

Caprera cocked his head to the side and giving Charles a sideways glance while cutting his breakfast and speaking. "We won't know until they have tested their mettle. No one knows their true self until they are faced with death."

Charles gave a wry smile, "If that is the case, I hope that my true self and I remain unequivocal strangers." Charles said lifting his cup in a toast.

Caprera laughed at his confidant's comment and raised his glass in return. Caprera expression changed suddenly and leaned forward and spoke in a hushed tone to Charles.

"What about America?"

The question of America was a sensitive one, all other nations that they had invaded had bent to their will, but the United States was far more difficult than anticipated. It was thought by Rome, that the American populace had become weak, and was growing disillusioned with their form of government. The Americans had proved to be more resistant to invasion and change than first thought.

"I must tell you Giovanni, that my former countrymen are quite a problem. Specifically it is not the military, but civilians who have been a *nuisance*" the word was a deliberate understatement.

Charles watched Caprera, but saw no outward signs of the fits of rage that the Emperor was given to have, so he cautiously continued.

"In the states that border the ground we have taken, gun store owners and department stores have been giving guns and ammunition away freely, to anyone who wants to fight against our cohorts. Militias have formed and evaded our patrols on the front lines; they are even blowing holes in our border wall with some kind of crude, homemade explosives. In Tempe, a crowd of what were believed to be townspeople watching a parade of our soldiers, pulled out guns and slaughtered thirty of our soldiers. It was quite the massacre, it seemed everyone was armed: men, women, grandmothers, children in strollers. When our reinforcements finally arrived, we could not find one gun among any of the houses we searched."

Caprera's eyes narrowed as he listened to the report. He sat motionless taking deep, long breaths and then suddenly slammed his fist against the table, sending plates and glasses tumbling to the ground.

"Boil them!"

Charles, who was used to Caprera's punishments, was caught off guard. "What?"

Caprera spoke through clenched teeth, "Boil them! We must make an example of their leaders, and anyone who would take part."

He slammed his fist again.

Charles spoke again in a soothing tone. "I think that might inspire even further revolt, I think enslavement would be more effective."

Caprera seemed to shake slightly from the display of anger, taking slow deep breaths to cultivate self-control.

"You are right... of course... Charles."

Charles nodded, "I will see to it that they are rounded up and sent to a work-camp in England."

Caprera had been exceedingly cruel in his campaign in Turkey, Syria and Tunisia. The Emperor had more than twenty thousand men, women, and children crucified in Turkey, and ten thousand in Tunisia to dissuade the last vestiges of the Vasekts from reorganizing. He had the Vasekt Sultan force-fed the remains of his son before he was buried alive, which cemented the terror he had instilled in the Vasekts. In contrast to the cruelty, he had schools built, educated women and made sure they had equal rights with men. Caprera envisioned an enlightened society, a jewel in the crown of the new Roman Empire. Tunis was chosen and renamed Carthage, as the area was known in antiquity. Caprera was an enigma, how his extreme cruelty was only exceeded by his desire to create a utopian society. He still hoped for Utopia in America. The Americans would gladly die for their freedom, something that was not present in the Vasekt territories; being free was not in the nature of a Vasekt.

"We must send more troops to America; we must make sure that it is never taken back by Washington." Caprera said with a calm earnestness.

"I agree, that is the only way to ensure that those states remain under our control." Charles said with another confident smile.

Caprera placed his hand on his advisors shoulder, "Charles, as usual you are great council. We would not be where we are without you. I also believe my daughter would appreciate a visit from you."

Charles stood up, nodded, and saluted, "I won't keep her waiting." He turned and made his way across the courtyard.

Charles kept track of all events; he was involved with every aspect of the government from economic to diplomatic. His unusual genius allowed him to have multiple high profile roles, while never overlooking anything. It was the same genius that catapulted him to fame as an adolescent, when even then the word *prodigy* seemed too light to describe his various talents. When he was 15, a private performing arts school production of the "King Lear," set in Saudi Arabia, was an avant-garde production that was a wild success. The play was re-written and directed by Charles, who also played the part of Edgar. Repeat performances were added, which was unheard of for any school. Word spread quickly among the theater community, and one year later he was directing Macbeth on Broadway, this time set in ancient Japan. After a year on Broadway he shocked the public and left it behind when he was offered early admittance to Columbia University along with a job. He attended The School of International and Public Affairs while teaching at the Barnard Department of Theater. He met and Married his first wife, Agnes, a student in the theater department who was a buxom twenty year old actress. She fell madly in love with him after witnessing his brand of bravado at a lecture he gave. Upon graduation he abandoned the theater completely, divorced Agnes and became a Rhode Scholar. Two years later he went to work for the state department; his intellect allowed him to advance through the ranks rapidly, gaining even more notoriety. He met his second wife Aria, the President of Mexico's daughter, while at the state department. He was next given the position of Ambassador to Italy, that and numerous affairs led to a second divorce. Everything had led him to Rome where he and Caprera were reshaping the face of Europe and the Middle East.

Charles quickly strolled through the garden and into the villa; his purpose was interrupted by the sound of music coming from a room down the hall. He walked across the marble floors to a large corner room. On the wall was a mosaic of Caprera's code of arms, a red shield with SPQR in gold letters with a Lion and Wolf standing on either side facing the shield. Underneath was written "TERMINATIO, CARITAS, IMPERIUM" (Determination, Charity, Power to Command). Dancing by herself across the red, blue and tan mosaic guilloche pattern on the floor was Caesaris Caprera. The sight of the Emperor's daughter always impressed Charles; she was of a slender build, and sleek features. Her wide hazel eyes locked into concentration that made her seem older than her sixteen years of age. Her mouth was small but ample and her lips were pursed in an expression of determination. Her full arched eyebrows, high cheeks and perfectly shaped nose looked as if her father had commissioned the best sculptor in Rome to make them. Her wavy strawberry blonde hair was pinned up to keep from getting in her face. She wore a blue sleeveless stolla that was embroidered with gold thread. Her long arms and legs were bent in what was a cross between ballet and the ancient Etruscan dance she was trying to recreate which made her seem taller than her diminutive stature. She twirled to see Charles standing there and grinned at seeing her old friend, and bent into a bow, her dress coming to rest over her slender bare feet. Charles, without hesitation, broke into applause, "Bravo!"

"Charles, dance with me!" Caesaris said extending her hand and turning her wrist to hold out an open palm.

An accomplished dancer as a child, and presently she was credited for starting the new traditional dance craze of the empire. Caesaris had created the dance for parties at the Basilica Caprera. Charles knew the dance well; he had been a routine partner to her since he was constantly present at the palace. Charles gave a slight bow and obliged Caesaris, joining her in the dance. He glanced over her shoulder at the room, it had been cleared of all furniture, and he could see the Holo-Def screen in the adjoining room was focused on Roman troop movements inside New Mexico. Charles gave Caesaris a playful scalding look,

"Does your father know you have cleared his conference room of all the furniture and hardware?" Charles was well aware of the answer, but asked it anyway.

Caesaris raised her right eyebrow, "Does it matter?"

"Yes, to your father, I believe it does." Charles chuckled.

"He can fix it when I am done. He is not my keeper."

Charles laughed again, louder than before, "I have no doubt of that!" He gathered himself and continued, "I was told that you were in Venice working on your restoration projects."

"I was. I have to speak to my father about his plan to change Salute into a temple for Neptune. Defacing that basilica is wrong; it is part of the city's history."

Charles shook his head, "My dear, Rome is now its history."

"Father said as much, but he yielded when I pressed him." She said with a self assured smile.

"As you did with the Vatican?" Charles meant it as more of a statement than a question.

Caesaris was determined and had more acumen than someone twice her age, making her as headstrong as her father. She was proud of what she had accomplished and was not ashamed to admit it. She decided to give Charles more ribbing.

"My mother did raise me to be a Catholic."

"Your mother died when you were very young."

Caesaris face changed to an expression of absorption, "What I can remember, she gave me my first rosary before she died. She told me to keep it a secret."

"I understand why, your father greatly disapproves; you know he feels Christianity makes those who practice it weak."

"Weak? Do I strike you as weak Charles?" She said teasing him.

"I suspect that if anyone thought of you as weak, they would receive a prompt shot to the chops."

Caesaris smiled and stopped dancing and gave Charles another graceful bow. Charles returned the gesture kissing her hand and nodded his head.

"Till we meet again"

Charles said as left the room. She was left standing alone, and no longer felt like dancing. Caesaris was always sad when Charles left; he had been her best friend since the rise of the empire. He felt like the older brother she never had, and his absence was felt when he left.

Caesaris adored her father, but was troubled at the same time. He had raised her until she was eight years old, when his duties as Caesar took too much of his time. Caesaris was then sent to a boarding school in the occupied Paris where she learned both French and English. Those were unhappy days for her in the beginning, but it is where she gained her love of art and dance. Caesaris had few friends until she reached the age of fourteen. Her classmates took notice of her, not only because of her elegance and comeliness; they took notice of her inner strength. It was these qualities that made her the talk of Rome when she returned. Her public appearances garnered almost as much attention as her fathers. She was nearly as important as the Roman government officials because of her prominence in the public eye; her leadership qualities were natural and unforced. She was sent as a good will diplomat to countries that had agreed to become part of the Empire, where she was also greatly popular, a weighty responsibility for a teenager. She related to Charles so well because, like him, she was also a prodigy, Caesaris had already graduated from Sapiens University with a degree in the humanities. Despite the public's perception of her as a leader she continued to anger her father by holding an ongoing friendship with the Pope. Caprera did not like Christianity; he believed in the gods of ancient Rome and worshiped them. He blamed his predecessors, the emperors Constantine and Theodosius, for making the Empire weak. He had an even harsher attitude towards Jesus, who he said turned a cross from a symbol of fear to one of worship. Caprera had restored ancient temples and brought about a new religion, which was a hybrid of the old religions and new age, of which he was the high priest. Caesaris then began to use her influence with her father to save Florentine and Venetian treasures that were based in biblical themes. Religion and love of Renaissance art was the main source of the friction between her and her father, who otherwise could not be closer. She did not inject herself into his policy of wars and security, and he let her have her pet projects.

As she stood staring at the intricate design on the floor, Caesaris heard footsteps approaching from behind, she turned to greet whoever it was entering the room. She lifted her gaze to see it was her father; he'd finished breakfast and was on his way to meet with the President of France, who was there to pay tribute. Caprera's eyes twinkled as he smiled.

"Why are you always practicing a dance that requires two people? When is my beautiful daughter going to take a suitor?" The emperor laughed. Caesaris crossed her arms in an accusatory stance "When I find one you don't terrify."

Caprera gave a gentle smile, "What happened to that boy in France?"

Caesaris rolled her eyes, "Marcel? You don't remember? You told him that at the last second the gods must have decided to make him a man instead of a woman." Caesaris said as she slowly began to walk away from him.

"Where are you going? I am speaking to you." Caprera gave Caesaris more leeway than he would of anyone else, but was slightly indignant.

Caesaris could see her father's frustration, "I am well aware of that fact." She said in the sweetest tone she could produce.

Caprera's anger melted under his adoration for his daughter. "Come and translate for me, the President of France is waiting in the Ceres room."

"I will, if you don't touch Salute." Caesaris said as she stopped and pivoted around to look her father in the eyes seeing if he would give up the old church in Venice.

He threw up his hands. "How can I refuse my daughter?"

She hugged him and laughed, "Easily and frequently as I recall."

"I had to make sure for the sake of Rome, that you did not jeopardize our image."

Caesaris leaned back to look up into his eyes, "That is the problem, when did you do anything for my sake?"

"Caesaris! You are the most powerful woman in the Roman Empire, you are waited on hand and foot and I permit your little projects."

"I still love you, and it is because of that I am going to translate. I trust that you won't choose another building in Venice for your temple?" The question needed no answer.

They walked down a long corridor with yet another intricate mosaic on the wall; this one was of Mars embracing Venus. They continued past the mosaic until they finally reached a large room at the end of the hall. It was a vast domed room with a few windows in the top of the paneled ceiling. The floors were polished black marble and the walls were painted maroon. The entire room had a mix of 21$^{st}$ century and ancient Rome. In the middle of the room was a marble statue of Ceres holding wheat, a gift that was given to the Emperor as a symbol of gratitude from the French government when he drove the Vasekts from France. At the end of the room were three large red velvet sofas. They were arranged in a half square so as to give a better view of the countryside.

Seated on one of the sofas was the President of France, Jean Marc Vichy, who was responsible for both his country's surrender, and subsequent annexation as part of the Roman Empire. Vichy was short and chubby; his face and hands looked like that of an infants and his fine, thinning blonde hair compounded the strange image, making him appear absolutely cherubic. Vichy knew France was not able to defeat Rome, so he decided to strike a deal that made him President of France for life; those who disputed were imprisoned or killed by the Roman government. Part of Vichy's duties was to travel to Rome on a regular basis and report to Emperor Caprera. In France he was a formidable leader, who ruled with an iron hand. The citizens of France either revered him or feared crossing him. He had several mistresses which he made no attempt to hide from the press. It was a role reversal when he came to visit Caprera, he lost all swagger and was reduced to a quivering mass of insecurity.

Seated next to Vichy was Sabrina Caprera, the Emperor's second wife. Sabrina was a strikingly alluring model and was on the runway at the age of fourteen years old. Her eyes were opal and her eyelids had a sleepy quality, her face was soft with a supple mouth. Her hair was golden blonde and swept over her face giving her an overall languid quality. Her unusual beauty had landed her several high profile ad campaigns across the globe; she had an ambition to match Caesar's. She had met Caprera at a party in his honor when she was just fifteen years old and they both fell in love not only with each other but the idea of what each could do for the other. Sabrina was accustomed to the lifestyle of a model and its excesses, which she brought to her new title as empress. Drugs and illicit affairs had been whispered about, but no one wanted to speak to Caprera about his new wife, so the whispers stayed just that. There was also friction between her and Caesaris, who despised each other for different reasons. Sabrina was envious of how the beauty of Caesaris, which she considered inferior, was considered as great as her own by the public. Caesaris despised that her stepmother was just one year older than she was, and the wanton party girl demeanor she displayed. Sabrina found comfort in all night parties and Raphaella, her constant best friend and constant companion from the modeling world.

Sabrina found Vichy repulsive, and although Vichy disgusted her, she took sadistic delight in making him squirm. She used all means at her disposal to torment him, and was quite effective. Sabrina was always conscience she was an Empress, and knew that both her power and beauty made Vichy apprehensive. Each time she received word Vichy was coming to Rome, she would find a particularly revealing outfit to wear. Sabrina would hide her revulsion and would touch his hand, shoulder or neck frequently; the intent behind her gentle touch was as malicious as that of someone throwing a punch. Each brush of her long golden hair might as well been a whip. Caprera entered the Room with Caesaris, which Sabrina took as an opportunity to make Vichy even more uncomfortable. She walked up to Caprera and gave him a blistering kiss while looking at the French President.

"Enough," the Emperor whispered in her ear not wanting to take part in one of her games. She looked into his eyes and gave a smile that was meant to convey her innocence, but instead was conveyed to everyone in the room as cruelty. She then glided over to the other sofa and stretched to her full length, the high cut white dress falling behind her to reveal her legs, drawing yet another scornful look from the Emperor.

Seated on the opposite sofa were Marco Napolitano and Senator Enrico Sulla. Marco was the Praetorian Prefect and the Emperor's first cousin. He was chosen out of all the members of the Praetorian Guard by the Emperor to command it. Caprera felt he could be trusted because they shared the same blood. The trust was well placed as Marco was also fiercely loyal to his cousin. He had joined the army to follow in the footsteps of his parents and cousin. His hatred of the Vasekts was perhaps the most acute of anyone in the Emperor's inner circle, save the emperor himself. After their retirement from the military his parents became police officers in Rome, both were on duty at Palazzo Montecitorio and were killed when the Vasekts destroyed it. The death of his parents blinded Marco with rage. In the war against the Vasekts he had gained notoriety for his time in the 9th Parachute Assault Regimen. In one battle in particular, his unit had been deployed into the heart of Turkey, the other units that were supposed to join them were mistakenly deployed over two hundred miles away. His unit was outnumbered one hundred eighty-seven to twelve. He killed ninety Vasekts and rescued his teammate who was the only other survivor of his unit. Because his unit had been able to hold off the enemy for thirty-six hours it allowed other units to come to their aid and ultimately win the battle. He was a hero, and a propaganda tool; Marco became almost as popular as the Emperor. His square jaw with a cleft chin was the spitting image of his cousins, his lean muscular frame and wavy dark brown hair made him the most sought after bachelor in Rome. He was also influential in the spread of paganism amongst the Roman public; he had adopted his cousin's faith and credited prayer and sacrifices to Mars and Apollo for his success in the battle. His speaking skills afforded him the adoration of his troops; some said he was an equal to his cousin with regards to giving speeches.

Senator Sulla was the oldest person in the room at fifty-seven, though he was nearly in the same shape as when he was in the military, but with deep wrinkles in his olive skin that ran the length from his jaw to his cheeks and deep furrows that ran from his forehead to the top of his shaved scalp, weathering due to many years in the Mediterranean sun. He was dressed in a traditional Roman tunic and sandals, having fully embraced the identity of a Roman Senator. Sulla held many of the same ideals as the Emperor, as a child he was a great admirer of the Roman Empire and was an effective soldier as well. As was the case with Marco he had gained notoriety in the war with the Vasekts. When the government was destroyed, he rejoined the army and quickly rose through the ranks due to his mastery of military tactics. Despite his advanced age he would advance from one rank to another in a short amount of time until he had finally achieved the rank of Colonel under Caprera. He and the Emperor struck a bond and there was not a battle that did not bear the influence of his council.

When the war was over and the Emperor and Charles Fletcher were planning the new empire, he was the only choice they could see as head of the Senate. His father had been mayor of Turin and he had first hand insight to politics. He was given nearly as much power as Charles Fletcher. In the event that the emperor became incapacitated, he would be given control of the armed forces. Senator Sulla also hid well his desire to be Emperor, although he would not move to kill Caprera, he would not turn it down if something was to happen to the Emperor. His nature was so secretive that he would never allow anyone to see him lose his temper in public; he did not want his enemies to gain any insight into what could manipulate him.

All three of the men rose and saluted the Emperor slapping their clinched fist above their heart and in Unisom chanting "Hail Caesar!" to the nodding approval of the Emperor who returned the salute. Caesaris walked in behind her father and threw a glare of disapproval at Sabrina who took pleasure in her daughter in law's distain for her.

"Jean Marc, my dear friend! It is good to see you!" the Emperor said grasping the President by the shoulder and kissing him on either cheek. Caesaris immediately translated her father's words and would do so with Vichy when he spoke to her father.

"It has been too long since we last saw each other Caesar." He said with a wide smile.

Caprera returned the smile, but his face slowly changed to a dower expression, "Tell me Jean-Marc, what is it that I have been hearing about protest in France?"

"It is nothing, we have been able to jail these criminals and stop their lies and deceit. The odd thing is" he stopped and stared at Caprera nervously, and then quickly changed his gaze to Caesaris, "the odd thing is they are not French, they have been coming from England somehow. We are trying to find them and the route they are taking to get into France. They have been distributing garbage stating that the true King of England is alive and will be coming to save not only England, but all of Europe. It is so silly that we have not been too worried about it." Vichy said in a slightly horse tone of voice.

Marco, hearing the charge, rose to his feet, "We will find them and make them pay!" the words were melodramatic, yet they did not seem so with the earnest expression of concern on his face.

Senator Sulla also rose, but in a much calmer manner "Perhaps these are just agitators, trying to build false hope among the ingrates who want to sever or treaty with France?"

Caprera was not pleased with Vichy's answer and sought to make his displeasure know. He spoke in a low, deliberate tone so that Vichy would understand before the translation.

"You seem nervous, if is nothing to worry about, then why the sweating?" he said, leaning in to get closer to Vichy.

The emperors meaning, and displeasure was not misunderstood. Caesaris was mildly curious, it was her understanding that the British Royal Family had been targeted and killed in Vasekt attacks. She wondered whom and more importantly why, anyone would spread rumors against her father? It was a question that would linger in the back of her mind.

# CHAPTER V

The office Ted Bulloch worked out of the most was the one at his home; it was where he felt comfortable making important decisions, like the one he was faced with. The entire room was a testament to his love of the west. His heavy oak desk was made in the prairie style, as were the two alabaster shaded square lamps that adorned it. On the wall behind his desk was a painting of buffalo on the plains by William Jacob Hayes. The rug on the wood floor was Navajo, its dark greens and reds intertwined, with bright yellows and blues incorporating several geometric and zigzag patterns. The windows were also designed in the Frank Lloyd Wright's prairie style as were the lamps and the doors. The office was situated in an old Victorian guesthouse, directly behind the main house, which had been converted to serve its new purpose. The office was a comfort to Bulloch, who always felt the west was a source of his strength. He did all of his thinking there and brought as much of his work back to the office as he could. With William West sitting in front of him, no longer disguised as the homeless man he collided with outside the Dirksen Building, once again he had to make an important decision.

Bulloch glanced upwards at the far wall across from his desk at a picture taken when he was sixteen at Clay Hodges' ranch in North Dakota. The old ranch, a testament to a bygone era, was a second home to him growing up. Bulloch was sickly during his early childhood in White Plains. He suffered from debilitating asthma and anemia. He spent much of his childhood in and out of hospitals and frequent visits to doctors' offices. He was taught whole grades by tutors because he could not attend class. His home became a prison, occasionally on a good day he could ride his bicycle. He became an avid reader to pass the time; his intelligence was on display when he read at least three books a week. His favorites were adventure stories and the Bible stories. It was suggested by his physicians that leaving New York for a less polluted, low allergen climate might lessen his problem, and in time he may outgrow the problem. His father owned a successful import export business and opened another division in Bismarck to export cattle to Canada.

Once Bulloch had been in North Dakota for a few months his health slowly improved and he began to explore. He rode his bicycle up and down the long country roads. He frequently would pass Hodges Ranch, stopping at the end of the drive and staring at the cowboys driving cattle into wooden pens. He marveled at how they were in control of not only the hundreds of cattle they were moving, but the colossal horses they rode. It was a ritual he repeated over and over; soon the ranch hands noticed the frail, pallid boy at the end of the old dirt road every day after school braving various types of weather conditions to watch them. Finally, the owner, Clay Hodges, drove his old beat up pickup out to meet him. He was in awe as he shook hands with the lanky square jawed, leathery skinned, old rancher in a denim shirt. His hair was as white as snow and spots on his hand gave evidence of their years of use. The thing he remembered most about Hodges was his smile; it seemed to brighten the overcast North Dakota skies every time he laughed. He told Bulloch to get his parents' permission and he would show him around the ranch. It was the eleven-year-old boy's dream to see that ranch, and after his parents spoke with Hodges, he had the chance to see everything up close for himself. He could still remember riding up to the tan ranch house with its gabled roofs, and its giant half circle window over a set of glass doors, for the first time. Its seventy rooms, the ranch log cabin style building that served as the ranch hand quarters, the original tiny ranch house built in the early 20th century, and the vast wide open space of the prairie. Hodges took Bulloch who watched the ranch hands work the herd, and rode on the back of a horse for the first time. He remembered that moment as changing him forever.

Bulloch's health drastically improved over the next four years, and Hodges suggested he work on the ranch as a cowboy, lifting weights in the ranch gym to build up his strength and stamina. Bulloch took the old ranchers advice, and transformed himself. His constitution became so strong that his family was able to move back to White Plains. He continued to go back to the ranch every summer until he graduated high school and went to Harvard. He and Hodges remained great friends until Hodges died at the age of ninety-eight years old.

It was the ranch in North Dakota that formed who he was, he learned the value of hard work, he learned the importance of having good friends, he fell in love for the first time there and in one notorious incident, at the age of seventeen, he beat a twenty-eight year old cowboy in a bare knuckles boxing match in the parking lot of a honky-tonk. During his last summer at the ranch he took part in transporting cattle drive from South Dakota to Utah. He grew to love the American West because of that trip, from driving the cattle to the trucks, to where he saw giant gray cone shaped sandstone buttes with coal seams in them, to watching a pair of beavers take down a birch tree, and to watching the landscape from the cab of a truck. It was because of his love of the west that Bulloch had devised the idea of a guerilla cowboy regiment. He knew that the cowboys knew the forests, mountains, caves, and canyons of the west better than any other group and would be an effective resistance to the Romans.

It was because of the rumors of a Cowboy Calvary being formed that William had sought out Bulloch. He had devised an elaborate scheme to meet Bulloch that had included growing an uncomfortably long beard, and living as a homeless person for weeks to meet Bulloch. Hours before he collided with Bulloch in front of the Dirksen building, William had doused himself in cheap whiskey to provide a more convincing performance. It was quite a change for William to put a phone in someone's pocket instead of picking their wallet or pinching their data manager. The plan had accomplished his goal; William now sat in Bulloch's office, showered and shaved. He had not yet won Bulloch's confidence; he had extreme reservations dealing with the nation's most notorious outlaw. Despite his skepticism, he was forced to listen to William because of what he had just handed to him. William had produced pictures of both the outside, and inside, of the forward Roman command center in Kansas City. It was hidden in a vacant mall in Shawnee. He had also accessed their mainframe and downloaded plans, schematics and intelligence onto a memory dot. The pictures that hovered over Bulloch's desk were stunning, better than any Intel that the Pentagon had produced. By virtue of what William had handed him, they had just gained an Intelligence advantage over the Romans and they were not aware of it; yet Bulloch questioned why William would go to such great lengths just to join the new regiment. His reservations were not altogether unfounded; William was the top thief on the F.B.I. most wanted list. Bulloch was also aware that William had never hurt anyone in a robbery, there was only one incident he had ever harmed anyone. William had stalked and shot his stepfather after he raped his little sister. As a result of the wounds, his stepfather bled to death. Bulloch's attention shifted between the intelligence in front of him and trying to read William's eyes. Bulloch leaned back in his brown leather chair and crossed his arms.

"Why should I trust you?" Bulloch said directly in his shrill voice. "You are a notorious thief", Bulloch leaned forward again and stared into Williams eyes "and may I add, a killer."

"I don't argue that I was a thief, but I have never, never been a killer!" William shook his head in disagreement.

Bulloch still unconvinced continued his line of questioning, "Your step-father is dead because you shot him. He bled to death where you left him, am I wrong in that statement?"

William could see that Bulloch was not going to be easily convinced of his sincerity, "He raped my little sister. As angry as I was, I just wanted to maim him, never to kill him. I shot off his hands and feet so he could never touch anyone again. It was outside his office, they opened at eight in the morning. It was just ten till eight when I shot him, the plan was for someone to find him and call 911. It was almost nine before anyone got there. I never wanted him to die."

Bulloch was unrelenting, "You must understand how difficult all this is to believe. You have had more sensational robberies than any criminal in the history of this country. There is more than just that, not only did you commit the crimes, you absolutely reveled in them. I have seen the videos you posted on the holo-def web, crowing about what you did. Whenever you had a big heist, you wanted everyone to know it was you who did it. All things considered, your character leaves much to be desired, and little to trust."

"Wow that really hurts, especially coming from you", the tone in William intended for his voice to sound jovial, but came out in a sincere tone of disappointment. "I could have left well enough alone, I did not have to go in to the lion's den and put my life at risk for my country. I used all my skill to get inside that base, knowing that if I made one wrong move I was dead. Look, I'll be honest, my family lives in Missouri, and the Romans are getting closer to them every day, that is part of why I did what I did, but I also love this country, and want to get rid of the Romans."

William learned why Bulloch had a tough as nails reputation as a reformer as he continued to press him, "Why bring this to me? Why not send it to the Pentagon, or the White House? Why the disguise? Why the cloak and dagger to meet me? Do you think I can get you a pardon? I will tell you right here and now I am not going to even utter the word when it is connected to you. Tell me really, why are you here?"

William was starting to become frustrated, but knew his reputation would be hard to overcome, "Because word got back to me about your recruiting for the secret cowboy regimen you are putting together." Bulloch let out a loud laugh, "Not so secret is it!"

William started to bristle under the line of questioning "It is! I have friends who know my experience on ranches as a cowboy, just as I know of yours. Word got back to me after your asking around. Come on, give me a chance! We both love the west, we both grew up on ranches and we both know what damage a bunch of well armed cowboys could do to the Romans." William's anger started to grow, he pointed at Bulloch with a jabbing motion, "You want the real reason I chose you, it's because we had similar experiences as kids, and I respect you. I respect your integrity; it's something that I didn't have a lot of until recently." William sat back in his chair resigned; satisfied he had given his best shot at trying to convince Bulloch.

Bulloch softened his stance somewhat, "Well I will say this for you Mr. West; you have already provoked the Romans ire. A team of Green Berets was ambushed and wiped out in Kansas City; we think it could have partially been revenge for their system being compromised. We did not know who did it, or what the extent of the breach was until now. By no means do we blame you for their demise."

William slumped farther back in his chair and spoke in a calm tone, "I want to help my country, I want to turn over a new leaf. I don't care if I go to jail when this is over; I just want the Romans off American soil. Look, give me this chance, let me do something good and right for once." William's voice and expression again conveyed sincerity.

Bulloch noted William's earnestness, but proceeded as if he were being lied to "Trust has to be earned, William. Even if I decide to let you be part of the regimen, it is not up to me alone. You will have to earn the trust of other key people. You will have to clear hurdles by being approved at each level, all the way up to the Oval Office. Understand this, if we do decide to allow you to be part of the regimen, you will be kept on a short leash; I will be watching you every step of the way."

William nodded but then realized what the artwork behind Bulloch was, "Is that a William Jacob Hays painting? I really like him; I stole some of his paintings from a mansion in Sandy once." William said staring over Bulloch's shoulder.

Bulloch scowled in disapproval. "That kind of statement will hardly help you."

William smiled, and almost laughed, but held it back at the last moment,

"Check the recent headlines, you will see that works of art that had been stolen around the mountain and south west over the last few years have been returned to the doorsteps of where they were stolen."

Bulloch was not expecting such a large act of contrition, "You returned them? How?"

William smiled again, "I stole them back and retuned them; you see, I now have more enemies than just the Romans", he laughed, deciding not to suppress it again.

Bulloch chuckled, unconsciously softening his stance, "Well, that kind of statement does help. I have always been a superior judge of character, and I believe that what you say is the truth. I am not promising that this is an absolute, but If you are willing to sign paperwork, confessing what you did, and the names of everyone you have ever sold stolen property to, including the people who assisted you, I believe we can convince the skeptics."

William sat silent for a moment, considering the proposal, divulging who bought the stolen artwork from him might keep them from killing him. He was not willing to give the names of those who were in his gang, epically Roost and his wife. William did not want to see the people he cared about in jail, and also because they thought he was dead.

William had become tired of stealing, he began picking up bibles in the different hotel rooms and reading them. He finally decided everything he was, everything he stood for, was wrong. Knowing that he would never be able to give up stealing while he and Cassidy were together, he devised a scheme where it would appear he was accidently killed. Keeping with his style of grandiose heist, he convinced his gang they were going to steal from Fort Knox by blowing a hole in the roof of a secret transport tunnel that ran underground and away from the building. William told Cassidy and Roost that he was going to use a rental truck to transport, and set up the explosives. Once he had the truck, and the plastic explosives, he blew up the truck on a deserted road three miles away from Fort Knox. Williams plan was to make it look to his gang as if he had been vaporized, and to the military, as if it was a failed attack by terrorists. The plan worked flawlessly and his gang believed he was dead, the story eventually made its way into the media spotlight after months of speculation if the explosion was an act of terrorism.

Now William was faced with a choice to betray his friends, or sacrifice himself. There was no question when he considered it; he would not betray his friends.

William gave Bulloch the most humble but stern expression he could manage, "I will give you the names of everyone I ever sold to, and the names of their go betweens. I am sorry; I can't give you the names of the people who helped me."

Bulloch was pleased, the question was a test, he did not want someone who would sell out their closest friends to gain favor, "I admire that, I suppose that it's good that you are loyal. I will go to bat for you William, don't let me down!" Bulloch said slapping his hand on the desk for emphasis and then extending it to William to shake.

William grasped Bulloch's hand and then grinned, "I promise, I won't let you down."

Suddenly, a thought occurred to Bulloch, "You're supposed to be dead. How did you mange that? They found your DNA at the scene!" He sat waiting for the answer, as if a great magician was about to reveal how he did a trick.

"The DNA was mine; it was in a plastic bag with samples of my hair fingernails, skin saliva" he paused "and other gross things. I spread it over the inside of the truck before I blew it up."

"I have to admit, that was an ingenious plan." Bulloch was truly impressed, but still wanted to know more "Why did you do it."

William sighed and sank back into his chair; he waited for a moment searching for the right words.

"I had everything, or at least I thought I did. The money, the beautiful wife, fame, the excitement and most of all, the challenge. The partying every night and the fame got old. I realized all I had accomplished in life was to steal things that other people had created or produced. I saw a bible in a drawer one night at a hotel we were staying at, that was when it hit me. I had grown up a Southern Baptist, my father was a Pastor, and I realized that I stood in defiance of everything in that book. I also thought of how disappointed he would be in me. I need this, I have cleaned my life up; I am trying to live by what I was taught growing up. Besides, there is only so much cocaine and rum a body can take!"

"This won't be easy. You have no military experience," Bulloch stood up from behind his desk and walked to the front and leaned against it, "You will have to undergo Marines' basic training, once you have completed that, you have just finished the easy part. Everyone will undergo a crash course in SEAL training, Ranger Jump School, Green Beret Training and Force Recon Training. You will be required to show your prowess at maneuvering a horse through rough terrain. The entire program will take ten months. Do you think you are up to the task?"

"Yeah, I do, but I need my horse, Slingshot. He is at a horse farm in Wyoming; I was working as a ranch hand there when the Romans invaded."

"If you are accepted, and you pass all your training," Bulloch smiled "I will fetch the horse myself!"

Bulloch headed for the door and motioned to William to do the same; "I had better take you in the main house and introduce you to my family."

William followed Bulloch out from the old Victorian guest house down the brick walkway to the historic mansion in front of them. Bulloch noticed a power company employee reading the meter on the side of his house. The man appeared young and clean shaven, with an athletic build. His dark eyes darted between Bulloch, William, and then back to meter. Bulloch held his hand up for William to stop, and then waved it, signaling him to back up. Bulloch then silently bull rushed the meter reader, who at the last second saw him coming. The man attempted to pull a small pistol out of his grey jump suit pocket, but it was sent spinning end over end when Bulloch thrust his shoulder into his chest with a thump, sending him backwards. The man ricocheted off the wall and stumbled forward, gasping to get air back in his lungs. He regained his balance and produced a butterfly knife from his other pocket. Bulloch rushed him again and grabbed his wrist, and then with his right hand landed a series of quick jabs to his face. William winced when he heard a loud crunching and popping caused by Bulloch's fist crushing the man's nose. The assailant's nose gushed blood and his vision blurred. Sensing that the would-be assassin was staggered, Bulloch reared back and delivered an uppercut squarely under his assailant's jaw. William could see through Bulloch's shirt the bulging muscle in his back and arms flex for the attack and then deliver the blow. The man's eyes rolled back in his head and he went limp, falling to his side. Bulloch quickly grabbed a garden hose and used it to hog-tie the assassin's hands to his feet. Seconds later the assassin regained his senses, and struggled against his bonds to no avail. William was shocked at how easily Bulloch dealt with the assassin. He knew Bulloch was an avid weight lifter and boxer, but had no idea at the power and skill he possessed in brawling.

"You won't get out of that knot!" Bulloch shouted in victory at his assailant. Bulloch brushed himself off, inspecting the damage to his brown three piece suit and not his person. "This is a brand new suit!" Bulloch said to an amazed William. He looked at Bulloch wide eyed.

"How did you know he was an assassin?"

"I called the power company out to scan for heat loss. It is costing me a fortune to heat my house. They read my meter last Tuesday when they were here! When I looked closely at him, I could see he had that blasted Roman haircut that Caprera insists all Praetorians wear." Bulloch said while continuing brushing himself off.

William was unnerved by what had happened. Over his criminal career he could pick an undercover robbery officer's face out of a crowd of hundreds. The Roman assassin was different; he did not have telltale signs that William could spot. He was not tense or stiff like the undercover FBI agents who attempted to catch him; the assassin was something completely alien to him. William realized that this was going to be unlike anything that he had ever seen before; a world where highly skilled operatives dealt in life and death with no remorse or pity. William turned back to Bulloch, still amazed at how handily he dispatched his opponent.

"Where did you learn to fight like that?"

Bulloch beamed. "Harvard Boxing Club, actually the toughest fight I ever experienced was when I argued against socialism with a pacifist in a debate. Things became too heated and we fought in a Yale parking lot. Fortunately we thought it was great sport and school officials present never reported it to the administrations."

William looked down at the assassin who obviously recognized William. He rolled over on his hands and feet to get a better look.

"You're William West! You're the most wanted man in America! Why are you here with a U.S. Senator?" The man said in an American accent.

"You'll never get a chance to report it you snake!" Bulloch guffawed at the assassin. "See William" he continued, "how they trained him so well he is still using an American accent!"

"This is why I have had to live like a hermit. I am a victim of my own success. I can't help that I am a celebrity and that people, whether they love me or hate me, all know me." William said in earnest.

"Wait until you meet Alex Wright, he is the only man I know whose vanity can exceed that sentiment."

Bulloch's wife, Elaine, a petite brunette, came storming out of the house as if she were ready to do battle with the invader, along with two of his children, boys four and six respectively who were the spitting image of their father, came out to see where the source of the clatter came from. Elaine first saw the Roman assassin lying in the hydrangeas, then her eyes lifted up to see William. She gasped at the sight of him realizing there was a notorious criminal standing in front of her.

"Ted, what is going on here?" Elaine said pushing her two boys back in the direction of the main house.

Bulloch walked over and hugged her, "Your surprise is warranted dear, but the danger is past."

Elaine pulled back, "What about him? What are you planning? Are you now in the business of hiding fugitives?"

"It is not what it seems. William has brought a memory dot to me that contained pictures and schematics of a Roman base in Kansas. We may be able to use his skills." Bulloch said looking back at William.

Elaine was even more suspicious of William because he had robbed two branches of the bank her family owned. She turned to William and looked at him with an accusatory glare.

"You're a killer, aren't you? How do I know my family is safe with you around?" her eyes squinted as if she were trying to concentrate hard enough to make William disappear.

"Don't worry, William; she has been like this since we were children!" Bulloch laughed. He looked over at his childhood playmate and college sweetheart. Elaine knew Bulloch well enough to trust his judgment and the look in his eyes told her that everything was going to be all right. Bulloch pulled his phone out of his pocket and started to call the FBI. He hung up when he realized they would place William under arrest before the Roman assassin. He thought for a moment and then dialed the President; it was going to take an executive order to keep William out of jail. Bulloch looked at William as the phone rang, although he would not say it to William, he knew the tide had turned.

# CHAPTER VI

Caprera walked the corridors of the Roman military headquarters, the Praetorium, with the Dux Americana, Yakiv Kravchenko. The Dux Americana was a lofty position; the Roman General in charge of military operations in the United States, and the second highest military post in the empire. Kravchenko was recruited by Caprera. As a general in the Ukraine; he was a brilliant military leader that had handily beaten the Russians when they invaded. Under Kravchenko's command the Ukrainians had actually taken land from Russia while driving them out. Kravchenko then partnered with an American ex-general to start the Mercenary Army: Credential Bond, which is where Caprera had first met him. They were contracted by the Emperor to take part in the invasion of America. He was promised a bigger role in the government by Caprera if he would come to Rome as part of the Legion. Kravchenko, whose hunger for power was only exceeded by Caprera, joined without hesitation.

Caprera and Kravchenko were a stark contrast in appearances. Caprera a debonair, charismatic leader; Kravchenko was tall, pale with an athletic build, his entire appearance menacing. His most striking feature was his eyes, one blue one hazel. Kravchenko's troops feared displeasing him, not wanting to be subjected to his disapproving gaze. Caprera and Kravchenko were both wearing golden molded breastplates, and fringe leather straps hanging just above their knees covering the tunic underneath. Both wore a modern pair of gold combat boots designed to look like they came from antiquity. Kravchenko's uniform did not seem to fit, but seemed too small here and too large there. Caprera's uniform fit him perfectly seeming to be part of his body, and accentuating the difference between him and Kravchenko.

The two moved quickly and silently from the main room to an adjoining corridor, and stepped in front of a steel door. A scanner recognized them and slid the door open. They stepped into a mahogany walled elevator, still not speaking a word, and descended. When the door opened again they were standing in a large segmented tunnel, tall and wide enough to fit three semi-trucks side by side. Each segment was about five feet in length, and painted by an artist; each one depicted a scene from Rome's history. A single line of LED lights ran along the entire ceiling of the tunnel. The tunnel was a feat of engineering that had claimed the lives of those involved. Caprera had instructed the slave drivers to kill all the slaves used in the project, which was obeyed. He next had the artist and slave drivers killed, so that no one but a few knew of the existence of the tunnel. Caprera was ruthless in his protection of secrets, but he thought it was justified, and believed it essential in protecting Rome's military.

Directly in front of them was a gleaming black chariot with a gold palmette pattern on the front. Hidden in the pattern were two headlights and a LED Incapacitator. The chariot's purpose was to transport them the length of the tunnel's three miles to the Imperial Palace. The two stepped into the chariot as it roared to life at the touch of Caprera's hand. He took the wheel and turned to his passenger finally breaking the long silence between them.

"The Americans are reorganizing their government; it looks as if they are strengthening their military for an assault. Why is this happening Yakiv?" Caprera said as he took the wheel of the chariot.

"With all respect Emperor, did you expect they would never try and regain the ground they lost?" Kravchenko responded in his gravelly voice, damaged from smoke inhalation in a house fire when he was a child.

Caprera was not fond of subordinates who would stand up to him, but he tolerated Kravchenko's lack of respect.

"Of course, Yakiv, I did anticipate that, it appears you and your commanders did not. Please don't test my patience."

Kravchenko looked straight ahead and spoke as if he had not heard Caprera's admonishment.

"We have a plan, the Americans will have to open a hole in their front to allow massive troops in, when they do, and they will, we will attack."

His voice was unafraid and somewhat defiant. Caprera bristled at the Kravchenko's tone of voice, "Are you still losing drones?" he countered, knowing the answer.

Kravchenko turned and faced Caprera, realizing he was being too confident.

"Yes, the Americans are very adept at shooting down drones. It's a pity they are not as good at repelling our forces, maybe they would still have their land." He said not wanting to appear weak.

Caprera smiled at him with obvious contempt, which made him more intimidating, "Make sure no more drones go down. We need our eyes on the Americans."

"Yes, Caesar." Kravchenko said in a submissive tone.

Caprera, satisfied he had made his point, softened his tone, "Intelligence tells me that George Vernon is coming out of retirement to fight us. I have never seen a man more loved by his troops, not even me. When we were fighting the Americans in Germany, we thought that his troops would give up, their morale gone; Vernon made a speech and they were fighting against us as if it was the first day of the war. Undoubtedly he will put Wright in command of some of the forces. Are you ready to fight against both Vernon and Alexander Wright? You and Wright have quite the history."

Kravchenko chuckled, "Wright has been a nuisance, but he will hardly stop me. All the articles he wrote about me and appearances at the United Nations did nothing to me."

Caprera did not believe a word of what Kravchenko said regarding Alex Wright, but humored him because he was a brilliant general. He decided to change the subject.

"How is the discipline of our troops?"

Kravchenko stood up straighter as if to emphasize a point he was about to make, "If your forces don't fear you, they will not respond in the way you want. Our soldiers fear what I will do to them more than dying at the hands of the Americans. Because of that, I will defeat the Americans no matter who they put in charge."

The chariot slowed down at a fork in the tunnel ahead of them and they veered to the right before finally slowing down and stopping in front of a large steel door. Both the passengers stepped out of the chariot onto the landing, their conversation clearly done. The sensor next to the door again recognized the pair, the massive door slid up; the groan of heavy machinery was audible as they walked through.

The Imperial Palace was opulent to say the least. It was surrounded on four sides by a defensive wall; each wall had two rectangular watchtowers in the classic roman style with barrel tile roofs. The exterior of the forty foot high walls were made of white marble, followed by a layer of three foot thick, reinforced concrete and finally another layer of marble on the interior walls. It sat on the former site of the Circus Maximus, like a phoenix risen from the ashes. The main gate was twelve feet high and fourteen feet wide.

There were two solid bronze doors that were embossed with a pattern of squares, each containing a frieze of a Roman god, Jupiter and Mars respectively. There were four security cameras that were placed at different angles around the door. A large Bronze circle hid a stacked projectile canon (SPC) behind it; three more similar SPCs' were mounted in each watchtower. There were two more such entrances with silver doors, but no friezes. The mammoth structure contained the even more mammoth Imperial Palace. A five-story building with ionic columns, holding up a pediment with a frieze, depicting the founding of Rome.

The structure was as much fortress as palace, it extended three stories underground in an impregnable bunker with three feet thick reinforced concrete walls. It was within the palace that Caprera felt safest. It was there he conducted nearly all of his business; the throne room was almost an identical design to Maderno's Nave at the Vatican, but without Christian imagery, instead adorned with pagan symbolism from ancient Rome. The room stretched the entire five stories and gave the room a distinct cavernous feel. In the center of the room was an ornate gilt throne, which Caprera would sit in from time to time, but he preferred to pace when he was speaking to his subordinates. Caprera and Kravchenko strode across the throne room to meet Caesaris standing in front of them with her arms folded wearing a black dress with a silver geometric design that recalled Byzantium more than Roman antiquity, and behind her, twelve of his personal body guards. The guards were dressed in traditional uniforms from Rome including red crests on gold helmets, chest-plates and even sandals. Caprera made a sweeping gesture from his chest and extending his arm,

"General, I don't believe you have met my daughter, Caesaris. I am sure she has news of one of her projects of which I am unknowingly blocking."

Caesaris was not happy with her father's immediate dismissal,

"Your description of me is flattering as ever. It is true; you have converted more churches in Venice to temples to the gods. Several of those you promised not to touch."

Caprera smiled and put his forefinger under her chin, "I am Cesar, and therefore I can choose to break a promise when it is best for the empire, even if I anger my beloved daughter."

Caesaris angrily brushed his hand away, "You aren't some dumb brute, you know the works of art you are destroying are treasures that can never be replaced. Why would you do that?"

Caprera spoke in a very condescending manner, "Their time has passed. We are now in another era, and greater works will be produced."

Caesaris shook her head and began to briskly stomp away when she heard a faint pop coming from overhead. She turned to see her father on one knee with one hand on the floor and the other clasped to his ear, blood oozing from between his fingers. Shouting and the sound of grappling came from one of the balconies above them. She looked up to see to Praetorian guards holding a young slave who was struggling to escape from their grasp, his eyes wide with panic and agitation. He appeared much more physically fit than slaves who were palace servants, his arms and legs were made up of lean muscle and his skin tone was not pallid from being constantly inside. One of the guards held up a high-powered rifle with a silencer, so that it could be seen below by Caprera. The Emperor gently felt his earlobe where the bullet had carved a nick into it. He motioned his guard to bring the assassin to him, and to Caesaris' bewilderment he had a fiendish smile on his face.

It became apparent to Caesaris that her father knew that the assassin was not a slave, and that he relished the thrill of the attempt on his life too much. The guards took him to the emperor, his feet dragging the ground.

"There are those in Italy that stand against you, and will defeat you!" he shouted.

The assassin was just a boy, not more than sixteen or seventeen years old; his face had not caught up with his longish nose yet. Caesaris wondered why someone that young would be used as an assassin, and who gave him the gun. She looked at her father still expecting to see mercy; after all he was just a boy that appeared only a year or so younger than she was. The expression she saw on her father's face was not mercy, but one of admiration.

"Who trained you, son? Was it a Praetorian, or was it Roman Intelligence? Whoever is responsible for recruiting you was wise; you are a strong young man. What you did took bravery; so much that it almost matches your treachery. Cesar is feeling merciful today; I am going to give you a chance to live, if you can kill me in a duel, you can go free."

Caprera stood up and took off his red cloak, and unsheathed his Spatha, a long double bladed sword with an ornate gold handle used in the old Empire, brought back by Caprera who was an expert swordsman. Caprera turned and addressed everyone around him while speaking to the would-be assassin as if he were on a stage.

"You are not praetorian, so I know that you have only had basic sword training. I will have one arm tied behind my back to be fair." His raised voice reverberated around the immense room as he projected it so all could hear.

Caprera held out his arm allowing it to be secured. A Praetorian guard ran over and attached Caprera's wrist to the back of his belt with a plastic zip tie. The guard then took out his sword and tossed it to the assassin who let it drop to the floor before hesitantly and clumsily picking it up. A circle of guards formed around the two men, keeping either from straying too far from his opponent. Caprera held his Spatha up to signify the duel had begun. He moved slowly, walking around the perimeter of the circle, like a lion stalking his prey. He spun the sword in his hand, all the movement coming from his wrist. The assassin was ashen and dry mouthed, he held his Spatha in front of him in a defensive stance, not quite knowing what he should do next. He moved counter to Caprera in anticipation of his attack, the only thing his terrified mind could conceive of doing. He watched Caprera's eyes, which were set and unforgiving, waiting for a sign of the first strike. Suddenly, Caprera smiled and then lunged swinging his Spatha low, aiming for the legs. The assassin lowered his Spatha to block the attack, allowing Caprera to spin his entire body raising his Spatha, and slice open the assassin's throat with a swift powerful slice. The assassin grasped the wound pressing to trying to stop the bleeding while trying not to drown in his own blood. He looked around the room, Caprera knelt down and held him as he began to convulse and finally fell still. The horrible sight lasted for a few seconds, but to Caesaris who stood watching from behind the throne, it seemed unbearably long. She was shocked at how her father took pleasure in brutality, the smile on his face as he stood up from holding his young victim. He then turned to address the room with the same fanfare as he had done earlier.

"How did this come to be? How did this young brave man get into the throne room? Can anyone tell me?" the question had a rhetorical feel to it.

Caprera then pointed at the head of his imperial bodyguard, Captain Victor Valerius.

"I now offer you the same opportunity. I know that because you are Praetorian, and the head of my personal security, that either you were complicit in the attack, or you are incompetent. I can't have either one as the head of my security."

Victor was broad shouldered and towered over Caprera, but visibly intimidated by him. He backed away a few steps before gathering himself. He knew his only chance of survival was to fight Caesar.

"Father no, don't do it! It's Victor!" Caesaris yelled, but her father had tuned everyone but his opponent out. He took his Spatha and cut loose his bond.

"I will use both arms this time, since you are Praetorian and are certainly a master swordsman."

Victor took two steps backwards knowing a full retreat would result in his being shot, he tried to reason with Caprera.

"Caesar! I beg of you, I did not have knowledge of this!"

Caprera used the blade of the spatha to point at Victor, "Incompetence is as bad as treason, and both have the same outcome."

Victor making no indication he was going to fight tried to plead again, "Please I have a newborn son."

Caprera dropped his spatha down to answer the plea "If you fight, even if you lose, I promise he will be taken care of; you have my word," he said, sounding as if he should receive a humanitarian award for his generosity.

Caprera raised his spatha in salute, Victor begrudgingly returned the gesture. They circled for a few seconds, each trying to anticipate the others actions. Caprera struck first, he slashed downward in an attempt to cut Victor's Achilles tendon, missing badly his blade striking the floor instead. Victor seized upon Caprera's prone position and slashed back, in a two handed upwards swing trying to hit Caprera's jugular vein; the tip of the Spatha missed its target, and sliced a valley above Caprera's right eye. The Emperor jumped backward in surprise, he had not realized that Victor possessed such skill. He gave his opponent a salute by raising his blade in front of his face and smiling; he loved the thrill of a life or death battle, which Victor clearly did not.

The two lunged at each other again, their blades striking and sliding downward against one another until the two of them were pushing against each other. Caprera kneed Victor in the side three times in rapid succession, momentarily knocking the wind out of Victor's lungs. Victor clutched his side gasping for air and stumbled backwards. Caprera, sensing weakness in his opponent, charged again lunging forward with his spatha, but was blocked by Victor who struck the blade hard knocking it backwards, again surprising Caprera. Both men were panting heavily, their eyes open to the maximum aperture; Victor hoped that his younger age would give him the upper hand if he could keep from being stabbed long enough. Caprera charged yet again, but was tripped by Victor, causing him to land face down, and prostate on the marble floor. Victor realizing that his best opportunity was in front of him, swooped in for the kill, but slid in the assassin's blood from the previous duel; taking him off his feet. Victor's elbow crashed against the marble floor, shattering it. Victor yelped in pain as his Spatha skid across the floor coming to a rest at least fifteen feet from him. He rolled over to see Caprera standing over him, smirking and then slowly pushed the blade into his chest. Victor did not cry out in pain, but let out a long deep breath, his eyes and Caprera's locked in a single gaze. He grabbed the blade with his hands, tying to pull it back out as his whole body shook with the strain. Caprera knelt down and whispered in his ear.

"Your child shall be under my constant protection." Caprera said to Victor, watching him cough and gurgled before finally going limp.

Caesaris had watched the whole duel, even though she did not want to, she could not release her attention from the spectacle that unfolded in front of her. Caprera slowly rose up from beside Valerius's body, his chest still heaving from the duel. It reminded Caesaris of a wild animal who had just finished feasting on its prey. The sight of her father, soaked in his own blood, and the blood of his two victims was shocking to her, but not as shocking as the wild look of triumph across his face. Caprera made no attempt to clean the blood from his body, but instead he licked away the blood from his lips, turning to walk to his chambers. Caesaris suddenly felt a burning nausea in her stomach, both from the bloody scene she had witnessed, and the cruelty her father exhibited and the pleasure he derived from it. She felt dizzy and a searing at the base of her skull caused by the strain. She ran down a nearby hall to an outside balcony where she fell to her knees and vomited. She then began to sob uncontrollably. She had never known her father to be cruel, nor could she have imagined the bloodlust he possessed. She wondered to herself if she had ever really known him. She gathered herself, wiping away the tears and walked back down the hall; she turned and looked to see the two bodies still lying on the floor. She had known Victor all her life, he had actually babysat her on several occasions while her father was engaged in battle, and there he lay in front of her, dead by her father's hand. What she had witnessed called into question if the gossip about her father was true. She had dismissed each rumor she heard with equal disbelief, but now all she knew was crumbling. Were there labor camps in Great Britain? Had he ordered the British Royal Family massacred? Was he as much of a libertine as had been whispered about? The rumors she had heard about his seeing blood in any dispute were obviously true, so what else was true about her father? Gasping for air and standing up straight, she resolved that she would find out who her father really was.

# CHAPTER VII

entral Florida was unusually cold for April; William rubbed his hands together to keep them warm in a defiant move against frigid air. He looked at the pine trees silhouetted against the brilliant orange sky. Sunsets are one of the few things that distracted him long enough to not think about the war, or his constant regrets about the past. It had been a blur since he had asked Bulloch for help in joining the new cowboy regimen. As Bulloch had predicted, William had faced opposition and he had to be cleared all the way up to General Vernon, who was convinced by Bulloch and Alex Wright that William's unteachable talents could be a great asset, but he would only agree if President Braintree approved William's enlistment. The President quickly consented after speaking to Bulloch and Wright, who were impassioned in their appeal.

The following day he found himself at Fort Knox for basic training, which ironically was the site where he had faked his own death. Nine weeks later, after merciless ribbing from his instructors, he began training for the cavalry that had brought him to the Ocala National Forest. The park had been closed since the invasion, not enough resources could be allocated to keep it open. The forest was expansive, and made a perfect location for training. The thick hammocks of trees, the wide open fields of palmettos, amber sand, and the rivers and streams mirrored the different landscapes the Cavalry would encounter. Their previous training in Boulder was more familiar to William, he knew the west; Florida was an alien world to him from its wildlife to its thick, jungle- like forests.

William's fellow classmate, Drake Obis, sat with an old short wave radio, his fingers gently pushing the keys on the tuner to try and find the right station. Each channel seemed to bring nothing but eerie high pitched whistles and static that seemed to be singing some long forgotten ancient song. As the sun sank lower in the sky and the shadows grew longer, William found the static un-nerving; he started to imagine that the frogs singing in the woods were trying to harmonize with the whistling noises. William scanned the tree tops not quite sure what he was looking for. He felt a sting on the back of his neck and quickly slapped it; the last of the bug repellant he put on three days ago had obviously worn off. The dark green uniform he wore gave enough protection to the rest of his body, but not his neck. The uniforms were modeled after nineteenth century cavalry uniforms, down to the Stetsons with crossed sabers and colored combat cords to signify rank. The material the uniforms were made of was very different than the ones used by the last mounted cavalry over one hundred years ago. The material was designed to insulate, cool in heat, warm in cold, was fireproof and hid body heat. Highly woven fiber made them nearly bulletproof. Optic sensors changed the color and camouflage patterns gradually as they moved across changing terrain. They were designed by the Fort Myers inventor Timothy Emerson, and were as vital as anything the cavalry would carry with them.

William began to tell Drake to move faster, but that had always resulted in the opposite. Drake stood up from his squatting position and pivoted to the left, trying again to find the right frequency, "Got it!" he exclaimed being thankful he did not have to keep up the search that had lasted twenty minutes. Thirty one, sixteen, thirty one, sixteen, thirty one, alpha, foxtrot, Yankee, a female voice, that was clearly automated, recited the string of numbers and letters over a channel that whined, cracked and reverberated. William had grown to despise the sound of the mysterious woman's voice.

"You know Drake, no matter how many times I hear that channel; it still creeps me out."

"I like to think of her in a bikini." Drake smiled and gave William a wink.

"Whatever works for you, Drake." William said with a chuckle.

He appreciated that someone had a sense of humor; it had seemed every one he had trained with was flatly serious. William thought at least Drake was confident enough to make jokes.

Six months had passed since cavalry training had gotten underway and it was hard for William to think of his life before he joined, it was like some kind of hazy dream. William had come so far, he had actually met the President and had signed a deal that allowed him to be part of the unit, but would make him stand trial when he was done, which is what William wanted all along, to clear his name. Jail is something William had come to accept; he knew there was a good chance he would not survive the war to make it to jail. Losing his life for his country was something he felt that would erase all the wrong he had done. William had been reading the bible every day and was confident in where he was going when his life ended. William was not suicidal, though- he had spent all of his spare time thinking about various scenarios that might take place, and how to survive them. Planning was the key to all of his successes, and William believed war was no exception. He was accustomed to accounting for every possibility; his philosophy was such that there should always be a contingency plan for every situation. He had read about Caprera's use of prisoners for propaganda and did not plan on being made a trophy by the Romans. If he was captured he would surely be marched out for the press and put on display like game killed in the hunt.

The training William had undergone had been arduous and completely unforgiving. No time off had been given to the trainees, and every day had only yielded an average of three to four hours of sleep. Some nights when all the exercises were completed the horsemen might steal five hours of sleep. Six hundred handpicked recruits had started the training and now it was down to four hundred and ninety. The batteries of tests they had undergone were especially taxing. Every Calvary member was required to undergo abbreviated, but intensive training for SEAL's, Green Berets, Ranger Jump School, Steeplechase School, and CIA field agent training. There were many trainees who were previously Green Berets and SEAL's who had to undergo the same training twice. In addition classes in Chemistry, Physics, Biology and meteorology were mandated to give the members of the Calvary better odds at surviving and even thriving. The troops were going to be re-supplied only when they came back from a mission that could last weeks or months. Knowledge of vegetation, wildlife and how to use everything they could scavenge would give them a better chance at completing their missions. Those who had made it to the six month mark were about to make military history. Never before had such arduous training taken place, not even the Praetorian Guard was so well trained in so many different fields.

William had been accepted by many of his classmates, but he was despised by nearly an equal amount. He had made some very good friends, Drake being his closest. Drake and William were the most relaxed soldiers among the entire Cavalry, a trait that was beneficial to them and allowed them to get along with each other. They were amused by the fact that Drake was actually hunting William before the invasion. Drake was a Texas Ranger, who had followed in his family's footsteps of military and police work. Drake's father was a homicide detective in Houston, and his great grandfather was the first black Texas Ranger. Drake had joined the army after graduating from high school and reached the rank of sergeant before leaving. He then attended Mercy College majoring in Criminology. He was part of the class recruited by Ted Bulloch as mayor of White Plains to rid the police department of corruption. Drake worked hard and became a narcotics detective, and was a star among his peers. Drake's smooth demeanor, dashing good looks and unwavering determination made him popular wherever he went. During his time in White Plains, Drake worked with Bulloch frequently and developed a lasting friendship with him.

Drake decided to move back to Texas and follow in his great grandfather's footsteps by becoming a Texas Ranger. He gained even greater notoriety by dismantling a drug ring that extended from Mexico into El Paso. The cartels, furious, put a one million dollar contract on Drake's life. A local gang made an attempt to collect by setting up an ambush in a narrow back ally that was the only entrance to an old warehouse. They followed him from home with two trucks loaded with gunmen and forced him into the ally. Drake not only survived, he also managed to disarm and capture all of the gang members, making him an instant legend and placing him among the greats that had served as Texas Rangers. His final assignment before the war was to capture William, after the robbery of eleven tank cars filled with crude oil, in ten different heists. He was able to catch several members of William's gang, but never William. On several occasions William, Cassidy and Roost just narrowly evaded Drake. Once William and Drake finally met, there was instant respect between them. Drake left the Texas Rangers, never having caught William (whom he never believed was dead). All the events had transpired to bring Drake to where he was, sitting in a clearing deep within a Florida hardwood forest, listening for a coded message to instruct them on what to do next. They only had a few months of training left, and the CIA training they were undergoing was one of the few remaining exercises. The wind was picking up, and the temperature falling; the pair was growing cold.

"This is Florida, right?" William laughed as he hopped up and down.

"Last time I checked," Drake responded with a smirk, "but you're welcome to check the map if you doubt me."

"You know Drake, it's moments like this that make me wonder if going low tech is a good idea. No GPS! I mean, what's up with that?" William said slapping a map with the back of his hand.

"You know, you're a genius, or so they tell me. I must be a super genius because I almost caught you three times" Drake said laughing "Anyway, use that high voltage brain of yours, Roman technology can even detect a hand held GPS. What the Romans can't detect, or stop is a short wave radio receiving a one-way message, using a one-time code, it is impossible to stop. Why else do you think we are using this antiquated Cold War technique?"

"I don't know;" William spoke in-between blowing in his hands "I just thought we were out here freezing our butts off so we could listen to some creepy chic read numbers over the radio."

Drake realized that William's youth was affecting him. Even though he was only a few years older than William, his maturity level was that of someone much wiser.

"Why don't you stop complaining, and grab a pen and pad and help me to decipher this?" Drake said in an authoritative tone.

"Head three miles to the northwest, coordinates: 29° 29' 4.37" North 81° 47' 15.79" West and tune to 10.150 megahertz at twenty-one hundred hours for further instructions." William said with his back turned to Drake, picking up a pinecone and hurling it into a small thicket of sapling pine trees.

Drake sat in silence for a moment, shocked that William had memorized the different codes and was able to break it down in his mind with no apparent effort. He knew from the profiling done on William by the FBI that he was smart, but the report gave an inadequate account of just how smart. Drake had realized that experiencing William's mind first hand was far more impressive than what he had read. Out of all the things he had seen William do, that was the most astounding. He stood up and stared at William for a moment before laughing.

"Son, I was never going to catch you was I?" He said in an epiphany.

"You never know, I could have gotten lazy and settled down in Texas, working at a nine-to-five job, using my own name." William said with a smirk.

"Who knew a cop and a crook would end up together in a forest in Florida, with guns and not shoot each other," Drake said in earnest.

With the sun having just set, the pair mounted their horses and made their way into the thick barrier of trees in front of them. They moved cautiously, the weeds and darkness made a dangerous combination, if a horse stepped in the wrong place, its leg could be broken. The sound of crickets and frogs singing together seemed almost deafening. William glanced to his left to see a white sand trail winding through the pine trees; it had clearly been made by a vehicle. Two tracks for the wheels left white sand, while the brush had been depressed by the chassis of the vehicle. The trail was fresh, and wound out of sight behind another wall of trees. "Pssst!" William signaled. Drake turned around to look at William, but spotted the trail and instinctively knew what William was trying to relay to him. Drake gently pulled on his horse's reins changing direction and the two rode down the sandy trail.

At the end of the trail was a clearing, a wide open field of maidencane grass surrounded by a dense circle of trees. In the center were several travel trailers in various states of decay. There were old aluminum and metal trailers, rusting from years of exposure. There were old fiberglass trailers, not quite white anymore and the paint on the logos faded to another color. Some had windows; others had boards where the windows had been. Some had doors; others had sheets covering the doorway. All the trailers were arranged in a row, about two feet from one to the next. Across from the trailers was a cluster of tents, some were big pop up types, others were nothing more than a tarp thrown over a rope between two sticks. A large bonfire, recently lit, sat crackling in the middle of the field. It was almost peaceful, watching small embers take flight against the darkening sky and the sound of crickets. William looked upon the scene as some type of caravan, possibly gypsies. The scene had a different meaning to Drake; he saw the extra propane tanks, the generators that sat silent, and the plastic milk jugs filled with gasoline. Stacks of unused household cleaners and over the counter medicines piled together. Drake knew this was no traveling group, but one that had taken up residence. He jumped off his horse and deliberately moved closer, pulling out his two pistols at the same time. William jumped off his horse and pulled his m-4 automatic rifle out of its holster mounted on his horse's side, it was an unnatural feeling for William, doing the hunting, instead of evading the hunter. He realized that Drake had seen something, and clearly there was danger, so he reacted accordingly. William knelt beside Drake; still not sure of what was happening, but trusting his former pursuer's judgment, he knew there was reason to be cautious.

"SuMas" Drake said with profound consternation, "The Roman's general, Kravchenko, took all of the Super-Max prison inmates and let them go free, *if* they promised to return to the American side of the front. They are a depraved bunch who can't go back and try to live in society because facial recognition software won't let them. They move in packs; some even have their families with them. There is usually some sort of chief or warlord who leads them."

William looked around trying to analyze the situation, "Let me guess, they're not hear for the scenery." William said in an equally frustrated voice.

Drake nodded in affirmation, "They raid smaller towns, the police are under-staffed because of the war and they just overwhelm them, prey on the weak. They steal guns, booze and pharmaceuticals and whatever they need to make meth. Their women come in behind them and steal supplies. They are probably here because of the isolation and the hunting."

"Great!", William whispered loudly ,"sounds like they are a civilized bunch. I'll bet they are *real* easy to reason with."

Drake glanced behind them to make sure they were not being ambushed, "You don't know the half of it-they are rotten to the core. They are usually made up of Whites and Latinos and are bigoted against all other races. Almost all the men have beards, and all the women are either workers to raise the children and cook, or there for the pleasure of the men."

William looked around at the camp trying to gauge what kind of resistance they would face, "How many are there usually?"

Before Drake could answer they heard the sound of palmetto leaves rustling. Instinctively Drake raised his pistols while William sank lower to the ground.

"Too many." Drake answered in a flat hushed tone.

They soon discovered what the source of the sound was as it moved closer. They could make out a group of ten to twelve men carrying guns, tromping through the brush. William noticed that the guns were not raised; the men had not seen them and were unaware they were being watched. Both Drake and William knew they were probably surrounded, and had no radio to call for reinforcements. William began to silently decry the training program for not letting them carry something that could signal an emergency. The duo slowly crept closer to the caravan; William spotted several children ranging in age from two to five years old running around, filthy and in dingy ill fitting clothes playing near several containers of unknown chemicals. William nodded his head to the right, so Drake would see the children; Drake returned a nod indicating he saw them. Drake wanted no part of a gunfight with innocent children in the crossfire; he made his way away from the scene, waving his hand for William to follow.

They slinked along carefully and slowly until they came upon a large tree, a gaunt pale blonde man with a long blonde beard sat underneath, shooting meth amphetamines from a cloudy syringe. The man's skin was spotted with sores, even on his cheeks and forehead, his blue eyes stood out surrounded by yellow corneas, they rose up to see the two soldiers trying to sneak back to their horses. He coughed and then let out a wheeze combined with a cry "Cops!" and then began coughing again. He stood up reaching in his torn jeans for a weapon, but he was too deep in the fog of intoxication. He shuffled his bare feet along the pine needles on the ground, his back shown red marks from the bark he had been leaning against. "Cops!" he cried out again in a horse voice.

William and Drake reluctantly accepted they were going to have to fight. The horde, looking to protect their home, charged forward through the brush, firing blindly as they went. Bullets hummed above the heads of William and Drake; accuracy was hard for them to achieve while running. William aimed his gun at the first SuMa out of the underbrush, but could not bring himself to pull the trigger. The image in his mind of his stepfather bleeding to death after he shot him caused him to hesitate. The man lumbering towards William reminded him more of a mastodon than a human. He was six foot five inches, long haired and bearded, wearing a tattered plaid shirt, his face was a leathery brown from constant exposure to the Florida sun. There was a pop from Drake's pistol and the man fell at William's feet, slumping forward like big game shot by a hunter on safari. He looked over at Drake, who flashed him an expression that indicated he wanted William to fight. The crack of gunfire from automatic weapons intensified as more SuMas came in from hunting greatly outnumbering William and Drake.

Drake un-holstered another pistol and began shooting with both hands, with much more accuracy than the advancing SuMas. One after another they kept dropping under Drake's return fire. In the midst of the battle, William heard a truck roar to life and he and Drake pivoted to see it as both headlights and floodlights came on, lighting them up in the fading twilight. William looked up in time to see another large SuMa lunging for him. His huge dirty hands quickly clamped around William's throat and knocked him off his feet. William tried to break the grip that was squeezing the life out of him, when he could not, he reached up and inserted his thumb in the man's eye, and depressed it into the back of the socket; William had the sensation of crushing a grape under his thumb when the assailant's right eye popped. The man stood up and screamed, allowing William to slide back and fill his lungs with air. He looked up to see the man, who looked almost the same size as the mastodon, charging again. Blood flowed out of the man's eye socket like tears, he screamed consumed with both anger and pain as he did. He was nearly back on top of William, when he fell over, having been shot in the back.

The gunshot came from another direction entirely, and was not from Drake's gun. William lifted his head up to see an athletic-looking platinum haired, blue-eyed soldier on horseback. His uniform was spotless, everything in its place, his white teeth were clinched and he was growling something through them, but William could not make out what under the popping and cracking of the gunfire. His pistol was polished, his aim steady and he fired while controlling his horse as if it were a Lipizzaner Stallion. Drake looked over and shouted "Walt!" at the sight of Capitan Walton George Smith.

The sight of him was dazzling enough to momentarily draw the attention of all the SuMas. They all stopped as if they had seen some mythical creature come to life, he in turn held his fire. Finally after the momentary silence, his eyes narrowed "Well, come on you bastards!" he screamed at them, seeming to jar them back to reality as they continued to charge. Six more SuMas jumped out of the back of the pickup, and charged along, firing their assault rifles as they ran forward. Drake and Walton continued to return fire; William finally roused himself to his feet, and saw his weapon lodged in a pile of pine needles. He ran to get it, hearing bullets fly past his ears; it reminded him of the buzzing of angry bees. He reached his gun and turned to shoot, not really aiming, but hoping to inflict damage. He was always the best shot on any ranch he had worked at, but target shooting and hunting was different than battle. William's barrage missed hitting anyone, but managed to shatter both headlights on the front of the truck. The loss of light was enough to send the remaining SuMas into full retreat, leaving their dead and wounded behind. Walton signaled to Drake to follow him as he galloped into the thick wood after them. William was left standing, looking at the carnage that had ensued, and wondering if he could really be a soldier.

The following morning all was silent and peaceful in contrast to the gunfight that had taken place the night before. The wind blew through the pines making a soft whooshing sound, and the sound of birds singing were the only things that could be heard. William left his tent, bottled water and MRE in hand, trying to go over the events in his head the previous night. If he was to survive, he would have to fire a weapon; His intellect would have to find a way to overcome his fear. He brushed the leaves off a fallen log, as they continued to fall like rain in the strong breeze that was blowing. As he sat down, he heard a horse voice behind him bark "coward!" He chose to ignore it; he had heard Walton Smith repeat the insult over and over since reaching the rallying point after the skirmish. The atmosphere of calm was shattered by the barb being repeated louder a second time. Walton felt that William had done nothing to contribute to subduing the SuMas, and was in fact a hindrance.

After William had lost sight of Walton, he had driven the SuMas into the approaching Calvary from the side, forcing them to surrender. Police from Ocala reached them an hour later, taking them into custody. Two school buses were brought deep into the woods on a narrow road, one for convicts, and the other for children and their parents who were not criminals. It was a proud moment for Walton, one of many in his career.

Walton walked from behind William and stood in front of him his face twisted in a snarl as he glared down at William who was looking off in the distance as if Walton was not right in front of him, doing his best to ignore him.

Walton leaned down and placed his face six inches from William's

"I don't know how or why you conned your way into this outfit, but you have shown you don't have the stomach for war, you need to resign right now."

William stood up and stretched "It's a beautiful day" he looked skyward, "yep, a great day to serve my country." William said as if speaking to himself.

Walton moved closer "You and your mutt of a horse need to leave now." he said as he poked William in the chest, and finally garnered a reaction.

William knocked his hand away, "You can say anything you want about me, but don't talk about my horse!" William said as he finally had all he could take of Walton's tirades.

"What are you going to do? I can kill you with one hand and you know it." Walton laughed.

William stood fist clinched in anger, but he knew Walton was right; he could not take him in a fight. Bulloch had been watching the confrontation unfold from a distance and decided it was time to intervene. He slipped in between them.

"Gentlemen, we cannot have you fighting. No offense, William, but you would not stand a chance. We cannot do anything that is completely intellectual, because, as smart as you are Walt, William is undoubtedly the smartest person I have ever met. What are we to do then? How is William going to defend his honor? How is Walt going to prove we are wrong about William? We are going to have a contest. Whoever makes it from Lake Dorr to Hog Valley first wins. The finish line will be the volunteer fire station. You will be going with only a compass, a map, a day's worth of rations, a flashlight, a knife and a radio, in case you are hurt or want to give up. Get to the finish first, using whatever method you choose. That will settle this. You both will have four days to get there."

William and Walton separated and stood there each waiting for the other to react first. William decided it was in his best interest to speak up in front of the others, he did not want to seem like a coward to them after his behavior in the firefight. He stepped forward turning his back to Walton and addressed the rest of the troops,

"I think that Walt will be afraid to lose in the race. He won't do it."

William decided to call Walt by his nickname which was popular with the troops. Walt's eyes momentarily flashed with rage, but he realized William was trying to prove his bravery and he laughed loudly. William let Walt laugh without stopping him, he wanted Walt to be overconfident.

Drake came up to William and pulled him aside.

"Look Will, I know that you want to earn everyone's respect, but you don't have to go through with this." William patted Drake on the shoulder and smiled, he appreciated that he was looking out for him. William knew, as he always did, he would find a way to win.

# CHAPTER VIII

Walton George Smith came from family accomplished in military tradition. He was part of a long chain comprised of distinguished military officers, which ran back to the American Revolution. His grandfather had been a two star general and his father worked in Army intelligence. Being a soldier was in his blood, and he knew better than most what it took to be a great warrior. It was because of that reason he believed that William did not have what it takes to be a soldier.

Walton, or Walt as his friends affectionately called him, relished the chance to embarrass William and expose him for the fraud he believed he was. Ever since he was a boy growing up in San Diego, he dreamed of the day he could join the Army. Walt was competitive by nature; he gave great effort in both school and sports. He was a gifted athlete who excelled in horseback steeple chases, swimming, and track and field, the latter so much so he was chosen to be on the U.S. Olympic track and field team at only sixteen years old. He won a gold medal in the decathlon, breaking the world records for javelin and discus throw in the process. Walt was offered countless endorsements, scholarship offers, and a guaranteed slot in the following Olympics, but his calling, he would tell anyone who asked, was preordained; he was to be a soldier. He enrolled in West Point after graduating early from high school. He graduated in the top two percent of his class, and then stunned his peers and mentors by opting to become a Green Beret. Walt felt his intellect, physical talent and shooting skill, which was an fourth in the army with a pistol, eighth with a rifle, could best be utilized by being in high-risk missions, hunting high-value targets. He proved his worth, leading missions ranging from secretly building and training resistance forces to capturing or killing high value targets. Walt's reputation grew with each success and he was considered one of the brightest and the best the Army had to offer. He was recruited by General Wright to join the Calvary, because of his background, his leadership and his horsemanship. With all of his success, Walt was still considered by some to be unhinged; his zeal for battle seemed too extreme at times.

The wind continued to blow hard against the forest, the sky was clear and there were no clouds, they had been swept away by gale-like blasts. Although it was a cool day, the sun had begun to warm the ground. Walt stood next to William; a crowd of their fellow trainees surrounded them, watching the two icons about to compete with one and other. The anticipation was electric, and the charge swept across the spectators. No one who volunteered for the Cavalry expected to see a happening like the one they were witnessing. The competitors were to climb up two very old and tall longleaf pine trees to retrieve a flag before they could depart from the start line. The trees had been dubbed "the twins" by the soldiers stationed at the camp because their gnarled trunks and twisted branches were almost exact mirror images of one and other. The flags were in fact old rags that had been tied at the top, and flapped in the stiff wind. Positioned in front of the tree were the two competitors, awaiting the signal to start the race. The fifty-mile race that ran from south to north gave the two competitors several different types of landscape to contend with from thick hardwood hammocks to wide open savannas, making it an extremely difficult undertaking.

William turned his head to inspect Walt who was wearing a standard issue olive t-shirt and olive camouflage pants. He had his backpack strapped on tightly and a pair of mirrored wraparound sunglasses. Walt was stretching as if he was about to compete in the Olympics once again. William chuckled at the ritual, which he could see was further enraging his opponent. William in contrast to Walt, was wearing his standard cavalry-issue grey pants and t-shirt with his Stetson. William did not stretch, nor hop up and down as Walt did, but instead squatted as a catcher does behind home plate, he examined a map he held out at arm's length in front of him. He was focused, not aware of what was going on around him, lost deep in thought. He occasionally looked up from the map, and over at Walt, who seemed to taunt him with his condescending smirks and nods. William had left his outlaw days behind, but he still loved to be the focus of attention, and the race was no exception.

Bulloch came striding from his tent and approached the two competitors, flanked by Generals George Vernon and Alex Wright, which sent a wave of salutes flashing through the crowd. Even William snapped to attention at the sight of Vernon, the single leader of the American Military forces against the Romans. Everyone there had great respect for Vernon, and treated him almost as if he was royalty, which the humble leader rejected. He was dressed in his field uniform with a Calvary hat, a sign of his support for the new undertaking. Bulloch strode in front of the two competitors and turned to the assembled crowd.

"Good Morning gentlemen, it is a fine day for a race, and before William and Walt undertake their challenge, General Vernon would like to speak to you."

He took two steps backwards to let Vernon be the sole focus of the troops. The towering six foot four inch frame of General Vernon was imposing, and he was almost always the tallest person in the room, which in itself had helped him to command respect, and made him easier to see, as was the case with the gathered soldiers. He stood silent for a moment, reviewing his troops before he spoke.

"Today you will witness what may be of great historical significance. Our two most famous soldiers are going to compete in a race. Some might think this kind of thing unorthodox or at the very least distracting. I respectfully disagree with those opinions. The competition between Private West and Captain Smith is the kind of thing that has made our country great, we compete with one another, but in the end we are all on the same team, we are all Americans. It is our desire to win, to be the best, while not stepping on our fellow citizens, which is what makes us who we are. Some in the Pentagon are referring to you as an experiment, a waste of time, a group of renegades; they think the vast range of backgrounds will make you an unmanageable group. I say that you should take their words and use it as a badge of honor. As of today, you will be known as the Renegades!"

There was a roar of approval from the crowd for the new moniker.

"It is our desire to grasp hold of the opportunity freedom offers to all of us, and to carve our own path as individuals; that will help us win this war. While you are all individuals, you have come together as a unit, a single force working in unison together. Some of you were with me in the last war, and you know I demand discipline, but encourage forward thinking. Private West and Captain Smith could have chosen not to let their differences ferment in their hearts, poisoning the ranks as one side or another was chosen. West and Smith have shown why we created this unit, and why it will be vital to the defeat of the Romans. These two men have chosen to compete, but when it is over, fight as Americans."

The crowd was silent after the speech, not from indifference, but reverence. General Vernon turned to Bulloch and smiled.

"Colonel, if you would please do the honors."

Bulloch nodded "Remember Gentlemen this is roughly fifty miles, you have three days, if neither of you reaches the finish line before that time, there will be no winner. Only use your com if there is an emergency."

With that, Bulloch pulled out his antique 1910 revolver and with a crack fired a single shot that reverberated through the woods .William and Walt began to scramble up the twins; there were no limbs to grasp for the first nine feet of either tree. William studied the tree for a moment and watched Walt climb, since the trees were almost identical. William smiled again watching Walt straining and going as fast as he could; William was fine with letting Walt do the work for him. Walt reached the top and triumphantly raised his flag and started his descent. William leisurely climbed the path that Walt had on the identical tree. Walt hit the ground and never looked back; he sprinted with long even strides, vanishing in the thicket of pine trees in front of him. William grabbed his flag and climbed down as calmly as he went up; when he jumped to the ground he turned to the crowed and tipped his hat, that was when he saw her, a tiny dark brown haired blue eyed soldier who was part of some other military training going on in Ocala National Forest. She turned and gave him a wide smile before turning and walking the other way with her unit. William had not counted seeing someone that he found so striking, not for her obvious beauty, but her earnest smile and the twinkle in her eyes. He was taken, and had read her last name *Willowdell* on her uniform  and decided he had to meet her. Instead of following Walt into the woods, he instead casually walked over to her and introduced himself.

"Hi there, I'm William. What's your name?" he said with his most charming smile.

Before she could answer, Bulloch bellowed at William "Private West! Are you going to bother to take part in the race or should I shoot you myself?"

William gave a tip of his hat to her not wanting to let the chance go by. He then focused himself to the task at hand and trotted off into the woods heading in a slightly different angle than Walt had gone. Absolutely no one watching believed William stood a chance of winning, with the notable exception of Ted Bulloch and Alex Wright, they had brought William in for his mind. They knew he was someone who could improvise in difficult situations, someone who could be adept at guerilla warfare. Bulloch watched William disappear into the same line of trees that Walt had moments before; a father of a newborn child could not have been more proud at that moment. William turned and looked back for a moment, he caught a fleeting glance of the soldier he had just introduced himself to, he saw her mouth words so that he could see it, but he couldn't quite make it out, he thought she said *be safe*.

William was always good at navigating his way from one place to the next, but he was more used to wide open spaces, the trees, thick brush and weeds of Central Florida were disorienting. He wished Roost were with him to help find his way. Roost had an uncanny sense of direction and of exactly how long it would take to get somewhere. William had marveled at the first time Roost bet him he could find a place within a quarter mile of its GPS coordinates, and he found his way to the location within one hundred feet of the GPS coordinates. Once when they were on the run in Colorado, Roost found his ways through the badlands and even through the Sand Dunes when a sandstorm blew up, all the way to the town of Alamosa where they had stashed money and supplies.

William wished he could tell his old friend what was going on, but it would have to wait until after the war, the he would try to make amends. William came to a thick line of sand pines in his way, he was unsure about entering them; he worked his way along the wall of bark and palmettos until he came to an opening. It opened up onto a piece of Florida Prairie, so wide that William could see the whole horizon. It was like he was on the planes again; he was truly surprised at finding such a stretch of wide open space. He was further surprised to see a heard of twenty buffalo grazing on the dry part of the prairie, they were originally native to Florida but were wiped out hundreds of years before. The herd of bison that William saw was from a hunting range, where they had been brought to be captive game for hunters, but had been released into the wild when the owners were killed in the Roman invasion. William watched them move among the tall grass and weeds, and thought about what must be happening in the part of the country he loved the most, the west. He had heard rumors that the Romans were constructing their own buildings and were destroying much of the west. It was the first time in his life he felt like he truly had a purpose; it seemed to him to be the reason God put him on Earth. He knew he had to win the race to gain the respect he needed so his fellow soldier's would trust him. He estimated Walt was probably far ahead of him, ripping through the brush, and he would have to use all his skill to catch him.

Walt had charged forwards through miles of loose sand, pine trees, grape vines and razor sharp palmettos in the area of the forest aptly named *Devils Bay*, all the while never slowing to a walk unless he had to clear brush. He finally stopped to take a drink from a clear plastic squeeze bottle out of his backpack at *Blue Sink*, a forty-seven-foot deep lake, formed from a sink hole in the heart of the forest. He sat at the water's edge on a makeshift dock made out of boards and plywood some enterprising fisherman had once put in some long forgotten fishing trip. The water was as deep a blue as he had ever seen, the old twisted oak trees grew just a few feet from the banks and wide swaths of vine spilled from the shore into the water. Walt found himself sitting looking at the scene for longer than he expected. While he loved the competition, the solitude it provided presented him with a different problem; he would become lost in thought. He turned over in his mind how the Romans could be beaten, what strategy would work best, and when he was not focusing on the war, how much he missed his wife and his little girl.

One thing Walt was sure of was that he had to beat and shame William, an army that allowed cowards in its ranks would surely fall. He saw no sign that William's lack of discipline would change, or that he would not freeze again in battle. If William did not quit when he was inevitably beaten, he could press his superiors to get rid of him, executive order or no executive order. Walt suddenly laughed out loud, sending an echo across the lake; he had the image of William trying to find his way through the same swamps he had just trudged through. In Walt's estimation, he should be hearing the rotors of a rescue helicopter flying overhead by nightfall, to extract William from being entangled in vine or having sustained a broken bone somewhere.

He took out his map and scanned it carefully; it was another ten miles to the Observation tower where he planned to spend the night. Once he reached the tower it meant he had traversed fifteen miles of swamps and forest, he estimated his opponent would only reach half of that if he was lucky. Walt looked at the dozens of tiny lacerations on his arm and the rashes from poison ivy; it was all worth it to prove his point. Walt believed that by the time he was done, William was going to prison where he belonged.

William had been walking in the same direction for three hours, through thick woods before he reached one of the main forest roads running north and south. He decided to follow it, even if it was a longer route, it meant less vegetation to contend with. Another hour would pass before William found what he was looking for, an unmanned ranger station that had been left vacant due to the war. As he suspected, staying on the main road yielded something of use. William approached the dark brown rough-hewn wood sided building, looking around for any sign that SuMas may be squatting or laying there, waiting for him. William surveyed the building from all sides before cautiously proceeding. The station had been constructed in the 1980's, a fact he knew because he had researched the park the previous night. William knew that Walt would be expecting him to take a more conventional route, and try to beat him in a foot race. Walt overestimated William's capacity for honor, at least with regards to competing. William had noted that nothing was specifically said about using what they found to win the race, just what tools they would be given. William examined the double hung windows on the face of the building. The blinds were all pulled down on the four front windows. In his past exploits he would have simply broken one of the panes and opened the window, but now he did not want to damage the building, he wanted it there for use after the war was over. He decided another way it would have to be found. He moved to the front door to see if it was possible to pick the lock; he found the white metal doors secured with deadbolts, and the addition of padlocks. He next moved to the utility building that had been a later addition to the building. Like many of the national parks utility buildings, it could be accessed with a remote controlled garage door opener; a fact which William realized from having broken into one and was planning to exploit that knowledge. He knew there was power to the building because, even though it was the middle of the day, a streetlight mounted on a decrepit telephone poll was lit. William glanced over to the oblong brown wood sign on a river stone façade next to the road; the floodlights mounted on it were on as well. He walked past the sign toward the station; William was surprised that its aluminum roof and stone façade looked as if it were still being taken care of; it made him feel almost as if there really was no war.

He followed the sand trail around the side of the station, and behind it, to the addition. On the front was a segmented white plastic garage door. William felt the same kind of satisfaction upon seeing it that he used to get when he got a particularly large haul from a heist, "Gotcha!" William said out loud to the building, as if it could understand he had found where it had been hiding the garage door.

William took his knife out, and his hand held radio. He took the knife and wedged open the casing of the radio, flipping it over. He then used the knife to wedge a circuit board from inside the radio. He unscrewed some wires and began to re-wire the radio, he would try squelching the transmit button, when there was no result, he would go to the next frequency. William continued the exercise of checking frequencies for fifteen minutes, before finding the right one. Finally, William found the right frequency, and there was the sound of clicking and whirring from behind the door, as it began to slide up to reveal what was hidden inside. William laughed out loud to himself when he saw a Ranger's Pickup sitting in the middle of the garage. The white truck had an LED light-bar with blue lights on top. Written on either side just below the hood in green block letters was *PARK RANGER*. On the door was an inverted brown arrowhead with the park logo on it. It had a well maintained appearance despite years of inactivity. Dry rot had not consumed the tires, even after sitting for so long a period. He walked over and peered in the window, there were no keys in the ignition. The garage was neat, everything in its place, if there were keys; William thought to himself, they would be hanging next to the door. He walked over to the door which had been painted white numerous times in its existence, and turned the knob, it was unlocked. He stepped through to what were once living quarters. There were two bare wooden nightstands and a cherry wood bed frame, with no mattress, only springs that were bowled out in the middle. The room was cramped, with only one window and bent venetian blinds with an empty closet three feet from the bed. There was a beat up old dresser that matched the bed, but with a constellation of scratches and nicks on it. William could see the outline of where a television had set on it for years, probably replaced by a holo-def screen at some point. The room smelled dank and musty from the years of not being used. William pulled up the blinds to see better as a plume of dust filled the air, each individual particle being illuminated by the sunlight pouring through the window. William coughed and moved through the next door, which opened up into the main lobby.

The lobby was a stark white room with three florescent light ballasts embedded in the ceiling. William flipped the light switch and they flickered to life, except for the last one that only had one good bulb. A reception area was built into the wall, with numerous brochures warped from exposure to cold, heat and humidity, sat in clear plastic stands on top of the desk. There were some bookshelves that had various books about the area intermixed with travel atlases. There was a table with a shadowbox built in to the top, slightly slanted. Various items from the area were on display including an arrowhead and wooly mammoth teeth. The whole scene gave William a feeling of loss, of the loss of normal daily life that the Romans stole when they attacked. He could imagine families, retirees and every day tourist coming in on their vacation and checking into the campground down the road.

William leaned over the desk and saw a set of keys sitting there, including the remote that belonged in the pickup. William smiled with satisfaction and snatched them off the counter. He quickly moved back out into the garage and pressed the button on the remote, which in turn caused a clicking sound from the truck as the locks opened. He quickly slid in and put the key in the ignition. The digital display lit up, but the engine did not start. There was only enough power in the battery to unlock the doors and light the display. The fuel gauge showed nearly a full tank of gas. William laughed again when he saw that it was a manual transmission on the pickup. He stepped out with the door open, and started pushing it out the door and onto the crushed rock seashell drive. Once the truck gained momentum, he jumped in, put it into second gear, and rapidly took his foot off the clutch. It sputtered to life and he pulled onto the road wondering what Walt was doing at that moment.

William raced down a long dirt road, creating a long cloud of orange dust behind him. He followed the telephone polls to a main road, from there it would take him to the finish line. The road was framed by two walls comprised of scrub oaks, slash pines, and palmettos, it was a rustic sight. William's mind was elsewhere, engaged in regretting the past. He thought about how he left Cassidy once again, he knew it was the right thing to do, but he felt guilt over how he did it. He missed her, but it was in a way more like someone misses a friend rather than a spouse. He also felt guilty for thinking about the girl he had seen that morning. She could not have been more than nineteen or twenty, a few years younger than William. She had a sweet air about here, something pure and pristine. As much as he tried William could not get the image of her smiling at him out of his mind, which amplified his remorse. He was still technically married, but he felt that faking his own death made it hard to file for a divorce. He was sure when the time came to pass Cassidy would not hesitate to sign the papers, once she knew what he had done. William knew that he and Cassidy were addicted to the rush of the heist; the drugs and alcohol were just an extension of that. As long as he and Cassidy remained together, they would never stop the life of crime, and would have wound up dead. He resolved to tell Cassidy and find the girl he had spoken to, for some reason he felt a connection to her. William shook off the notion of love at first sight, he was not the type for that, but nonetheless, he felt something for her.

His foray into self incrimination was forgotten when he saw two propeller planes like the ones used in air races. They swooped in front of him just above the treetops. Two more planes came roaring behind them, and circled back around, and vanishing behind the tree line. William stood dumbfounded at what he had just seen when there was a deep and resounding boom, suddenly the ground rumbled below the truck. He slammed on his brakes and jumped out to see a large ball of fire floating upwards, becoming thinner as it did, finally dissipating into nothingness. William decided it must have been one or more of the planes crashing, practicing some kind of maneuver for some sort of show. He wondered why they were in a closed national forest, and why practice there of all places. He started to turn around and go help when he looked over and saw a set of gates to another dirt road with signs making it clear he was next to a bombing range that was used by the military. As he looked at the gates he again heard the roar of a propeller plane, this one had a much louder sound, William tried to identify it, but could only come to the conclusion that it sounded like a racecar engine. Seconds later two more planes appeared over the road, much faster this time and different than the first planes, these were larger and looked to William as if they were designed based on old prop planes from the mid twentieth century. He could see rivets in these planes made of steel or titanium he could not tell which, but he could clearly see the bombs attached to the bottom of the wings. They looked like old planes he had seen images of as a child, it befuddled him. Again there was another thunderous boom as the planes released their ordinance, and another fireball rose from behind the trees. William was not sure what was happening, had another plane crashed, or were they on some sort of bombing run? William stood there for a few minutes, waiting to see if more planes came, or if there was another explosion. Nothing happened, so he decided it was time to continue with the race. He was mystified though about the planes, why was the Air Force using long outdated technology, when the Romans were so advanced, he thought. It made no sense to use antique planes, they had no advantage except their old electronics and machinery were immune to some newer technology. He climbed back in the truck, wondering what it all meant.

Walt had made excellent time; he had traveled nearly fifty miles on foot in less than 72 hours. He had only stopped to sleep for two hours the previous night, and had managed to eat while he traveled. He had become both dehydrated and fatigued; only able to walk the last few miles of the journey. When he came upon the  rows of modular tents and armored vehicles that had been moved from the start of the race, he saw normal morning activates, the horses being fed, soldiers heading in and out of the showers, and others eating breakfast. What Walt did not expect was to see William standing there directly in front of him, waving and grinning. The sight of William enraged him and revived his strength, and he sprinted towards William, shedding his backpack as he did. He sprung into the air with the strength and speed of a wild animal attacking its prey; he landed on William, punching him in the face repeatedly. Walt then put his hands around the throat of the dazed William, and squeezed. William, tried to push him off, but to no avail, he felt around on the ground for something to hit him with, but found nothing. Suddenly William's training took over, and he cupped his hand and thrust it as hard as he could against Walt's ear. Walt yelped as his eardrum popped, and he let go of William. William gasped for air as he rolled away, and clambered to his feet. If he was going to die, he would die fighting. He ran towards Walt with his fist raised. Walt grabbed him by the arm and hurled William to the ground.  William spun around, ready for the next assault when he saw Walt softly chuckling to himself. "Congratulations, now you're ready to be a soldier" he said holding his ear, trying to keep blood from dripping onto his neck. William had proven to Walt that he was not a coward by fighting back, and thereby winning his respect.  He walked over and patted the coughing William on the shoulder and then turned and walked away. William felt the bruises on his face, and felt the scratches on his neck; this had not been what he thought it was going to be like to be a soldier.

# CHAPTER IX

The vaulted halls of the Imperial Palace were, to anyone who witnessed them, the epitome of the architectural achievement of the new Empire. The marble floors were adorned with squares arranged in a wide circular pattern .The circles were black with each square hollow, giving the impression it was black with a thick white line surrounding the square. The squares surrounded a circular black and white geometric pattern; the circles were repeated over and over down the hall. Each arched doorway was adorned with two ionic columns, followed by marble sculptures of great former emperors on the interior walls of the dome. The public was given tours of the palace twice a month, thus it was given the designation of *Basilica*, a large Roman public building, which Caprera relished; he wanted to reclaim the term from the Church.

It was down one of the halls that Charles Fletcher quickly strolled through, his footsteps echoing as he walked. He continued the pace until he marched into Sabrina Caprera's bedroom. She did not sleep with her husband; he slept for only three hours a night and did not want to be disturbed. Sabrina was on her side, stretched to her full length on a gold lectus, her head resting on her outreached arm. Her hand was placed on a gold threaded pillow, as if it was on display. She looked up to see Charles standing in the doorway and smiled

"Please come in Charles." She said in a content voice.

He nodded and stepped into the spacious room with its half barrel ceiling and coral walls covered with mosaics. On one wall was a tile mosaic of Pan playing his flute surrounded by dancing nymphs, on the opposite was Neptune causing the sea to wash Vasekts off a cliff. There was a canopy bed in the corner of the room and a large holo-def screen near the doorway. The room also contained a large classic Roman style vanity, and a cavernous walk in closet. Sabrina moaned as she rolled to her back and stretched while inspecting the tiles on the ceiling.

"What can I do for you Charles" she said in a yawn never making eye contact.

Charles was hardened by years of being around beautiful actresses who all wanted to be with him because he was a famous director, but Sabrina's unusual beauty and unorthodox manner affected him, though he would not let it show.

Charles smiled and spoke with his usual debonair manner "Empress, I have a proposition for you."

Upon hearing his words she sprung up, "You're propositioning *me* Charles? I am truly flattered."

Charles smiled, still exuding confidence, "You have a great deal of influence with your husband, perhaps even more than I do. You see, Empress, this is why I need your help." Charles said ignoring Sabrina's suggestive tone.

Sabrina stood up and glided across the room to a nightstand, she opened a drawer and pulled out a small mirror and a jar made of black marble, which contrasted the white marble floor. Inside the jar was her personal supply of cocaine. She poured some of the contents out onto the mirror and began arranging it in neat parallel lines. She started to lean over and stopped herself, giving a playful glance to Charles.

"Would you care for some?" she said being genuine in her generosity.

"No, I never touch the stuff, it gives me headaches."

Charles rebuffed the offer without offending her by saying what he was thinking: that the habit of cocaine snorting was truly depraved. He touched two fingers to his forehead as he did so giving his signature charming smile.

Sabrina was undeterred "Excuse me for a moment please."

She proceeded to take in the powder through a gold straw designed for the purpose of snorting cocaine. She stood up and flipped her long honey blonde hair back and giving Charles her complete attention. Charles again started to explain why he was there.

"Empress…"

"Please, Charles," Sabrina cut him off, "call me by my name. We don't have to be so formal with one and other, do we?"

Charles again smiled, intrigued by the forbidden conquest within his grasp, but again focused on his task.

"Very well, Sabrina. Your sister-in-law is greatly embarrassing your husband, and you by proxy. As queen of England, she needs to be demure in her actions, she has hardly been that. She has shown the entire world what a first class floozy she is, a back alley French prostitute has more class than Julia. The parties she has at Buckingham palace often turn into full-blown orgies. She mocks the very crown that she wears on her lovely little crimson head and smells of gin and tequila most of the day; now I am hearing rumors that she is doing something horrible with young English girls she sees on the street. It's you Sabrina, who can change this. You alone have the power- speak to Giovanni; convince him to remove Julia from the throne." His tone was resolute and stirring.

"Why would I want to do that?" Sabrina sighed, "What good would come from Julia leaving England?" Sabrina inched closer to Charles as she spoke in a manner meant to intimidate.

Charles, in turn, moved closer to her, "You could convince him to put his daughter on the throne in her place." Charles said in a low throaty voice to neutralize her attempt to intimidate him.

Sabrina's expression changed, she had not considered that she could rid herself of Caesaris. The extreme disdain between the stepmother and daughter was mutual, and the fact that Sabrina was nearly the same age as Caesaris compounded the sentiment, and made being in the same room nearly unbearable for both. Sabrina let out a chuckle at the idea and smiled at Charles, looking at him without breaking her gaze. Charles was again taken aback by her crystal blue eyes; they had a sleepy, half shut look to them, but were strikingly alluring. He chuckled in return to mask his attraction. Charles beamed with confidence even though he was uneasy; he stepped closer to her in order to regain dominance.

"You see Sabrina, with no competitor for his affection; you will be quite the influence."

Sabrina moved closer again and stared up into his eyes, "Charles, you are a smart man, and I trust you. I will convince Giovanni that she should be the new queen of England. I am grateful to you for the idea. I did not think you cared about how I felt Charles," she said, touching her hand to the breast of his blazer.

Charles gave Sabrina a sideways look and gave her his most charming smirk. "Quite the contrary, I care very much about your feelings."

He turned to walk back across the long marble floor, having achieved his goal, when he was stopped by the sight of Sabrina's reflection in a full-length mirror. She was sitting on the lectus and had removed her shawl revealing her long blue dress with a plunging neckline. Her hand was patting the gold cushion and she had the smile of a crocodile about to devour its prey.

Sabrina cooed, "Charles, please come sit and spend some time with me. It will be worth your while, I promise. You won't be disappointed." The invitation was obvious.

Charles hesitated for a moment and then turned, enthralled with the conquest. "How could I turn down such a kind invitation?" he said as shutting the ornate brass door behind him.

Charles Fletcher's office was an eclectic mix of clean classic roman lines, and ornate Victorian furniture, a dichotomy befitting his personality. An ancient mahogany parlor table sat in the back of the office with a marble bust of Cicero on top. A three door Victorian bookcase sat to the left back corner of the white room with a vaulted ceiling. In the bookcase were leather-bound copies of The Prince, The Art of War, Julius Cesar, Macbeth and the Taming of the Shrew; each book was at least over a century old. Charles sat behind his Victorian pedestal desk, clear of paper and pens. A holo-def screen took up the far corner; in the middle were the remnants of his lunch: a sirloin steak, a pineapple, a quart of pecan ice cream and a bottle of scotch. The only reason Charles was slightly overweight, and not morbidly obese, was an almost inhuman metabolism, that burned everything he consumed. He sat, reclined in his chair, cigar in hand, holding court with Senator Luigi Corioli. Charles was a stark contrast to the senator; he wore Caprera's own design of the traditional grey suit combined with the roman toga, while the senator wore a full toga. Charles was relaxed and exuded power, while the senator was quiet and measured both in his words and actions. Charles looked at Corioli with an acute stare.

"Senator, it is my strong belief we can have Julia removed from the throne." Charles' conviction and salesmanship were second to none.

The senator was not easily moved "You act as if that is so easily achieved." Luigi said, rubbing his curly auburn bearded chin.

Charles leaned forward and smiled in his easy way, though his stare was no less intense, "Senator, you have my solemn vow, Julia will be removed, and Caesaris will take her place." Charles held up his left hand while placing the right over his heart for emphasis.

Luigi bolted from the antique red velvet chair, and shot a look of disbelief to Charles. He paced to the front of the room, his head hung looking at the floor, but seeing something else. He stood, motionless for a moment, pondering the idea of Cesar's daughter sitting on the throne. He realized she was more than capable, and admired around the world, even where her father was considered a tyrant. It would be perfect, but Luigi had trouble believing the emperor would give his consent. He stood upright and straightened his lean frame before turning to Charles.

"How, Charles? How did you manage to orchestrate this?"

Charles chuckled, "I haven't completely pulled it off yet old man," his expression became serious again; "But give me time, I will."

The senator stood staring at the floor "Caesaris fits perfectly into the plan." he said as if Charles was not in the room.

Charles sensed his plan was working, "She does, doesn't she?" he said, feigning as if the idea were the senator's and not his own.

Luigi still stared at the floor and spoke again as if Charles were not there, "Is this the right time to do this? I am still shocked at the Americans' determination; I think it safe to say no one would have expected they would be putting up such a fight. Our allies in Congress are being discovered and arrested. The new President openly mocks him, even though we occupy a large portion of their country. I think Caesar may not be open to suggestions," he said pondering the cons of the plan.

"I know. I am immensely dismayed at the way the cowards are singing like so many canaries under only slight duress. Our inability to hold their loyalty is an embarrassment to the empire. I think Cesar is going to be angry with our so-called allies who take money from us, pledge their undying loyalty to Rome, and then betray us. I know the Emperor, perhaps better than anyone else you see, and he needs an outlet for his anger. His sister has been a disgrace in her role as queen; she will be the one to feel the brunt of his displeasure."

Luigi was perplexed, "Then why now? Why are you going to invoke the name of Julia in the middle of a crisis?" his confusion was genuine.

"Because he needs someone to direct his anger at old man, and I don't plan on it being me. Julia has caused us enough headaches, having her undoubtedly confined to her home will be a breath of fresh air." Charles said as he leaned forward to extinguish his cigar in a Victorian porcelain ashtray decorated with hand painted purple flowers.

Charles quickly looked up upon hearing the sound of the Praetorian guards outside shouting "Hail Caesar!" followed by the abrupt entry of Caprera in to the room. Both Charles and Luigi sprang to their feet beating their fists to their chest and blurting out "Hail Caesar!" simultaneously. Caprera weakly returned the salute, and placed his hand on the shoulder of Luigi.

"Senator, it is good to see you. I am sorry to interrupt, but I need to speak to Charles in private."

Luigi nodded his understanding at the same time he made eye contact with Charles. Luigi passed Caprera as he exited, stunned that the emperor looked so disheveled, his appearance was always impeccable, but the impression his appearance gave was that he had not slept, or eaten in days. Caprera slumped into the chair that Luigi had been sitting in moments before him. Charles looked at his appearance and pressed a button under his desk that turned the picture window behind him from clear to a solid grey, he did not want anyone seeing Caprera in a weak moment.

The emperor looked up with a weary expression, "What is going on, Charles?" he said in a demanding voice.

Charles leaned back in his chair and spoke in a matter of fact tone "We have lost a battle, Kravchenko should have planned better, and our so called allies in Congress were less than sincere in their devotion to us." He then sat silently waiting for Caprera's reply.

The emperor leaned forward, his face contorted, "That was *my* plan, not Kravchenko's, and that is not what I was asking." Caprera's voice was clearly masking anger.

Charles continued to speak in the same tone, "I can't help you unless you tell me what you mean. Is Caesar upset with the quality of my work?" he said leaning forward in his chair.

Caprera looked dumbfounded, "Charles, I am surprised you don't have any idea why I am upset." He said leaning in, growing tired of explaining the situation.

Charles was not sure of what the reason was, "Is it the recent behavior of your sister?" Charles said, hoping that was the issue, and not his recent visit with Sabrina.

With that Caprera pointed and shook his finger at Charles as if he was the cause of his troubles, "She is out of control. I am sure you are aware of the liver washes. Does she really believe that she will not age, or that no one would find out? We have to remove her, there is no other choice. The English people are becoming more of a problem. You can't hide the parties, or young girls going missing after being in Julia's presence." His face grew red as he thought about his sister.

Charles was taken aback by the level of Caprera's anger, he had not anticipated his response, and it was evident that he had been considering Julia.

"What do you propose?" Charles carefully probed.

Caprera stood up walked in a small circle, sat back down and then looked up with a resigned expression.

"Send the Tenor" Caprera said in a melancholy tone.

Charles knew what the request meant. The Tenor was the empire's most accurate and prolific assassin.

"The Tenor! Are you sure? She is your sister, your flesh and blood. Have you thought this through?" Charles did not want the death warrant to be thrown back at him by Caprera in a fit of regret at some later date.

"There is no other way." Caprera said with remorse "She is a monster. I had indulged her other habits until this latest problem. The day she took the first girl off the street, she ceased to be my sister. I have no doubt in what I order. Give him a position as a royal bodyguard. Make sure it looks like it is from a natural cause." Caprera said not bearing to make the arrangements himself.

"Very well." Charles said hiding his disdain for Julia, "Whom are you considering in Julia's place?" he said moving his plan forward.

"What do you think about Caesaris taking the throne?" Caprera said changing his tone.

"I could not think of a more capable young woman. She is capable of administrating large projects. We would not have to manage London from here anymore. I think she would rule with honor, and honor her father."

Julia Caprera's beauty was not diminished by her forty one years, her olive skin, pale blue eyes, titian hair and long slender neck, looked nearly the same as they did twenty years earlier. It was because of her appearance that her fractured mind latched onto the idea that rubbing her skin with the liver of young girls kept her youth intact. She rode the streets of London in an unmarked black limousine, past illegal underground clubs at closing, searching for the perfect victim. The one she was looking at was an old steel warehouse outside of Canary Warf. The area had been a center of commerce before the Roman invasion, now the businesses were boarded up, windows broken. Glass and steel buildings that were once jewels of the district, were now tattered and dull, like the rest of London which was as dreary and downtrodden as any point in its long history. No one came to the wharf anymore, the homes in the area were vacant, it was no longer an approved area for living; yet rebellious Britons made their way past soldiers and gilded screamers to parties or *Balls* as they called them. The fact of the matter was that the Romans had been turning a blind eye to the movement because it provided Julia with what she desired. The abductions had provided some of the most horrific crime scenes since Jack the Ripper. The British public had grown suspicious of Julia, rumors had persisted she was involved in the murders. It compounded the misery and despair the public felt since the invasion.

The music coming from inside the warehouse was distorted and muffled as it permeated through the rusting walls, only the thump of the beat could be heard and felt. Julia sat staring at the building twisting her hair between her fingers with excitement. She was always accompanied by three royal guards, two to do her bidding, and one chauffer to stay behind and protect her. It was no different than any other of Julia's hunting trips, the nondescript limousine trolled past the warehouse, hordes of young people dressed in Victorian clothing, poured out the side door flooding the street. They scurried off in all directions to avoid capture. Her almost nightly routine had changed though, she had confided in a new guard, personally sent by her brother for her protection. She was grateful he was looking out for her, just as when they were children.

The guard, who she only knew as Victor, was tall lean with broad shoulders. Julia kept positioning herself in the way of the rear view mirror, adjusting her black toga to be more revealing, as she had been admiring Victor since his arrival. His piercing cobalt hued eyes were topped by thick bushy eyebrows; he looked back occasionally and smiled at the queen and said "Your Majesty" with a cockney accent. They slid past the club, Julia pressed against the glass in anticipation. "Her! She's the one, I must have her!" She said tapping against the window while pointing to a girl who shared her complexion and hair color.

Victor nodded and pulled down an adjacent alley. As soon as the car stopped, Victor began to sing from the opera "Lucrezia Borgia" and turned quickly shooting the two guards with her. Julia screamed in horror, as the guard sang louder to cover her cries.

He covered her mouth with his hand and spoke with an Italian accent "By the way, my name is not Victor", he said as she struggled to free herself.

Her eyes then focused on his right hand as he produced a syringe gun and injected her with a non-detectable toxin designed to cause a brain aneurism. He sang softly into Julia's ear as he injected her. She struggled for a few seconds more before she began to shake and convulse, as quickly as it began, it was over; her limp, lifeless body lay on the limousine floor. The two guards, unbeknownst to them, had been transferred by an order from what appeared to be Julia's own hand, and were not officially with her. The assassin was pleased with the results of his work; he had disposed of a monster and her two accomplices. The Tenor began to sing again as he climbed back into the front of the limousine and proceeded to drive back to Buckingham Palace, where he would transfer the guards to a van that would take them to a crematorium. The Tenor would place Julia in her bed, where the servants would discover her in the early afternoon.

Caesaris stood gazing out her window at the expanding skyline of Rome, the new high rise buildings her father was constructing, adorned with four columns attached to a corresponding corner, each pair framing glass windows and colossal friezes inside a triangular pediment at the top. Three of the new sky scrapers were the tallest in the world, their construction allowed them to sway with strong wind or earthquakes. The buildings were a symbol of Rome's return as the home of the world's elite engineers. As the aqueducts were in antiquity, the new skyscrapers were a marvel of structural engineering, giant turbines on the roof of each building powered the entire structure. They were constructed on the backs of slaves, many of which perished during construction, but provided limitless round the clock labor to quickly complete the new buildings.

Caesaris was not looking at the skyline; her mind was still focused on her father. Every time she saw him, she remembered the joy he took in killing his two opponents. Even her wardrobe reflected her mood; she wore a long black Stola dress and black Palla, as if she were in mourning for the childhood memory of her father. The dress gave the appearance of a death shroud, wrapping completely around her, from the crown of her head to the instep of her foot. She had sunk into such a profound depression that she abandoned her projects, and had not much of an appetite since the incident. Her father had come to her to try and mend the damage, but he could feel the distance that had never existed between them before. She had grown increasingly isolated, not even seeing her friends. She had wished she had not been there when the assassin tried to kill her father, now she wished she were anywhere else but home. There was a light knock on her door.

"Caesaris?" Charles Fletcher's voice floated through the brass door.

Caesaris was surprised at how glad to hear her old friend she was, and threw open the door. Caesaris had quite a different room from her stepmother. There were no mosaics, but paintings by Titian and Pallo Uccello, which she had rescued from her father's edict to destroy any art considered not to glorify Rome. Her desk, which had belonged to Benedetto Croce, was placed against the large picture window in her room. Her bed was small by the palace's standards, and there was no holo-def screen, she preferred to read or paint. There was a small, green, renaissance style couch against the far wall for the expressed purpose of sitting with visitors. Charles noted the difference between the stepmother and daughter's personal styles were evident as he entered the room. Charles immediately noticed the sullen mood that had Caesaris in its grip. He had always been fond of her and felt a responsibility to care for her.

"You know, I always preferred Titian to Michelangelo." Charles said trying to lighten his friend's mood.

Caesaris had held her feelings in, afraid to let them out, and a suspicion that had lingered in the back of her mind. She had no one else to confide in.

"Charles, I can't help feeling that my father had something to do with my Aunt's death. I know it sounds like I have lost my mind," she paused for a moment considering her words, "maybe I have, but I cannot stop thinking about it." She glanced up at Charles waiting for his judgment.

"She had an aneurism," Charles said touching her shoulder, "how could he have possibly done that? I know there are drugs now that can could be twisted and used for such purposes, but that seems unlikely." He said in a soothing tone.

Caesaris gave a faint smile of appreciation before sinking back into the gloom that held her, "I am not sure what I am going to do next. I feel empty."

The words caused Charles to feel a pang of sadness for her. He wondered if he had picked the right time to present his plan, but he also feared that if he did not she may fall into a deeper depression. Charles gently lifted her chin up with his forefinger and looked into her eyes.

"You are good and virtuous, Caesaris. There are few as pure as you, which is why I believe you can serve a greater purpose." Charles' tone was serious but delicate.

Caesaris held Charles in such high esteem that the words had the effect of distracting her from her despair, "What purpose? What do you mean?" She said uncovering her head.

Charles stood up and spoke as if he were delivering a soliloquy, "I think that you are the perfect choice to be the new Queen of England.

You will, of course, need to convince your father that you should be on the throne. You can achieve that with my assistance," he gave a self-congratulatory smile before continuing, "You could finally carve your own path, and not have to compete with your step mother. Yes you are very young, but you would not be the first young queen of England. I believe you have the strength, the courage to lead, the intelligence, the integrity and most importantly, the air of Royalty. What do you say?" Charles waited for her answer.

# CHAPTER X

Roost Roberts and Cassidy West walked at a brisk pace through the sagebrush and tall prairie grass as they traveled east. The land was flat and wide open, except for the occasional tree or hill, and the sun was constant, giving no relief from its heat. There were wide, bright swaths of yellow from the wild daisies and Mexican hat flowers, giving evidence that spring had arrived. Roost and Cassidy had been keeping their path on the wide-open plains for days, as they attempted to escape from Roman occupied territory. The pair was cautiously hopeful, having crossed the border from New Mexico into Texas they had left the most heavily occupied territory behind them.

The Romans had only been sending a Centuria, a unit consisting of one hundred Legionnaires, patrols to search for Americans to enslave. Each Centuria was backed by light armor and drones; they covered an area of five hundred square miles each. The legionnaires were spread too thin trying to cover the area and had allowed Roost and Cassidy to slip through. The pair had been forced to keep moving on foot; Roost's horse had been felled by Roman gunfire while they were fleeing from a patrol. In their journey they had seen horrible things, experiences they wished they'd never witnessed, and would never forget. A husband and wife, in their late seventies who was traveling with them, decided they could not go on and both resigned themselves to their pending demise. The couple, Tony and Amelia, who had shown them pictures of their children and grandchildren, just stopped and sat alongside of a dirt road in the desert. They both were gray haired, but in good shape for their age, but their lack of youth proved to be deadly, at least in their own minds. They were weary and decided they could not go any further than that dirt road in the middle of the desert. Tony and Amelia were from Pittsburg and had saved their whole life to move to New Mexico, they both had worked in the steel industry and had dreamed of the day when they could retire and move west. They had been in their dream home for four months when the Romans invaded, they laughed, saying they should have retired to Miami instead. Cassidy pleaded with them before Roost finally pulled her away. The vision of them just sitting there waving goodbye was a fresh vivid memory in Cassidy's mind. She could never forget the look of resignation on their faces; she did not understand how anyone could just decide to die. She had always been good at persuading people to do things, it is what made her a great con artist, but she failed to change their minds. She thought that maybe, if she had tricked them, they might still be alive. It was too late and as Roost had kept telling her, they had to keep focused on their own survival.

Both Cassidy and Roost had green canvas backpacks with sleeping bags tied on the top. Roost looked more the part in his brown Stetson denim jacket, jeans and cowboy boots; Cassidy looked less the part, she wore a long sleeve black hooded t-shirt, short cut off jeans and black tennis shoes. Her nails were freshly painted black; her perfect makeup was hidden by an oversized pair of sunglasses.

Roost scanned the horizon in front of them; he felt they were not as far as they should be,

"You know, we could have got an extra hour head start, if you hadn't spent an hour on painting your face" he said in a matter of fact, non-scolding way.

"A girl has to look her best at all times," she said patting her hair, "even in a crisis." Cassidy responded with an upbeat tone and contagious smile.

Roost chuckled, "I'm sure the Romans will find a special place for you if we are captured." he said shooting a mischievous glance at her.

Roost and Cassidy had always gotten along, and had always enjoyed teasing one and other, even in their situation they still kept up the jovial banter. Cassidy looked around seeing nothing in every direction.

"Where are we?" she, like William, had learned to trust Roosts uncanny sense of direction, but it felt to her as if they were at sea in a lifeboat, looking for land.

"We are heading for a town called Muleshoe. I checked the GPS a few minutes ago; it is about a mile ahead of us." Roost said pointing the way.

Roost pushed the brim of his worn brown Stetson back with one finger so he could get a better look ahead of them. In the distance the edge of the town sat against the prairie, as if the streetlights and little brown houses with doublewide trailers had grown out of the ground. The image shimmered in the heat, almost making Roost doubt if it was real, or a mirage.

The town's five thousand residents had evacuated in haste, leaving behind their possessions, and the starving livestock to fend for themselves. It was a scene that had been repeated all over the west. Roost took off his hat and wiped the sweat from his forehead with his jacket sleeve. Cassidy could see the heat was bothering him.

"Why are you wearing a jacket in this heat, does your cowboy image mean *that* much?" she said coyly. Roost lifted his arms and looked at the sleeves.

"I couldn't stuff it in the bag. I have been wearing the thing till it's all beat to hell." Roost knew the Romans could not be far behind, and they were going to have to work hard to evade them. "I know you're cute and all Cass, but I'm serious about the Romans catching us while you're getting all gussied up." Roost voice conveyed the strain he felt.

Cassidy gave him a condescending sideways glance, "We aren't all born as beautiful as you Roost. You are quite good at pulling off the whole ruggedly good looking guy thing, with the mustache, blonde hair and blue eyes you are hard to resist." She said grabbing his upper arm with both hands and pulling him close.

He gave her a hard look, "Knock it off Cass; now is not the time." Roost was still feeling pangs of guilt over having a romance with his best friend's widow.

Cassidy knew what was bothering him, she had felt it too, "He has been gone for over three years. When are you going realize what we have is beautiful, and it's what Will would have wanted for us?" Cassidy said, attempting to ease his apprehension.

"Well, it ain't that easy. You just don't steal your best friend's girl." he said in a calm resigned voice.

"Roost, I am *your* girl now." Cassidy said running in front of him, lifting her sunglasses and leaning down to look up at his face and catch his gaze. Roost nodded and placed his hand on her shoulder.

Cassidy smiled warmly, "I miss him, too, but I am a different person now, I was greedy and selfish and stealing was wrong. William's death was not meaningless; you and I both are better people. William was brilliant and funny and he made stealing a rush. You have to admit the fun was gone without him."

"I know, I just…, I don't feel…., I feel like I am betraying him with you." he said struggling to convey his feelings as he looked forward at the town again.

Cassidy walked next to Roost and turned to face the town with him, "You're not, what we have is different than what I had with William. What I had with him was fun and a wild ride, but that was all it was. I did not connect with him like I did with you; he did not understand me like you. Roost Roberts, you are a good man! You did not do anything wrong and I love you!"Cassidy gave Roost a playful bump with her hip.

They started off for the town again when Cassidy suddenly stopped and bent over, "Owwwww! Damn! Something just bit my shin!" Cassidy said hopping on one foot and reaching for her other leg. Roost moved in front of her.

"Stop! Hold still! Let me see." he grabbed her hand and quickly pulled her to the other side of him.

He looked at her shin and saw two small puncture marks that were oozing blood. He spun around and looked down to see the slit eyes of a diamond back rattlesnake staring back at him, coiled and shaking its rattle.

"Now you shake your damn tail! You're supposed to do that before you strike!" Roost yelled at the snake and kicking dirt on it.

He heard more rattling behind him, and Cassidy cry out again, he pivoted back in the other direction in time to see her bitten by two more rattle snakes and realized the pile of rocks they were standing in was a nest. He looked down to see another rattlesnake strike at his boot. He threw off his backpack and slung Cassidy across his back, and then sprinted away from the snakes. He gently set her down after he was sure they were clear of the vipers.

"Let me see" Roost said examining the four bite marks on Cassidy's leg. Cassidy could tell her predicament was serious by the way Roost examined her and gave a sheepish smile trying to comfort her.

"What do we do?" she said wanting the truth.

He looked her in the eyes "It's not good, but we have about an hour to find anti-venom. All these prairie towns have it we.... Damn! Not now!" Roost looked up to see a Roman drone flying in the distance.

"What?" Cassidy said thinking Roost was referring to her snake bites. Roost cupped his hands around his eyes to see better, "It's a camcopter, and *damn*, the Romans won't be far behind. They must have picked up on the GPS," he said scolding himself.

Cassidy stood up and dusted herself off, "Let' run to one of those houses. We could...."

"You are not running anywhere that snake venom will go straight to your heart and pump through you. Climb on my back." Roost ordered.

Roost held her in a fireman's carry, running in short strides because of the extra weight. The town was surrounded by trailers on its outskirts, which looked like some kind of barrier wall. Immediately to the left of the trailers was a large dairy farm, which would be the first place Roost thought they would check. He was running faster than he thought he could, his adrenaline pumping. He knew that he had to get Cassidy anti-venom, which would be at a hospital, or a doctor's office, but getting out of sight was his first priority. He ran past the dilapidated trailers, and up to an unpainted wood fence, he followed it along from a trailer until he found a rusty latch and opened the gate. They went around a silver propane tank spotted with rust, flush against the side of the trailer, and stepped over a broken red tricycle missing its pedals, before moving into the street.

The houses across the road looked all the same, ranch style homes built in the early 1960's, all were covered with false, grey and tan brick fronts, all had porches and all had their venetian blinds closed. Roost could see rising over the rooftops, the roofs of two stories houses on the next street. He decided a two-story house would provide more hiding places.

"We are going to have to break into one of the houses on the next street over." He announced to Cassidy.

She slid off his back, looking behind her to see if they were being followed, she suddenly had an idea.

"Have you already forgotten? Remember all those times we were hiding out? We used to sleep in houses that were for sale." she said giving a slap to his shoulder for emphasis.

It suddenly came back to Roost, "That's right! Realtors almost always left a spare key to get in so they could make sure the house would be seen. Hang on."

Roost quickly lifted upward with his knees, and threw Cassidy across his shoulders again and ran hard. He used the street rather than to try and cut through a yard, he stopped to look down the street and its rows of houses.

He then saw a for sale sign. "There!" he pointed.

He glanced back to see the drone was moving in on the town. Roost did not know, but he felt that the Cam-Copter must be searching on a grid or pattern. He knew they had a few minutes before the Roman troops would be there. Roost ran again, he could feel Cassidy's leg sweating, her body trying to get the poison out. Roost was concerned, but tried to hide it.

"You okay?" Roost asked.

"I feel a little nausea, but I don't feel *that* bad." Cassidy's voice had grown weaker

"Good, now just sit here while I look for a key."

Roost set Cassidy down on the brown lawn, dead from a lack of watering. He quickly moved to the front door and lifted up a green plastic welcome mat with a picture of two mallard ducks on it. Roost face grimaced in frustration at the lack of a key. He slapped the mat back down in disgust. Roost eyes scanned around him, there was no planter, and there were no plants near the door. He regretted not pushing to go further south to a suburban ghost-town where there were hundreds of abandoned four bedroom homes; victims of the financial crises earlier in the century.

Roost trotted back to Cassidy, they were going to have to keep moving. He picked her up and put her as high up as he could in the fireman's carry and moved back into the street, running down to the next street, to his disgust, there were no homes for sale. Roost looked left and right, there was nothing on the street; he again ran to the next intersecting street. Roost was growing fatigued, and Cassidy seemed heavier with each passing second. He stopped to look, before he looked to the left, Cassidy tapped him on the shoulder and pointed to a two-story house for sale. They again moved, Roost began to breathe harder and harder as the raced towards the house.

Roost again set Cassidy down gently, he was alarmed at her pallor, but winked at her to try and keep her spirits up. The house looked different than the others; it was red brick in the front, with two white posts holding up the white wood façade to the front porch. The second story was white wood with two windows. The roof was covered with grey shingles, unlike the brown ones on the surrounding homes. A single birch tree, no more than five years old was planted next to the concrete driveway. *Sticks out like a sore thumb,* Roost thought to himself as he looked over the house. He went to the front porch like the previous house, and as with that house there was no key under the doormat. He was about to walk away, and then he spotted a dead plant in a brown plastic hanging pot. Roost reached into the pot and felt around; he pulled out a case that had been buried in the dirt. The black case was the type used for hiding keys; he slid it open and shook the key out into his palm.

"Got it!" he said holding the key up so Cassidy could see it.

She walked over as Roost unlocked the door, and they quickly moved through, aware they only had moments to hide from the Romans. Roost locked the oak door behind him and fastened a chain on the door. The house was completely empty, even the curtains were gone. The blinds were all open, Roost darted from one window to the next, letting the blinds down. He felt trapped, and worse he realized that he was violating William's rule of always having an escape route before you hole up somewhere. Roost then sharply missed William's presence; he would have known what to do in the situation. It was strange to him at that precise moment he would miss his old friend so much, and that he tried to recall his words to Roost in past dilemmas. Roost redoubled his efforts and focused on survival, he at least knew that was something William would have done.

Cassidy sat on the stairs and listened to the clatter and crash of each set of blinds being lowered around the house. She tried to take her mind off the nausea by looking around the room. The living room was bare, just grey carpet and a gaudy ceiling fan. The front door was heavy, there was no peephole, it was not necessary in such a small town. As she looked at the room, it started to spin. She lay back on the stairs and covered her eyes with her arm in an attempt to stop the spinning. She had trouble believing all that had happened to her had really taken place, and that this house in a tiny Texas town might be where she was going to die. Then it occurred to Cassidy, it probably was where she was going to die.

"Are you okay?" Roost said as walked back into the living room. She looked up at him with bleary eyes.

"I will be." Cassidy's smile was not as convincing as it had been previously.

"We need to get you upstairs." Roost picked her up in his arms and carried her up the stairs.

He gently set Cassidy down in the upstairs bathroom, on the floor in front of the toilet. There were no windows in the room, and he left her to shut the blinds upstairs. He felt time was slipping through his fingers and that with each passing moment the situation was more and more bleak. Roost dropped the last blind and went back to check on Cassidy. She was lying on the white tile floor, her face pressed down against it. The coolness of the tile was soothing to her. The air was hot and hard to breathe upstairs; the air conditioner had not been run in months and there was a buildup of heat in the house.

Roost walked back out to the bedroom window. He parted the blinds with two fingers and peeked out at the street. He noticed all of the houses were un-touched, so the Romans had not searched Muleshoe yet. It was eerie to see all the houses, with no cars parked outside. He wondered how big a force would be sent to search the town? Roost wondered how long they could wait before trying to break into the hospital. He thought maybe it would be better to let Cassidy be captured, that way she would live. He immediately dismissed the idea; she would rather die than become a slave. Roost had trouble absorbing everything that had happened, it was hard to comprehend. It all seemed like a bad dream, but he was determined to survive. He concentrated and cleared his head of the fog that occupied it. Roost was even more determined to make sure Cassidy survived. He had finally found someone he truly loved, and he was not going to lose her.

Roost decided he was going to make a break for the hospital; he went upstairs to get Cassidy when he felt a low rumbling under his feet. It was faint at first but grew stronger, next came the groan of heavy engines. The noise grew louder, and Roost knew they were moving in close. He ran to the front window and peeked out, unable to see anything, he ran to the side of the house that was facing where he thought the noise seemed to be coming from, to his horror he saw a screamer, Mars face extended to its full height, slowly rolling down the street. He had never seen one, but he had heard from eyewitnesses the story of what they could do to the human body. He then saw Legionnaires flanking the Screamer on either side. They were not heavily armored, just the ornate gold chest plates and gold helmets.

The screamer turned as it aligned itself with the street and caught the sun's rays, sending a blinding glare into Roost eyes as bright if it came from a mirror. He instinctually let go of the blinds, purple spots floating in front of his eyes. He blinked and then rubbed his eyes in an attempt to get rid of the spots, to no avail. Roost then moved to another window and slightly separated the blinds to see a Roman soldier standing just a few feet outside of the house, staring in his direction. In alarm Roost pivoted and flattened his back against the wall. He could hear voices speaking Italian, growing closer. He tried to move as silently as he could from the wall to the stairs, painfully aware of the sound of his boots each time he stepped on the wood floor.

He quickly ascended the stairs, and moved directly to Cassidy. He saw her, arm draped over the back of the toilet, and the outside covered with fresh vomit running down the front, where she had not quite hit her target. Roost was sure the Romans were coming in, and looked around for something to clean the toilet with; he did not want to unpack Cassidy's backpack, which sat next to her. He reluctantly took off his jacket and cleaned the toilet, not wanting to leave any evidence they were in the house.

He very softly closed the lid, hoping they would not check if they came inside.

Roost picked Cassidy up and moved her to the master bedroom; he darted back and grabbed her backpack. He froze for a moment when he heard the bang of the Romans using a metal ram on the door. He could hear the front door cracking, and about to break altogether. He did not see any visible access to an attic; it was likely the soldiers would check there anyway he thought. He then moved quickly to the window and pulled the blinds up slightly, he carefully opened the window so as not to make any sound. As he turned to pick up Cassidy he heard the door finally shatter under the strain of the Romans battering it.

Roost could hear the voices of the soldiers entering downstairs, laughing and talking casually. He lifted Cassidy's chin up with his forefinger and knuckle and motioned with his other hand to the window. She gave sarcastic thumbs up sign and dragged herself out onto the roof. Roost then grabbed the backpack and slid it out to Cassidy. Roost started to climb out after her when he realized he left his jacket lying on the floor next to the toilet. He crept as fast as he could back to the bathroom. He snatched the jacket up from the floor and quickly put it on, and turned to go back to the window. He stopped and snapped back behind the door at the sight of a Roman soldier moving from the stairs into the hall. He listened to the sound of the legionnaire's footsteps moving toward him, then away again and once again toward him. Roost waited a moment and slowly peered around the corner; the soldier had gone in the opposite direction and disappeared into one of the rooms further up the hall. Roost slipped off his boots and ran across the floor and out the window onto the asphalt roof.

As he and Cassidy lay flat against the nearly unbearable hot roof, he reached back into the window and lowered the blinds, carefully shutting the window. He lifted the backpack onto the second story roof and then pushed Cassidy up; she flopped down limp, and rolled over. Roost carefully climbed up so that there was no noise, boots in hand. He turned to look at Roman soldiers huddled in a circle in the street, talking about something, but unaware of him and Cassidy.

Roost thought for the first time that he might die; all he had seen running from the Romans; the people taken as slaves, the death and destruction, he always knew he and Cassidy would escape. He had seen the look on the faces of people as they realized they were going to die, he did not want to die that way. He resolved that if he was going to die, it was going to be on his feet, fighting even though he had no weapon, and that it meant certain death, he would not die on his knees. He looked over at Cassidy who was lying flat on her stomach with her head on the backpack. She looked over and managed to smile at Roost, trying to put him at ease. He felt the opposite of at ease, Roost felt the most helpless he ever had, he did not want to die, or watch the woman he loved die on a roof.

Roost started looking around for an escape route but there was nowhere they could go without being detected by the Romans. He clinched his fist and gritted his teeth in frustration, ready to give up when he heard someone gagging. Roost crawled to the side of the roof and peered down to see a soldier in black body armor, holding a knife to the throat of a legionnaire. The soldier was Morrison Lyons, who had snuck up behind the Roman.

"Camminare con me se vuoi vivere!" Morrison said in Italian to the soldier, which translated into *walk with me if you want to live.*

Roost watched him slowly walk the soldier around the air conditioner and past some brown plastic trashcans to the other side of the house. Roost lost sight of them but then heard a muffled report, and another. He rose up, to see two Roman soldiers, dead as the grass they were lying on.

Morrison walked back out the front door, with the soldier still in front of him so to keep the Roman SPR's from firing. He turned around to scan the area and looked upwards; he saw Roost's head peeking from above the roof. Morrison raised his silenced MP7 sub-machine gun, and lowered it when he realized Roost was a civilian. Morrison raised one finger to his lips in a shushing sign, and then motioned with his hand for Roost to get back down. Roost nodded his understanding to the stranger, and slid back to Cassidy.

Morrison lowered the dark wraparound glasses on his forehead over his eyes. He then unzipped a pocket and produced a pair of black earplugs. He put them in one at a time using his free hand. He then started walking in the direction of the idling screamer. Roost lifted up from his hiding place to see what was happening; he saw two other similarly armored knights crouching in between two houses across the street, one of them, tall and hulking with close cropped brown hair and thick bushy eyebrows and a nose that looked as if had been broken a dozen times; he was holding the biggest shotgun Roost had ever seen with his own eyes. He looked to his left and saw another on a roof, a few houses down, with a high-powered rifle trained on the Romans. Roost could clearly see that they were waiting on Morrison for the command to attack. He was amazed over how peaceful everything seemed, he could hear the breeze blowing, and it was an otherwise beautiful day. It was the kind of silence that made a person notice it, like the kind of quiet before a storm.

The screamer sat dormant in the street, as if all was normal. Morrison gave a signal to the two knights across the street; in turn one of the knights pumped his arm, sending the message to the sniper down the b. Morrison stepped onto the road, his arm tight around his prisoner's neck. The Romans raised their SPR's but they froze because of the fail-safe chip in Morrison's prisoner. The other knights fell in quickly behind Morrison as the Legionnaires began falling to the ground under precise gunfire. Morrison was deadly with his shot, taking slow aim, and always making head shots. The knight with the shotgun was less carful, shooting as fast as he could. A centurion came running from behind the legionaries; he was slowed by the gunfire, but not stopped. Roost tried to get a look at the centurion, he had heard of the horrifying Etruscan death masks on their faces and of the indestructible armor, but he could not get a good look without exposing himself. The Centurion continued forward, resolute in his task. The microphone in his helmet barked a command to the speaker's in the legionnaire's helmets, which heeded the call to retreat.

Roost then saw the Screamer turn slightly toward the soldiers, followed by a hum and a loud pop, and then the screamer started screaming. The LED eyes started flashing, cycling through the different wavelengths, catching one of the knights off guard. He started vomiting from the flashing lights, looking at them without his protective sunglasses. The different colors flashed faster and faster, making the effect more intense.

Roost hid his eyes, when the ear splitting noise started, originating from the LRAD in Mars mouth. He clamped his hands over his ears, but it could not block out the noise. He had never heard a noise as loud or as painful; sounding like a jet engine, metal scraping against concrete, and a high pitched tone, all at once. Roost's eardrums twitched and began to spasm. A sharp pain, like he had never felt before, came from deep inside both ears. He rolled back over and looked down the street. The Screamers thirty-millimeter machine gun had opened fire, shredding the knight who had been caught in its path, to something that was unrecognizable as human. Roost thought it looked closer to raw hamburger than the remains of the soldier. He next saw something coming, flying low. He realized it was a missile a split second before the screamer's raised head blew up in a flash that sent shards flying in all directions.

The sound stopped, but all roost could hear was a loud ringing in his ears. He looked over at Cassidy, who had her hands still over her ears, but had passed out. He put his hand on her chest to feel for a heartbeat, which was there, but was weak. Roost then turned again to the battle in the street; he saw more of the knights coming in from behind the screamer, walking with legionnaires in front of them, shooting the other legionnaires who began to flee between the rows of houses. Morrison walked towards the Centurion, who could not fire his SPR, and threw it aside. Morrison tossed the Roman soldier in front of him and likewise threw his gun away and smiled. Roost could not believe what he was witnessing; his concern for Cassidy had momentarily been replaced by amazement.

The Centurion broke into a full charge, and ran at Morrison, who continued to walk at a normal steady pace. The centurion came up fast, grabbing Morrison with one arm and raising the other one far behind his head, ready to land a blow. Before the centurion had a chance to strike, Morrison flashed a knife out of its sheath, and drove it in a small space between the centurion's helmet and armor. The stunned centurion released his grip on Morrison's arm, stumbling down the street. In vain he tried to dislodge the knife, but the damage was done, his carotid artery had been severed. He crouched to his knees holding one hand to the ground, and then went limp. There was a crashing noise behind a house from the camcopter falling, the brain interface link with the centurion severed.

Roost stood up and waved to the unknown rescuers.

"Help please! I need to get my girlfriend to a hospital right away! She is dying!" Morrison looked up at Roost and motioned to two of the knights down the street.

"Get her to the Runner."

He looked down at the legionnaire he had been holding by the neck, he was very young, and traumatized to the point he was shaking. The big Knight, Kenneth Gains, walked towards him, pulling out a pistol to shoot him in the head. Morrison saw the intent in his eyes and stepped in front of him. Morrison pushed the outstretched pistol down.

"Ken! Stop! Don't shoot him!"

Kenneth thought Morrison was joking. "Come on Morris! Step out of the way so we can give him a pop!" He said with a ghoulish smile.

Morrison reached down and picked the legionnaire up by the arm, "Look at him Ken! He can't be more than sixteen years old. Caprera forces young men into service when they are still just children. Are you going to start killing kids now? What about our code?"

Kenneth lowered his gun in disgust, "Right, I'll let the boy live. But you owe me a Roman." Kenneth said poking his finger in Morrison's chest. Morrison laughed, he had grown to admire Kenneth, especially after he had carried him when he was hurt in Kansas City.

"I will give you two, but right now we need to find out what is wrong with that woman who was on the rooftop."

Morrison said as he ran towards Cassidy who was being carried out of the house by Roost and the sniper who was on the roof down the street. Morrison looked at Cassidy and turned to Roost.

"Don't worry; I won't let her die on my watch. It's not how the Knights of the Clock Tower do things."

# CHAPTER XI

The Renegades, mounted on horseback, moved into the outskirts of Oklahoma City. They were three companies in number: Arizona, Utah, and Colorado; all were expert equestrians. They all moved forward in perfect synchronization, knowing what their roll was, and were prepared to execute it. They were there because a chance existed that survivors were in the city, and in desperate need of assistance. It was the perfect place for the first test of the Renegades, the situation was one suited to their skills. They were led by General Wright, who was with them, but would stay behind the forward forces with a smaller unit in a command roll.

The air was eerily still, not even the prairie wind blew in; the horse's hooves on the road were the only sound. The sun was about to set and the buildings that lined the street began to cast long shadows. The city had become perhaps the largest ghost town in the history of the United States. William, taking everything in, looked at a church steeple in front of him, silhouetted by the orange sky and purple clouds; it was such a tranquil scene that it reminded him of his childhood with his father. He sensed he was dropping his guard, and fought against it. This was not the place to become too relaxed, he thought. William had been in situations where he could have been caught, and spent the rest of his life in jail, but that paled in comparison to the looming specter of combat. He had undergone months of rigorous training with the others, and felt prepared as any of them, but he still did not think of himself as a soldier. William believed his other skills would benefit the Calvary, skills that only he possessed. He shook off the strange contentment he was feeling and forced himself to focus on the task at hand. He looked at the others around him, it was so odd to be on a mission; he was not afraid, just bewildered.

The temperature was falling, as it would sometimes do in early May once the sun goes down, but no one seemed to notice. The Renegades were well trained and committed to their mission, the weather would be a minor distraction. Fog started to rise off the river and obscure the cityscape around them. Arizona Company kept moving forward, everyone's stomach sank as they moved closer to the city, anticipating what atrocities they might find. There had been no communication with anyone inside Oklahoma City for nine days. A few survivors had escaped and reported the Romans taking people who had not evacuated from their homes. None of the survivors knew where those people were taken, or what they had done to them. The abductees in all probability had been taken as slaves.

A pack of stray dogs, nine or ten in number, was the first indication of the devastation ahead. They looked at each one of the riders as they passed, with a desperate look that showed longing and fear.

"Poor devils!" Bulloch said earnestly as they passed by, "We will have to do something about them once we have secured the town". No one else spoke; they remained vigilant, looking for survivors.

The company moved into the Bricktown side of the city, which contained several old red brick buildings constructed in its heyday during the 1890's, combined with the Renegades; it looked like a scene from one hundred and fifty years earlier. A clock in the square had stopped at 3:01am, marking the time the Romans cut the power to the city. Time had stood still it seemed for this area, which would have been empty at the time of the invasion. They crossed a small bridge with green triangular steel arches, which took them to California Street, where a restaurant in what used to be an early 1900's apartment building had been ransacked; there was no sign of anyone being there.

Bulloch rode his horse straight through the front doors which had been smashed and torn off their hinges. He leaned forward on his horse as they passed through the opening. He looked around in the half light, the bar was still fully stocked and the smell of spoiled meat filled the air.

"Is anyone in here? It's safe; we are the Mounted Horse Cavalry of the United Sates Army! We are here to rescue you at the command of the President!" Bulloch's valiant words echoed through the restaurant, with no reply.

He carefully moved his horse up and down the aisles of booths, checking them as he went. The others watched him from outside, holding their breath, not knowing if Bulloch was in harm's way. He looked at the questioning faces staring back at him from outside.

"No Joy" he said as he trotted back out the doors.

Disappointed, the company moved forward and fanned out, with the fading hope of finding any survivors. Side by side they rode, stretching out in a long line, covering more ground. The sight was truly inspiring, had anyone been there to see it. The fog grew heavier, visibility dropped to nearly thirty feet. Not seeing as far meant that they were even more vulnerable to snipers, they could not see them, but if there were snipers, they could hear the hooves coming up the street. The thought crossed Walt's mind, but he considered it cowardice and a violation of duty to turn back. He looked to his left and right checking for signs of jitters among his unit. What Walt saw from William was not jitters, but a relaxed manner that was just as dangerous.

"Look alive, Will!" he barked.

William saluted from the brim of his hat. William's expression acknowledged to Walt that he realized he was not nearly alert enough. They passed a convenience store that had obviously been looted after the Romans had sacked the town, or the Romans had looted it themselves. The front windows were nothing more than long jagged shards of glass, the doors held open by a pile of dented soup cans and an overturned candy display. Empty foil bags and plastic bottles left a trail of litter from the front door to the street. There was also what appeared to be dried blood in the doorway. Blow flies buzzed around the riders, due to the rotting garbage and spoiled food. William shook his head, he looked at the expressions of those around him; they all knew something horrible had happened there. Was the looting done for survival, and if it was, where were the unfortunate souls now? It was probable they all were abducted, or dead. Despite the grim surroundings, not one of the Renegades had given up hope, and believed they would still defeat the Romans. They knew devastation was to be expected. This was a store where people shopped while going about their daily lives, and now it was a dismal monument to the loss of the familiar.

As the group moved forward, they transitioned from commercial surroundings to residential. There was not a door that had not been left open, every house, car, shed, trailer and business; nothing had been left untouched by the legionnaires. The Romans were sadistically meticulous in their search for people to enslave. It was apparent that people had been ripped from their hiding places, the riders tried not to envision what took place. Slaves were a commodity to the Romans, and they were not going to be denied a bountiful harvest. The Romans had left supplies, tools and weapons behind which was odd by their standards. Emperor Caprera had taught his soldiers to scavenge anything useful. The scavenged materials saved the shipping of supplies from the empire. Caprera himself had built an army with scavenged weapons when he defeated the Vasekts. Walt, a student of Caprera's methods, knew that the Romans had deviated from their normal procedure. The deviation signaled something had changed the Roman protocol.

"Caprera never leaves anything behind." Walt said as he leaned over to General Wright. Wright nodded, acknowledging what the Capitan said was true. Walt's ability to analyze a tactical situation was unparallel among the troops.

"Intelligence should have known about this." Wright said to himself, more than in response to Walt.

The question remained, why did the Roman's change their protocol? General Wright realized he had gone further into the city than he should have and pulled back with his escort.

"You are in charge, Captain", he said to Walt as he circled back to the rally point.

The unit continued along the same route, the streetlights flickered on, casting an amber glow on the road and brick buildings. William looked back at Walt to see if he was alarmed, he was as focused as ever, only considering the mission. Walt saw his expression and sensed William's concern. He spoke to the entire unit through his com-link.

"Oklahoma City converted all their streetlights and traffic signals to solar power; they are on a separate grid."

They came to an intersection where a traffic light swayed in the wind, turning from green to yellow to red. William thought the sight was surrealistic, the lack of cars in the street, no noise and the open doors in every direction. He felt as if he was in a movie, or a strange dream. The reality of the situation was too aloof; again he struggled to gain focus. William decided he had to concentrate on contributing to the mission; he decided he would use his mental prowess to achieve that goal. William scanned the devastation as they rode, reconstructing what must have happened in his mind's eye. He deduced from the lack of bodies that most of the citizens did not put up a fight, and that the Romans must have brought screamers when they invaded. There were no tanks in the streets, or police cars; William took this to be a sign that the Romans did salvage the tanks and police cars for some purpose. He also feared it could be that the police fled, and the National Guard never engaged the enemy. He knew from the debriefing they received before the mission, that spy satellites had shown the Romans moved southwest with over 100,000 slaves jammed into semi trucks. William had been looking but saw no signs yet of where the trucks had passed, and they were on the south side of the city.

The com link crackled in their ears, Utah Company reported they found a nursing home, where the staff had been taken and the elderly left to die. Some still survived, but most had died, and were decomposing in their beds. William looked at Walt for a response, but none came; he stared straight ahead, Walt's focus was on the mission. William prodded Slingshot and moved up next to Walt.

"Why don't you let me scout some of these places out? You and the boys continue on the path you're on." William said.

Walt gave William a quick glance over. "Are you alert enough?" he said still concerned with William's focus.

"I am now," William said pushing up the brim of his hat with his forefinger "I am going to stay within a mile or two of the rest of the company." His voice was clearer and he had shaken the malaise that had overtaken him.

Walt knew William was a better horseman than anyone in the company, and could cover more ground on his own. He nodded his approval and William cut off a side street and disappeared from sight behind a hill.

William galloped off through an older residential neighborhood. The streets were lined with broad oak trees and antique streetlights. Part of the city's attempt to connect with its beginnings. The homes were constructed from brick and built in the early 1900's; the scene was the same there as the other part of the city, open doors, signs of people being drug from their homes. He could tell the difference between the homes where the inhabitants had evacuated, and those who stayed behind in a vain effort to protect their homes. The homes that were evacuated looked as if they were untouched, with the exception of the open front door, and a spray painted x on the door to show it had been checked. The homes where the residents had been taken, some had windows that were broken, and their belongings created a path from the front door. Some of the homes had burned down, a byproduct of struggle with Roman soldiers. Looking at the scene caused William to feel profound sadness at the devastation around him. These were peoples' homes, he thought, some of which could have been in a family for years. All the personal history that was taken from them was truly heartbreaking to him.

William came upon a drainage ditch at the bottom of a hill, in it piled together were hundreds of bodies, the very old, the very young, and the disabled, killed and disposed of because they had no value as a slave. There were children who had been shot holding hands with each other, elderly with the look of shock still frozen on their face, as it was the moment they were murdered. The cruelty of it seemed incomprehensible to William. These people had their lives stolen from them, not allowed to die with dignity or mercy. Children never having a chance to grow up and experience life as God had intended. William looked around him at the ruin that the Roman force had left behind. It was at that moment that all the things he had been told, all the stories that seemed too horrible to be true, all the images he had seen on TV; in that singular moment it all became a reality. Anger as he had never felt, manifested itself in a burning in his gut. Whatever sadness he had felt before was now had been transformed into seething rage.

The stench from the ditch and the countless blowflies, were enough to make William ill. He gave Slingshot a nudge to go, he did, sensing William's distress. William rode hard till he was far enough behind him to not smell it. He sat for a moment, letting his horse catch his breath. William looked up in front of him to see another startling sight, he saw a statue of Jesus crying, a memorial to the child victims of the 1995 bombing of the Murrah Federal Building. He thought the statue might as well been for the victims of the slaughter he just saw. He couldn't help feeling that his arrival at the statue was not accidental. It seemed, he thought, to be a message to him that his whole life, everything he had done since the day he was born, had led to this moment. The whole situation was more than he expected, being in combat he had prepared for thoroughly, finding mass graves never occurred to him. William thought that if any good had come from what he just witnessed, it was that his resolve to defeat the Romans had been strengthened. He thought to himself: now he had no problem pulling a trigger to kill another man. Suddenly, a calm came over William, the kind of calm that made him an unequaled thief. He took a long look at the memorial in front of him before he finally turned to inform the unit about the ditch. William did not want to pass by the grave on his way back, he would have to bring his comrades to it he did not laze it for satellite plotting. Twice was more than enough to look at a heap of decaying corpses. He was going to have to move on.

As he made his way back, William noticed a bright, silvery light in the fog. The light was emanating from a side street situated between two old brick warehouses that belonged to a mattress factory. He also heard a faint hum that made him realize he had to investigate. Carefully, he and Slingshot slowly made their way down the alley. William emerged on the other side of the two buildings; he saw a Roman command unit like he had infiltrated in Kansas City. Hundreds of Legionnaires were preparing for their next operation. The uniform of the legionnaire was an impressive sight. Designed to look like the uniform from Roman antiquity, the body armor had several features. The Helmet was gold, with a domed top and rounded flap that extended down to the shoulders and out. Two face guards stretched from the cheeks down to the chin. A small visor wrapped around the front of the helmet to provide shade. A hidden lens could be slid down from inside the helmet to shield the soldier's eyes from the sun. A display showing targeting and weather conditions could be viewed on the lens. The same lens also worked for night and infrared vision.

The Chest plate of a legionnaire was the same color as the helmet. The armor was a titanium alloy, which was effective in stopping bullets and shrapnel. The crimson and gold armor was segmented for easy movement and aesthetics .The boots were designed to look as if they were separate from the rest of the armor, but they were actually connected. The boots had an ornate pattern on the front. Some could even be considered a work of art, usually depicting a soldier or a Roman god. The uniform also had a tracking device and vital signs monitors. The armor was a symbol of Rome's restored might. They all carried the standard firearm for a legionnaire, the Stacked Projectile Rifle. Their sidearm was a standard 9mm recoil pistol.

The Legionnaires were led by highly skilled Centurions. The Centurion wore a full body armor suit that was highly advanced. The black suit was sleek, and glimmered in the light. It was made of metallic glass and was stronger than titanium and as flexible as rubber. There were robotics inside that aided the strength of the soldier, making them twenty percent stronger than normal. The faceplate was just that, a sculpted face, inspired by Etruscan death masks. The eyes were wide and slightly slanted with the corneas in the center. The nose was one constant line that ran from above the eyes to a point just above the thick lips, set in a slight smile. White pinstripes surrounded the eyes, eyebrows, nose and lips to make them stand out. The face did not look remotely human and was meant to strike awe in enemies and subordinates alike.

The nerve center of the base was a semi truck attached to a fifty-six foot mobile command trailer. It was red with the letters SPQR in gold surrounded by a gold laurel wreath. A set of retractable stairs descended from the back of the trailer. Such an opulent display was part of the intimidation strategy that Emperor Caprera had used to conquer nations without firing a shot. Seven Screamers next to the command center sat silently, as if they were great beasts, in slumber before being awoken for their terrible work. William touched his com-link to inform Walt, but it did not respond. The Romans were jamming all communications but their own.

William realized that he was going to be seen if he stayed visible outside of the ally. He backed Slingshot behind the wall to keep from being detected. He quickly dismounted and removed his anti-material rifle from the saddle.

"Go back." William said to the horse, knowing that he would find his way back to the main body of the cavalry.

The horse did as it was told and trotted off in the opposite direction. William's heart was racing, something he was not used to feeling. He had always remained cool in a heist, even when they went wrong. Never before had he faced a situation where not only his survival was in doubt, but also the lives of countless others. He could hear the murmur from the Romans, which reminded him of a nest of angry hornets.

William took off his hat and strapped on the rifle. He crouched down to the asphalt and slowly lowered himself to the ground so that he could move closer, and devise a plan on how to escape. He crawled painstakingly slow, moving only a few feet over half an hour. He had evaded authorities looking to arrest him many times, what unnerved William was that none of them had sought to end his life. He realized he might not have to fake his death again, this time it might occur for real. He again thought of Roost and Cassidy, but to his surprise, he also thought of the girl he saw in the Ocala National Forest when he and Walt were about to race. He again realized he was losing focus and forced himself to redouble his concentration.

He worked his way over to a shrub that was growing in a planter on the curb. He slowly peeked over the top of the shrub to evaluate the situation. Out of the mobile command center emerged a Primus Pilus, the centurion in charge of the Praetorian. The commander was wearing a full battle suit, an encased motorized suit of armor that was almost indestructible. The suit was black with a red plume on the helmet. On the front of the helmet was a sculpted face, just like the other centurions, designed to intimidate enemies in battle. A Primus Pilus would only be in armor and in the field if a major operation was going to take place. William decided he had seen enough and rose up into a squatting position and attempted to make a quick duck walk back behind the warehouse. His toe caught a hole in the asphalt, causing him to pivot and crash into pile of old rusty mattress frames on the side of the building. The pile spilled onto the ground making a chorus of ringing sounds. William's heart sank, he did not bother to look back to see if he had been detected, he knew his position had been revealed. Seconds later bullets slammed into the wall in front of him, showering him with fragments of hot brick.

William scrambled behind around the corner his eyes darting from one thing to another in hopes to find something to save him. He saw a manhole cover a block back from where he was. He reached into his pocket to pull out his magnet. It was a useful tool he had with him in all the robberies he had ever committed. It could be used to help hold screws, short out electronics and, as he was about to do, lift things. William sprinted over to the cover and placed the magnet on top of the cover he tried to pull it up with it, but the cover was too heavy. He pulled his knife out and franticly worked it between the cover and the street. He was able to pry it open.

He dove, head first, into the opening grabbing onto a wrung in the wall. The inertia caused him to swing into the wall, knocking the air out of him, and bashing the back of his head against it. He climbed upwards toward the lid, still unable to breathe, and in pain. He pushed up on the manhole cover sliding it back into place with all the strength he had left. While he pushed, his vision began to narrow into a dark tunnel until he could not see, and he passed out.

William slowly awoke; momentarily confused he remembered the manhole cover, and then blackness. Alarmed, William suddenly thought to himself, what about the Romans, how far away were they, how long had he been unconscious? He looked at the ceiling of the sewer above him as he laid there, grey concrete faintly lit by some light source. He then thought: where was the manhole cover? William realized somehow he had been moved. He did not remember moving, but must have mild amnesia, he reasoned. He pushed himself up with his arms to sit up, it was then he saw why he had moved. Staring back at William were four children, dirty and two caked with dried blood. The oldest could not have been more than ten years old, and the youngest appeared to just have begun to walk. The shock in their faces was unmistakable due to the hollow stare all but the baby displayed. William was in shock, too, but realized he had a duty to the children, to comfort and rescue them.

"Thank you for pulling me back here, that must have been hard." The children stood where they were, not responding.

"My name's William, I am here with the Cavalry to help you. What are your names?"

There was a silence as the children, shellshock from what they had experienced, were hesitant to trust William.

"Come on," he said with a smile, "You wouldn't have helped me if you thought I was one of the bad guys?"

The oldest child, an ashen, black haired, ten year old girl with haunted eyes stood up and ran over and hugged William. She understood what was happening more than the other children, and the impact was more acute for her. She sobbed deeply, losing her breath, as she clung to William; he held her and did not say a word until she stopped crying. Once she had stopped William wiped the tears from under her eyes.

"You're going to be okay, now what's your name? You don't want me yelling *hey you* all the time right?"

Her dark eyes looked into William's; they looked as if they should belong to someone much older than her tender age. The other children watched in silence, still numb from shock. William knew that the children's parents were likely dead or enslaved, and that for their survival, he had to give them hope. He did not want to give false hope, but he had to find a way. He smiled again as he held onto her never averting his gaze from hers.

"I promise that all of you will be okay. God let all four of you survive, so he must have something in mind for you."

"My name is Wendy," the girl finally spoke in a whispery tone.

William picked up his hat and raised it up and down on his head, "Pleased to meet you Wendy, who's with you here?" The girl, trying to be strong wiped her eyes and proceeded with introducing her companions.

"That's my brother Herbert, and over there are Avery and Stuart." She said in a calmer, steadier voice.

William crouched down resting his arms on his knees to come down to their level, "How did y'all get here?" William asked in the gentlest tone he knew how.

"We were hiding at home when the soldiers came after us. My brother and I were in my closet. My dad had a gun and was shooting at the soldiers, when we heard a loud noise and then he yelled like he was hurt. My mom screamed his name a few times and then we could see the soldiers take her. I grabbed my brother's hand and ran out the back door. We have a big tree in the back yard, so I climbed it while he held on to my neck. We could see the other houses on our street, they took some of my friends out of their houses and shot them", she paused for a moment as if she were re-living the experience in her mind, "they took them and threw them in a ditch with other people who had been shot. The soldiers started shining lights in the trees, so I climbed down with my brother and ran to the ditch. We climbed beneath all the people who had been shot and hid until the soldiers went away. Then we went to a tunnel under a bridge and have been hiding in here. We met Avery and Stuart in here." Wendy said as if it had happened to someone else, or she was recounting a story she had been told.

William sat in silence, stunned at what atrocities a little girl had spoken about in such a matter of fact way. He realized he could not let his shock be sensed by the children.

"Was it the same with you Avery?" William said gently. Avery nodded and wiped his eyes and tried to follow Wendy's example.

"They took my Mommy and my Daddy. I heard them call my parents names, they made fun of us because we are black. They hit my daddy hard. He yelled really loud. I was hiding under my bed, one of the soldiers looked at me told me not to move, he whispered don't come out until they were gone, and then they left. When the sun came up I ran to a tunnel, and crawled in. I found Wendy, and she has been taking care of us."

He looked drawn and weak, and William knew he was hungry and probably dehydrated. William had found a part of him that he did not know existed; he never knew he could talk to children. He realized he had to get their spirits up if they were to survive.

"How old are you?" William said smiling at him. Avery held up five fingers to indicate his age. William gave him a pat on the shoulder and turned to Stuart.

"How about you Stuart?"

"They took my Mommy and Daddy" he said with tears streaming down his face. "Their names are Ted and Lisa Chang! You have to find them! Please can you find my Mommy and Daddy?"

The crying became more hysterical and mournful; William knew not to ask any more of the child. He reached over and hugged Stuart, letting him cry until he was through. William felt anger in him welling up again, not even when his sister was raped had he been so enraged. William wanted to kill every Roman he saw, but again he calmed himself. He knew if the children were to survive he would have to be able to think clearly, which was a difficult enough task with his head still throbbing. He said a quick prayer asking for guidance, and then addressed the children.

"We are all going to get out of here. There is a reason we all found each other, whatever that reason is, God knows why, and we have to trust him."

William looked around at their surroundings, the stark walls and fading light, he had to formulate a plan to get them all out alive. He reached into his pocket and pulled out a small flashlight to get a better look.

"Are we very far from where you found me?" William asked. Wendy shook her head no and pointed to the direction they had come from.

"Stay here I am going to go take a look around. I promise I won't leave you," William said.

He could see that the children did not want him to leave, but he knew that to survive, he had to find the best way out. He shone the light behind them to show smaller pipes where storm water runoff was routed; none of them could make it through that. William headed back to where they had come in, hoping to find another way out. He checked his weapons as he went, holding the flashlight in his mouth as he inspected them. All of William's guns appeared to be in good order he concluded. He came to the ladder and manhole where he had come in. There was a sewer vent off to the side of the manhole he could look out of if he leaned out from the ladder. Carefully grasping a ladder wrung with one hand and the edge of the vent with the other, he peered out.

William peeked out of a storm vent at the Roman encampment; suddenly he realized what they were in front of, a propane gas company. Next to the building were four colossal white cylinders; they were tanks which contained eighteen thousand gallons of propane each. Parked twenty feet behind the tanks was a bobtail propane truck.

"I thought these guys were supposed to be smart." William said aloud to himself while he surveyed the area.

William sat for a moment, shaking his head in disbelief over the Roman's disregard for enemy attacks. Walt had told him the Rome's arrogance would be their undoing, now he understood why. The number of legionnaires appeared smaller than usual, around three hundred soldiers and only two centurions. The centurions had their helmets off so they could speak face to face making them vulnerable. There would be at least two more units of ten each searching for him William estimated, and he had to get the children past them, he thought as he slid his nineteen millimeter anti-materiel rifle off his shoulder. The red and silver armor of the Legionnaire was arrogance itself; they had no camouflage properties whatsoever, the Romans almost seemed to be daring someone to attack them. Their overconfidence was so profound, some of the soldiers had set their weapons down, and the Centurions had complete lack of situational awareness. William knew this was going to be the chance they needed, that would allow them to escape. William crept back over to the children, who now hung on every word he said.

"Everybody listen carefully, in a minute you are going to hear a really big boom. When you hear the boom, climb up through the hole at the end of the ladder as fast as you can and follow me. Do you understand?"

All but Herbert nodded; he was confused but not terrified like the other children. William climbed up the ladder and slowly slid the manhole cover open and took aim at one of the middle propane tanks. He glanced over at the mobile command center, the five personnel transports, the generators, the five screamers and the four tanks all sitting idle, all within blast range.

"I've had enough of these guys." William said to himself.

He slowly took aim at the closest propane tank though his scope, held his breath, and squeezed the trigger. All of the Roman's turned towards the report from William's gun in one final uniform act. William watched for a split second as a white light flashed, at the same moment he dove back into the manhole as the tank exploded. The ground shook, less than a second later the other three propane tanks blew simultaneously, shooting fire a thousand feet into the air and flooding into the manhole. William scampered backwards to escape being burned, feeling the heat on his face and filling his nostrils. He watched the flame move across the ceiling, and stop, like it was looking at him, and then retreat back out of the manhole. Finally the propane truck blew sending another smaller, but no less deadly fireball in the air. He could hear the clanking of shrapnel cutting into the surrounding buildings. Sirens came to life from all the car alarms in the surrounding parking garages. A shower of burning ash and cinders filled the air. William climbed up the ladder and waved for the children to follow, he pulled them out one by one as they climbed to the top.

"Run that way, just as fast as you can!" shouting as loud as possible over the sirens and horns.

He pointed to the path between the mattress factories from where he came and again shouted.

"Run that way" to be sure the children did not freeze out of shock and fear.

The children did as they were told and ran, not looking back, their legs going faster than they ever had before. William turned back around to see the propane foundry in a pile of rubble, masses of black smoke rushing out into the night sky. He then turned to see the mobile command unit had been thrust on to a factory roof more than half a mile away; its state resembled a crumpled foil wrapper. There was no sign of the soldiers who had been there, but the units on patrol had rushed back to the scene. William was wrong in his estimation of how many Legionnaires had been searching for him, there were what seemed to his count to be one hundred and fifty soldiers. Their numbers were small compared to the Renegades, but the stacked projectile guns made them more than a match for at least three hundred soldiers. William was trying to formulate a plan, when he realized there was only one thing he could do, run.

William's heart raced and he felt the cool burning of the adrenaline in his chest as he sprinted to catch up with the children, leaping over hot shrapnel as he ran. Wendy yelped in pain when her foot caught a piece of brick that had come from the obliterated foundry. William grabbed Wendy and scooped her up in his arms, seeing she had twisted her ankle. The wind carried the smell of burning wood and chemicals, and made him cough as he ran. Wendy yelled something to William, but her cries were overpowered by the alarms and gunfire that filled the air. They ran for nearly half a mile when William finally heard Wendy's frantic plea. "Herbert is back there! We have to go back! Please we have to go back" she screamed in hysterically, tears streaming down her face.

The Renegades had seen the explosions, and all four hundred and fifty members came charging towards them, including William's horse, who knew instinctively to stay with the Calvary. William quickly mounted slingshot in one continuous motion. Bulloch saw what his intentions were and grabbed his arm.

"What could possibly possess you to ride head on into gunfire boy?"

"A child was left behind!" William said yanking his arm back.

Bulloch could see William was going to take an unnecessary risk, "The child is probably already dead William; you have to let it go."

William ignored Bulloch's plea, instead he turned and shouted "yah!", and he galloped back, headlong into the battle.

Gunfire was erupting from both sides; William could feel the heat and hear the hum as the bullets passes his ears. One bullet was so close to his left ear, he lost his hearing momentarily; it was quickly replaced by a high pitched ringing. The stacked projectile bullets would be set to explode when they were near their target, but none of them were set to hit William, but they still shot past him. One oversized SPG bullets grazed William's in shoulder, sending him head first off his horse. Slingshot skidded to a stop and came around for William. He grabbed the saddle horn and swung himself on with a hopping motion as Slingshot ran by him. William sighted Herbert who was standing by himself, crying out in fear. It was apparent to William there was only one thing he could do. He tied off the reins on the saddle as they approached the toddler and with Slingshot in full stride William leaned down with both hands and snatched him from the ground, and in an instant he had the child. Slingshot then turned around and thundered towards the Renegades. William was clutching Herbert with one arm and holding Slingshot's reins with another, although the horse did not need direction where to go. A projectile bullet exploded behind William, showering his back with tiny bits of hot shrapnel, and knocking him out. Everything went black again.

William awoke in the back of an old Stryker armored medivac that had been pulled out of scrap and restored for action. He struggled to focus on the doctor's face in front of him, his vision still blurry.

"Hello sleepy head," she said as William struggled to focus on the people standing in the room.

"The kids?" he said groggily.

Bulloch leaned forward to him. "They are all fine Will. That was one of the bravest and most ill-advised examples of heroism I have ever seen. I don't know how you do it; you should be dead right now! You even held onto that boy while you were unconscious!"

William sat up and looked at the doctor "concussion?"

The uniformed grey haired physician smiled, "A mild one, you need to take it easy for a couple of days" she said flashing a light in his eyes.

William groaned "Will it kill me to move?" it was more of a rhetorical question as he sat up, his head pounding.

The doctor waited until she made eye contact, "It could. At the very least you will have severe headaches. "

William knew about the headaches already, "I can keep going then, we can't waste time." he said rubbing his temples.

Bulloch gave William a congratulatory pat on the shoulder, which did not aid his headache.

"We have a good idea what the Romans are up to Will. We were not supposed to survive this; it was a setup, an ambush. This was supposed to be the demise of the Renegades on our first mission; Caprera could not produce better propaganda than that. We also know that there are moles inside the Pentagon; they altered the satellite data so that it appeared the Romans were gone. It won't be long until we find them." Bulloch said with his usual delivery of rhetoric.

William now questioned their survival, "How did you stop the Romans?" he said still trying to process everything he had seen in the previous six hours.

Bulloch smiled to himself; William truly had changed, anyone else would have been bragging about their accomplishment

"Well, after you vaporized eighty percent of their troops, it was not a monumental task." Bulloch laughed. "We also had a secret weapon. She is even a better shot than you!"

"She?" William was taken aback and coaxing another hearty laugh from Bulloch.

The laughter of Bulloch made William feel more at ease , he was glad Bulloch was the one who he saw first when he awoke. His new friend had made him feel better and for a moment, forget the horrible atrocity he saw, the one that would always be present in the back of his mind. There would never be a day where he did not feel sorrow and regret over what he saw. At the same time he was grateful that the incident had strengthened his will, and that he was able to rescue the children in the sewer from a fate like those in the ditch. William felt something else, something he had not felt before; for the first time since joining the military- he felt like a soldier.

# CHAPTER XII

Arizona and Utah Companies, frustrated after two days of uneventful patrols, had regrouped in Enid, Oklahoma. The hope of finding and engaging a Roman unit had not come to pass, mostly due to a unforecasted dust storm; in the process they had run out of supplies. The dust was still in their nostrils and they had a chalky dryness in the back of their throats. The sand was everywhere, even in their ears. Sleeping bags, which had been used to cover the horse's heads, became as much sand as fabric. Water had been used to flush out eyes and mouths, and was gone quickly, leaving none to drink. The Renegades had no choice but to come in to replenish their supplies. After their success in Oklahoma City, they were now going to embark on their true mission, to get behind enemy lines and disrupt the Romans. If it were not for the sand storm they would have been well on their way, now they were facing a setback. It was going to be harder to find a way in now, there would be extra Cohorts of Roman soldiers looking for them, since there was a problem keeping anything in the Pentagon a secret.

Enid was a natural choice for resupply because two Green Beret units, and the resurrected 2$^{nd}$ Armored Tank Division, were stationed in Enid to guard the colossal grain elevators spread out across the small town. Intelligence reports had shown that the Romans were planning to break through the front lines and raid agricultural centers, thereby causing a food shortage inside the unoccupied states. It was in front of one of the mammoth white Grain Elevator that William sat. He was situated on a loading dock, his legs dangled over the worn concrete that had countless coats of white paint on it over the decades. He was peeling and eating an orange for his morning's breakfast, his head still feeling the effects of the concussion. He watched Walt going through his morning routine of pushups, pull-ups and various kinds of sit ups. Walt had even added a three mile run while they were in Enid. William had come to admire Walt's tenacity, but like everyone else, he also thought he was not completely sane.

William had just shaved using a knife and shaving cream, a trick he had perfected in his days on the run, and was feeling refreshed. William's philosophy had been that you were less likely to seem like a criminal if you were well groomed. He wanted to leave his image as a thief behind him; he was keenly aware that he was still seen by some of his fellow Renegades as just that, a common criminal. He had garnered some goodwill from his actions in Oklahoma City, though, and there was a growing feeling among some of the troops he was not a phony and that this was not a con on his part.

William stared across the street at another white grain elevator; he always was impressed by the sight of them, the way they stood out on the barren prairie like a pyramid or colossal statue. It had a long cylindrical shape with the ruffles in it; the center section was composed of tin, painted over countless times. There were small square windows in rows of four that rose above the top of the silos. On the side of the building the word *Cooperative* was written vertically in old brown faded letters. The building had looked much the same for the last one hundred and twenty years, when it only accommodated rail cars. William had never been to Enid, all the running around the southwest and high plains he had done, and he had never passed through the town. The town had a main street with brick buildings that had stood since before the great depression some still had the original company names written on top of the buildings in faded paint, making them resemble something found in ancient ruins, like hieroglyphics or a cave painting. Enid was quiet, even before the war it did not have much activity. It was this lonesome quality that made it seem sad to William, it was not a ghost town, but it was not far from becoming one. The tiny strip malls and various fast food restaurants sat vacant. A few brave business remained open, providing services for those who chose to stay behind.

William watched as a white semi backed up to the dock with incredible swiftness. The driver stopped just inches shy of the weathered rubber bumper attached to the dock, as if he sensed it by instinct. It reminded William of how Cassidy could handle an eighteen-wheeler. The sight of daily commerce seemed serene and comforting after what he had witnessed in Oklahoma City. William had struggled to clear his mind of what he saw, splitting time between cleaning his weapon and reading the Bible, and yet he could not forget the atrocities he saw. He also tried to forget the anger he felt towards the Romans, the fact that he wanted to kill so badly scared him. As a Christian, he did not want to feel that kind of hate, it ran contrary to what he was supposed do. He knew it was war and that was what was expected, but his thoughts kept going back to his stepfather, and if he had meant to kill him or not. He wondered if he had been lying to himself all of the years that had come and gone since that day.

The morning was cool and the sound of trains in the distance signaled that the Romans had not completely stifled American Commerce. He was also inspired by so many men and women who were working in a place where they were in constant danger of being killed or captured. While he was pondering the courage of the people working to keep food flowing to the rest of the country, he heard a soft voice from behind.

"I hear you are looking for me." William slowly turned to see who was talking, to his surprise it was the girl he saw in the crowd in the Ocala National Forest, the same one who had been in his thoughts since he saw her. She was just over five feet tall, but had a long and elegant frame, not stocky. Her blue eyes, shimmered in the morning light, her shoulder length hair was light brown. Her skin was a honey brown from being in the sun for the past few months. Her mouth, small and demure, was nonetheless, full and pink. Her smile was warm and genuine, and lit up her whole face. She wore makeup, but so little it was barely detectable. She wore a cavalry uniform, just like William's, which indicated she was somehow a part of the unit now. William recognized her, but did not want to seem too eager.

"That depends, who are you?" he answered her question with his usual charm.

She gave a wry smile "I am the girl who saved your life." she said boastfully.

William looked around in a playful way as if there was supposed to be someone else he was meeting there, "You're Phoebe Willowdell?"

She lifted her hat  and shook her hair, setting it next to William and then sitting next to the hat, "The one and only." She said with pride while not being arrogant.

"I'm William West." He held out his hand, which Phoebe took in her slender hand and gave a gentle shake.

"I know who you are, everyone knows who you are." She said in a soft spoken yet strong voice.

William's tone became more somber, "I wish I could say it was for the right reasons." he said staring off into the distance.

Phoebe saw that she had touched a nerve "I saw how you went back to rescue that boy. It won't be for the wrong reasons for long. What you did was the bravest thing I have ever seen in my life." her voice was uplifting to William easing his grim mood.

He continued to speak as he looked off into the distance as if he were viewing his own past, "If you know who I am, then you know what I did to my step-father." He finally turned to make eye contact again.

"I know he raped your sister, I know a little about that," she hesitated for a moment turning her gaze downward, "I was molested by my uncle several times when I was eleven years old. My aunt threatened to kill me if I told anyone. My parents found out when I was twelve; I was leaving the house with my rifle to go kill both my aunt and uncle. Yes, William, I know how you felt."

She looked back up again to gauge his reaction. It was a difficult thing for her to divulge, but she had heard what William went through in Oklahoma City, and she felt he was a kindred spirit. William was staggered by the revelation.

"That happened to you? That must have been hard to deal with." It was more of a statement of sympathy than a question.

Phoebe smiled "It was, but it made me who I am now, there is no sense in dwelling on it." her voice was resolute and it had the desired effect on William.

He looked over at her with an expression of gratitude, "That is a really good way of looking at it, maybe I need to look at things that way." William was impressed by Phoebe's inner strength.

Phoebe smiled and spoke in an upbeat tone, "I think that you already are."

"Hey, thanks for the support. I need that right now"

William smiled appearing easy going, at the same time trying to emit as much charisma as he could. William wanted to ask her if she was seeing anyone, he wanted to tell her that he had never been so struck by anyone as he was the first time he saw her, but he stopped himself. He was still married to Cassidy, that would be an obvious hurdle, and he had never let himself love fully, he had always held back. He knew that if he got involved with Phoebe, it would be different. William decided it was best to keep his feelings to himself, although he could not stop trying to impress her, no matter how hard he tried. Phoebe could at least be someone he could talk with.

"Hey, how did you wind up here?" William asked coyly, knowing she had killed 48 Romans from nearly a mile away.

Phoebe cocked her head and shot a knowing look at William. "The President asked me to join the Renegades, and I am here to teach you boys how to shoot," she said standing up again and posing with her gun.

The sight drew a laugh out of William, she had a sense of humor too he realized, it would be even harder for him to resist. Cassidy had a propensity for moodiness and could go from playful to angry in the blink of an eye. He could tell Phoebe was not like that. William was still impressed by how good a shooter she was.

"Bringing your spotter with you?"

Phoebe raised an eyebrow, "I didn't use a spotter."

William was sincerely impressed, "Wow! Are you serious! You made forty-eight head shots from a mile away with no spotter. You must almost be as good a shot as I am!" the words were meant to be a compliment.

"You think you are a better shot than me? Is it because I am a girl?" Phoebe said with a wide smile.

William smirked and then gave a cocky smile, "No, it's because I'm a better shot than everybody else."

"Oh my! Is that a fact?" Phoebe said in a gasp placing her hand on her chest and feigning amazement.

"Very funny! Care to see who the better shot is?" William now was feeling the same sensation he used to feel when stealing with Cassidy.

Phoebe was profoundly confident in her ability, "What's in it for me?" she said in a condescending tone.

"What do you want?" William who was as equally confident was willing to put anything up,

Phoebe glanced over to the stables, "Well, that horse of yours is impressive. If I win, we switch horses."

William laughed, "You mean Slingshot? Okay, but if for some reason I lose, like my arm breaks; Slingshot is loyal to me." William's confidence was never lacking and he became boastful.

"What do you want?" Phoebe smiled politely

In an instant, William decided he might die and never get a chance to be with Phoebe, and all of his wavering on how he felt would cost him his only chance.

"If I win, you buy me dinner when all this is over." he waited silently for her reaction.

"It's a deal!" Phoebe again grabbed William's hand to shake it as she stood up. "By the way, you know I was the youngest ever champion in both the United States Practical Association's Shooting competition and the National Rifle Association's championship." she added in with a tone of false sincerity.

William was taken aback by Phoebe's entire being. She was petite and well mannered, but strong at the same time. She was covered up, head to toe, but yet she was still beautiful. William was surprised at how he felt towards her, there was a definite attraction, but he felt more connected to her as someone who seemed to understand him. With Cassidy it had been lust at first sight, he thought, and she never had been acquainted with the concept of modesty. He watched Phoebe as she walked away, graceful and poised. She looked back over her shoulder and gave him smile and opened and closed her hand in a small wave; it was an image that William would not soon forget.

At an unused golf course a few miles away from the forward command, William and Phoebe stood ready for their contest. They had convinced the owner to let them use the golf course for the exhibition. No one had used the golf course in over a year, yet the owners had kept it in shape, refusing to let it fall into disrepair, it was their way of being defiant of the Roman invasion. The green was lush and well kept, the trees were trimmed, and no leaves were on the course. It was on the longest straightaway that the shooting contest was to be held. It was lined on either side by a combination of Elm trees and Dogwoods. The wind was not blowing as hard as it usually did on the plains, making it a perfect day for long range shooting.

Behind Phoebe and William stood a crowd of nearly fifty people, who had gathered to watch when word got out that William West was in another contest. At first Walt, Drake, and Bulloch were supposed to be the only observers, but word spread quickly and others flocked to see the contest. There was *Meaner* Colter, a lean, square jawed, squinty eyed former park ranger, former Superintendent of Yellowstone National Park. Lance Best, former Marine fighter pilot and astronaut who enjoyed any contest and eagerly awaited the match. Nearly all of Arizona Company had rushed over when the news reached them.

The resident golf pro stood in his khaki pants and green golf shirt, his cap covering his eyes as he faced out looking at the green, wondering if the two soldiers could actually stop his shots from landing there. He reared back his titanium driver and swung with a clean swooshing sound. From one-hundred yards away Phoebe fired her first shot with an old M-4 rifle with no scope. She stood rigid as a statue, she only shuddered very slightly when she pulled the trigger. The ball seemed to jump straight up when it was hit, leaving two smaller uneven parts to fall to the ground below. The crowed collectively gasped at the sight. William stepped up, using the same weapon loosely holding it in contrast to Phoebe. His expression was not as focused as hers and played to the crowd, a habit that he knew was not humble, but still loved. Walt walked up to him and put his hand on his shoulder.

"Do you really want to do this? Think of the embarrassment of losing to a young woman."

William looked back at Walt and winked at him, "I won't lose. I learned to shoot on a ranch in Wyoming from a bunch of cowboys!"

He then nodded to the golf pro to hit another golf ball.

With the strike of the driver, the ball sailed through the air, William waited until the ball began to descend and fired his shot, sending the ball streaking to the ground. William turned and bowed to the applause of the crowd.

Phoebe stepped up and held up two fingers, indicating to the golf pro to drive two, one right after another. One ball made a perfect arc in the air followed closely by the second with speed that seemed more than natural, phoebe shot both balls in less than two seconds, splitting one in half. The crowed was stunned for a moment and then roared at the feat. All eyes turned back to William, who was focused on Phoebe, he watched her stroll back over to a brown folding chair and take her seat, crossing her legs and holding herself in a ladylike posture. She turned her head to William and gave him a smile that at once conveyed both good-natured taunting and encouragement.

William, feeling the pressure held up three fingers, indicating he wanted three to be driven. The golf pro set three golf balls on three separate tees and swung at them as fast as he could. The balls all followed the same trajectory and made an arc towards the green. William moved quicker, less casual and more intense, he fired three shots in less than three seconds. As before, all three balls streaked downward. William turned to Phoebe and bowed and held his arms out towards the spot they were shooting from as if to indicate it was her turn to match him, he was sure that she would not be able to do it. William reasoned that she may be accurate from long range, but there was no chance that she was as fast as him.

Phoebe smiled and never said anything to William but instead held all five fingers on her hand up to indicate she was going to shoot five golf balls being driven toward the green before they could hit. There was a low murmur among the spectators wondering if Phoebe could shoot that well, it seemed to be an impossibility to be so fast and have that degree of accuracy. The owner of the golf course, a former pro-golfer in his late sixties walked over next to the golf pro. He looked the part his brown skin was leathery from years of being in the sun, and he seemed eager for the next shot. He drove two tees in the ground in front of him placing the balls on them at the same time. He raised his straw hat up so he could see better and nodded to his employee to start swinging at the three balls teed up in front of him. Five balls flew through the air, two close together, the rest were spread out. Phoebe moved just slightly as she aimed at each one, hitting them in rapid succession, splitting some and just striking others. It was an incredible display of shooting that sent the crowed into wild applause. William took of his hat and wiped his forehead, now feeling that he could not match her, he thought of quitting, but knew that he had to go on as a matter of honor.

William had not actually believed that Phoebe was a better shot than he was, even with the number of kills in battle she had already. William nodded he was ready to shoot, he moved with lightning speed, splitting one ball, hitting three, and missing the last one. He groaned in defeat, and looked over at Phoebe who tipped her hat, beaming with pride; to William it seemed as if she was glowing. She walked over and held out her hand in a show of good sportsman ship. William shook it, ignoring the calls behind him from Walt to those he bet with to "pay up".

William smiled at Phoebe. "He loves apples, but I don't think Slingshot will let you ride him." William had lost his horse in the contest, and came to the realization he was falling in love with Phoebe.

# CHAPTER XIII

Arizona Company had been instructed by the coded message from the eerie voice on short wave to travel to a point south of Amarillo, Texas to Palo Duro Canyon. It had taken several days for them to arrive. They reached their destination just before dawn, they dismounted and waited near Lighthouse Hoodoo, a large red rock formation near the coordinates which they had been directed to stop. Just like the Ocala National Forest, there were no rangers on duty because the war had forced budget cuts. It had been treacherous for the renegades entering the canyon in the dark of night. The horses had to be lead down the narrow path on foot, although the horses had been chosen for their temperament in battle, an encounter with a wild animal at night could have spooked them and caused a rider to be thrown.

The dawn began to break over the canyon casting long shadows, although it was early and still cool, the temperature would soon be over one-hundred degrees. There were patches of green sagebrush, dotted with yucca plants, sweeping up the sides of the red craggy walls. Oblong grey rocks littered the landscape, sometimes balancing on top of a red rock formation. Islands of young oak trees were mixed in with sprawling old and dead oaks. The shear red cliffs rose up into columns of rock formations that seemed to be reaching into the sky.

William felt at home among the red dirt and rocks, he had spent so much time as an adolescent in the southwestern wilderness, hiding out with Cassidy and Roost in places like the Palo Duro. It had been months since William had seen the atrocities in Oklahoma City, and yet riding alongside Phoebe he had managed to forget for a little while. He had taken in all the sights on the ride to the canyon, the bison, mule deer and bobcat. He did not even care that Phoebe had been riding Slingshot. Walt had mentioned to William that he believed they were heading in theater, which William welcomed; he wanted to make the Romans pay for what they had done, for justice sake.

William gently nudged his horse and moved up alongside Bulloch, which he had grown to respect and for whom he had a genuine affection. He looked at the determination on Bulloch's face, a change from his jovial nature. William knew there was a problem,

"What was in that message that has you so concerned?" he said observing Bulloch's expression.

"I see you have added mind reading to your repertoire." Bulloch said with a slight chuckle.

"You know why we are here." William pressed.

Bulloch stopped his horse and turned it towards William, "No, it was the name of our contact, I am familiar with it."

William interrupted, "Ice Swan?

Bulloch weighed if he should tell William not wanting to compromise the agent

"Ice Swan is above top secret. All I know about Ice Swan is that it is a name synonymous with removing various threats to the United States over the last several years." He decided that there was no harm in telling William since their communication with civilization was very limited.

"Let me guess, we are heading into major danger. Well bring it on! " he felt after the shooting competition with Phoebe he could inflict damage on any Roman unit they encountered.

Bulloch gave his full toothy smile, "That is strong bravado for you isn't it Will? Is Walt rubbing off on you?" Bulloch chuckled.

The conversation abruptly stopped when they spotted the headlights of a black SUV approaching, the glare cutting through the half light. The vehicle came down a dirt road that had been encroached upon by snakeweed and lavender basket flowers. William and Bulloch glanced at each other with a look that expressed their eagerness to find out who Ice Swan was and why they had been ordered there. The black SUV rolled to a stop and cut its engine. The windows were heavily tinted and the driver, or if there were any passengers could not be seen. William and Bulloch placed their hand on their respective side arms. A tall, sleek woman emerged from the vehicle. She wore a brown cowboy hat from which her jet black hair flowed out from under. Her eyes were dark amber and her skin was auburn. She wore Native American jewelry around her neck and was dressed in a plaid button down shirt, khaki shorts and work boots. She was stunningly attractive and walked with confidence.

"Colonel" she said addressing Bulloch as he and William both dismounted and approached the mysterious woman.

Bulloch strode over with determination, "Ice Swan?" Bulloch said unsure after seeing the contact's appearance.

"Yes Colonel, I am code name Ice Swan." She said with a nod and extending her hand.

William studied her for a moment, she was not what he expected, "Comanche?" he deduced from her appearance, and the region of Texas where the canyon was located.

"Cherokee actually, but I was not sent for my ethnicity." She turned back to Bulloch, "Time is of the essence." She said and handed him a small rectangular device.

Bulloch stared at the gadget in his hand, "A field tablet? This will be detected by the Roman's sensors if I use this! I hope its importance is worth the risk."

"That is a low yield field tablet. It can't be detected. It contains information about a Mercenary Army operating out of Mexico called Credential Bond," she said, leaning against the SUV and scanning the rock formations around them for Roman spies.

"I know all about Credential Bond. I know about Ben Waterman leaving the Joint Chiefs of Staff when the U.S. went to pacifism and created the merc army with Kravchenko, waiting in Mexico to pounce when they had the chance. I would like to make them face a firing squad!" he said with a level of passion William had not seen since Bulloch had been jumped by the Roman assassin at his home.

"We have had reports of a group of soldiers in black body armor in Kansas City and around the southwest. They usually are near where the Romans are conducting operations. They have been seen traveling in Roman Runners, but not wearing Roman uniforms. We have fresh Intel they are in Amarillo. You are to intercept them and capture one or more for interrogation." Ice Swan said coolly.

William was impressed by her, and thought she must be highly intelligent to be so focused. Ice Swan then gave a gracious smile to them.

"I have opened up the cow camp cabins, your company can take time to shower and eat, but you need to get moving as soon as possible."

She then moved to the back of the SUV she opened the hatch and brought out two large boxes of food, ammunition, and first aid supplies. Bulloch signaled to Walt to get the supplies, he nodded and sent two renegades over to retrieve them. William and Bulloch were both impressed with her demeanor and taken aback by the appearance of the agent; She looked as if she could be model, not a hardened field agent. She could sense their surprise and chose to ignore it; she knew that her appearance was part of why she was so successful. It did not matter that to her if they knew she could have had a career as physicist, people opened up more when they believed she was vapid and shallow.

Bulloch slapped William on the back, "Until you walked right into a Roman forward base, Ice Swan had given us the most information on their military." He said to William, bringing him up to speed.

Ice Swan smiled at William and threw a bottle of water to him. He grabbed the bottle and gave a wide smile to her.

"That was good work in Kansas City. I watched your videos online whenever you posted one; I knew you were more than just a thief and a pretty face," she said, placing her hand on his shoulder.

Phoebe had been sitting on Slingshot close enough to hear what was being said, and to her surprise, she did not like seeing anyone flirt with William like Ice Swan was with him. She was glad to see William turn and remount his horse, and not engage in the flirting.

Phoebe had made a checklist of reasons she could not get involved with William: he was a thief, he was older than she was, and he was probably going to prison for a very long time after the war. None of the reasons seemed to matter. When she caught William's attention as he leaned back in the saddle, and he smiled, it brought her to a realization that not only was she attracted to him, she had never had such strong feelings for anyone else. She shook it off and turned her attention back to the mission.

The Renegades, after being debriefed, had made their way to Amarillo, more specifically to the area where the soldiers in black had been seen. They had ridden past the line of graffiti covered Cadillac's half buried at the *Cadillac Ranch* on the way. William had joked that if the Romans won, they would replace the cars with chariots. Half of the citizens of Amarillo had moved away, being so close to the front lines it was not a safe place to live. The towns remaining residents were defiant, refusing to let the Romans disrupt their daily lives, and willing to put up a fight if they came for them.

The Renegades made their way to the center of the city riding down the brick paved streets. The light was fading into an amber glow on the horizon, and the streetlights had just flickered to life. The streets they traveled on had led them through residential neighborhoods; some of the people still in their homes came out to see them. Some cheered, some held U.S. flags or "Don't Tread on Me!" flags, some offered them food or water, but hope could be seen in the eyes of every one of the people. The experience had given them a greater sense of purpose, seeing the faces of those whom it was their duty to protect had inspired and emboldened them.

Arizona Company was the smallest of the Mounted Cavalry units, comprised of highly skilled soldiers, numbering twenty in total. They split into two groups to search the downtown area. William's group was lead by Walt, and contained both Phoebe and Drake among others. William again had been given the task to act as scout, a job he would have felt better about if he still had Slingshot. He rode up Ninth avenue past the old Santa Fe building which used to contain the offices of the Potter County Government but had been turned into a four star hotel. He winced as his horse's hooves made noise on the bricks below them and reverberated off the buildings. William stopped for a moment, frustrated by the noise, he looked around for a path that would be on grass or dirt, but all he found was brick and pavement. As he looked to his left he noticed an alleyway that ran between two old brownstones circa the early twentieth century. He slowly moved his horse closer to see a Runner, covered with what looked like a giant burlap sack that had been woven together out of several smaller covers; the front end of the runner was completely exposed, as if it were set up for a rapid getaway. William moved down the alley to get a closer look at the runner when the unmistakable sound of a bullet whizzing past his ear re-focused his attention. Before he could turn around there was another shot that ricocheted off the front of the Runner. William could not hear the report from the gun, so he deduced it was a silenced weapon being fired from the Santa Fe building from its trajectory. He realized a sentinel must have spotted him approaching the vehicle. William decided not to try and engage them but instead went into a full gallop down the alley till he bolted through and emerged on the other side. As he rode past the bus station where waiting passengers watched him go by in disbelief, a Walk/Don't Walk sign erupted in a shower of sparks next to him; he was still being targeted by a very quick sniper. He hung on to the horn of his saddle and threw one leg over till he had only one foot in the stirrup and was hanging on the other side of his horse, completely hidden from whoever was shooting at him. William hung on the side of the horse until he was safely out of range.

Walt saw William coming, hanging from one side of the horse, and instantly knew there was trouble. William righted himself and approached Walt. Walt galloped over to William waiting for a report. Walt drew up his weapon from its holster on his horse.

"What the hell happened!" Walt barked.

"Santa Fe Building, one, maybe two snipers. There is a runner in an alley, when I approached the shooting started." William said as he straightened his hat.

"We can't wait for the other unit; we will have to stop them ourselves!" he said checking his gun to make sure it had no sand in it and would not jam.

"What! Ten of us!" William thought it suicidal to ride into sniper fire facing an unknown number of legionnaires.

"Don't be a coward!" Walt growled.

William was about to take Walt to task, "I am not."

"Willowdell, Obis, West, you're with me." Walt shouted over William, "Everyone else attack pattern gold, center on the Santa Fe building!"

Walt led the quartet bounding, in a leapfrog type maneuver where they covered one and other, riding from building to building for cover; until they arrived at the brick building facing diagonally opposite the Santa Fe Building. The streetlights had been shot out by the time they arrived, leaving only the fading light to spot their attackers. Walt peered around the corner of the building to see three men clad in black body armor, who in turn saw Walt and opened fire. As soon as he dove back behind the wall the shooting stopped. There was yelling from the Santa Fe building, but it was hard for Walt to decipher. A black ball rolled up behind the Renegades, prompting Walt to yell.

"Pitchball!"

The ball was a small robot that could be thrown over walls or around corners to train it's camera on the enemy so the operator could know how many were at that position. Drake quickly scooped it up and deposited it in a square trashcan bearing the city seal. William looked at the old police station down the street.

"You know, this is one time I wish the police were around," William joked.

Drake smiled "I'm insulted! What do you think I am?" he responded.

Walt was clearly irritated by the joking during combat, and flashed a twisted grimace to make his displeasure known. Walt looked around, for anything to gain the upper hand. He then saw the tan six- story bank building across the street; it was only half the size of the Santa-Fe building but was the highest point where they could cover the street. Using sign language, Walt indicated they needed to get to the roof of that building.

William, Phoebe and Drake simultaneously nodded their understanding. Walt sprinted across the street and jumped onto the roof of a parked SUV and sprung up to a wide ledge that ran the length of the building. He came to a window and shot it out disappearing inside. William in contrast, calmly held his hand up for Phoebe and Drake to wait. He jogged across the street to the front door, took out his knife and worked in between the doors until he had disengaged the lock. He swung the door open and held it wide bowing with his hand extended at arm's length, in a sarcastic display of courtesy. Phoebe and Drake heeded the invitation, sprinting across the street and through the open door. They made their way down a dark hall and into the darkened stairwell; they could hear Walt climbing the stairs, his steps hard on the concrete above them. They put on their night vision glasses and ran up the stairs. When they reached the roof they saw Walt flat against the edge looking for shooters in the other building. He turned to see the trio and signaled for them to get down; they quickly complied and crawled on their stomachs next to Walt.

He pointed to his eyes indicating he saw the shooters, and then spoke using hand signals at the same time holding up his fingers to indicate how many he saw.

"One on the roof, four or five on the ground. Drake, you're with me, you two cover the roof and the ground." Walt whispered.

William grabbed Walt's arm. "You're nuts! You're outnumbered!" he said with sincere concern.

Walt gave a sly look to William and gently pulled his arm back, "No Will, were not, we've got Phoebe!"

Walt signaled to Drake to follow him and they disappeared through the rusty steel door of the roof access. William signaled he would take the roof Phoebe could take the street. They both sat motionless and silent looking through their sights, waiting for a target to hit. After a few minutes the sniper on the roof of the Santa-Fe building moved to the edge. William saw him and pulled the trigger as the sniper threw himself backwards. He had seen William at the last moment before he fired saving his life. William hit the ledge where the sniper had been. He was shocked that he missed a target that wide.

"That sniper was as big as a house! How did I miss him? I mean he was enormous!" William said to Phoebe, but speaking more to himself.

Gunfire erupted in the street below them as the two groups exchanged fire. Walt's plan to have a second group of Renegades flank the building had worked. The soldiers in black were pinned down and could not fight their way out of their position. Walt and Drake started to move in but were stopped in their tracks when without warning the windows on the second floor of the hotel exploded outward with a roar and crash, sending shards of glass flying in all directions. The blast was from heavy machine guns firing from inside the building. The building had been fortified and was an impregnable fortress, the mammoth guns roared shredding everything in their path, including asphalt and steel. Phoebe could not see any of the soldiers firing the machine guns, she shot next to the gun on one side, then the other, and the gun continued to shower bullets on the ground below.

The exchange of gunfire continued for half an hour until a brown compact car containing a mother, father and two little girls; desperate to escape the area, sped in between the two groups. The gunfire stopped as the family squatted down in their seats to keep from being shot, and darted down the road. William had put his head up in time to see the car go by them. After the car passed, Phoebe had a soldier in her crosshairs, he had moved slightly so that he could see the car, now she could see the top of his head. William suddenly grabbed the barrel and pushed it upwards as she shot sending the bullet away from its intended target.

"What was that for?" Phoebe said in complete surprise.

William continued to push the barrel down "Don't you get it? They stopped shooting!" he said pointing to the silent guns.

"What?" Phoebe was unsure what William was saying.

William laughed, "They did not want to kill innocent bystanders."

Phoebe started to understand, "What does that mean?"

William stood up in plain sight, "Romans or Mercenaries would not care about collateral damage. I don't think these guys are the enemy! I'm going down there." he left his rifle sitting next to Phoebe.

Phoebe was horrified and pulled at William's arm, "You're going to get killed!"

He looked down and winked at her, "Trust me this is going to work."

William flashed a confident grin at Phoebe and ran to the door; moments later he had reached the street.

"Don't shoot, I am coming out! We are American soldiers!" William said waving his arms with his hat in hand. He threw his sidearm at his feet "Don't shoot!" he repeated as he slowly walked into the street.

He inched forward, towards the Santa-Fe building when the figure Phoebe had targeted to shoot started walking towards him. The soldier was

Morrison Lyons, who like William had ignored the calls by the Knights not to enter the street. Morrison lowered his MP7 and walked forward to William. He extended his hand to William.

"I'm Major Morrison Claret Lions, and you are either very brave or very stupid." He said with a smile.

William returned the gesture and smiled, "I've been known to be a little of both," he said shaking his hand.

Morrison scanned William noting his Emerson Suit "Why are you wearing a uniform in combat that has no armor?" William pushed his hat up with his finger, "We have the armor; we just don't like wearing it. Slows you down," he said reaching down to retrieve his pistol.

Morrison was truly glad to see the Pentagon was creative in their approach to the Romans. He was even more pleased to be speaking with someone in Special Forces.

"What is your outfit?" He said, looking at the other Renegades on horseback.

"Newly formed U. S. Mounted Cavalry, they call us the Renegades." William spotted the Knights slowly coming from behind cover. "What are you guys? Navy SEALs? Delta-Force?"

"No, not exactly." Morrison hesitated for a moment.

William was perplexed and a little concerned with the hesitation, "Well, what exactly are you?" he said still trying to be polite.

Morrison had felt like he was betraying his country at times, but it had not been so pronounced until that moment, but he still believed in what he was doing. "We are the Knights of the Clock Tower. British Knights." William was skeptical and surprised at what Morrison said "What? You don't sound very British." his face made it more apparent than the question that the story was hard to accept.

Morrison sighed, remembering what he thought the first time King Owen told him about the knights.

"I'm a Green Beret; I was rescued by the Knights, now I am one of them. Trust me, I know it sounds nuts, but it's true."

Kenneth had elected himself to find out what was going on and walked over to see why Morrison had stopped shooting, and was now talking to William. As he approached them, he recognized William

"Aren't you William West? You're in the American Military now?" Kenneth said in a tone that was not flattering.

"I'm a Yankee Doodle Dandy." William said with a wink.

Kenneth was instantly offended, "The American's must be desperate if they are using this one. What, they had to take the likes of him? Accepting criminals now, are they?" he said stepping forward to intimidate William with his huge frame.

William realized that Kenneth was the sniper on the roof who moved so quickly he could not hit him. He was astounded at how someone so muscle bound and tall could move with such agility.

William would not let himself be intimidated and smiled at Kenneth in defiance, "Aw, you know, they did what they had to with me. Hey, by the way, it looks like by the looks of you the Brits are letting big dumb morons into the armed forces." he smiled even wider after the insult.

Enraged, Kenneth lunged forward at William; Morrison immediately wrapped his arms around him and pulled him to the side.

"Let it go K, he got you, it was a good one, now let it go!" Morrison said as he tried to suppress his laughter.

William tried not to laugh, "Yeah K, no hard feelings right." he held out his hand which Kenneth reluctantly took, as he scowled.

William could not resist another verbal jab, "Oh Yeah, you're the big guy I almost shot on the roof." He added after releasing his grip.

Kenneth growled at the remark "Oi! If it had been me shooting at you, you'd be dead!" he glared at William who was clearly enjoying antagonizing Ken.

William was about to needle Kenneth further when he was interrupted by a voice from behind him.

"William West. I know who you are." King Owen said as he came from behind cover.

"I seem to be getting a lot of that. Who are you?" William said turning around with a smirk of impatience.

"I am King Owen Badon."

"*Right*, you're the king of England. I'm Arch Duke Ferdinand, pleased to meet you," William said impatiently.

King Owen gave a slight smile, "You are witty, just like they say you are, but you are also exceedingly brave from what I have seen."

William rolled his eyes and curtsied sarcastically, "Thank you *your majesty*. That was very nice of you." he was sure that King Owen was in fact, a soldier who had gone insane.

Bulloch, who rode up with the rest of Arizona Company, recognized King Owen from meeting him years before at an event he attended at Buckingham Palace, when he was still just the Duke of Sussex, when the press referred to him as the *Warrior Duke*. He immediately dismounted and gave a half bow. Bulloch realized that Owen must be King since the British Royal Family was reported to be dead.

"Your Majesty, it is good to see that at least one member of the royal family has survived." Bulloch said with vigor.

William was stunned, "What? You mean he is the King of England?" he said as disbelief washed over him.

"Yes, William, he is. I met him once at a dinner at Buckingham Palace. He is a soldier; he trained his whole life to be one. He wanted to make his mark, knowing he would never be king." Bulloch looked over at King Owen who nodded his agreement. Bulloch was energized by the discovery "He is the last great hope of Brittan. He is the rightful blood holder of the throne," he continued speaking in a high shrill tone which conveyed his exhilaration that King Owen was alive.

"Wow, I feel like a royal jerk! Pardon the pun." William said holding out his hand, breaking etiquette.

King Owen grasped his hand and shook it, showing no signs of being offended by the gesture. William realizing what he had done took a step back and gave an awkward bow. King Owen smiled at the feeble but well meaning attempt at etiquette. He held up the palm of his hand to stop it.

"Please, you never have to bow to me William." King Owen had still not adjusted to the trappings of being the sovereign.

William was still stunned and mortified, "Thank you, your majesty." he said relieved he had not caused a diplomatic crisis.

The King placed his hand on his shoulder, "William, please call me Owen. We are all brothers in arms."

The thrill of finding King Owen started to fade and Bulloch had questions. "I must ask; why you are here?" Bulloch asked King Owen.

"Until the United States is whole again, we cannot defeat the Romans. Only with your help can we free the United Kingdom."

William was still trying to put everything together in his mind, "How did you get here?" he said still reeling at the revelation that he was speaking to a king.

King Owen was still cautious in what he divulged, "Texas, by the way of Germany." He knew Bulloch, but William he did not know yet, and did not know if he could be trusted.

Bulloch continued his well meaning line of inquiry, "It seems you are well-funded."

King Owen carried himself in a way that held both Bulloch and William captive, he had a detectable air of nobility whether he admitted to himself or not; they stood there silent, waiting for the secret of how he came to America.

King Owen considered himself an excellent judge of character and William seemed to have changed from the brash, self promoting robber that used to be a fixture in the news. He made the decision to trust William.

"My uncle foresaw the end and convinced the CEO of the Crown Estate to have the revenue from the entire royal holdings placed in a secret account, in my name, since I was out of the country. A few members of the House of Lords who were sure to be executed followed my uncle's example and donated their fortunes. I found out through an email from the cousin of the CEO, which was sent right before the fall of my country."

As Bulloch and King Owen were conversing, William received another shock as he saw a familiar face. Roost had made his way outside; he had been staying with the Knights after they rescued him from the Romans. His eyes came up from the ground to meet William's. William took long strides over to see Roost, whose shock was profound seeing William back from the dead.

William stood in front of Roost smiling, trying to think of something to say. He was about to open his mouth when Roost struck him square in the chin, sending him tumbling to the ground.

Roost pointed angrily at him, "I'm sorry Will" Roost said pointing angrily, "You had it coming! That was a lousy thing to do!" he said before he turned and walked away.

William brushed himself off when he next saw Cassidy standing in front of him; she was frail and still recovering from the rattlesnake bites. She was dressed in men's military clothing consisting of a long sleeve tan waffle shirt and brown camouflage pants. It was the first time he had seen her in public without makeup, so he knew she had been through something traumatic. He hoped it was not from his faked death, and that she had not been slowly withering away mourning him. William stood there for a moment, when he was about to speak, she slapped him across the face and walked away.

# CHAPTER XIV

I t had been agreed that Arizona Company and the Knights of the Clock Tower would travel together on the next mission. The Knights had desired to be invisible until the moment of their choosing, but King Owen believed the moment had chosen them, and the time had come to become known to the world. Both the knights and Renegades sat in the hotel lobby, the gothic motif that had persisted since the 1930's was riddled with bullet holes. The far wall from the front doors contained a mural depicting the history of the southwest; it had been spared any major damage. It still was the most comfortable room any of the Renegades had been in for months. The terrazzo floors were cool and the interior itself was unusual. The ceiling consisted of a hand molded and painted plaster tiles that formed a brown and bronze check pattern intersected with diamond shapes containing geometric flowers. William noticed that the brass and bronze chandeliers, although art deco in design, reminded him of something else. The long narrow shards of glass from the top row and the smaller narrow shards were opaque with a golden tone to them. The ends of the strips of glass had two lines that met in a point, making it appear to William as swords and daggers underneath. As he was looking at the ceiling he was joined by Drake, who had witnessed William's greeting from his best friend and his wife. Drake sank into the brown leather sofa next to William and smiled. He looked up at the ceiling where William had been looking

"You know" he said unsolicited "If I were a king, and I was looking for a building in Texas that resembled a castle, this would be it. Have you seen the outside of this building? It looks like it's right out of medieval times. King Owen must be pretty smart, look at how solid this place is, it's like a fortress. Battlements on the roof, granite and steel, this building is not going to come down easy. Now, if you'll excuse me, I am going to go see if the King will let me stay at Buckingham Palace when this is all over."

Drake gave William a pat on the shoulder and walked off. William appreciated what Drake was trying to do, he was a true friend. He glanced back down at his holo-def bible, looking for guidance in the situation he was in.

William looked up to see Roost and Cassidy together and realized why they were still with one and other. He felt glad they were together, but longed for the days when the three of them were inseparable, but he knew those days had to be in the past. King Owen walked past William reading the expression that was on his face and sat next to him.

"I find solace in that book when I am troubled. It has been a great source of strength for me. Believe me; I know what it is to be troubled." King Owen said seeing what William had in his hands.

William leaned forward and groaned. "I led my wife, my best friend, and my family to think I was dead. Not a really good move on my part."

"I had wondered why Roost and Cassidy felt the need to hit you." King Owen said being somewhat amused.

William looked at Roost and Cassidy as he spoke, "You know, they have every right to be angry with me, but I wish they could understand why I did it."

"What was the reason? It seems a selfish act. You don't seem to be self indulgent"

"As long as Cassidy and I were together, we were headed to an early grave. Booze, drugs and robberies don't get you a long life."

King Owen nodded his understanding, "If they cared about you, they will forgive you. I lost my entire family a few years ago; I would be overjoyed to find out any one of them was still alive, even if it had been a deception."

William was appreciative of the advice, "That is very insightful, a good quality for a king."

King Owen smiled, "Let's not get carried away."

William looked around at the destruction, the tiny pieces of shattered glass, where pipes had been shot, and flooded the lobby, and the fact that there was a maintenance crew, complete with blue shirts bearing their name on the left breast, working in the hotel that had been taken over by the knights.

"How did you manage to get this hotel? Did you have to break in here?" William said knowing that his question was not what happened.

"I own it; I bought it through a shell company, Domboc Holdings Incorporated." King Owen explained, "How else do you think that we had remote control forty caliber machine guns mounted all the way around the second floor. That was the answer you were fishing for, wasn't it?"

"I'm sorry; I didn't think you would come right out and answer me. I guess I was used to deceiving people for so long it became a habit." William answered regretfully.

"We are all creatures of habit I am afraid. I don't fear the war we are fighting; it is being a king that frightens me. I have trained to be a soldier my whole life, how can I rule in peace after that. I don't want to be like Caprera." King Owen stared straight ahead as if seeing a scene that had not yet happened.

"Well if you're going to be like Caprera, you better start stocking up on togas." William said with as serious an expression as he could manage.

King Owen erupted in laughter, a sound so rare that all the knights stopped and watched him and William laughing. He had not laughed since his family had been killed, he had been like a machine, with one purpose, drive out the Romans, destroy Caprera and his works.

Cassidy watched, angry that William managed to laugh with her in the room. After all he had done to her and Roost he had the nerve to laugh in front of her, she thought. She gave William a look across the room he had come to know all too well; it was a look of complete disgust. She stomped off to an open elevator and never looked back up at William. Roost saw the exchange; he could see that William was truly remorseful for what he had done. He walked up to William, winked and sat down next to him.

"Your Majesty" he nodded to King Owen as he sat down.

"So you joined the military, never saw that coming, Will." Roost spoke with his easy manner.

William laughed, "Neither did I, but it is what I wanted. Here I am. I'm a soldier now."

Roost gave him a wry look, "It sounds like you are a damn good one from what I am told."

"Who told you that?" William, who was never humble, was sincerely embarrassed.

"Everyone, Will, everyone. I heard what you did for that kid in Oklahoma City; that was a brave thing to do." Roost said in a tone that conveyed his understanding of who William had become and why he had left.

Bulloch strode into the room and approached King Owen giving him a bow as he stood in front of him. King Owen shook his head, he had made it clear to everyone that no one there had to bow to him, he disliked the practice, and although he was king, he had still not grown used to it.

"Please, Colonel, there is no need to bow."

"I am sorry your majesty" Bulloch stood up in embarrassment "I am afraid it is ingrained in me, and I can't seem to untether myself from the practice."

He handed King Owen his field tablet "We need to speak in private." King Owen stood up to follow Bulloch but turned back to William and Roost before he did.

"William, I must know, how did Roost get his name?"

William chuckled looking over at Roost "When he was at the University of Wyoming, he climbed a flagpole outside the stadium to impress a cheerleader. The following Monday the school paper put a picture of him on the front page with the caption *Roberts Roosts* and the name stuck."

King Owen looked at Roost with a look like he had uncovered a state secret. He and Bulloch moved hurriedly into the stairwell, the door slamming shut behind them.

Cassidy sat, staring at the embers floating inside the fireplace in front of her, still in shock over finding out that William had faked his own death. She sat silently, Roost had intentionally stayed away to give her time to absorb everything. William, who was reassembling a lock he had found in a maintenance room, looked at her sitting there the flames reflected in her blue irises. He remembered how he had fallen in love with her in the first place, how they met on her father's ranch, and how hard it was to leave her. He walked over and eased himself on the couch next to her.

"I am sorry Cass; I should have done it some other way. I guess I just didn't have the heart to leave you to your face. I wanted a new start, to stop taking what was not mine, and start contributing to society. "

A single tear rolled down Cassidy's cheek. She looked at William with both reproach and fondness.

"I thought you were dead. You made me think you were dead, Will! I mourned for you. I actually felt guilty for not being with you when you died." She said in a low voice, never looking up from the fire.

"I know." William sighed, "One day I decided I just couldn't do it anymore, I tried to tell you and Roost, but even though I lost the desire to steal, I couldn't stop myself. I would see you and Roost and the looks on your faces, it was like a drug. I wanted to be an upright citizen, and as long as you and I were together, I was going to keep stealing." William looked at Cassidy as he spoke even though she still stared into the fire, "You know it was fun when we worked as a team. I loved you so much, but that was what we were, Bonnie and Clyde in a non suicidal, non psychotic kind of way." He chuckled.

Cassidy smiled slightly, she reached over and touched William's hand, looked him in the eyes and spoke.

"I am glad you're not dead, and I understand why you left. I knew something was gone between us, all we had was the next heist, and physical attraction. Right before you died," Cassidy stopped for a moment to gather her composure, "I mean before you left, I thought about our future. I realized we were never going to have a normal life. There would never be two kids and a yard. I also thought would we still be trying to steal when we were in our fifties? There was no future in you and me, only a dead end. Roost was there for me, and we fell in love. Roost would not even look at me for months out of respect to you." Cassidy pulled her hand back as if to sever a connection. "We looked to you for what to do next, and when you were gone, the stealing stopped. I never knew that I could make an honest living; I never had a real job in my life. It felt good to make an honest living, even if it was only as a waitress." Her tone of voice was equally as cold, "I spent a lot of cold nights alone feeling guilty about you before I let Roost in; I felt like I was being unfaithful. It was just very hard when I saw you riding up today. It was harder than when the Romans invaded, it was harder then when you died. I almost died when we were running from the Romans; I was bitten several times by numerous rattlesnakes. They tell me that I was unconscious for four days and that the venom may have scarred my heart. It gave me a new outlook on what is important. I already realized that we were both going to die if you had not gone, but I had not forgiven you yet. You were right to leave, and look at you now! You're a hero!"

William chuckled and gave her a sideways glance. "Come on Cass, I am not a hero."

Cassidy gave him a less harsh look, one of admiration, "You keep running into gunfire to save people from what I understand."

"Only twice, well three times." William said with his most charming smile.

"I believe that qualifies you, Mister West." She said sitting up and smiling.

"Are we okay Cass?"

"It's strange, you are so brave with everything you do, but you did not have the guts to tell me it was over. You're lucky I am not the psychotic ex-wife type. But no, Will, we will not be okay for a while. What you did really hurt, and was really mean. It will be a very long time before we are *okay*." The last word was biting in its tone and delivery.

William did not know what to say and he blurted anything out, "Technically we are still married."

Cassidy gave him an unfeeling stare, "We will take care of that when all this is over with."

William now regretted what he had done more than ever, "We had a lot of fun didn't we? Those were good times." he said as he stood up to leave. There was no response. William shook his head in frustration and turned back to Cassidy.

"Cass, we are good people, you me and Roost, we just did bad things. Now we all have a chance to start over and redeem ourselves. No one is going to care about what we did in the past; all they are going to care about is what we do for this nation." William looked up at the mural on the wall "I did not realize how deeply I love this country until it was invaded." He then looked down at Cassidy, "Look Cass, I thought you would be okay, I did not know how bad you would be hurt, if I could I would take it back. I will always be sorry for what I did to you." He said and then turned and walked away.

As the Renegades prepared their mounts, the knights were busy shutting down any technology they did not need. Instead of using technology to lure the Romans to them, they were going to have to be undetectable, like the Renegades. The four knights who knew how to ride, including King Owen, were given horses. The rest would follow behind in two runners, and stay out of sight during the day. William was about to mount his hose when Phoebe walked over and kissed him on the lips. He stopped for a moment, feeling both surprised and elated.

William reached down inside himself to keep calm and then spoke to her, "What was that for?"

"That was for not letting me kill an innocent Soldier." Phoebe said as she patted his chest, "and I am giving you your horse back."

"Wow, thank you." William said not sure if the kiss was a thank you or if it was something more. "That is really nice of you."

Phoebe jumped into the saddle and rode off following those who had already gone ahead. William watched her ride off, but heard two sets of hooves coming up behind him, he turned to see Roost riding towards him wearing a Calvary uniform and holding Slingshot's reign.

Roost nodded towards Phoebe "She's is a good woman, Will, I wouldn't let her get away." Roost said, leaning down to hand William the reign, "She asked me a lot of questions about you."

William was shocked to see Roost in a uniform. "What are you doing in that?"

An unmistakable look of determination was in Roost eyes, "I had to fight Will; I can't go home and do nothing, one day I may not have a home to go to anymore. Besides, I always loved those old cavalry movies with the Duke."

William still was in disbelief, Roost couldn't just put on the uniform, it had to be given to him, unless he stole it. "Come on Roost, how did you get the Emerson Suit?"

Roost laughed, knowing what William was asking "I asked Colonel Bulloch if I could join. I really want this Will."

Surprised that Roost was allowed in, William thought out loud, "You've had no training."

Roost flashed an assured look at William, "You've forgotten Will, I was a criminology major, and I interned with the ATF. I am not completely untrained. They let me in for the same reason they let you in, we both have special skills that no one in the military would have."

William started to utter "How..", but Roost cut him off.

"It was an executive order from the President on the recommendation of General Wright and Colonel Bulloch."

William became amused at the thought of him and Roost in the Army together, "Wow, I never thought you and I would ever work together on anything honest. I am glad to have you back partner." he then changed his tone. "What about Cass?"

Roost shared William's concern, "She is going to Dallas; they are going to check out her internal organs to see how much damage the Venom did to them."

"Don't you want to be with her?"

"She insisted I go."

William nodded and the pair without speaking bolted off to catch up with the rest of the Renegades. They came up to Phoebe and slowed their pace until they were all galloping at the same speed.

"What do you think, Roost?" William yelled to Roost on the other side of Phoebe, who looked back and forth between them.

Roost smiled, "Home on the Range sounds good to me."

The pair started to sing the old cowboy song, which was a tradition they had when they were embarking on long rides. Phoebe laughed, and decided to join in. The three of them rode west, heading to the coordinates that were given to them, heading into the heart of Roman occupied territory, New Mexico.

# CHAPTER XV

Caesaris felt her heart pound while she rode to her coronation; she was both thrilled and apprehensive at the same time. She was about to be crowned Queen of England, but many questions lingered in her mind. She wondered if her ascension to the throne would be accepted by the British people. How hard would it be to convince them she was not the same as Julia? Would she be able to escape her father's long shadow? The questions had been haunting her, but nevertheless the coronation would go on as planned.

With all that transpired she was glad to be in England. She had been shocked by her father's actions with the two would be assassins, but still, she knew they were trying to kill him, and she could not extinguish her love for him. The sight of her father reveling over the lifeless bodies of his prey had driven her away from Rome to London. Caesaris had not seen much outside of Buckingham Palace since her arrival in London. She had heard the persistent rumors of Slave camps in the northern part of the United Kingdom; normally she would have dismissed them; slavery after all–she reasoned– had been designed to allow debtors to repay their debt. But after seeing her father's brutality, she was starting to have doubts. Caesaris wondered if perhaps she had convinced herself that all the whispers about her father she had overheard growing up were untrue. Much that she had believed to be true, seemed to be a mirage, and those she had trusted and counted on may have been a part of the deception. She had been a party to slavery, and it gnawed at her. It seemed so benign the way it was explained, but now she had to know what was factual. She planned to tour the country after the coronation, in search of the truth, no matter what it was.

She waited in the State Carriage Britannia, a black coach with intricate gold patterns. In recent years cars had been used instead of carriages, but she decided to revive the tradition to indicate she respected Brittan. It had four gold lamps, adorned with sheets of hand- carved crystal, equally as intricate. The undercarriage was gilded with twenty-three carat gold, and the gold roof bore a gilt carving of four lions acing as legs for a pedestal that held an exact carving of the crown. It was pulled by restless Windsor Grey horses, they seemed to Caesaris as if they knew she was not the true Queen, and wondered if the public would react in the same way. She had chosen the coach because it had never been used in a coronation, and more importantly, because Julia had not used it. Her aunt had chosen to be crowned in Trafalgar Square, in a ceremony that was more Roman than English. Julia had wholly thrown herself into the traditions of ancient Rome, even having dormouse and lamprey served at the coronation banquet. No one in England shed tears for Julia when she died, and they were glad she was buried in Rome, not under British soil.

Caesaris took pains to make sure that, though she was Roman, English traditions would be observed; and so she sat in front of St. Peter's Church at Westminster. She looked at the old gothic stone church with its giant rose window, flying buttresses and stained glass. The walls of the building were weathered from centuries of perpetual English rain; some of the stones made up dark beige patches, with light sand colored stones standing out among them, looking almost like pieces of a puzzle that were out of place.

Caesaris was used to buildings that were hundreds, even thousands of years old, she had championed the restoration of Venice, but this was different, this building had charisma, Westminster Abbey called to her. She felt a tangible yet unexplainable connection with the building. An intense feeling of belonging fell over her, so strong it startled her. She wondered if it was because she was trying to break from her father and Rome, was it because she had found a place where she could be who she wanted to be, or could it be providence? She had kept her mother's wish and been a quiet, yet dedicated, catholic. Upon her arrival in London, she had converted to the Anglican Church, because she was to be the leader of the church. She was more than ready to embrace the British traditions, and she also believed she was ready to lead. The idea when she was a child that her father would rule over a new Roman Empire, and even more unthinkable, that she would be Queen of England would be farfetched to even the most imaginative of children. She thought about all the events that had led her to that place and to that moment, and how each step of the journey seemed to prepare her for becoming Queen.

Her coachman, who wore a black and gold three-corner hat, a powdered wig and a red coat with gold garnish, turned the jeweled handle on the coach door to let Caesaris out. She extended her hand to help her down from the coach. She stepped out on to the old stone path leading to the entrance, staring up at the Abbey all the while. Her dress was simple, but formal enough for the occasion. It was white silk, embroidered with threads of gold making up complex patterns, flecked with pearls. The scoop neckline was encrusted with twenty-four carat gold beading, as was the bottom of the short sleeves. She wore matching white satin opera gloves. Around her neck was a twenty-eight carat diamond necklace that came to a point of a single large teardrop diamond. Her strawberry blonde hair was pulled into a bun, and she wore a diamond crown worn by Queen Elizabeth the second in her coronation. Her eyes were cast downward in a gesture of humility; her long supple lips were pursed in similar manner. She did not want to appear arrogant or give any impression that this was a Roman victory. Julia had done enough damage to them, to their collective psyche Caesaris decided.

The crowd of Londoners, who had gathered there out of curiosity and resentment not jubilance, let out a collective gasp at the sight of Caesaris. She had been shielded from the media by her father and not much was know about her outside of Rome. She looked the part of a Queen, unlike Julia, who although striking in her appearance, was less than stately. Everything seemed to fit, the slight chill in the air despite it being the second day of June, the slate colored sky, which looked as if it was the middle of winter and Caesaris, who carried herself the way the royals used to, when there were still royals. The onlookers had not expected to see a Roman dressed in such an accurate display of English refinement. Despite her regal appearance, the crowd was still largely hostile; one unseen heckler shouted "Go back to Italy!" the taunt prompted raucous laughter from the multitudes of onlookers, and concern from the nervous legionnaires patrolling the streets.

Caesaris concentration was unbroken, she walked towards the ancient church doors, Praetorian Guards on the left dressed in their molded breastplates and gold helmets with red crests, and the Grenadier Guards, with their famous red uniforms with their tall black furry bearskin caps, stationed on her right. Each group was an acute contrast to the other, both in dress and in manner. The Grenadiers had been made to swear allegiance to Cesar, and had small explosive implants surgically placed next to the left carotid artery, which could be remotely set off if they ever turned against the Romans. There was no doubt about who was truly in control of the day's events.

Caesaris decided that having either the Robe of State made of Crimson Velvet or the Parliament Robe being carried behind her was too ostentatious a spectacle, humility would have to be observed, she concluded, in order to win the hearts of the British people.

Caesaris walked down the long isle running through the middle of the church. Her eyes glanced upwards at the fan vaulted ceiling with its bewildering carvings and long inverted spires, capped with gold tips. She thought it looked like a beautiful cave with gilded stalactites, she was truly enraptured. She tried not to pay attention to the Roman dignitaries who made up most of the seven thousand guests in attendance, but she caught glimpses in her peripheral vision. In the front row was her father, in his military uniform, gold breastplate, and complete with gold laurel on his head. Sabrina Caprera was next to him, wearing a Scarlet dress with a plunging neckline and back that left little to the imagination. Her lipstick was the same brazen hue of red, and she wore her hair up sprinkled with tiny cut rubies. Her overall appearance was both disrespectful to Caesaris, and to God. Next to them was President Vichy with one of his assorted mistresses; he had been escorted by a nameless redhead for the coronation. His infantile features were accentuated by the fine blonde hair having been flattened against his head with styling gel.  On the next row were several Roman Governors, from conquered provinces such as the recently restored Carthage and Armorica, beside them was Charles Fletcher, beaming like a father of a newborn child.

Caesaris continued her march to the heart of the sanctuary, flanked by the Bishop of Durham in his white robe bearing a wide red stripe with a cross made out of gold thread and a large gold cap that had two points shaped like a spade, separated by a valley in between. He was seventy-five years old and wore wire rim glasses and was not in the best of health. She could hear a high pitched wheeze that repeated every few moments emanating from the bishop as he took a long piping gasp for each breath. She was flanked on her right side by the Bishop of Bath and Wales, who wore a white robe with a red scarf and red cap shaped like a upside down diamond. He was a younger man of thirty-two years, who was visibly nervous, perspiring as if he had been running in a race. Both bishops carried croiser staffs, which symbolized them being the Sheppard of a flock.  A choir of boys attired in white robes sang Handel's *Zadok the Priest,* accompanied by the Royal Philharmonic orchestra, which had been a tradition prior to Julia's coronation. Caprera had allowed the Anglican Church to remain in place, because he did not see Christianity as a threat to Rome, but he vowed he would stamp it out if it became one.  Behind them was an army of crown bearers, dressed in red satin robes, carrying various crowns, to be used in the ceremony. Trailing the Crown Bearers were the

Bearers of the Crown Jewels and the Sword of State. Caesaris looked ahead and saw there, situated in the middle of the vast room, was King Edwards Chair. The chair had been a staple of previous coronations, until Julia's. Next to the throne was the Archbishop of Canterbury, who wore a gold cap similar to the Bishop of Durham, a gold robe with several ornate patterns mingled together and a red stripe running down the front to match his red collar. He was a stout fiery eyed man with a ruddy completion who looked older than his fifty years. Unlike the Bishops, he showed no signs of nervousness.

Caesaris moved forward to the first throne she was to sit on in the ceremony, the Chair of State, an ancient mahogany chair. The chair's four feet were carved lions, leafed with gold. The complex carvings in the chair had worn down over time, making them nearly invisible. Caesaris eased herself into the chair, at which point all other members of the ceremony fanned out to various parts of the church, only the Archbishop was left next to her. He turned to the congregation and spoke in a booming voice:

"I here present to you, Caesaris Caprera, your undoubted Queen! Wherefore all of you who are here today to do your homage and service, will you do the same?" There was an affirmation from the crowd. He then turned to Caesaris, "Will you solemnly swear to govern the subjects of the United Kingdom and Great Britain?"

Caesaris felt the magnitude of the words, and felt as if not only was it a coronation ceremony, but a transformational passage. No longer would she be a shrinking violet, afraid to do anything but plead with her father for what she wanted. Even though it all seemed like a dream, she knew this was where she belonged. It was truly happening; she was to become the Sovereign of England.

"I *solemnly promise* so to do." Caesaris said with heartfelt sincerity and enthusiasm that echoed through the chamber.

The Archbishop continued to bellow the words of the ceremony "Will your power be used to cause law and justice, in mercy, to be executed in all of your judgments?" His voice reverberated around the church.

Caesaris words held no less emotion, "I will do so."

"Will you, to the upmost of your power, keep the Laws of God, and true profession of the Gospel? Will you keep and protect the Church of England?"

"The things that I have promised this day, I shall perform and Keep, so help me God." she turned her head slightly so that she and her father made eye contact; that he would understand her resolve.

A bible was handed to her, but no more was said to keep from drawing her father's ire. They were about to remove it when she grabbed it and gently kissed it, returning it to the bearer. It was a moment of defiance her father could not have mistaken. Caesaris stood up and made her way to the platform which held King Edwards Chair. Like the coronation chair, it was a worn mahogany; the red seat cushion had been replaced numerous times. The base of the chair contained an old gray stone from Scotland that ran the length of the seat known as The Stone of Destiny, it was believed to be the rock, as told in the bible, where Jacob rested his head and had a vision of the ladder to Heaven.

She sat carefully in the chair, noting it was as fragile as the previous chair. Four attendants rushed over and held a gold canopy over Caesaris head. Four Maids of Honor, dressed in blue sleeveless silk Roman dresses appeared seemingly from nowhere. The quartet was made up of her closest friends, who proceeded to remove her jewelry and her cloak the Colobium Sindonis, a white linen gown that signified purity before God. She looked at her friends and wondered if she had really ever known them at all. The Archbishop then produced the Ampulla, a small solid gold eagle perched on an ornate pedestal, its wings extended to their full span. It had the appearance of a symbol, more than that of a realistic portrayal of the bird of prey. He very carefully tipped the figurine so that oil poured out of the beak and into a solid gold spoon with four minute pearls on the handle. He proceeded to anoint Caesaris by pouring the oil, which smelled of roses and cinnamon, onto her hands, her chest, and her head. He then turned and handed the Ampulla to yet another attendant who scurried off, and returned with a pair of Spurs. The presentation of the spurs was a part of the ceremony that in the past had been performed by The Lord Great Chamberlain, a position that had been abolished under Roman occupation. The spurs were made of solid gold and were touched to each heel very gently, and then touched by Caesaris. Next, were the swords of state, covered with rare jewels and handles plated with gold representing: spiritual justice, temporal justice and mercy.

The Maids of Honor came sweeping in again to remove the Colobium Sindonis and place a robe called the Supertunica on Caesaris, a long gold cloak with gold lace that looked like something a cardinal might wear at a

Vatican ceremony. Woven in were such varied items as shamrocks, pink roses, palm trees and plum colored thistle. On top of the Supertunica they hurriedly placed the Pallium Regale; another gold robe, also decorated with the shamrocks, but it also had fleurs-de-lis, green thistle, with four eagles, woven from silver thread, each in a corner and lined with red velvet. Finally, the Armilla, a similarly decorated gold scarf was draped around her shoulders.

Caesaris sat back down, going through the motions of the ceremony as if it were a carefully choreographed dance, which is how she had envisioned it. The Archbishop approached again, this time with the Sovereign's Orb, an iconic globe that had been seen in paintings and photographs of Kings and Queens for centuries. Caesaris knew its appearance meant she was about to at last become the Queen of England. The Orb was gold, ringed with various gems, enclosed with two diamond encrusted lines, another similar half circle ran across the top and a gold cross projected from the top, which was also encrusted. She was then given two gold scepters, one with a dove and one with a cross.

Finally, the moment that made the entirety of the ceremony relevant, the moment that would make Caesaris relevant, the moment that the Archbishop placed St. Edwards Crown on her head. The crown was heavier than she expected, over four pounds weighted down by gold and large gems, it was crimson, encircled by four jewel encrusted fleur-de-lis, and four crosses Patée, four pearl lined and jewel filled bands rose from the ring and converged on top to hold a smaller version of the orb. The Archbishop stood back and exclaimed in an even louder bellow:

"*God Save the Queen!*"

At which point the crowd of mostly Romans awkwardly joined in the cry a second after the Archbishop, not quite knowing what the proper action was in the coronation, followed by thunderous applause. Caesaris then stood up, emotions surging through her, and made her way to her throne, an oak chair covered with gold leaf and cardinal red velvet cushions. The arms sloped down from the back; on the end of each was carved the face and outstretched claws of a griffin. On top was an intricate rococo style pattern of flowers and vines carved into the wood. Her maids of honor rushed in and removed the Supertunica placing the Purple Robe of State upon her shoulders, and there they remained to manipulate the eighteen-foot train. Caesaris had chosen not to wear anything as ostentatious as the robe upon entering the Abbey, but wanted to keep the tradition alive in her coronation.    As she sat, the bishops, lead by the archbishop, raised their voices in unison pledging their allegiance to the crown. Caesaris, leaning forward and lowering her eyes, gave a nod of acknowledgement to the clergy.   St. Edward's weighty crown was then removed from her head, and replaced with the red velvet diamond and pearl encrusted Crown of State, which like the previous crown contained a smaller version of the Orb at its crest.

The ceremony was elaborate and impressive on a grand scale, but still missing the members of the Royal family and nobility who would have been present in the past. There were no dukes or duchesses, no lords or ladies, only those who were loyal to Rome.   Then the precession made its way out of the church, led by the sword bearers, Queen Caesaris carried the Orb and the scepter with the Cross as she followed. The gathered congregation and choir sang *God Save The Queen* as she left, the words on a large holo-def screen near the exit for the benefit of the gathered Romans whom most of chose not to sing.

Caesaris was helped back into her coach, the robes having been removed; she carried a bouquet of white lilies, which she held in one hand as she turned to politely wave at the onlookers. The waves were not reciprocated and she noticed something she had not on the way to the coronation. In the crowd were young people, dressed in Victorian and Edwardian era style dress with some differences.  There were girls wearing petticoats, and silk dresses with sloping shoulders, there were side lace boots and both broad brimmed hats adorned with flowers and feathers, and demure bonnets. The striking thing was the material; some outfits were blood red, head to toe while others were vibrant colors with bright plaid patterns overlaid. One girl Caesaris saw wore a silk dress of bright canary yellow with dark green plaid, pagoda sleeves complete with matching bonnet, gloves and parasol. The hairstyles of the girls ranged from long hanging ringlets to green and purple hair dyed to match their dresses, most though had platinum blonde hair.  She also saw boys dressed in similarly colored frock coats and trousers sporting matching top hats or bowlers and cravats. Some of the young men wore solid black suits, and had the hair to match. Caesaris was fascinated by the sight of them, the fashions covered every inch of exposed flesh except for their faces, it was quite different than the revealing Roman fashions being sold in the stores. She realized that this was open rebellion to Roman occupiers. They were exactly who she needed to reach in order to be a successful leader, she thought.  She also found the look intriguing, how such restrictive, formal clothing, could seem so informal and stylish.

As the procession moved its way through the streets of London up Victoria Embankment, over to Northumberland Avenue, around Trafalgar Square, through Admiralty Arch, and down the mall, young people in clothing from a bygone era were everywhere. They stood out against the background of the commonplace people who made up the mass of the crowd. Something else stood out, hundreds of legionnaires, holding SPR's and strategically positioned gilded screamers, making sure no attacks, or protests took place. Caesaris was distressed that the parade was literally for a captive audience, she wanted to be Queen, but there was a melancholy feel to it all. Instead of carriages behind her, as in the past carrying other members of the Royal Family, her father and high ranking Romans were carried in Runners, constantly vigilant, looking for attacks. She could not help but think of the Roman parades which had the sole purpose of displaying Roman might.

The carriage finally arrived at the Buckingham Palace; gone from the gates were the famous coat of arms, although it still remained in the center pediment on the front of the palace. The landmark was synonymous with Brittan, even so, it was neo-classical with it is ionic columns and entablatures; it was like a building that could have been found in Rome, and it felt familiar to Caesaris.

The sea of people gathered outside the gates parted for the carriage to pass through them. The carriage stopped just inside the gates and turned so that the Queen could wave to the crowd. What she saw instead were several giant red banners with yellow block lettering several stories high, being unfurled on buildings in the area near the palace that said The True King Lives ; the crowd let out a collective roar of approval, sending a frenzied wave of exuberance through their midst. A football style chant of " *True King*" emanated from the exuberant crowd. The refrain grew louder and louder as more and more people joined in until it was like a fist, striking the Roman troops over and over again. The display made the Romans visibly nervous, a few legionnaires were pelted with garbage, but they could not see who did it. The roar of the crowd grew and pushed up against the Roman barricades, taunting and pointing at the legionnaires. The crowd became so ecstatic that a centurion ordered the five screamers surrounding the crowd to suppress them, fearing the protest would turn into a riot. They hummed to life and raised their golden faces high above the fray. As quickly as the crowd had become jubilant, with equal swiftness they became terrified, they realized what was happening; revelry subsided and confusion and fear took over. People started rushing to escape, unintentionally trampling over those poor souls who had fallen in the surge of the stampede. Some climbed the Victoria Monument, seeing the giant fountain as their only salvation; the Angel of Justice on top of the pedestal had been replaced with a similar statue of Julia, who seemed to smirk at them. They scampered up in hopes of ascending to the top and rising above the crush of humanity. The wails and cries grew to a crescendo in anticipation of the weapons being used on them. There was a rush to exit back down the mall, but the way was cut off by a by a green wall surrounding the circumference of the roundabout and all three streets were blocked by screamers and fifty legionnaires. The people were trapped, with nowhere to go, their desperation had become palpable.

Queen Caesaris, seeing the panic, and the screamers about to be unleashed on them, threw open the carriage door and sprang to the ground. There was a strange feeling in her, one of greater responsibility than she had ever before known and despite the fact that it was a chaotic situation, there was no other choice for her, she had to act. She walked to the gates, where two Grenadiers were positioned, watching with horror at their fellow citizens being overtaken by panic.

Queen Caesaris came up behind them and yelled at them.

"Open the gates and come with me!" in a voice loud enough to be heard over the roar of the crowd.

The guards spun around not quite sure who had leveled the order. Since the Romans had taken over they were little more than props, part of the scenery. They hesitated for a moment, but looking at the determination in her eyes, they knew that there was no other choice, Julia had never so much as looked at them, and they could sense the new Queen was different. They swung open the famous black wrought iron gates, topped with the Omni-present gold fleur-de-lis and a replica of the Orb at the apex. The Queen calmly, but briskly walked out, followed by the guards, who made their best attempt to remain stoic among the panic, wondering if they might be shot down by the Romans. The people, as they caught sight of Caesaris, were stunned, they stood and watched the Queen stomp forward, undaunted, in a straight line towards the centurion who had ordered the Screamers to attack the crowd. The onlookers grew silent and parted in front of her, not sure why the young Queen from Rome would risk her own life. A wave of silence spread as quickly as the panic had before it. The Queen created a wide birth as she moved forward. She walked directly in front of the Screamer and fixed her eyes on the centurion, who was standing next to it. She stopped a few feet in front of the centurion and spoke to him in a loud voice so that the crowd could hear.

"Shut them down. Today is my day; I will not let you ruin it! Am I perfectly clear?" her voice had an air of authority that surprised even her.

The centurion stared in disbelief for a moment before speaking. "This must be done. This is for your safety."

Queen Caesaris stood still projecting her voice, "Not for my safety. Perhaps the fear you felt, but not for my well being." The crowd now hung on her every word.

The centurion was clearly uncomfortable. "I have orders that must be obeyed. I am sorry."

"I am Queen now," she said stepping forward "and you *will* shut them down. If my position as Queen is not enough, I am sure you are aware of who my father is, *or shall I remind you?*"

"Very well, we shall stand down. My apologies, your majesty." The centurion said backing away, clearly intimidated.

The centurion waved his hand in a downward motion and the screamer pilots retracted the hydraulic arms. Caesaris then turned and walked back the way she came to the palace gates. She walked with a regal air, one she had spent a lifetime acquiring, but now finally able to put into use. Her father had always stated that she would have made an excellent successor, but only a man can be Caesar.

A murmur swept through the crowd; they had witnessed the daughter of Caesar, their new Queen, standing up to the Roman troops. It would not be shown on the BBC evening news or retold in the papers, both of which had become propaganda tools for Rome. It did not matter that it would not be broadcast, thousands had witnessed her stand, and word would spread among the people.

A lone voice somewhere in the crowd shouted "God Save the Queen!" a chant that was sporadically repeated by some among them.

Others were unsure of her motives, but believed she was at least different from Julia. With one singular action, Queen Caesaris had begun to win the trust of her subjects, no matter how small. It was a first step. She walked back to the State Coach Britannia and climbed up, displaying dignity and grace as she did so, and they continued on the path into the palace courtyard. The crowd quickly dispersed, helping the injured as they went, until only a few remained outside the palace gates. Some among them had a feeling they had just witnessed history.

The coronation banquet was waiting for the seven-hundred invited guests, set up by an army of British servants who had previously worked in the palace. The staff was demanded by Queen Caesaris because they were familiar with the inner workings of the palace. Julia had used a staff composed of slaves dressed in sackcloth robes, which were taken from all over Europe and had no knowledge of the palace history or traditions. Watchful Praetorian Guards were posted everywhere food was being prepared for fear of it being poisoned. Cameras in the kitchen were trained on the five star chefs busily preparing the food for the feast.

The banquet was being held in the Palace Ballroom, which would have a Coronation ball held the following night. The room was chosen, due to its colossal size, in total it measured one hundred and twenty feet long by sixty feet wide and forty-five feet from floor to ceiling, more than adequate for the occasion. The red carpet had an endless pattern of dark red squares with lighter red circles contained inside each square. There were six giant crystal chandlers suspended from the ceiling, which impressed Caesaris each time she saw them. Candelabra lamps were located on each side of enormous framed tapestries giving them just the right amount of lighting. The ceiling contained giant gilded plaster moldings shaped like flowers. On the long tables were, gilded dinnerware, and silver gilt plates awaiting the first course of the meal, glasses filled with champagne awaiting the first toast to the new Queen and ornate Rococo center pieces and candelabras of gold depicting the Four Seasons, as well as Neptune, Mercury and Bacchus.

The gathered guests were seated in red velvet chairs, not staring at the work of art that was the banquet table, but buzzing about the Queen's actions outside the palace gates. The room hummed from the din of the gossiping guests. She had always been active in public life in Rome, but never had she displayed such nerve as she did in backing down the centurion and the Screamers. The guests whispered in not-so quiet tones to one and other: What would Caesar's reaction be? He had not entered the room yet and there was speculation that he was presumably with the Queen, lecturing her on what she could and could not do under his rule. All speculation ceased as Queen Caesaris was announced, the guest stood up and the musicians in the gallery broke into *God Save the Queen.* She emerged from the east gallery Lead by the Sword of State, which was being held by a servant. Behind her were her father and Sabrina, Charles and the Dux Britanniarum, Jacopo Severi. The Dux was in full military dress, including a gold chest plate with a depiction of Romulus and Remus. He had stringy black hair that was parted to one side; his face was thin and narrow with deep pockmarks. His eyes were narrow and dark and seemed to be holding his long thin nose in place. His neck seemed too lean for his muscular build, and he walked as if the applause was for him. He had commanded the Legion that conquered Brittan, the act of which earned him the Dux title. He was feared in every corner of England; he had spies everywhere and controlled the people through intimidation. His agents had almost killed King Owen in Germany, but had missed him by moments and killed two of his advisors. He had also been a frequent guest to Julia's chambers and her "parties" at the Brighton Pavilion. The group made their way to the head of the table and stood there awaiting a toast from Caprera. He took his glass from the setting in front of him and held it high.

"To Queen Caesaris, who this day proved she truly is her father's daughter. *Long may she reign!*"

"*Long may she reign!*" the guests repeated raising their glasses.

She looked around at the guests, their faces did not show happiness or anger, but anticipation, awaiting what she was going to do or say next. She looked around the room making eye contact before she finally raised her glass and spoke.

"I feel sorrow at the loss of my aunt, which is how I came into this role, nevertheless I am grateful for the position I now hold. I shall do my best to serve as Queen and improve the quality of life for all Britons. *To Britain!*"

The guest echoed "*To Brittan!*" except for Severi, who considered the throne little more than a symbolic position, used to placate the British people.

After the third course had been served, the Queen and Charles Fletcher circulated the expansive room, speaking with each guest as the musicians played the Four Seasons by Vivaldi, her favorite piece. The servers brought out porcelain plates for pudding, signifying the feast was nearing its end. As they made their way back to their seats, Severi stood up and bowed to Caesaris, taking her hand with a kiss that lasted long enough to make her recoil it in revulsion.

He took a step towards her "I hope we can work closely together your majesty. Let me do the work for you. I can make it easy for you." He gave a smile that betrayed his intent.

Caesaris glanced over at Charles, who nodded his support. "I appreciate your kindness, but I plan on being very involved with the welfare of my subjects."

"I plan on visiting you every day and keeping you abreast of my actions. It is my duty."

Charles, sensing the tension, moved in and gently took the Queen's elbow, guiding her forward, "My apologies, General, we must not neglect our other guests."

The look of insult on Severi's face, and his blazing eyes were enough for Charles to make a mental note of it. He kept an enemies list, and the Dux had just been added. Caesaris took her seat at the head of the table, as a group of bagpipe players, in full Scottish regalia including kilts, came out as the final part of the banquet. Caesaris sat looking across the room examining the familiar faces, and those of the servants. The servants moved and spoke with a melancholy manner that showed they had broken spirits.

"Charles, we must involve more British citizens in the management of their own country. Even if Rome has conquered Great Brittan, we should not be so cruel as to destroy everything they hold dear."

Charles looked at Caesaris in astonishment, it was the first time he had ever heard her use the word conquered to describe the state of England. He had heard her refer to Rome's presence as aiding England, but never more than that.

"Why do you say that?" Charles probed. He looked at her expression and knew she could not speak freely.

"Your Majesty, it would be my distinct pleasure to discuss it with you after the banquet."

The Queen's sitting room was one of the smaller rooms in the palace, but no less impressive. Caesaris had instructed the staff to furnish it with Victorian items. When Julia had possessed the room it was not recognizable as a room in Buckingham Palace, but would have looked to a visitor to it as if it were a temple in honor of Venus. There were no traces of its state under the previous ownership. Caesaris had made an effort to recreate the style of the room when it was owned by Queen Victoria. She had incorporated some art she had rescued from her father, Venetian paintings and sculptures and the painter and sculptor her father hated the most, Michelangelo.

Caprera blamed Michelangelo along with Da Vinci and Botticelli for destroying the image of Roman antiquity, and replacing it with a weaker Christian ideal. Despite the additions the room was distinctly British; there were no traces of Roman influence. In the center of the room hung a brass gas and electric chandler with fleurs-de-lis on the arms made to look like leaves. Three round smoked glass shades were intended originally for gas, and had been altered to allow holographic images of flames in them. A large circular mahogany chess table sat underneath it. The chess pieces were silver and gold, depicting characters from Alice in Wonderland, a book Caesaris loved since she was a child. On the wall opposite the windows was a portrait of the young Victoria, along with a portrait of the young Elizabeth the First. A Mahogany desk was pressed against one wall with a dormant laptop on it. It was a room where Queen Caesaris felt at ease.

Charles, whose eyebrows arched in concentration against his furrowed brow, sat on a floral pattern Victorian parlor sofa deep in concentration. He was listening to Queen Caesaris, who had pulled close a parlor chair that matched the sofa. She leaned in so that they could speak in hushed tones. The rain, cascading against the balcony windows, ensured no laser microphones could be aimed at the room from outside and eavesdrops on the conversation. The sun had just dropped below the horizon, and its glow was faintly visible through the summer rain shower. The rain cast a constantly scrolling amber pattern over the room so that it looked as if slow ripples of water were running over everyone and everything in the room; the effect was almost hypnotic.

"Charles, I have to know," the Queen looked around still afraid her father had the room bugged, and would find out what she was asking, "who is the true king?"

Charles' eyes flashed to the left and then right, scanning the room again before speaking. "That is a good question isn't it?" he leaned in closer and lowered his voice "We think it is Owen Badon, eighth in line for the throne. We now know he was out of the country when the rest of his family met their unfortunate demise."

Caesaris felt a twinge of sadness, remembering how it was when her mother passed away, "Where was he when they died?"

"He is, or was a member of the Special Air Services. They were on a mission in France and that is the last trace we have had of him."

Charles waived his hand in the air indicating they had lost him to the wind. He withheld that at her father's behest, the Tenor had almost assassinated King Owen in Germany. Caesaris sat silent for a moment, absorbing what she had just been told when she leaned in and spoke again.

"He is a soldier? What else do you know about him?"

Charles in turn leaned in again to answer the question, "From the reports I have seen he is exceedingly brave, and equally as virtuous. He is smart enough to disappear well, and equally smart enough to stay hidden. He could be in England as we speak."

Caesaris grasped Charles forearm and spoke in a stronger voice "Is my father trying to kill him?"

Charles looked at her with a long stare that suggested she already knew the answer, "I do not know. I am your father's friend, and I am your friend. But I do not control the whims of Caesar."

Caesaris realized that her responsibilities as queen had begun, even as the celebration of her crowing was still fresh, "Do you think he will try and kill me? King Owen?" The words seemed odd to her having just been coronated Queen of England.

"I don't believe so, besides, any man who looks upon you and is not smitten is blind." Charles said with a devil-may-care grin.

Caesaris changed her expression considering what Charles said, "Well I am afraid General Severi may be too smitten with me."

"That man has the moral proclivity of a love-sick alley cat!" Charles guffawed at the idea.

Caesaris smiled and then her face grew dire; Caesaris looked at Charles with a purposeful gaze and leaned over to whisper to him.

"Even if my father does not acknowledge it, standing on the backs of the British will only drive them to fight against Rome. They are my people now and I will not let Severi brutalize them."

"You are taking on a powerful and dangerous enemy in Severi."

Her expression was unchanged, "I am aware of what I am undertaking."

"Your father will not approve."

"Let me deal with my father."

Charles returned to his jovial disposition "You always do your majesty!"

Charles then leaned in again with the same serious tone as before. "It is the nature of anyone who has not known tyranny to rebel against it. The people, who have only known tyranny, don't reject it when one tyrant replaces another. But the people who have only known freedom, and are force fed tyranny will spit it back into the face of the tyrant."

"You mean my father?" Caesaris looked at Charles, puzzled over the cryptic statement.

Charles gave her a long silent stare before his expression changed again "of course not" he smiled, "Severi is fermenting rebellion."

"The people in the street dressed in those clothes!" Caesaris said remembering the young people, around her own age dressed in the Victorian style garb.

Charles nodded and let out a murmur, signifying his recognition, "Those kids are called Chords, something to do with their clothes. They reject the Roman ideal of beauty by wearing restrictive Victorian and Edwardian style clothing."

"What about the work camps north of London I have heard whispers about?" Caesaris looked at Charles as if he held knowledge of all her father's secrets.

"There are some things that are best left unasked. If you do pursue that question, do so without your father or Severi's knowledge." Charles leveled his most serious gaze at her yet.

Queen Caesaris was unsure of Charles; he seemed to be discouraging her from investigating the rumors, while at the same time telling her how to go about it. He was her most trusted friend growing up, like an older brother; but she was now Queen, and he seemed to her, duplicitous if not manipulative. She wanted his advice, but she was ready to strike out on her own. There were too many questions that needed to be answered, and too much at stake. She decided her first order of business as Queen would be to remove Severi's boot from the neck of England. Her problem, as it presented itself in her conversation with Charles, was whom she could trust.

An idea crystallized in her mind, "Charles, I need a list of former Parliament members who I could add to my staff as advisors. Can you get that for me?"

Charles stood up and bowed, "Your majesty, your wish is my command."

# CHAPTER XVI

William shot up and sat erect emerging from a deep sleep. He spun around to see his brown leather cavalry saddle behind him, relieved to see where he was, which was not in Oklahoma City. William used the saddle's memory foam seat as a pillow and slept on top of his sleeping bag; he despised the sleeping bag, which was hooded, and felt like a death shroud to him; the case was the same with most of the renegades who had worked on a ranch at one time or another. They were instructed to sleep in the bags because the camouflage patterns, and insulation would hide them from the Roman drones. The troops felt their Emerson suits were better at hiding them, and disregarded the order. It also made sleeping with a weapon easier, not having to crawl out of sleeping bag to shoot.

William, Phoebe and Drake had a running contest who could shoot the most drones down. The contest had almost made the issue of being spotted moot. If it were not for the fact shooting a drone down alerted the Romans they were in the area, they could have, as Drake stated "slept in bright orange clothing," and not worry about the constant supply of drones to shoot out of the sky. The Renegades had become so used to the trio shooting down drones; they had found it easier to sleep at night. William was not one of those who could sleep well.

William had been having nightmares about the ditch full of corpses in Oklahoma City, causing him to wake up frequently and had been volunteering for watch duty every night, but that stopped as soon as Roost joined. Roost, who felt he had to do something to prove his worth; to prove he belonged, had been taking on one or two watches every night. William had reluctantly capitulated so that his friend could prove himself to the others, who were skeptical of Roost's value to the unit, just as they had William's. With William's nightmares coming almost every night, he was just glad he had managed to patch together three or four hours of sleep. He had started to feel weary from the lack of sleep, and it had slowed him down. He looked up at the prairie sky and the endless stars above it made him relax; combined with the surroundings, the gentle breeze blowing and the crickets softly chirping were enough for a wave of serenity to wash over him. William had never been one to let his nerves get the better of him, and he did not plan on starting at a time that was crucial he let nothing unnerve him. He laid his head back on the saddle and watched the night sky, he had developed a habit of counting shooting stars while he rested, and if he could not sleep at least he could relax.

The Renegades had been trying to find a way through the heavily fortified front lines without being detected, it was decided that they would have to ride south, turn north, and try to cross the southern front line in Texas and make their way to an unknown destination in New Mexico. The mysterious voice on the number station seemed to know where they were at and would send coordinates located nearby, wherever they were at the time. They were just south of the latest coordinates sent to them. The little ghost town of Toyah, Texas had been abandoned since 2013, but provided what they needed. William felt strange being there; he and Roost had used the town as a hideout more than once when the Law had been bearing down on them. The town had several artesian springs, where the horses could be watered and canteens could be filled. They were outside the old brick high school built in the early 1900's. The two-story building was sturdily built, and despite being deserted for ages, it had held together well. The building had been turned into a gym in the late 1950's deviating from its original purpose. A few years before the Roman invasion, William and Roost had taken on the gargantuan task of fixing the flooring and reattaching the corrugated metal roofing. The roof had been ripped off due to one of the tornados that frequent the area in summer. They had cleaned out mounds of pigeon droppings from the interior and replaced the broken windows. They had hidden several gas generators on the property to provide them with electricity when they needed it. The windows had since been boarded shut making the grand old building seem even sadder.

A set of steps lead to the porch framed by two old wood columns with flaking white paint. Behind the columns were the front doors, which were also boarded with plywood. Above the porch on the brick façade was written in tan molded block letters **19 HIGH SCHOOL 12**, signifying both the year it was built and its designated function. It had once been the center of learning for the whole town, kindergarten through the twelfth grade, but now a reminder of how many towns in the southwest had dried up during the great depression. Toyah had never recovered and was nearly a ghost town for most of its existence, and it had come to a point where it was worthy of the name.

William decided that he would get up and relieve his old friend. Roost was sitting on the worn bottom step resting momentarily; he had been walking around with Drake on patrol and the lack of sleep had started to take its toll. William walked over; the moonlight was bright enough to see without the aid of a flashlight. William looked at Roost's expression, he was fatigued but did his best to hide it'

"Hey there Roost, are you okay?" William said sitting next to him.

"I'm okay," he continued to stare out into the night determined to remain vigilant.

"Are you sure? You look a little haggard there amigo."

Roost ignored the question and instead leaned forward and turned his head to look at the school behind him.

"The old 1912 hideout. You know Will, there is something we should have done when we were repairing this place, we should have fixed the pipes so that we could have running water right now," he said, chuckling.

William nodded "Kind of weird being here with these guys huh?"

"Yes it is Will… yes it is."Roost said with a smile. He rubbed his eyes, trying to stay alert, "You're alive — the Texas Ranger who was chasing us is now riding with us — and we are here with the King of England and his knights. It doesn't get much weirder than that."

"Yeah, I kind of see your point." William chuckled and then looked at his weary friend, "Get some sleep Roost."

"I am fine, why don't you go back to sleep?" Roost said, and then realized the answer before William could speak. "Nightmares again? It has been years since you shot your stepfather, and we both know you didn't want to kill him."

"A nightmare, but a new one, Oklahoma City, it was pretty bad."

"Well at least you're not trying to lose them in a bottle of whisky now." Roost turned his attention back on the horizon, remaining vigilant.

"I don't know, maybe the nightmares are punishment for what I did. Maybe I deserve to be tormented."

"Come on, Will," Roost said turning to William, "neither one of us believes that. I have seen you reading that bible of yours over and over. You're not the same as you used to be when we were robbing. You've changed."

William appreciated Roost's observation; he felt he was not alone in his reformation though, "You have changed, too. You and I were always basically good deep down, but we let the thrill of stealing keep us from realizing that we were hurting real people. But now you're out here trying to prove your worth. I know you didn't go through the training, but you found your way here without a GPS or a map. That is something that no amount of training could produce."

Roost smiled and shook his head; trying to remain humble he changed the subject, "Did you see Drake's face when I told him this was one of our hideouts?"

"I think he was upset because it was so obvious." William laughed.

Roost looked at him with a deadpan expression, "I am surprised the man will talk to you at all. The way you used to taunt him when he was chasing us." he said in an equally flat tone.

"I didn't know he was the one chasing us, besides how did I taunt him?"

Roost looked at William in disbelief, "Come on Will, when we stole the genie to fix this roof, you had us break back in to return it with a picture of yourself with *Thanks for the lift* written on the back."

"Well, maybe a little." William said with a wry, cocky smile

Both William and Roost heard the distinct sound of footsteps approaching. They both sprung to their feet and drew their side arms. They could see the other Renegade assigned watch duty, on his horse about one hundred yards away, but were not sure whose footsteps they were, until a figure appeared in the moonlight. The footsteps belonged to Bulloch, who was awake and had heard William and Roost talking, he had managed to brew a cup of coffee somehow and was sipping it from an insulated cup while reading the field tablet he had been handed by the enigmatic Ice Swan. The faint glow illuminated Bulloch's face. Roost and William slid their guns back into their holsters, relieved that they were not being ambushed, and saluted Bulloch. He had a look of exuberance tempered with concern.

"Colonel?" William said wondering why he approached them in silence. Bulloch looked at the field tablet again and held it up.

"About an hour ago this beeped", he said gently shaking the device in his hand, "there was a message. Apparently General Vernon has taken back Charleston, and inflicted heavy damage on the Romans.

The damage Bulloch had referred to was truly significant. The Romans had invaded Charleston, South Carolina and Wilmington, North Carolina a few weeks after the invasion of the southwest. They used their Mars class submarines to overtake the two cities. The colossal submarines were designed not to launch missiles, but to carry massive numbers of troops and armor. The black subs, over two hundred yards in length targeted the two towns due to the strategic value of their deep water ports. Because their military bases had been shut down during the previous administrations budget cuts, it ensured little to no resistance. The Romans had seized both cities in a matter of hours, and all the towns and coastline in between. There had been no attempt to retake the cities since the invasion, only to create a front they would not cross, a front which the Romans had been slowly pushing back each week. The Romans had become over confident and had dropped some of their defenses in and around Charleston. Stationed at what used to be Charleston Air Force Base was Credential Bond, a mercenary army comprised of Serbian, Venezuelan, South African and Ukrainian soldiers of fortune. The latter made up the majority of the army, as was its leader General Kravchenko, the Dux Americana. The Credential Bond barracks were alongside the Praetorian barracks at the Forward Base Dubbed *Caprera's Spear.* A team of Navy SEALs made their way to the Roman Base through the sewer system; they entered through a pipe that opened onto the Cooper River. The forward base was surrounded by a twenty-foot high, seven-foot thick reinforced concrete walls, adorned with Ionic columns, Doric friezes and pediments. The overall look was as if Rome had sprung up on the banks of the river. The base covered a staggering five thousand acres, a feat that was the trademark of Roman engineers.

The SEAL team cut a hole in the pavement above them then placed inside the wall a combination of C-4 bricks and HMX bricks with delayed timers. They slipped back out the way they came shortly before the plastic explosives detonated. The tunnel collapsed from the explosion, killing two of them, and vaporizing the barracks housing both Credential Bond and Praetorian Guard alike. Seconds after the blast, to the horror of the remaining Romans, two of the Mars subs opened to reveal American Troops and R-1 Petraeus tanks. A joint CIA and Special Forces operation had captured the subs only a few hours before, keeping captured key Roman personnel at their post so that all appeared normal. A battle ensued to re-take Charleston, which Wright's forces did in a matter of three hours.

The Romans sent troops and armor down I-17 from Wilmington, as General Vernon had predicted, to come to the rescue of the Charleston forces. General Kravchenko, in a panic, had ordered swift deployment of the backup. He had not realized that the retaking of Charleston, as great a victory as it seemed was a decoy. The Roman Base in Wilmington, *Caprera's Sword*, was emptied of nearly all its forces in the rescue mission. Ten minutes after the last of the convoy had passed over the Highway Seventeen Bridge; it was detonated behind them, leaving no way back across the Brunswick River. General Vernon had had given the task to General Henry Hardin of finding and placing snipers, former military and present, and inserting them in the forest. Hardin amassed over five thousand snipers from around the country, supplied them with firearms. The snipers, along with Special Forces troops were placed in the forest. Special Forces bombarded the convoy as it sped down the highway, weakening them along the way. By the time they had made half the journey, the armored vehicles were badly damaged. The vehicles began to break down and forced them out on foot. The snipers, who were nearly invisible in their gilly suits, began picking off legionnaires. The casualties were breathtaking, even with their SPR's, the Romans were not able to slow the carnage. The Romans continued their forward push, until they came to a section of the highway that was blocked by felled trees and tractor-trailers. It was at that point, half way between Wilmington and Charleston that it became a bloodbath. Special Forces unloaded all of their missiles seemingly from every direction. People emerged from their homes, with weapons that had been hidden from searching Romans, and joined the massacre. When the shooting stopped over two thousand Legionnaires and Centurions had been slaughtered. Only a handful of Centurions managed to escape. The U.S. forces had only lost twelve soldiers in the entire battle; it was the first major victory since the Romans had invaded. Word of the victory spread quickly to a jubilant nation, and now it had reached the Renegades.

William and Roost stood captivated, listing to the report of the battle being read by Bulloch.

"That's great news, Colonel!" William said slapping Roost on the back.

Bulloch's endless grin faded into a scowl as he looked at William, who had suddenly realized the problem with the transmission to the field tablet, "The signal! The Romans probably detected the signal!" William said snatching the hat off of his head and slapping it against his thigh. Bulloch looked around at the sky wondering if they had already been detected.

"We probably should move at first light." he said as he looked out over the sleeping bags spread out in front of the old school building.

William put his hat back on, and focused his attention on the western horizon, "only one way to go, through the mountains."

Roost knew what William was suggesting and the danger it held, "The Guadalupe Mountains? Make a run straight into New Mexico?" Roost said turning and looking in the same direction.

William pushed up the front of his hat to look around better, "You know how fast they move, Roost, there is no way we will outrun them in the open. We will have to ride through the Delaware Mountains, and then up through the Guadalupe Mountains, we can head to Cassidy's Cave (a hideout named for Cassidy) to regroup." William smiled to himself, it was like old times and he and Roost were together again.

"That is over fifty miles of mountains to get through! We will move at a crawl. How are the Runners supposed to make it through there?" Roost said still reviewing the terrain in his mind.

William was sure it was the way to go and had to convince Bulloch of it, "Why don't we ask Drake?" he said pointing to the Texas Ranger who had finished guard duty and was sleeping propped up against a tree.

"Fine! Let's ask Drake."

"*Drake, hey Drake!*" Booth William and Roost yelled in a loud whisper.

Drake lifted his hat from over his face and looked at them with aggravation "We better be about to get killed." he said not happy to have his slumber interrupted. He stood up and brushed himself off and walked over glaring at William and Roost, he momentarily averted his gaze to salute Bulloch.

"Now what the hell is going on here?"

"Will thinks we need to ride straight through both the Delaware Mountains and the Guadalupe Mountains till we get to New Mexico. The Romans were probably alerted by Bulloch's field tablet receiving a signal. What do you think?"

Drake turned and faced the same direction as William and Roost; as if they all could see the mountains had they been just ten feet away from them. He rubbed the back of the neck as he envisioned the route.

"That's like fifty miles of mountain riding. That's a good way to get killed." Drake said as he looked at the horizon.

Roost quickly turned to William, "See, Drake thinks it's a bad idea too!" He said triumphantly.

"It's a bad idea," Drake quickly interjected, "but trying to fight Roman armor on horseback is a worse one. We have no other choice but to go through those mountains." He said giving Roost a consolatory pat on the back.

Bulloch listened to the arguments and came to a decision that he thought was prudent. "William, get everyone up, we need to come up with a plan and then move out. We are going to ride through the mountains." he said hoping to get a head start on the Romans.

The Renegades were bleary-eyed and stood in a semi-circle around Bulloch, Colonel Colter and King Owen. The trio stood on the top step of the high school entrance, lit by several solar powered lanterns, all eyes focused on them. Colter stepped down one step, squinting as if daylight were shining in his eyes, and addressed them.

"Okay everyone listen up! We have got one hell of a ride ahead of us," he barked in his gruff voice "At o-six hundred hours we are moving out, we have reason to believe the Romans now know our position. We have not received new coordinates where we will rally yet, but it's probably in New Mexico. We are going to enter through a ridge that runs both across the Delaware Mountains and the Guadalupe Mountains. We will have to ride hard not to be caught. Another group of you will be going with the Brits to Dallas as a decoy. The King and a few of the Knights will ride with us. You have one hour to get ready and mount up. Now the King would like to address you."

King Owen stepped forward, his resolve on display as usual. "We face an overwhelming task, to penetrate the Roman's fortified front lines, and then enter into hostile territory where we will have no help. I tell you, the reason we take such a risk, is because the outcome is so important. We must not and cannot fail. My knights and I have seen the devastation that can be inflicted if Rome is left unchallenged. Most of my country has become a vast slave labor camp. Everyone lives in fear they will be snatched from their homes in the dead of the night if they do or say anything against the Romans. My people live in unbroken misery and despair, and this too awaits your county unless we act. You already know that what we do now is a dangerous undertaking. I am proud to fight alongside you, together we will free the states taken by Rome, and then together we will save England."

The weight of what the King said brought nods of agreement and a quiet grunt of approval from the soldiers.

The pre-dawn light cast a sienna glow over Toyah; the town was deserted but still had a lived-in look. The old water tower had been knocked over years earlier by a tornado, but most of the town still stood, some parts dilapidated, and some pristine. A white, two bedroom house with an aluminum roof that sloped down over the front porch, stood as it had since 1910. The only signs of change with the home were the long since outdated satellite dish on the corner of the house and the prickly pear that had over grown the roof and half the length of the porch. There was a small cemetery that was surrounded by a rusted rod Iron fence, that still bore the name of its origin: **The Rogers Iron Company, Springfield Ohio**, and it's patent date: **November 22, 1881**. An old red fire truck was parked, rusting, next to a fire hydrant hidden by weeds, just as it was when the town was abandoned. William and Roost had been captivated by the charm of old prairie town, and it was by far their favorite hideout. The morning had reminded them of the good times, which now seemed to be in the distant past, yet the duo was glad they were working on the right side of the law.

The Renegades were saddling their horses, as were some of the knights, who had exchanged their black body armor for the sand and clay camouflaged Emerson suits, including King Owen. The optics on the suit and the camouflage patterns it produced were highly impressive to King Owen. They came to the conclusion that they would have to break off into two groups; the majority of the knights would act as a decoy, taking the runners and making a dash straight out on I-20 and into Dallas, taking with them the Cavalry members who had become ill, injured or exhausted. The horses and equipment were given to the knights who had riding experience; they would continue on to New Mexico with the Renegades.

The Romans had built a massive base in Taos using it as the staging area to take over the United States. The fortress was given the name of New Pompeii. Caprera had envisioned a city in the vein of its namesake bordering the base. Most of Taos had already been leveled in anticipation of the new construction. It was from there that the invasion of Oklahoma City was mobilized. Taos was the likely destination of the Renegades, although no one could say for sure. The trip in total stretched over four hundred miles, snaking through what would be considered dangerous territory without the presence of the Romans. Drake was sitting on his horse next to William who was leaning forward on his saddle, watching the knights getting into the cavalry gear.

"You know how weird this is for me to be here with you and watching the King of England mounting up?" Drake said pushing the brim of his hat up, a habit he had picked up from William.

"Yeah, I kind of know where you are coming from." William said flashing a smile.

"Where do you think we are headed? Taos?" Drake said looking at the gathering clouds above them.

The smile faded from William's face, "Yeah, I don't know about that, I don't know if we are going to go head on into a massive fortress like that. But I have been wrong before. It's making it through the mountains without being caught that worries me."

Drake smiled with the easy charm that had made him so popular, "Come on West, you and Roost managed to get through there before, so it can be done."

"That was without a war going on," William turned to look behind them at the growing clouds, "and the weather was never like that."

Drake smiled and nodded "I know things are bad, but there is not another bunch of guys," he turned to see Phoebe ride up next to him, "and a girl, that I would rather face the entire Roman army with."

"Come on Drake, you're the only one good enough to give me any real competition with a gun, it ain't you who has to worry, it's the Romans." Phoebe said with a laugh.

Drake and William were amazed after the grueling pace they had been keeping, how Phoebe could remain so perky. Drake glanced over Phoebe's shoulder and saw Bulloch conferring with Meaner Colter, about the course that had been plotted, and Colter with the grimace and squint plastered on his face, it was hard to tell if he was concerned or not. Bulloch was the Reason he was there, and the person he trusted more than anyone.

"Ted Bulloch really is the most honest person I know." Drake said as he watched him.

Phoebe quickly glanced behind her, "In what way?" she said with true interest.

"When he was mayor of White Plains, he had every organized crime kingpin, corrupt politician and fat cat business owner in his office offering money, sometimes with actual cash in a briefcase, and he never took it. It turned into assassination attempts right after he turned all those bribes down, but he never once thought about taking any of it."

Phoebe turned her horse around to face the same direction as Drake, "No wonder so many people he worked with volunteered to ride with him." She said with a new found respect for Bulloch.

William was still looking at the sky, but listening to the conversation, "Well I am glad that he got Drake to join, he saved my hide in the Ocala National Forest. I froze like a frightened bunny when the SuMas attacked; he took down about ten of them in under a minute. Shooting double fisted," William changed his focus to Drake and winked.

"Good looking and ambidextrous to boot!" Phoebe quipped.

The wind began to pick up and William turned back to look at the dark mass growing in distance, lightning illuminated the clouds, revealing the huge cloud tops. He had become adept at judging when weather would turn bad over the years, a skill that was useful in more ways than one. He and Roost had used storms to cover their tracks numerous times and both of them could identify the different types of clouds and what kind of conditions they would bring. William glanced at Roost who was also looking at the storm and then made eye contact and shook his head no, which indicated to William he had the same impression, the storm's nature was going to be violent.

The rain caught up with the riders a few hours after they struck out for the Delaware Mountain Range, and had extended ahead of them the whole sixty miles of the dirt roads they were traveling on, making it a muddy and miserable experience. The rain at times had been blinding, a wall of murky green water came upon them just as they reached the base of the Delaware; visibility dropped to only a few feet and made the treacherous ride even more un-negotiable. The water was black and unseasonably frigid. The wind blew hard and seemed to be howling at them as if its goal was to knock them off the mountains. A flock of crows caught in the wind's teeth were frightened and confused by it; they flew in wild circles, sometimes colliding with one and other. The rain had seemed to come from all directions and made it hard to know if one was still heading in the direction that had been intended. Roost had brought his horse alongside William at one point, and mentioned that he thought a tornado was passing within a mile of them, but they could not see it. William had also quietly made sure that he was never too far from Phoebe, that her horse would not bolt or throw her.

The rain and wind had them all shivering, though it was summer, the temperature was falling at a steady pace. They never stopped to put on rain gear, or try to warm up, the storm had given them an advantage over the Romans, their armor could not follow down such a steep and muddy road, and the drones could not fly in such hostile conditions. The ride had been hard hunger and fatigue was only compounded by the damp and cold, but morale never waned, each was as committed to the cause as ever.

Once the Renegades had made it into the Mountains, they abandoned the main roads, traversing near the top of the mountains, weaving their way through Yucca plants and car-sized orange boulders. The rains finally ebbed a full two hours after they reached the mountains, and twelve hours after they left Toyah. They came to a road, overtaken by weeds and grass, as they climbed higher and moved further into the mountains. It was a narrow trail that ran along the ridge, nearly at the summit, it was an old service road used for maintenance on the wind turbines that had long since been disassembled. The turbines had become obsolete almost immediately when Timothy Emerson invented the perpetual motion turbine. The remnants of the road were lined with juniper and pinon trees. Despite the presence of muhly grass, sandstone colored mud flowed in small streams across the trail. Cattle drives had been undertaken through the Delewares in the past, but they were never done at such a high elevation, or on such a slither of land.

William and Roost rode in front, as they had negotiated the mountains four times in the past, and in fact were the most qualified to lead the way. William noticed a difference from past trips through the mountains; there were no antelope or deer. Previously when William and Roost had gone into the mountains, they encountered herds of antelope, numbering, at William's estimation, over one hundred head. He noticed something else as well, the horses were jittery, even Slingshot, who was the most unflappable horse he had ever seen. William looked back at Morrison, who despite his skill at nearly everything else seemed to be struggling to keep control of his horse, who was clearly spooked. William dropped back and grabbed Morrison's horse by the bridal.

"Hey why don't you come up to the front with us and I can give you some advice on how to control your horse, okay?" William offered.

Normally the idea of anyone trying to tell him he was not good enough would have angered Morrison, and he would have challenged them to a fight, but in this case he subdued his pride and took William up on his offer. The situation they were in did not afford any time for defending ones honor.

"Only if the King comes with us," was the only caveat that Morrison had.

King Owen, overhearing the conversation, looked back at Kenneth, not wanting to leave him alone. The gentle brute smiled.

"Don't worry about me mate, why don't you let them go show you how to ride a pony," Kenneth said to Morrison, but was looking at King Owen, both of them chuckling.

Drake nudged his horse gently and filled the gap between them, "Don't' worry, I won't let him get lonely" he said laughing.

William guided Morrison to the front and positioned him between him and Roost, with the King directly behind them. William was about to start a lecture on the effect ways to control your horse without making it hate you, when he heard a sharp snapping noise that reverberated around them, then a moment later, another distinct snap, followed by the clattering sound of stones skipping down the mountainside, striking other rocks as they went. William turned to ask Drake if he knew what the sound was; at that moment it happened. The ground shifted underneath Drake, Kenneth and two renegades behind them. Drake's and William's eyes locked, they both knew what was happening, but neither one of them could do anything. A second later the ground started to slide at a rapid rate, the horses and riders seemed weightless for a moment, hanging just inches above the crumbling ground. William and Drake held their gaze; a look of resignation to his fate fell across Drakes face. Another second later the whole side of the mountain shifted, rushing downward, swallowing up the horses and riders with it in a wave of debris, boulders and rocks showering down on them. Trees and rocks rushed by until suddenly it stopped, a single pinon tree stood in the spot where Drake and Kenneth had been, as if scenery on a stage had been moved for the next act. Despite the drizzle of the rain that began to fall, a dust cloud billowed up from the canyon below; obscuring the remaining riders view of what had happened. The whole incident had happened so fast, no one could react to save them; it was little comfort to those who witnessed it.

William immediately knew what had taken place, hard rain had saturated the ground, which on the steep hill became too heavy and gave way, creating a craggy grave for the horses and riders below. Landslides were not common in the Delawares, but too much rain in too short a time had made it inevitable. Morrison, seeing what happened dismounted and went searching in his saddlebag for equipment to repel to the floor below. King Owen rode over to him and placed his hand on Morrison's shoulder.

"It's too late for them; there is no way they could have survived that." King Owen said with William nodding in agreement behind him.

"We can't just leave, they could have survived!" Morrison said emphatically as he rummaged through the bag.

"Ken is my oldest and truest friend, but he is gone. We have to keep moving." King Owen said grabbing his arm and pulling him back.

"No!" Morrison said yanking his arm back, "I am going down there to see if anyone is alive!" He said his eyes full of rage.

King Owens's expression hardened, he placed his face inches from Morrison's "Sir Morrison, I order you not to go down! You took an oath to obey my command!" he said in a booming voice.

Morrison stopped, his head hung low, and in what he considered defeat, climbed back in the saddle. He knew King Owen was right, even though he felt like he was abandoning Kenneth, who had carried him on his back in Kansas City, and saved his life.

The Renegades all stayed where they were, frozen in shock at what they had just witnessed, no one spoke a word. They were all prepared to die, but to die in a landslide was not what any of them had envisioned. The suddenness and finality of the event was hard to comprehend. In less than ten seconds, they had lost four lives, not to enemy fire, but to a lumbering, soggy mountainside. A feeling of despair hung in the air at their lost brethren. Colonel Colter's gruff shout broke the silence.

"More could go at any second. I will lead the others on this side back around the mountain. We will meet you at the summit of the next mountain over." his rough voice echoed through the canyon below as he shouted to Bulloch.

It had been hours since the landslide, but the shock over what happened still lingered. Despite the soggy conditions, William had managed to build a campfire by using rocks to elevate it off the ground and built a wall behind it to shield from the wind. They had scavenged for dry kindling, which was an accomplishment at an elevation of over one thousand feet. He welcomed the menial task; it helped to not think about the tragedy he had witnessed. The distraction was short lived; he had finished the job and had time to dwell on earlier events. He sat staring into the fire, as did Phoebe, Roost and King Owen. They listened to the hissing and popping of the damp wood, and watched the ambers float off into the night like fireflies. Normally the Renegades had avoided starting campfires, as not to signal Roman drones where they were. But in this case, everyone was cold and the fire acted as a beacon for the other renegades who were trying to find a way around the mountain in the dark. Under any other circumstances, the whole scene would have been considered breathtaking, the red glow in the west fading and giving way to the ascending stars. Bulloch stood with a pair of night vision binoculars, scanning the mountain where they had been for any sign of the riders approaching, and seeing none. Morrison stood at the edge of a steep cliff, staring back towards the area where the landslide had taken place. Although he could see nothing in the darkness, he watched and listened for a sign, as if perhaps someone had survived and would call out for help or come stumbling out of the darkness, but no one did.

William punched at the controls to his suit, trying to reverse the cooling coils and turn on the heat, which was drawn from the wearer's body heat, and amplified. William stopped what he was doing long enough to see King Owen staring into space.

"I am sorry, Owen," he said looking over at the King, who had literally lost his best and oldest friend, "I know it must be hard."

The King's gaze was fixed on the fire and never looked at William, "You never get used to losing loved ones. No matter how many times, the sorrow still finds you," he said flatly.

William could see the agony in the face of King Owen, "Dad always said that it is hard when we lose someone, but when we get to Heaven, we will all laugh at how silly it was."

Phoebe smiled and nodded, "My grandma used to tell me the same thing," she gave a gentle smile "it is hard to remember that in moments like this one."

King Owen forced a smile at the efforts to comfort him, "It is something I will try and remember", he was still visibly shaken, but he fought showing it; he was King and if he were to break down, his knights surely would lose confidence in him.

Walt came over and sat with the rest of them, an unusual action, since he usually spent every spare moment he had working out, or reading about military strategy. He took off his hat and looked around at the faces staring back at him.

"I know that you are upset over the loss of our friends. It is a damn shame they died the way they did, if you are going to die, it is better to do it in battle and not something that seems so meaningless. The way we honor them is by completing the mission they were on; we kick the Roman's asses off the continent. I am proud to be doing that with this bunch. I have not heard a complaint out of anyone, not even when we lose someone, which is something you don't find every day."

Walt then stood up and patted William on the shoulder, "Seems like a good time to check the airwaves for our latest orders while we are on top of a mountain" and then he walked off into the darkness. The rest of the group sat speechless, but agreed with what Walt said.

Bulloch turned and shouted "They're back!"

The rest of the Arizona and Utah Company had made it safely around the other side of the mountain. In the meantime, William had pulled his radio out and was trying to find the right frequency, but what was running through his mind was Drake. The radio reminded him of training in the Ocala National Forest with Drake. He had become good friends with him, closer than anyone else while he was training. William tried, but could not escape the look in Drakes eyes before he died, like Oklahoma City, it would stay with him the rest of his life.

# CHAPTER XVII

The Coliseum had stood for over a thousand years, falling into disrepair in the Middle Ages, serving Rome in various states, primarily as a quarry after a major earthquake in 1349. It had been preserved by the Catholic Church after hundreds of years of steady decay, a place where martyrs had met their end, a place where the young religion had begun to spread. Its next purpose was to serve as a tourist destination for decade after decade. It was visited millions of times by those who tried to imagine what it must have been like in its heyday. Since his childhood, Caprera saw it as a sad reminder of the glory that once was Rome. The marble peeled away from the exterior leaving exposed bricks and black stains, like a discarded half-eaten piece of fruit rotting in the center of the city. It was a disgrace that he vowed to himself one day he would right. Ever since that day he had dreamed of seeing it restored to what it was intended to be, the centerpiece of the Roman Empire.

When Caprera first came to power, restoring the Coliseum was his first priority. He and Charles Fletcher had devised a plan to resurrect the Coliseum and the Forum, which would help provide jobs to the twenty percent of the population that had been unemployed. Funds plundered from conquered enemies and tributes from neighbors paid for the projects. Extensive geological searches were undertaken to find new quarries to mine the massive amounts of marble required for the restoration. In a few years, not only had the Coliseum been restored, an entire new level was added, along with giant holo-def screens and holophonic sound system. New padded seats were installed with both heat and cooling coils. Despite the updated amenities, the exterior appeared exactly as it was in the structures prime, with the exception of an additional level. Statues of mythological figures were sculpted with as much delicacy and detail as their predecessors during antiquity were, and placed in the arches that wrapped around the façade, as it was in the past. Instead of retractable canvas banners projecting from the roof to provide shade and shelter from the elements, it had giant marble slabs that slid in and out like the iris of a camera, widening and contracting based on the weather. It was a stunning display of engineering and design that was harbinger that Rome would, as it had in ancient times, return to its role as the most powerful country in the world. When it was dedicated, Caprera led a parade of children who were crippled by the war with the Vasekts and those who had lost their parents to the conflict. They gathered in the center of the arena, which was a touching display to all who witnessed it. He told them their sacrifice had allowed Rome to be reborn and that they would always be taken care of by the Empire.

As it was when it was reopened, the arena was the center of attention. Caprera's Imperial Box, like the restored Coliseum, was as modern as it was dedicated to the ideal of classical Roman design. The whole unit was open air, but was still climate controlled. Banners of crimson and gold bore SPRQ, written vertically on them and adorned both sides of the box. Seated in the center were Caprera and Sabrina on thrones carved from marble, with complex carvings depicting floral and wildlife designs. An eagle, with wings spread adorned the top of each throne, one looking at the other. Heavily padded red leather seats made them much more comfortable than their hard exterior appeared. A row of female slaves stood at the back of the box, clad in small white tunics and sandals. The slaves brought food and drink and tended to every need. Sabrina had five slaves in total, including a pair of twin red haired ten-year-old girls taken from England. The twins were her *Shoe Girls*, there to take off her sandals when she sat and put them on when she was ready to stand. They were quiet, and dare not speak, keeping their eyes cast downward for fear of being punished by their mistress. Sabrina wore a flowing white halter top and long black skirt designed to look like a toga her bare midriff separated the two. Caprera was dressed in his General's uniform, which he preferred to the ancient robes worn by past emperors. Directly behind him was a Praetorian who bore his standard, also topped with an eagle that matched those on the throne.

Caprera felt that battle was the most honorable way a man could prove his worth. Combat, he conjectured, brought forth the truest form of one's self. Only when faced with death or injury, did you truly know what your limits are. He sanctioned hand-to-hand combat matches, which were a reflection of his unflinching philosophy. The combatants were from a variety of fields and backgrounds. Slaves, who wished to be free before they had paid their debt, or were prisoners of war, were given a chance to fight. Professional athletes, soldiers and even ordinary citizens were also given the chance to face combat in the arena. The only stipulation was the combatant must have minimum qualifications to fight. Martial arts, athletic build, or combat experience was each in its own right acceptable criteria. Combatants were paid a fortune to fight, they lived in a palace constructed for them and were given slave girls to do their bidding. The rewards were great because the risk was equally as great, it was commonplace for a combatant to be killed or crippled in a match; there were no rules, except one: there were no draws. The combatant who reached one-hundred victories was given a position in the government with a high salary, usually as a propaganda tool appearing in public service announcements and dedications of restored buildings. The gamble for the contestants was that each match was drawn at random; none of the combatants knew who they would fight before the match. With such chaos, a two hundred fifty pound, six foot five inch former wrestler could draw a one hundred fifty pound former praetorian guard. The crowds had grown to love the taste of blood; they descended into a frenzy when they sensed a combatant was about to meet their demise. Romans had embraced Caprera's philosophy that it was better to die in a struggle, than live in weakness, suicides among the sick and elderly had grown more frequent. The brutality of the coliseum had become the embodiment of the new Roman philosophy.

Charles Fletcher, wearing a grey toga-suit, which he deemed appropriate since he had returned from England; he had jokingly told Caesaris once *When in Rome* with regards to his attire. He entered the imperial box and stepped between the two thrones, leaning over he spoke to Caprera.

"All is taken care of in London. I helped Caesaris find advisors she believes hold the same philosophy she does. Even though they are British, they are loyal to Caesar." Charles whispered.

"Charles, as usual you have positioned everything perfectly. However, we need to discuss our setback in the United States, but now is not the time." Caprera said without removing his gaze from the brutal contest. Charles nodded, "Caesar" he said respectfully as he backed away.

"Good to have you back, Charles" Sabrina said with a suggestive smile.

"Thank you Empress." he nodded in acknowledgement.

Charles walked across the marble floor to an expansive red velvet Lectus that was on the far left side of the box. He peered out into the sunshine at the two combatants; one, a lanky dark haired man with a pinched face, who lay prostrate in the sand, bloodied and blinking at the sky above, the chiseled military specimen above him moving in to inflict more damage.

Charles then glanced back at the throne platform, moving towards him was Raphaella, Sabrina's best friend and constant companion. There were whispers reverberating around Rome that she and Sabrina were more than just friends, and that the relationship extended to the Emperor. Her career had begun at the same time Sabrina's had in the modeling world, but her true talent was as an actress. Her hair, black and slightly wavy, fell to just below her cheeks and framed her oval face and olive skin. Her mahogany eyes were partially obscured by long thick eyelashes which were set below her round eyebrows that were slightly arched. Her nose was wide, but perfectly shaped and complemented her full lips. Her figure was the type that must have inspired the Roman Artists who sculpted Venus, Charles thought. She wore a white halter top with a long black skirt, matching the one that Sabrina wore. Raphaella glided to the edge of the Imperial Box and leaned over the side looking out over the sea of adoring fans, allowing them to catch a glimpse of her. She then sashayed over and sat down next to Charles and with a slight tilt of her head gave him a knowing smile, as if his secrets were open to her. Charles, never at a loss for words, turned to her.

"Raphaella isn't it?"

He was perfectly aware of who she was, as was everyone else. She was one of the most famous women in the world, having achieved acclaim as an actress. She was perhaps the most popular actress in the world; her acting ability was not overshadowed by her appearance. In fact Raphaella's films were still popular in the United States, despite Roman aggression. She had split time between Los Angeles and Rome prior to the invasion of America.

Charles again smiled at her, "If I ever do a production of Othello again you would be absolutely perfect for the part of Desdemona, you wouldn't disappoint me now would you?" he said with the ease and charm that made him such a magnetic presence.

"Charles," She purred, "I have recently heard things about you." she slightly raised one eyebrow.

Charles gave his best surprised look, "Really? What sort of things have you heard? If it's good it's all true, if it's bad it's probably true, but I will tell you they are scandalous lies."

Raphaella slipped her feet out of her shoes and swung her legs onto the couch and stretched them behind her placing her arm on its top, putting herself on display for all to see.

"They are all good. I would like to find out more for myself," she said, lightly patting his arm.

Charles looked across the box at Caprera's cousin, chief protector and Raphaella's current suitor, Marco Napolitano, who was keenly aware of the conversation taking place between the two. Charles shifted his weight so that he was leaning away from Raphaella.

She ignored his retreat and moved in closer, "Marco is not my Keeper" she said, laughing.

"That may be true," Charles said with a smile, "but he may keep me somewhere if you don't sit back a little." he said in a placid tone.

Raphaella glanced over at Marco and made sure he saw her, then slid closer to Charles, "You aren't afraid of him are you?"

"In a word my dear, yes. He could quite easily kill me, and I am afraid I would not be much of a challenge. I am not a fighter." Charles said cautiously glancing at Marco.

"If you aren't good at fighting, what are you good at Charles?" Raphaella said continuing to flirt and inflame Marco.

Raphaella looked over at Sabrina who was looking back at them and smiled, "I am glad you helped Caesaris", she said with sincerity to Charles.

"Why is that?"

"I think she is sweet, and Sabrina is jealous of her and treated her terribly. I love Sabrina, but it was wrong how she made Caesaris miserable," she said, looking away from Sabrina.

"Really? Is she aware of how you feel? I understand you two are very close."

"No", she said with a melancholy tone, "that is one thing that I don't dare tell her".

Charles raised his eyebrows "Why is it you feel you can tell me?"

"You have an honest face"

"My dear, you flatter me, you're hopelessly misguided, but you still flatter me." He said chuckling.

Charles and Raphaella both stopped talking when they saw Caprera rise up from his seat. At the end of each contest, he made a statement, or had some sort of demonstration. The demonstration that was about to be held was one the bloodthirsty crowd loved. It was known as *Judgment*, Caprera brought out three prisoners, usually escaped slaves, who had committed heinous crimes and would offer mercy or execute them, and the latter was the more frequent outcome. The crowd was stunned into silence when three young prisoners were marched out in sackcloth uniforms, followed by two praetorians who had their weapons trained on them. A nervousness could be felt from the crowd as they watched them take their places. The prisoners were two seventeen-year-old boys and a fourteen year old. The two seventeen year olds had beaten a four-year-old boy to death by repeatedly punching and kicking him. The pair had been arrested multiple times before for offenses ranging from car theft to battery. They looked much older than their age, they both wore the popular short Roman haircut, they were both over six feet tall and had sturdy frames with broad shoulders, their faces were defiant and angry; their eyes were fixed on Caprera and full of rage. The fourteen year old was on a similar path, car theft, assault, and shoplifting. In contrast to his two fellow prisoners he looked much younger than his age his hair longish and messy. He looked as if he had been living meal to meal, appearing to be a wisp of a boy. It was his boyish appearance that was so shocking to the crowd; he looked as if he should be frolicking on a playground, not taking part in Judgment.

Caprera walked out of the shadows of the Imperial Box into the light, the mid-day sun burning above. He descended down a set of marble steps from the box to a platform just above the field. His gold chest-plate shimmered in the Mediterranean sun, casting its reflection around the Coliseum. The crowd still sat silent, waiting for Caesar to speak. A microphone was embedded in the chest plate, and was activated remotely by a soundboard operator in an unseen control booth. He stepped forward; his piercing eyes locked with the prisoner's eyes and caused an involuntary shudder to run through them. Caprera then lifted his eyes up and looked around the arena as if to make sure everyone was paying attention. After a few moments taken for calculated dramatic effect, he spoke.

"Honor is a simple concept. Yet we find that there are some who do not have the capacity to grasp honor, some are so selfish they take and never produce. They will never know the joy of a triumphal ceremony; they don't realize there is no honor in the things that are the coward's path. There is no honor in preying on a helpless child who, for all we know, could have grown up to be great among Romans, what was stolen from you, the Roman people, we will never know! There is no honor in taking something you have not toiled to earn. It is this lack of ability to contribute to the greatness of Rome" Caprera waved his arm in a sweeping motion toward the crowd, and then turned again to the three wide-eyed, ashen prisoners. "It is this choice to dishonor us all that is the true crime." He then slammed his fist down on the Balustrade in front of him and growled "A young mother has wept night after night for her son, taken by those who have not chosen to sculpt a statue, or fight for the glory of Rome, or plant crops to feed us!" He pointed at them as he looked at the faces around the Coliseum, "They have chosen to be takers, those who do not produce; the lowest of society. Slavery is not an option for them; they would only steal from or even *kill* their masters. What is to be done with them then? What punishment is there that would change them, and purge them of the cowardice and greed that has rotted their soul? There is only one punishment that will cleanse them, *death*!"

With the emphasis on the word, he drew his gold plated nine millimeter recoil out so quick no one seemed to realize what was happening, and fired one shot each into the forehead of both seventeen year olds with blinding speed, the report from each shot reverberated around the marble walls in turn. They slumped over and fell, one on top of the other. He fired another shot, what seemed less than a second later, at the feet of the fourteen year old boy. The boy shook, his eyes filled with tears. He looked up at Caprera as he panted, and his spindly legs struggled to hold him up. Caprera, in contrast to how he drew the pistol, slowly returned it to his holster, his eyes never breaking contact with the boy. He then spoke directly to him.

"I have spared your life. You are young enough to learn honor, and in time, you may become one of Rome's greatest citizens. Honor young man, is not just a word, it is a way of life. I will free you so that you may bring honor to us. One warning though, should you decide that you still want to take the coward's path. You will return here, with your parents, and you all will share the fate of the two that lie at your feet. Now go, return home and live with your loved ones and stop scrounging like a dog in the streets, there is no honor in it."

Caprera turned and began ascending the steps, at the same time the crowd erupted into a roar of approval. He turned back and raised his hand in a wave of acknowledgement. He scanned the crowd, focusing on each individual as he did. Their faces shined with adoration for him; people who in the not too distant past had called themselves Italians, now called themselves Romans adopting his vision of the new empire. They were willing to follow the Emperor anywhere; he had delivered them from their darkest days into a new era. Their gratitude had made him the most powerful man in the world. He had rid his mind for the moment of the lingering thought that there had been numerous assassination attempts on his life, for the moment there was only his glory.

Sabrina had averted her eyes from it all, not wishing to see the carnage. Charles had noticed her reaction, and that of Raphaella, who seemed shocked and delighted at the same time, although she did her best to hide the latter.

Raphaella feigned horror, and turned her head.

"It is so brutal!" she said with emphasized distain. "Yes my dear, it is brutal, but it is Cracker Jack at keeping the crime rate down." Charles said with a devious smirk.

The crowd continued to chant Caprera's name, but he was about to undertake a meeting that would change his mood.

In the Basilica Caprera, the Emperor sat in front of the holo-def conference screen, SPRQ hovered in front of him as he waited for the uplink to connect. He sat in the marble throne constructed specifically for the room. The White House had agreed to a brief holo-conference between the two leaders. Suddenly the image changed on the screen. Before him was the image of the President of the United States leaning against his desk in the Oval Office. President Braintree was a short, balding, bespectacled and contentious man. He would not have been considered handsome by even the most lax standards, but what he possessed was a superior intellect and a brash charisma. He brimmed with self confidence, so much so that Caprera could feel it through the satellite link. Braintree chuckled heartily at the sight of Caprera.

"Loose something Giovanni?" the reference was clearly to the recent U.S. military victories over Rome.

Braintree's swagger was so infectious that the Emperor could hear the presidential aides laughing in the background at the remark. Caprera, stung by the barb, struggled to maintain an outward appearance of serenity. His voice was low and monotone as he spoke.

"Mr. President, I am here to offer you a chance at peace. If you surrender, we will allow you to stay in office, and to work with Rome. If you think about it, we are not so different. Your government was based on Roman law, your architecture in Washington is based on Roman design; clearly we have much in common. It will be in the best interest of your people."

Braintree stood with his arms crossed his tie loosened and his sleeves rolled up. He strutted around to the front of his desk and again smirked at Caprera.

"First of all, they aren't my people. I was elected by them to get our Roman houseguest out. Second thing, no one in this administration is going to lick your sandals like my predecessor did." President Braintree's demeanor continued to exude boundless confidence; "Now I have a counter proposal for you sir. If you pull all of your troops out, return all of the prisoners you have taken, and release England; then we won't come after you."

He said further infuriating Caprera. The Emperor sat still for a moment, he did not want to reveal his indignation; it would be a sign of weakness. He began to laugh softly to himself before finally looking into the screen.

"You think you stand a chance against us, against the full power of Rome?"

Braintree cocked his head and leaned forward towards the camera, "Yes sir, I do, and I think you do too. We are the United States of America, and what you have in a long history of Imperial domination, we have in America being not just a place, but an idea. We are the Constitution and the Declaration of Independence. We are schoolchildren dreaming of what they can be in a limitless society. We are baseball in the spring and football in the autumn. We are high school proms and Thanksgiving Day parades. We are the country that survived the great depression, won World War Two and was the first to put a man on the moon. You are smart, Giovanni," the constant use of his first name by the President tried Caprera's patience, but he continued to sit idle "you have to know this is not going to end well for you if this continues. We are going to defeat you, as a matter of fact, when we take Rome, I am going to have the Third Infantry Drum and Fife Corps play Yankee Doodle on the steps of your bunker! Now sir, if there is nothing else constructive you want to offer, I have to return to the business of dismantling your empire." With that the screen went blank, and Caprera went into a rage.

He flung a gold basin at the screen, shattering it. He turned to Charles his face red and his nostrils flaring, his eyebrows and mouth both flattened in the same line, he swayed forward slightly with each beat of his pulse. He spoke with quick shaky breaths.

"We must crush them. We must mount a new offensive and take the center of the country, and then we will see if that puny toad laughs when there are not enough coffins to bury his soldiers! I must speak to Kravchenko now!" He emphasized the last word by slamming his clinched fist into the arm of the throne. Charles remained calm and spoke in a low, soft voice.

"I am sure that President Braintree does not know the wrath he is about to incur. I will have a new screen brought in and let General Kravchenko know you would like a word with him."

Hours after the ill-fated conference between Caprera and the President, Charles sat in his usual place in Aqueduct, the premier nightclub in Rome. Only the elite of the Empire were admitted into the club. Its very existence was a propaganda tool to help glorify Rome; the press was frequently given access to the club to disseminate glamorous images from inside to the world at large. Aqueduct was a spectacle of colossal proportions. Housed in what used to be the French Embassy in the Palazzo Farnes, a high renaissance building that was allowed to remain thanks to the fresco's of Annibale Carracci, which depicted the *Loves of the Gods*. The pagan images fit in nicely with the Emperors philosophy. The gallery was one of the few rooms that was untouched, except for a few couches and air scrubbers; the room was the same as it had been for centuries. The maze behind the building was nearly the same, but the hedges had been allowed to grow larger to hide the unchaste activity that frequently took place there. The rest of the building was another story altogether. The map room, which contained giant frescos of world maps, was the best example of the change; in its center was a faux marble stage, raised by four hydraulic lifts disguised as ionic columns. Four slave girls, painted white, wore white wigs and white contact lenses, to give them the appearance of a marble sculpture. They were forced to dance six hours a night, every night. Holographic torch lamps lit the dark corners, in which were tucked private tables. The tables were black, surrounded by white velvet chairs. It was at one of these tables that Charles sat, tucked in the corner. He was anxious to be away from Caprera since he was humiliated in his holo conference with the President. He had a bottle of scotch in front of him and a porterhouse steak, a chef was kept on staff just for Charles late night meals. He looked out at the toga clad revelers dancing under the holo-beam lights, as he watched them; he was surprised to see Sabrina and Raphaella dancing with each other in the middle of the crush. He chuckled as he realized that apparently he was not the only one avoiding Caesar's wrath. The duo spotted him and smiled and each gave him a small wave. The pounding music was almost hypnotic, and Charles found himself deep in thought, he was so engrossed that he did not notice anyone moving towards him.

A long sleek figure dressed in black Toga approached Charles's table, two Praetorian Guards tasked with ensuring Charles's safety moved forward to block the approach. Charles glanced up at the woman, her jet black hair worn up and her dark amber eyes glistening in the half light.

Charles motioned his protectors back with a motion of his hand, "Don't worry gentlemen, if she is an assassin, this might just be worth dying for." he said intrigued by the alluring visitor.

She eased herself in front of him taking a seat, and spoke to Charles directly: "I want to be your chief advisor." the matter of fact tone was bold and demanding.

Charles lit a cigar and gave her a skeptical look. "That is a little forward. Don't you think dear, that you ought to introduce yourself before making demands?" he said shaking the wood match out that he had just lit.

She gave sly expression to him, "My name is Camille Swan." She said leaning in closer to Charles, "I have a certain skill-sets that you may find to your interest."

Charles smiled and spoke in a condescending tone, "And what makes you believe that I would be interested in having you as an advisor, aside from your lovely appearance?"

She put her finger on her lips and cast her eyes toward the ceiling as if she was trying to find a reason, "Hmmm. Because I worked on the Variable Specific Impulse Magnetoplasma Canon", a smile that could only be interpreted as self assured spread across her lips.

Her posture conveyed that she had something she knew Charles was desperate to obtain. Rome had been racing to beat the U.S. to the development of a VASMIC, the plasma canon and any advantage was crucial to their winning the arms race. Charles had stopped laughing off her claims and stared at her face, looking for evidence of her honesty.

"Is this of the 1934 teleforce variety?" he said probing to see if she knew of the weapons origins.

Swan's eyes narrowed as she leaned further forward across the table, "Yes, and I saw a working model, a successful full working model." she said in a hushed voice followed by another knowing smile.

"You worked on VASMIC? Are you a physicist?" Charles said with great interest, leaning forward, his tone having grown serious.

Swan eased back into the couch and outstretched her arms along the top of it "Among other things." She said with a confident tone of voice that Charles knew hinted at a background in espionage.

He raised his eyebrows and scanned her with his eyes, "I can venture to guess the sort of things. Who are you? You speak perfect Italian, no trace of a foreign accent, but if you worked on VASMIC you spent time in the U.S. working in a D.A.R.P.A facility. You can't be Roman, we would have known if someone in this country were working for the U.S. government. Judging by your appearance you are in your early to mid twenties, so you must have been recruited by some intelligence agency for the skill-set you have not yet told me about." Charles' deductive reasoning was more than sound; his genius was effortless, taking Swan somewhat by surprise.

She gathered herself, her demeanor never showed any cracks, if she was not an agent in the field, her abilities would have made her a great actress. The fact of the matter was that Ice Swan loved the danger and the games, she knew the risks, and she also knew details about everyone she came into contact with. She also knew that Charles Fletcher's weaknesses were his vanity, and the female of the species. She reached over and touched his arm and spoke to him in English,

"Let's say I have spent time in the U.S. but was born in Spain. Does that work for you?" her voice was smooth as she gazed into his eyes.

Charles chuckled, "I think that is a good arrangement. I would like to discuss this further with you in private."

Swan held up her finger and wagged it, "I don't kiss on the first date."

Charles was amused by the gesture, "I assure you Miss Swan, I have no intentions of pursuing my prurient interest," Charles looked over at Sabrina and Raphaella, "at the moment." His expression unexpectedly changed to a stern scowl, "You come here, and ask me to give you a job, which is fine; you can't be working for the CIA, Mossad or MI6 being so forward. I will bring you aboard, you will report to me and tell no one anything about who you are, not even the Emperor. As far as they will be concerned you are a secretary. You will report to my office tomorrow morning at 6:00 A.M., and Ms. Swan, please dress less conspicuously."

Swan nodded and smiled, "I guarantee you will be pleased." She stood up to walk away when Charles stopped her by grabbing her wrist.

"In the event I am not pleased, I will wring the life out of your lovely throat with my own hands; I will have your remains incinerated at such a high temperature that your DNA will be destroyed. It will be as if you never existed, but let's not think about such unpleasant things." Charles' charm resurfaced as he released her from his grasp, "You must stay here as my guest, it will not do well for my reputation if everyone sees such an attractive young lady leave without me."

Swan withdrew her arm, trying to resist the alarm she felt, "If you insist." She said with a warm and genuine smile that was in reality, neither. She looked around the room at the slaves tending to their owner's needs, "Where are your slaves, Charles?"

Charles gave an amused smile "I value my solitude too much for slaves."

"I wonder why that is?" Swan said goading him.

Charles laughed, "My dear, it is my sincere hope that you will find out one day."

# CHAPTER XVIII

**B**oth colonels Coulter and Bulloch stood in the clear morning air, listening to Walt explain how they were going to evade the Roman forces that were undoubtedly bearing down on them. The field tablet Bulloch was carrying had received a message from Ice Swan, forwarded from the pentagon, instructing them what was to be their next target. They had managed to make it into New Mexico undetected before the message was received. The eerie voice on the number station had chanted out a code through the static and high pitched whines, to their next set of coordinates once they had penetrated the state, and then no more instructions had come. It had been days since they reached those coordinates, and the last transmission. The lack of orders had had left them moving around the same area south east of Santa Fe. Some had begun to wonder out loud if they had been abandoned. The message from Ice Swan was a relief, and had been a boost to morale.

The renegades were anxious to engage the Romans; after all, the collective logic ran it was why they had been brought to New Mexico, in order to wage a guerrilla campaign. They had made camp overnight along an ox-bow on the Pecos River which was swollen over its banks due to the monsoons that had had soaked the area. It was a good location to make camp, but now it had to be evacuated because the Romans had surely detected the message being transmitted, even if it they had not deciphered it.

William and Roost sat on a pine tree that had fallen, the saturated ground unable to support its roots. They both ate their breakfast sitting on the rough bark. They took in the scene unfolding in front of them with amusement. When William and Roost had pulled cons to set up a heist, they liked to pick a personality out of the crowd and study it, and try and decipher what that person was thinking through their gestures and expressions. They were once again engaged in the practice, except this time plying their trade on the Renegades. Phoebe soon noticed the duo chuckling to themselves beneath their breath, like a pair of schoolboys whispering something about their teacher and trying not to be caught. She quietly moved up behind them and it became immediately apparent why they were amused. She could see Walt's animated description of his plan, waving his arm in wide swings demonstrating where the Renegades would move to and from while attacking the Romans. They were just out of earshot of the conversation, but would occasionally hear Coulter and Walt growling at each other in the more heated moments. It reminded William of his youth working at a ranch in Wyoming, and a particular incident. He encountered two badgers fighting over a female growling in a similar manner as Walt and Coulter. William, Roost and Phoebe enjoyed the whole scene even though they were in the teeth of the Roman territory. What made it even harder to resist laughing was Bulloch repeatedly stamping his left foot on the ground in an attempt to warm it up. The Emerson Suits had one major flaw, no heating element in the boots, which Bulloch was keenly aware of. He circled around Walt and Coulter stamping his foot and then looking up to see if anyone had noticed.

Moments later their focus shifted to King Owen, who had finished his morning swim and was walking towards them. Roost looked at him with bewilderment, how could anyone swim in the cool temperatures they were feeling, especially when it was in the frigid water of the Pecos River. He shook his head at the sight of the dripping wet King "Pardon me your majesty," he said in a tone that deliberately sarcastic tone "but isn't a little chilly for swimming?" King Owen stood there not yet having put his shirt on and gave small smile.

"Roost, I am from England, this *is* the kind of weather we swim in. Notwithstanding, it would be bad for a king to forgo bathing and have a tarnished image," he said with wide smile.

King Owen had grown closer to both Roost and William, and it had helped ease the loss of his oldest friend, but he had become accustomed to loosing those he cared about and would not let it hinder him. He noticed the presence of Phoebe and quickly put his shirt on, old fashioned in his demeanor he felt obligated to apologize.

"Forgive me Phoebe; I did not see you standing there."

Phoebe smiled with the bright warm smile that made her so popular.

"Don't worry about it your majesty, I am used to seeing this bunch of riffraff half naked, or completely naked, besides it's not like you're hard on the eyes."

William and Roost were surprised that the comment actually had caused him to blush. King Owen had grown to admire Phoebe, her constant positive attitude, even in the face of tragedy; she was without a doubt the best shot he had ever seen. He also marveled at someone as tiny as she was could be so dangerous, when it came right down to it and the circumstances demanded it, she could be a cold unfeeling killer, never hesitating to dispatch her enemy. She was always at the ready, never keeping her rifle too far away and keeping two nine millimeter recoil pistols holstered on her hips, handles facing out. He had seen her shoot down a Roman drone in darkness, without night vision, using the canopy of stars in the night sky to detect it. The shot was the most amazing he had ever seen from anyone. His main thought, was to get her to return to England with him as a Knight. She was the only one he could think of that could take Kenneth's place. With his friend's death he had no one left in the world who knew him since he was a boy. He was also preoccupied with the new queen who had been placed on the throne. He had heard the accounts of her coronation over the short wave radio William was carrying. It seemed from all indications she would be different than Julia was, and that she seemed to be loosening Rome's grip on his people. It could be a deception though, as the forced labor camps still existed north of London. Nevertheless he was intrigued by the account given on Voice of America telling of her stand against the Romans outside Buckingham Palace. King Owens's train of thought was interrupted by the sound of Walt's voice barking at them.

"You three are with me." He stood there for a moment glaring at them

"Well, where the hell is the salute!"

The trio quickly stood and saluted. Walt turned his tirade to King Owen.

"Well do you mind being used as bait, maybe that scares you, or maybe you have you forgotten what it is to be a real soldier?"

The words were biting and disrespectful, but Walt had little regard for what he considered a ceremonial figurehead position. King Owen stepped forward standing face to face and stared down at the slightly smaller Walt.

"I am not afraid to be a target, and if you were not needed, I would bloody you with my bare hands so that you would have no doubt I know what it means to be a soldier!"

Walt laughed out loud and gave King Owen a slap on the shoulder, "That's the spirit. We aren't going to let them know you are with us right now, but soon. Now if you're ready, let's go give them a taste of death and destruction!"

Bulloch, who was busy preening his uniform, had overheard the exchange between Walt and King Owen. He strode next to the King and did his best to resist the urge to bow. He shook his head and glared at Walt.

"Your majesty, are you sure this is wise?" Bulloch said, wanting to make sure that the commitment was made out of sincerity, not an urge to protect his pride.

"God has given me a purpose bigger than any title I hold, if I die while we fight then I am glad it will be for the greater good; to answer your question yes, I am sure." King Owen said as his anger subsided.

Bulloch nodded his understanding and mounted his horse. He hoped that King Owen would have a chance to keep his word.

After three agonizing hours of waiting in the Santa Fe National Forest for Roman forces to arrive, the Renegades, were unprepared for what they saw. From their vantage point on a hilltop, what looked to be an entire armored cohort had been dispatched to deal with them. Walt counted twenty screamers, forty Hades Tanks and five armored carriers loaded with twenty Legionnaires each. He then looked up and saw two drones flying ahead of the cohort.

Walt grinned like a Cheshire cat "This is better than I expected, they are sending a lot of legionnaires for us to kill".

He put down his binoculars and took in the scene of the orange dust being kicked up by the approaching convoy on the old dirt road and laughed again.

"Corporal Willowdell, would you please do the honors and shoot down the two drones that are heading our way, get their attention by missing the second one, before you inevitably shoot it down."

Phoebe unsheathed the rifle she used for shooting while on horseback, a smaller Polish-made bolt action model she had chosen from over one hundred she tried out when she was recruited by Bulloch. She scanned the sky for the daytime drones that were painted light blue to camouflage in the setting. If she was patient, they would reveal themselves to her. She had developed an uncanny sense for finding them by waiting for them to pass in front of a cloud, or seeing the heat rippling from their engines. After a minute had passed, she raised the rifle up and looked through the scope, her hand on the trigger and her elbow extended out with the other extend out almost at arm's length, her other elbow slightly bent. She left both eyes open as she tracked her target, a faint smile materialized on her lips as she readied herself. She shot and quickly swiveled her torso to the extreme right, raised the barrel five degrees and shot two more quick shots. It was so fast it was almost inconceivable, and even more inconceivable that she would hit her targets. A few seconds later the two drones she shot came crashing to the ground and exploded in two fireballs respectively, a result of the munitions they were armed with.

Walt turned his horse around, "You need to go to the other side of the ridge and meet Colonel Bulloch, Corporal, and you will find another armored cohort heading our way."

Walt then turned and addressed the two companies that had been placed under his command. The faces staring back at him had a mix of apprehension and morbid curiosity, most of them had considered Walt a great soldier, but as a leader, he was considered by most to be too mentally unbalanced to lead. Colonel Bulloch and General Wright had gone against conventional wisdom and designated Walt as the commander for this battle, raising him to the rank of Major. He glared back at his detractors through his pale blue eyes with equal intensity.

"We are going to whip the Romans, stick to the plan, keep together with those who have been tasked with the same objective. I know you are a bunch of rugged individuals, but we get slaughtered as individuals, as a team we kick ass! One more thing, when you kill a Roman, cut open his right shoulder and dig out the restrictor chip that keeps them from being shot by the SPR's."

It was a ghoulish order, but one that all the renegades knew was necessary, but their hesitance to follow Walt's battle plan overwhelmed their willingness to follow orders. They were all silent, just staring at Walt, when William trotted Slingshot forward and yelled.

"Yes sir!"

It was a sign of loyalty that had weight with the other Renegades, considering the rocky history between Walt and William.

The others followed suit, almost simultaneously uttering "Yes Sir!"

They moved their horses and separated into the teams that were assigned to them, vanishing into the forest of ponderosa pines covering the ridge. Walt nodded to William who in turn saluted him, and was joined by Roost and Morrison in the salute. They turned and galloped through the trees, knowing that chances of surviving this skirmish were unlikely. Few of the renegades wore any body armor, and they were going against at least two armored Cohorts that they knew of, probably more were coming. William looked up at the old growth trees stretching high above as they rode to their assigned position; he wondered if there had ever been such a battle during the history of the West. His unit had been developed with the precept that they would use unconventional warfare, but William wondered had anyone actually conceived that they would be engaging tanks and screamers? He had set his mind to the task of formulating a plan, as he always had when he was a thief. Roost recognized the expression.

"All right Will, what's the plan."

William usually would try and feign a smile to keep Roost from worrying, but it seemed pointless to him in light of current circumstances. He stood up in the saddle and took a long look around before answering.

"I am trying to figure out how we are going to beat a bunch of tanks while we are on horseback," William said with a dire expression.

"Who elected him leader? If you have forgotten, I outrank you both!" Morrison said, spinning around and looking back at his comrades.

"Okay what is the plan?" he said in a serious tone of voice, but the sarcasm was apparent to William who looked at the ground to keep the smile on his face from being seen. Roost leaned back in his saddle and crossed his arms as if he was ready to listen to a long story.

"The plan? The plan." Morrison realized he did have any more of a strategy than William, "Well, my plan is to let him come up with something. But you have to clear it with me. Okay?"

William and Roost leaned forward and saluted together "Yes sir" they said in an obviously exaggerated serious voice.

"Great, we are marching to our doom here and I get stuck with a pair of clowns," Morrison said intentionally loud so that he could be heard as he turned around.

"That hurts me Morrison!" William said in the same semi-sarcastic tone, "Wow, and just about when I was going to ask for your input."

"Alright, stop! I'll bite", Morrison whipped around "This had better be good, or I will personally beat you within an inch of your life."

William pushed the brim of his hat up with his finger to see Morrison better, "Don't take this the wrong way, but you are a terrible equestrian. However, Roost tells me that he has never seen a faster draw...."

William was interrupted by the muffled boom of a tank firing and the sound of a shell cutting through the air, followed seconds later by an explosion two hundred feet behind them. William knew his plan would work; he just had to get them to safety so he could explain it.

Bulloch and Phoebe heard the sound of shells crashing into the forest growing closer; they had been trying to convince King Owen to go with them to the rally point northeast of the forest and get out of harm's way.

Bulloch had argued that he was the best symbol of hope for the British people, to no avail. Because of his battle experience, King Owen felt he should be in the fight, and despite Bulloch's most impassioned plea, he had decided he was going to join the fray. King Owen knew what Bulloch was saying was true, that he was the best hope for England, but he knew that without the United States at full strength, hope was lost for the United Kingdom. King Owen was not assigned to a team; he would have to partner with Bulloch and Phoebe. Bulloch resigned that King Owen would fight, his focus switched to formulating a plan. He took account of their surroundings, weighing everything in his line of sight. A thought suddenly occurred to Bulloch as he surveyed the terrain, to have a chance they would have to move to a higher elevation, just below the top of the tree line.

Bulloch gave a victorious "A-ha!" before turning to his companions, "Phoebe can target the Legionnaires who undoubtedly will be coming for us if we climb up to the aspens on this mountain. We will…"

"You and Phoebe", King Owen interrupted, "climb to that level, I am going down there." He said pointing to the now visible advancing column.

"Why?" Bulloch said in a less than polite manner, realizing it was suicide.

When King Owen turned to face Bulloch, he knew why; his eyes burned with the intensity that let Bulloch know he was not going to be dissuaded. He softened his stance and let King Owen Speak.

"Because I know how to kill Romans, and if I don't, we lose; then Britain loses," he was interrupted by an explosion close enough for them to feel the concussion, "They are using cluster shells! We need to move now. We don't have time to waste debating this!" the tone from King Owen was inspiring to Bulloch despite his reservations.

"All right, I know it is better to die in battle than cower in fear," Bulloch said slapping his hat on his head "I would do the same thing as you are; your majesty. Now let's go cut this Roman cancer out of this National Park!" he said with restored enthusiasm.

Phoebe pivoted her quarter horse and sprinted up the narrow trail meant for hikers that had become unkempt with no one to manage them. She maneuvered through fallen trees and sapling pines growing in the middle of the path, and was soon out of Bulloch and King Owen's sight. Bulloch as he looked at the approaching forces, unhooked a black shotgun that looked like a combat rifle and slid a round black canister underneath, he looked at King Owen and nodded he would follow his lead. They let the horses go up the trail behind Phoebe, which the beasts were all too willing to do, frightened by the explosions that grew ever closer. Bulloch and King Owen crouched down and crawled into the juniper brush in front of them and waited silently for their prey. King Owen vowed silently to himself, that he would not let harm come to Bulloch, because the U.K. needed him in Washington when this was over.

On the opposite side of the mountain, a column of tanks and screamers made its way up the rocky forest road that had become more mud than dirt, their treads sinking in the mire as they crawled forward. Two cleanup units on foot consisting of five legionnaires and a centurion each, followed behind the armor, their boots caked with gray mud. The second unit trailed about one hundred feet behind the first; they stopped and stared, confused by the sight in front of them. Slingshot, with William draped across his saddle, walked into the trail in front of them and stopped. They quickly raised their weapons, and then after a few minutes lowered them wondering if William was alive. William's head was on the other side of the horse and his feet dangled over the side facing the Romans. Slingshot stood there silent except for the occasional snort; the Romans were confused as they approached him. As they crept towards Slingshot, Morrison came up behind the centurion and jabbed his knife in the slot between the helmet and the armor, severing the jugular, the legionnaires started to raise their guns when William spun up in his saddle and shouted.

"Gotcha!" the legionnaires spun around and saw William and Roost smiling, with their guns trained on them.

William smiled with pride "We've still got it." he said relishing the old days, he slid off Slingshot and nudged Roost with his elbow while keeping his gun aimed at the surprised Romans, "Go ahead, you know you want to say it!"

"Stick 'em up!" he said in a stern voice moving his gun in an upward motion. Roost smiled wider thinking about how they used to pull a bank job.

The soldiers dropped their SPRs and raised their arms above their heads. Morrison knew enough Italian to make out the racial slurs being hurled at him by some of the soldiers, and just laughed. The rest of the column kept moving forward but he knew that they would soon notice the Legionnaires' absence. Roost and William swiftly herded them into the juniper scrub next to the path. William quickly and skillfully mounted

Slingshot, and scanned the woods for enemy troops. Roost mounted his horse in the same manner as William, making it look effortless. Morrison went into the bushes and untied his horse and mounted the palomino horse after much labor and frustration.

Roost looked at William and Morrison, "Now what do we do with them?"

The question was a valid one, and one William had not fully thought through. Unlike the times when he was planning a heist, there was no time to test things, to consider every detail. He had to think fast like he did in Oklahoma City; the decision became clear to William when the sound of armor rumbling up the path caught his attention.

"Quick, herd them to the east."

The trio pushed them forward through the thick green bushes, Morrison kept turning back and looking behind them, he could not believe that the roar of the heavy engines could be so close and they had not yet seen the tank or screamer that was making it. At that precise moment a tank burst through the brush and crushed the legionnaires walking in front of William and Roost. They had no time to run before the armor bounded on top of them. The cowboys moved their horses so quickly they were untouched even though it missed them by less than two feet. Morrison was glad he decided to bring up the rear; knowing he would have never been able to maneuver his horse out of the way of the charging armor. He also realized they had not been seen as it passed.

"Roost, Will, head back down the path the tank came up!"

William and Roost did not waste time to acknowledge Morrison, but instead tore off into a full gallop downhill. Morrison followed them at a slower pace; he met them halfway down the path the tank had carved. They slowly rode down over crushed trees and brush, keeping a sharp focus on their surroundings to make sure they were not being targeted. When they reached the bottom of the mountain, they came to a stream, inside the banks of which appeared more like a river because of the days of relentless rainfall from the monsoons. The water was as gray as the soil around it, being full of eroded mountainsides that had washed down in to it. Morrison intensely started at the rushing water.

"It's time we did what we came to do on this mission! We are going to bring those tanks down here," he turned to William, "can you ride fast with me on the back of your horse?"

"No problem, but let me get this straight first. You want the tanks to shoot at us?"

"Listen to me, the plan will work, Walt was right." Morrison said dismounting his horse.

William held out his hand, "Well, come on then, let's go!"

He swung Morrison up behind him and they charged back up the mountainside, Roost following right behind them. Morrison brought his gun up to bear on the tank that was directly ahead of them and opened fire. The tank kept pushing forward for a moment and then suddenly stopped; its turret began to rotate around towards the trailing riders. They pivoted and went full gallop downhill till they reached the bottom. They turned around in time to see the tank stopping and aiming at them.

"We have got to move, they are going to fire!" Morrison barked.

They plunged their horses into the swift moving water that came up over the top of the horse's legs, and moved at an angle so that they were not directly in the line of fire. Then the tank opened fire, filling all of them with adrenaline and causing them to shudder. The thump from the shells concussion was only surpassed in its deafening report, and by the sound of the cluster shell exploding behind them, they all looked over their shoulders to see hundreds of smaller explosions scattered through the air, they could feel the heat on their faces, but they were far enough out of range not to be hit by shrapnel.

The tanks rumbled downhill and into the creek, where they slowed down and finally stopped, the engine roaring in protest, as they sank into the soft creek bottom, water rushing over the top of the ten-foot high tank. The hatch opened and a legionnaire slowly raised his head out, peering around sure that the riders had fled, He was surprised as he heard Morrison yell at him.

"Fare cadere la sua arma ed uscire" which was bad Italian, but clear enough to the legionnaire who turned around and faced him to understand.

The legionnaire gripped his SPR just beneath the hatch; he acted as if he had not understood the command to drop his weapon. He decided that Morrison could not kill him with one shot, if he just drew his gun he would kill all three of them, which also were his last thoughts as Morrison shot him in the throat, severing his spinal cord with one shot. Morrison saw him flinch just before he tried to pull the gun and the look in his eyes, which betrayed his intentions. Roost was horrified at what he had seen, he was about to voice his objection when he saw the gun in the dead soldiers hand.

"How did you know?" Roost shook his head in disbelief, "He did not move until you shot him!"

Morrison smiled, "The same way you and Will knew that horse of his would distract those Romans," he said keeping his weapon trained on the hatch, "I could tell because I have seen that look a hundred times before."

Morrison abruptly stopped speaking at the sound of clanking from inside the tank, followed by four SPRs hastily thrown through the hatch.

"Don't shoot!" came from inside in a thick Italian enunciation.

Moments later the four Legionnaires came out one by one, their arms raised over their heads.

William shook his head, "Great Morris, now what do we do with them?"

"You know you are a real fool," he glared at William "Do you know that?"

"I've been told." William turned back around and focused on the problem at hand. "Which one of you speaks English?"

A tall hawk- nosed soldier with dark circles under his eyes spoke up "I do."

"You and your pals strip."

The legionnaire was not quite sure of the meaning. William motioned at him again.

"Disrobe, take your clothes off!"

There was a moment of hesitation before the soldier translated the order. William watched as they followed the command.

"But for Pete's sake don't take your underwear off!" he said realizing he had left out the caveat.

The soldiers stood shivering in the icy rushing water, watching their armor and clothes float downstream.

"Well get up here!" William ordered the legionnaires, "Morrison, do you have the stomach to cut the chip out of their shoulders?" he said knowing that having the chips could save them.

Roost could not believe the callousness of his old friend, he then realized that William saw things even worse than he had, and that they changed him forever. Morrison did not hesitate and quickly dug the tip of his knife into the first legionnaire's shoulder, popping out the chip and dropping it into his hand; he did the same with the next three soldiers, each one yelping in pain as he did. William waited until Morrison had finished his unpleasant task and then shot in front of the Legionnaires' feet.

"You tell Caesar William West is coming for him! Now, go on, git!"

They started to run back to where the Romans were, William shot in front of them again. The legionnaires clearly understood the message and ran in the opposite direction. Roost stared at William.

"It's good to see your vanity is still intact Will, but *go on git?*" he said unable to conceal his amusement.

William looked insulted, "You got to say Stick 'em up."

Morrison stared at the pair of cowboys, "Both of you, both of you are goofy." he observed, somewhat irritated at their joking in the midst of battle.

The conversation was cut short by the low roaring sound of a tank rumbling through the woods, as it snapped trees at their base. They scanned the woods for a moment and decided to move into the tree line on the other side of the banks. The sound continually grew louder, intermixed with the sound of SPR's being fired, it was clear to Morrison that the sound was coming downstream from them, but in his mind it was headed for the creek, and he was correct. They could make out the figures of Bulloch, King Owen and Sergeant David Mesquida running out of the woods on foot and plunging into the creek; seconds later a tank and several legionnaires appeared giving chase.

"Let's draw their fire from behind that boulder!" Morrison said sprinting to a house sized sandstone bolder a few yards from where they were. William started to walk out and aim at the Romans.

"What's the big deal Morris? We've got restrictor chips."

William's question was answered by the sound of SPR's being fired at him and the explosive projectile going off about twenty feet behind him. He sprinted to the bolder and flattened his back against it.

"The chips don't work at this range," Morrison smirked at him. "Aren't you supposed to be some kind of genius or something?" he quipped.

Roost ran over while in a squatting position, projectiles exploding above him, until he finally dove behind the bolder. Morrison carefully scaled the rock in order to look over the top. When he peered over, he could see the second tank had sunk in barrel first and the hatch had already been opened. He suddenly saw the other legionnaires taking aim at him; he slid down the rock with no regard for injury. There was another barrage of SPR fire, sending chips of rock and dust flying over the heads of the three Renegades. Morrison could also hear the crack of gunfire coming from the woods on their side directed at the tank, which had become a shelter for the Romans to fire behind. Morrison turned and grabbed William and Roost by the shoulder.

"We've got to move now. They will be calling this in, if we are not already being watched by satellite or blimp. King Owen is over there and I promise he is thinking the same thing".

They attempted to move, but the hail of SPR fire was overwhelming. They swung around and reverted their aim back to the woods where they had come from. Morrison ran out from behind the rock and opened fire taking down two of the legionnaires, he counted a total of seven, but knew there could be more than that. He rolled back to the safety of the boulder.

"I count seven" he said followed by the sound of gunfire coming from the woods where the other Renegades were, "Now!" Morrison yelled.

William, Roost and Morrison all ran out and opened fire, then they realized why the Romans had been shooting into the woods. Three legionnaires were left standing while the others were floating in the creek, as they watched them turn to open fire, the remaining legionnaires turned from shooting at the unknown sharpshooter to shooting at them. As the legionnaires changed their target, another one fell; Phoebe was picking them off from high ground. The remaining two, realizing they were outgunned, threw down their weapons and threw up their hands in a panicked surrender. William, Roost and Morrison then saw Bulloch holding his weapon on the Legionnaires and shouting something in Italian, which they could not make out. The Roman soldiers obeyed the command and knelt down threw off their helmets and interlocked their fingers on top of their heads. Sergeant Mesquida went over and bashed them in the back of the heads with his rifle knocking them out. He pulled plastic zip ties out his pocket and quickly went about restraining the two soldiers. He then pulled duct tape out of his other pocket and covered their mouths.

"Be glad this is all I am doing to you!" he snarled in his thick Tennessee accent.

Mesquida had resisted the urge to execute them though he felt there was good reason. He had been with four other Renegades in Utah Company when a cluster shell hit their position, he had gone ahead of them on foot to scout a path when the explosion occurred, he ran back to find carnage so complete that he had trouble telling the human body parts from the horses.

He was left without a mount when he found Bulloch and King Owen, who he joined. A decorated captain in the Navy SEALs, he had taken a lesser rank to join the Renegades. Having grown up on a horse farm in Knoxville, he was eager to join the non-conventional warfare unit and use all of his skills. Now he was the last one from the group of SEALs he joined with. He controlled his thirst for revenge and changed his focus.

"Was that Phoebe who shot the Romans?" Bulloch nodded an acknowledgement but had other concerns on his mind.

"We have to do something about that poor devil."

He nodded to the one legionnaire who lay face up in the water unable to move and gasping for air, his lungs were slowly filling with fluid,

"We can't let him suffer like that."

It was something that they all knew had to be done, to be merciful, but no one could stomach the idea. Morrison moved toward the dying man.

"I'll do it"

He took aim, looking in the soldiers eyes who gave an almost undetectable nod; the others turned their backs, despite all they had seen it was still hard to watch a life be snuffed out. A single shot was all that was needed; the pop of Morrison's pistol let the others know the grim deed had been done.

William had been away from the scene, oblivious to the coup de grâce that just took place. He was focused on the mountainside waiting to see if Phoebe was coming down, if she was okay. Bulloch saw William looking upward and knew what he was thinking.

"William, by all means see if she's alright."

William did not answer, instead put two fingers in his mouth and gave a loud whistle. Slingshot came trotting over to his master hearing the call, and gave out a snort acknowledging that he was ready to work. William mounted him in one sweeping motion and they galloped into the forest.

King Owen stood looking at the Roman corpses that had clumped together on a juniper scrub, swallowed by the swollen stream. A crimson blob pooled underneath the bodies and slowly drifted into the main flow of the stream. He stared at them for a moment and then raised his gaze to the bright powder blue sky filled with wispy clouds.

He shook his head "How can a place of such beauty be filled with so much death?" He was speaking to himself, but Roost overheard him.

"It's the Code of the Forest, everything has its place, its purpose," he pointed to the vultures already circling overhead "every creature knows exactly what it has to do to survive; but it is always about survival and death."

King Owen nodded, "I believe it is, as God intended it."

Bulloch was looking at the vultures at the same time; he despised the idea of leaving any soldier, even Romans, to be devoured by the scavengers, but he had no choice. He waived his arm.

"Let's move to the next rally point. William and Phoebe will find the way there."

William was still absorbing the fact that he had lost seven of his friends in the battle, and an eighth had lost both of his legs. He came upon Phoebe and watched her for a moment, realizing for the first time since they had met they were alone. He noticed that both of their Emerson suits had become yellow and white from the optics picking up the blaze of aspen leaves above them and the snow white bark that surrounded them. William felt both the moment and the longing for Phoebe he had held inside for months. He dismounted and moved closer to her, until he was staring down into her eyes.

"I know this is sudden, but I want to be with you. If God allows us to make out of this alive" he hesitated slightly, "is there a future for you and me?" Phoebe said nothing, but closed her eyes and lifted herself up on her tip toes to gently kiss William on the lips. They embraced and held the kiss for a moment among the falling leaves and the sound of the wind. Phoebe pulled back and stared into William's eyes.

"Of course there is ,Will; you must have known how I feel about you? I love you, and not because you are a famous thief, but because you are a good man."

William was relieved to hear the revelation, that he had not imagined Phoebe's glances at him, or the way she had touched him.

He laughed, "That's good, because I fell in love with you when I first saw you in Ocala!" William did his best to regain his swagger "It would have been discouraging if you didn't! It's good to see I haven't lost my touch."

Phoebe gave him a playful slap on the arm "You are still conceited though aren't you!"

William laughed "True, but right now I am worried about us kissing, do you think they will get rid of us?" The sarcasm was apparent in William's voice as he looked around pretending that they were being watched.

He had let himself think about a life after the war for the first time. He had thought about being happy, but had not believed it could ever happen again. Another realization then occurred to him.

"I may be in prison for a while; I don't want that kind of life for you." William said in a melancholy tone, letting reality creep back into the moment like a dark cloud.

Phoebe looked at him and smiled. "If you don't get your butt shot off, I doubt anyone will want to see you land in jail. You are a hero now, Will, and not some folk song stick it to the man anti-hero, but the real thing. I don't think I will have to wait for you, but even if it came down to it, I would." she said with a wide reassuring grin.

William felt better, but he was increasingly distracted from the smell of burning plastic and rubber filling his nostrils, and the clouds of smoke on the Horizon.

"We better catch up with the others; it won't be long before the next wave of Romans show up wanting to get even with us."

William and Phoebe came to a clearing in the trees; it was a breathtaking sight that caught them off guard. The hazy silhouette of the mountains miles away, and the hills dotted with evergreens and yellow aspens, blanketing everything all the way up the mountain. In the middle of it all was a clearing with a pristine green field. Then they quickly refocused as they spotted a convoy of tanks and screamers, winding their way up a two lane road about two miles from them. Phoebe slid off her horse and moved to an outcropping on the cliff. She raised her rifle and looked through the scope.

"There are maybe fifteen or twenty pieces of armor, and there are at least four centurions, I see four drones at three, eleven, twelve and nine o'clock…"

Phoebe stopped speaking at the sight of two plumes of debris streaming in the air from a pair of hills that were intersected by the road that ran between them. The explosions had the look of a splash; it was if the hillsides were pools of water that had a stone dropped into them. The explosions reminded William of volcanoes erupting. There were two more rapid explosions on either side; the hillsides which were saturated from the previous few days of rain, came plummeting down on top of either side of the road in a landslide, crushing the tanks and personnel underneath them. Seconds later the sound of the explosion traveled to where they were, violently reverberating off the mountainsides. The drones, severed from their masters, spiraled out of control and came crashing out of the sky. William slid off Slingshot, hopping up and down in elation.

"Walt did it! That crazy, wonderful, psychopath did it!" he said picking up Phoebe off her feet and bear hugging her and laughing.

They were stopped by the sound of two more explosions, they turned to see smoke rising from behind a mountain further up the road from the other explosions. Walt's plan had worked perfectly, he had used Colter's knowledge of the Santa Fe National forest to draw the Romans in and execute a series of ambushes using the weight of their armor and the rain soaked ground as weapons. All of Walt's years of studying military history and tactics had paid off, the feat of beating Roman Armor without air strikes or artillery was such that it put Walt and Caprera on the same level of military genius. The Renegades had dealt a decisive blow to the Romans in the heart of Roman occupied territory. It was seen as an impossibility by almost all at the Pentagon, yet Walt had done it.

Watrous, New Mexico was a tiny town situated on Interstate twenty-five between two other small towns, Las Vegas and Wagon Mound. It was an area where mountains and forests transitioned and struggled not to give way to the encroaching desert planes. The streets were interspersed with stone homes that were decaying; some were no more than the façade, the other walls having fallen long ago. Some homes and business were pristine, looking as if they had only been there for a short while. The town had been founded in the 1850's and boomed when the Railroad came through the town in the 1870's, it had not changed much since the early twentieth century. Yet the tiny town was where the instructions from Ice Swan had directed the Renegades. The area had a few ranches that were on the wide open plains, which at one time had been successful, but had fallen into disrepair since the Roman invasion.

The Renegades were making their way from various parts of the Santa-Fe National Forest in separate groups to the rally point. William and Phoebe were following the trail of Roost, Bulloch, Morrison, and King Owen. William saw that they had an extra set of hoof prints; he realized it must have been Mesquida's horse. William and Phoebe were coming down a hill to a sea of wide open beige grassland, dotted with green junipers. William spotted a bison ranch in the middle of the grass valley. He stopped and pointed it out to Phoebe.

"I can't believe it. Do you see that?"

He galloped downhill to get a closer look. What William saw was a giant heard of fat buffalo with their young. There were some big ones with black heads that weighed nearly two tons, and small orange colored ones with nub horns, sticking close to their mothers. All of them were growing thick wooly brown coats for the coming winter. Phoebe was not a rancher, but knew there was some significance to the herd.

"Is there someone there taking care of them?"

"It looks like no one is there." William looked and could see no vehicles or signs of any ranchers.

"They have survived out here on their own?"

William nodded "They have thrived on their own" he made a clicking noise with his mouth and Slingshot turned around "Let's take a closer look."

They galloped to the mesh fence that had been stung from one old log post to another; the fence looked as if it stretched a mile. It encircled the property that included a small creek, the water source for the more than fifteen hundred head. There were a few large cottonwoods which had kept them cool in the summer. There was also an old wooden barn that had not been painted for years as the faded patches of red indicated, and it had a distinct lean to the right. It looked as if a strong wind could knock it over. On the property was a two story brick ranch house built in 1982, designed to look like it was built in the old west, but had an artificial feel to its appearance. One of the buffalo, the largest one, which William took to be the heard alpha male, charged the fence making a deep guttural noise as he did. It stopped short of crashing into the fence and gave a heavy guttural snort through its enormous nostrils. His head was completely black in contrast to his hulking brown body. His coat had already grown in for the winter, even though fall had just begun. He scratched his enormous hooves on the ground and grunted. He was more animated than any buffalo William had ever encountered.

"He is a frisky one isn't he?" William noted.

Phoebe was not used to dealing with beasts like the buffalo and was nervous that it might knock down the fence, "He is a little scary. Should we move back?" she said as her hand instinctively reached for one of her pistols.

"How do you do that?" William Chuckled.

Phoebe flashed an annoyed look at William "What do you mean?"

"How do you stay perky when you are about to shoot someone or something down?"

"I do no such thing!"

William realized it was a line of questioning he should quickly abandon. "If you think this guy is scary, you should have seen Slingshot when I first got him. He kept kicking people in the head without warning. The ranch owner was going to shoot him when I asked if I could have him. That was scary. This guy is a prime example of where the term *to buffalo someone* comes from."

The beast moved nearer to them and William leaned down and held out his hand. There was the sound of air rushing in and out of its lungs, as the buffalo sniffed William's hand. After the inspection there was a snort of approval.

"I think he likes me" William thought for a moment before speaking again, "He looks like a Chester doesn't he? I am going to call him Chester."

"You're naming him?" Phoebe was both amused and perplexed.

"You never know when you will need to call a two thousand pound buffalo," William explained in a tone that insinuated it was self-apparent to need a two thousand pound buffalo.

William reached into his pocket and pulled out a granola bar, feeding Chester. He let out a grunt of approval as he took it in his mouth. He let William pet his immense head as he chewed the treat he was given. William looked back over his shoulder at Phoebe.

"See, now we are good friends."

He gave Chester a final pat on the head and then turned Slingshot back to the northeast and galloped off to the Rally point.

The Renegades had gathered at the Watrous Post Office, a small white, shingled roof building with a single mailbox sitting in front. It had been left untouched by the Romans and was right off the interstate which was eerily silent and blanketed in some stretches with tumbleweeds and sand. William and Phoebe rode up to see King Owen, eyes wide with urgency pleading to Bulloch and Coulter.

"This man," King Owen said while pointing backwards at Walt "This man can help me free Britain, this man can help me build an army! We have need of him!"

Bulloch remained calm "I understand your point your majesty, but we have a mission to finish."

King Owen gathered himself "Don't misunderstand me; I have no intention of him abandoning his mission. But I can't risk him being in harm's way." he spoke in a low but sharp tone.

Walt swaggered forward, full of confidence from his battle plan yielding a greater victory than anyone expected, and because he was the focal point of the conversation.

"With all due respect your highness, who the hell said I would go with you?"

King Owen slowly turned to him, the anger visible in the narrowing eyebrows and mouth set in a slight scowl. He could not believe what he was hearing; were the rumors about Walt's sanity true?

"Why would you turn this down? You are the biggest single warmonger I have ever met!"

Walt crossed his arms and stared flatly "I love my country. I have no desire to become a British Subject."

King Owen with effort calmed himself, "A British subject! I would give my throne to you in exchange for my people's freedom!" his tone was restrained but his demeanor was no less intense.

Coulter stepped in between King Owen and Walt.

"All right that will be enough!" he growled in his scratchy voice. "Stop clucking like a couple of old hens! We have a mission to complete, and I am sorry your majesty, we need all hands on deck, so Major Smith stays in the fight!"

King Owen nodded; he had been accustomed to taking orders before becoming King and felt that Coulter owed him no respect as a King, only as a soldier. Coulter turned to the gathered Renegades.

"Ten Hut" was barked out as he walked towards them.

"At ease. Who did that? It's not like we are a regular outfit. When did we suddenly get discipline and finally start following protocol?" Coulter said in a half joking tone.

Coulter looked around driving his point home about the lack of respect for military regulations among the Renegades, especially those who were in the military before they joined.

"Colonel Bulloch is going to brief you on our next mission, and who is going to be assigned where and when."

Bulloch strolled forward, hands clasped behind his back and gaze aimed at the rocky ground, when he had found a mark that was suitable to him he looked up to deliver the daunting news.

"Here are our orders: some of you will be heading north of Taos to prepare an ambush at the Rio Grande Gorge Bridge. The rest of you will be infiltrating a Roman Data Stream station, and acting as the bait for the ambush. I will not lie, both will be dangerous, but most of you who are going to the Data Stream station will not be coming back. You have been assigned according to your background and skill." Bulloch stopped for a moment, seeming to be choked up, "I want to say to all of you, before we leave on this mission; it has been the greatest honor of my life to serve with you," he said relaying the fondness he had for them all.

The Forlorn Horsemen, as they had dubbed themselves consisted of William, Roost, Bulloch, Morrison, Mesquida, Walt and King Owen. They prepared themselves, saying their goodbyes to their friends and recording messages to be given to loved ones if they did not return. William and Phoebe stared at each other across the crowd, unable to say goodbye because they were not supposed to be together. William gave his best smile and tipped his hat, he leapt onto Slingshot signaling to the rest of the group it was time to move out. The rest of the group followed suit and began to ride out. William looked back at the faces of the Renegades who were going to take part in the ambush; they were melancholy and downtrodden, but still resolute. William pulled hard on Slingshot's reigns and the horse stood up on his hind legs, William took off his hat and held it high above his head in one hand, reign gripped in the other. The Renegades roared in approval at the stunt. Slingshot came down gracefully and the pair rode quickly in a circle before racing off to catch the rest of the group. William smiled to himself as he rode, having not showed off on a horse that way since he was seventeen years old. He hoped that he would survive to do it again one day. Phoebe watched as they rode off, hoping it was not the last time she would ever see William.

The Forlorn Horseman emerged from among a hardwood forest of various scrub pines onto an outcropping of Sandstone near the bottom of a green hillside. They had tied their horses just out of sight, in the midst of the tree line. They crawled on their stomachs across the rock that had thousands of minute holes, which had the same effect as a cheese grater on bare skin. Crawling was unavoidable in order to avoid being spotted by Roman surveillance. William made a sucking sound with his teeth every time his hand was sliced into by the rock. Roost nudged William.

"Do you want to do that a little bit louder? I don't think you've alerted the entire Roman Legion yet." Roost chided in a loud whisper.

They all stopped short of the outcroppings edge, and stared at the spectacle in front of them. The data beaming station was a solid square concrete building with a single steel door. On top of the building was an eighty-one foot bronze statue of Caprera depicted as Mercury, arms outstretched, winged helmet on his head, winged ankles above his feet. The body was sculpted with ripples and bulges that were reminiscent of the sculpture by Bologna which had inspired it. In the statue's cupped hands was a laser that beamed data to a stationary airship in the stratosphere. Based on a stolen design by Timothy Emerson, it was a marvel of design. The saucer shaped airship had solar cells covering its top and at night conductors would produce electricity from plasma, powering the rotors that kept it aloft. Emerson had correctly theorized that plasma existed in the upper stratosphere at night, making the aircraft possible. Data was beamed back and forth across the laser beams that bounced off it.

The station was specifically constructed for controlling drones and robots. William was awestruck at the sight of the statue; he patted Roost on the shoulder.

"And people say I'm vain!" he said in a whispery laugh.

Bulloch and King Owen crawled up beside William and Roost. King Owen was angered by the sight of Caprera depicted as a god.

"God grant me justice for my family and people!" King Owen said aloud but no one else heard the plea of righteous anger.

Bulloch rolled over on his back to address the others. "Anyone see an entry point beside the door?'

William chuckled again, "The air vent, on the roof, the door is just a key code and optical scanner system." He nudged Roost again "See those cameras, are they Swiss?"

"Why yes, Will, they are Swiss." Roost said as he lifted his head up slightly.

William smiled at Roost, "Do you see the angle they are tilted at?"

Roost scowled back at William, "Will, what are you getting at, you know they are not tilting down. Why don't you just say it?"

"Because I'm the smart one, and you're the good looking one, it's my job."

"You know, you can be a real jerk sometimes." Roost complained loudly enough that the others could here.

Bulloch looked at them, "Do you gentlemen have something you would like to share with us?"

Both William and Roost fired an exasperated stare at Bulloch; William nodded an affirmative response to Bulloch's question. Bulloch waved his hand for the group to crawl back into the trees; he knew that the pair had a plan on how to infiltrate the beaming station.

The group huddled together, some squatting, some kneeling, in a circle among the trees behind a large boulder.

Bulloch spoke to the group, "William and Roost have some skill at this, they were experts I believe." The words were both a concurrent compliment and a slight.

"Roost and I know cameras better than any security expert in the world. The cameras are Swiss; they have infrared, night vision, backlight correction and five filters to make the image as clear as possible. They are state of the art, but they have one major flaw, they don't tilt up and down, just side to side. The air intake vent and door are both on the east side of the building, in the middle of a wide open field."

The rate that William disseminated information and formulated a plan held the others spellbound, except for Roost who had grown accustomed to William's genius over the years.

William continued, "The significance is that the one thing it can't filter out is direct sunlight, and it can't tilt down to shade the lens. If we approach from the west as the sun is setting, all the camera will see is a big white and yellow glare, like someone shining a flashlight in your eyes coming out of a darkened room."

Morrison had been listening intently, and was impressed with the plan, but he still had lingering doubts.

"What about the drones? They won't be affected? How do we get past them?"

William smiled he had thought of that, and had devised a plan instantaneously on the spot, that was worthy of his greatest exploits.

"A few miles back there is a ranch that has about fifteen-hundred head of Bison that are thriving on their own. We are going to drive the herd here, and use them as cover to get to the air intake. Roost and I can get in easily after that. One thing I need to know," he looked at Bulloch "what are we doing once we are inside?"

Bulloch pulled the field tablet out of his pocket and held it up, "Apparently, you can clone a hard drive located in the system as a backup with this. The drive is located in the left arm near the top. With the information we will get from this it will give us an intelligence advantage over the Romans."

Roost nodded at each gauging their approval, satisfied he grinned, "Let's go do it then!"

The removal of the herd had proved to be the hardest part of William's plan; the buffalo had gown quite comfortable in their captive surroundings and did not feel motivated by freedom to leave the ranch. It took some time to get them moving, it was only by William luring the mammoth buffalo he named Chester out with granola bars, did the rest of the herd follow the old bull. The trip was relatively easy back to the beaming station. William, Roost, Morrison and King Owen were tasked with infiltrating the station; their various skills were the most suited to the operation. Morrison was anxious and wanted to act quickly.

"Okay, Will, how are we going to do this?" he said as they watched the herd move into the grassland and began to graze.

"We need the herd to want to stick right with us. We need Chester, and we need his scent if we get separated, so the others will want to stay with us."

"I don't like the sound of this." Roost said shaking his head.

"What do you mean scent?" Morrison said reacting to Roost's look of disgust.

"We need his scent on us."

"How do we do that Will, huh?" Morrison's tone had a cutting sound.

"I know how." Roost said still shaking his head.

Morrison moved closer to William in an intimidating stance "How?"

"We cover ourselves with his manure."

"Hell no, Will!"

"I know it's gross, but it's the only way to pull this off."

"I am not covering myself in buffalo crap!"

"There is no other way."

Morrison was struggling to restrain his urge to yell, he spoke in a harsh whisper through clinched teeth. "Find another way!"

"Fine, you stay behind then." William said in his best attempt at reverse psychology.

Morrison was about to yell when he looked over to see King Owen behind Chester, picking up fresh manure and then spread it on his arms and neck.

"What the hell are you doing?" Morrison finally let the yell burst forth. King Owen walked over and looked him in the eye. "I have done much worse than this to escape the Romans and get to America, and I will do anything to free my people."

Morrison shook his head in disbelief, and spoke to himself. "Great! Just Great! I am stuck with a bunch of crazy people." He reluctantly picked up some of the droppings and spread it on himself.

William looked over at him with a big smile "That's the spirit! Now don't you feel better?

The herd moved just as William said it would, Mesquida, Walt and Bulloch watched with amazement as they approached the beaming station. They came right up to the vent and William and Roost took out their tools and went to work.

William looked at Roost "Wow, they actually used Phillip's head screws on the outside of the vent!" Within seconds they had the cover off the air intake;

William stuck his whole torso in and looked up. "It's wide, this must suck in a lot of air to cool the servers."

Roost stuck his head in after William. "Looks like it only runs about ten feet up."

William started to climb in when he was stopped by King Owen, who grabbed William's arm. "If I call you, it means you have to stop whatever you're doing and get out," the gravity of the statement was well understood by William who nodded his understanding. He and Roost crawled into the rectangular duct. They placed their backs against one side and their feet against the other and shimmied up. William facing one direction and Roost below facing the opposite direction they came to their first obstacle, an air filter that was fitted with steel rods. William examined the filter with the same care that a neurosurgeon uses before making the first cut. He looked closely at the bolts on the filter.

"Great, these are metric! They use Philips heads on the outside, and metric on the inside, makes no sense! Do you have a metric socket Roost?"

Roost reached into his bag and produced a leather case containing the required wrench "Here you go."

"Now we're in business. I forgot how much fun this was!" William said gleefully absorbed in his work.

"Will."

"Yeah?"

"I'm glad you're not dead."

William stopped to look down to acknowledge Roost, "Thanks Roost, me too." He smiled "Just like old times!"

"Sure, just like old times." Roost said with a smile.

Outside King Owen and Morrison were growing increasingly concerned with each passing moment. The sun continued to sink lower and lower in the sky, and at least one drone that they knew of had flown overhead. King Owen focused on scanning the horizon for more drones, but his mind drifted to Kenneth, and why Caesaris was restoring some of the British traditions. Although Kenneth was gone, he knew Morrison was as loyal to the cause as Kenneth, and was the best soldier he had ever seen. He and Morrison had a bond, so much so that neither one spoke. They instead used hand signals to communicate, ingrained in them by their special forces training. King Owen kept a close watch on the open vent, which was just a foot above the ground, the herd hid it well, but it still made him nervous. He was used to laying in wait to attack, but not so they would remain hidden. His train of thought was broken when he saw Morrison pointing two fingers towards his own eyes, signifying he saw something; he then pointed to the north, and held up four fingers. King Owen turned around, remaining in a crouched position, he saw four legionnaires standing two hundred feet in front of them.

The legionnaires were born in Rome, and had never seen a buffalo before. They were sightseeing more than they were patrolling. Morrison raised his gun slowly preparing to fire, when King Owen grabbed the barrel and pushed it down, he held up his fist in a signal to hold his position and not shoot. Morrison thought they should strike before they were found, but followed orders and lowered his weapon. The legionnaires began to walk closer and King Owen wondered if he should let Morrison shoot, if they moved much closer they would undoubtedly be discovered. The legionnaires drifted closer and closer, to the point he could clearly hear their voices. He was sure that he was in full sight of one of them, but he had not been noticed yet.

King Owen was about to signal to Morrison they should attack, when a runner came barreling up behind the legionnaires, a centurion stepped out and began yelling at them. They snapped to attention and saluted by pounding their fist over their heart. The centurion continued barking orders for a moment, and then he walked back to the runner, turned around and barreled back in the direction it came from. The Legionnaires, seemingly disappointed turned and walked back across the field, after a few minutes they disappeared across a hilltop. King Owen and Morrison looked at each other; the expression on both of their faces was relief. Suddenly William popped out of the vent.

"Let's Go!" he said emerging from the duct, startling both King Owen and Morrison.

Roost followed and they quickly attached the vent and ran west into the glare of the sun. William stopped and turned to the others as they moved back up the hill. He laughed at the site of the others covered in filth, and the miserable expression on their faces.

"I don't know about you, but I could use a shower!"

# CHAPTER XIX

The Forlorn Horsemen had barely slept since they left the beaming station. Wanting both to continue their mission and avoid the Roman patrols that were likely to rush to the station. They had hastily rode off, leaving the herd of buffalo behind. In the fading sunlight they had made their way to the top of a ridge and Bulloch had beamed the data they had stolen from the Romans to a Pentagon satellite. There was one last message that was received when the transmission was complete. It said:

MR. WHITE WILL ARRIVE AT DAWN. MR. LONG IS READY FOR HIS ARRIVAL.

William, who had escorted Bulloch to the ridge, had seen the cryptic message on the screen, but had not worried about deciphering it; he was more concerned with his survival than trying to crack the code as he normally would. He felt the enormity of the task they were about to undertake, there was no more time for games.

William, Roost, Morrison and King Owen had stopped to wash off in a stream before continuing on, still filthy from the last mission. The smell proved to be stronger than their determination to ignore it. The sat near the stream and ate a quick meal before moving forward. With each passing moment the sense of doom among them grew more palpable, but it did not deter them. The group moved quickly through the forest, a full moon lighting their way through the combination of thick underbrush and clustered pines. They had tried to sleep to the sound of owls hooting and crickets so loud they sounded like some kind of high-pitched machine, working at a never ending task through the night. The air was also bitingly cold, making sleep no more than a momentary occurrence. After three hours of attempted rest, mostly for the horses, they were on the move again, taking up the dangerous task of riding through the forest at night. The most dangerous wildlife was active at night in the forest, but that was not at the forefront of their minds. The ride into the heart of the Roman colonization was the overwhelming thought each one of them held in their mind. William wondered if he died, was all he had done for nothing. He prepared himself, accepting that he may die and the next sunrise he saw could be his last. A strange feeling of calm was growing inside him, despite the bleak circumstances, he felt that it was God's will for him, and whatever happened would be for the greater good. He was grateful that he had a chance to apologize to Roost and Cassidy; he had never imagined that Roost would end up joining the Renegades. He looked up at the sky as they passed through an open clearing and at the millions of stars above, it reminded him of being on a ranch when he had run away at fifteen years old. There was some guilt on his part that Slingshot may die; it was his choice to join the Renegades, not his horse's. If things go bad, William thought to himself, he would dismount and let Slingshot go free. He looked up at the sky again and noticed a faint glow in the east that signaled dawns pending arrival, astronomical twilight was beginning. William gave Slingshot a gentle tap with his heels, and trotted up next to Bulloch.

"We need to pick up the pace, look at the sky." Bulloch glanced upwards, and then down at his watch.

"About an hour and a half to sunrise?" he glanced back at the others

"We need to pick up the pace. Roost, get out the map."

Roost dutifully produced the map from a saddlebag and used a reading light over it.

He studied it for a moment, "We are about five miles from Taos."

"Eight Klicks, Private" Walt quickly corrected him.

The group weaved through the trees faster, their horses breaking into a gallop when they could. The smell of dampness still hung in the air from the monsoons, even though it had not rained for days.

William looked at the sky again, "Weird, there are no drones this close to their biggest base," he said thinking to himself out loud.

"Roger that. They don't think anyone would be crazy enough to get this close. I for one am looking forward to doing some damage." Morrison said from behind.

Walt who was next to Morrison let out a loud laugh "You are my kind of soldier. We are going to tear their throats out! We have the element of surprise and after we tear up their town, they will follow us right into the ambush!"

William felt somehow comforted by the words, he hoped he could be as half as brave as the two former special forces soldiers were.

"I would not want to go on a suicide mission with any other bunch of guys" he declared in a jovial tone.

The crushing feeling of dread that had sat like a weight on William's chest had completely left him, his mind– his greatest weapon– set to work on devising a plan. He stopped for a moment and waited for Roost to catch up with them. Roost's face had an expression of trepidation carved into it, he was less sure of the outcome. Unlike William, he had not been able to shake the feeling of dread. Doubt still filled his mind, and he thought about Cassidy and not ever seeing her again. He looked at William and stared at him for a moment the worried expression did the speaking for him, no words were necessary. William knew how he felt; he had the same kind of feeling when he rode into Oklahoma City. Roost shook his head as he looked at the trees around him growing more sparse, indicating they were growing closer to their destination.

"I don't know if I can do it, Will."

William gave Roost his most reassuring smile "I thought the same thing, when you get into the battle you will react, you will want to fight."

Walt who was in earshot, pulled on the reins of his horse and swung him around. He sat up straight in his saddle and looked at Roost with an unwavering stare.

"Every soldier is scared when they go into battle," Walt leaned forward and smiled "any soldier who says he does not is a damn liar! You are no coward Roost, I have seen you put your life in danger, this is nothing new, except you will be killing a bunch of those skirt wearing Romans!"

The words had their desired effect, the words bolstered Roost and he felt more certain.

"Thank you Major, I needed to hear that" Roost said nodding to Walt in appreciation.

They turned their horses and galloped back to the others, back into the thicket of trees. The glow in the eastern sky was faintly brighter, like a clock counting down to the end of a game; all of the Forlorn Horsemen were aware of it. They finally came to the edge of the woods and down the hillside to a clearing where they could see Taos, streets abandoned, some of the buildings on the main strip were in the process of being torn down, including Kit Carson's home. Then they saw it, just beyond the main part of town was a new city being built, rising above the old town. The sight of the city that was already large enough to house a million people, was both awe inspiring and dispiriting. It was one of Caprera's dreams, New Pompeii, a masterpiece of architecture and art. It had been built at the cost of the thousand year old pueblos that were flattened to make way for the new marvel. The budding city was perfectly laid out on a symmetrical grid, the villas in various states of construction were two and three stories, all with terra cotta tiles covering the slanted roofs. They all had front porches with triangular pediments held up by two ionic columns. The streets were made up of polygon shaped stones, there were street lamps perched on top of Ionic columns. In the center of the city was a vast Piazza with a sixty-foot Marble colossus of Caprera at its center, his stoic face turned to the east. At the far end of the piazza, directly behind the statue was the *Pompeii Lodge* a seven-story palace that was a cross between Tuscan and Native American. The slanted roof, like the Villas, was covered with tile; the walls were covered with large redwood timbers. A large balcony extended across the entire third floor, and it was held up by redwood sculptures of Minerva, Proserpina, Ceres, Vesta, Maia and Diana. Right above the porch, the roof arched into a triangular pediment with a frieze of Caprera leading the invasion of the United States. Extending out from under the balcony was another roof, slanting down over the main entrance. The Main entrance itself was comprised of two large pane glass doors framed by a redwood sculpture of Atlas and Hercules holding up a triangular pediment. It was a stunning sight; it was built to be Caprera's personal vacation palace, just as the whole town was to be a vacation town for Romans. A ten-story hotel was being built adjacent to the Lodge in the same style. Not far away was a Terra Cotta shaded outdoor amphitheater that could seat forty thousand patrons. There were nightclubs, bars, and a building that was clearly intended to be a brothel. An impressive, giant park with a running track; there were two Olympic pools next to a five hundred thousand square foot marble covered fitness center. There were statues of satyrs throughout the city, signifying its hedonistic purpose. Dispersed on rooftops throughout the city were batteries of stacked projectile cannons, making an air attack almost impossible. Even in the half-light from the lamps the renegades stared in wonder at what the Romans had done.

"This can't be real," William whispered to himself; he felt as if he had been transported to Italy seventeen hundred years earlier, despite the 21$^{st}$ century technology. Bulloch and King Owen were equally stunned; both had visited the ruins of Pompeii and were shocked at the uncanny resemblance to it. The city itself was daunting, but the Forlorn Horsemen gathered themselves; they were not intimidated. Northwest of the city were dual two hundred foot high military compounds, each modeled after the Parthenon. The compound was dubbed the *Limitanei Americana* after the frontier bases in the original Roman Empire. The entire complex stretched over nine miles in length and was home to fifteen thousand legionnaires and four thousand Praetorians and support troops. It was the largest Roman military base in the United States, surrounded by a fifteen-foot high chain link fence topped with razor wire. It contained hundreds of Stacked Projectile Batteries like the ones in New Pompeii, as well as screamers and Hades tanks. There were large barracks in the classical Roman style, hangers housing hundreds of drones and fifty stacked projectile robots. It was like two separate cities, but joined into one larger whole. Bulloch was stunned; there was no satellite imagery of the massive construction that had to occur to build an entire city. He realized that moles in the Pentagon and at the CIA had compromised the data on Taos.

William unsheathed his rifle and looked back at the others.

"I have a plan," he smiled and the others knew he was going to get them through the mission.

"We don't have to ride up to the gates, look at all the cameras placed all over that town. Come on guys, do I have to spell it out? You have the most famous man in America," William pointed to himself "a U.S. senator and the King of England!" William pointed at King Owen as his eyes darted around for reaction from the others. "Oh come on! Where do you think those cameras go? They will come out in force to capture us, they will want to use us for Propaganda or as bargaining chips" he smiled again "but the rest of you they will defiantly kill."

Bulloch laughed out loud, "It's so simple, but William is right. The rest of you need to get to the bridge for the ambush. The three of us will draw them out, the rest of you can add to our effectiveness on the ambush."

Walt sneered "With all due respect Colonel, I think you need me."

"No Walt, we don't", Bulloch said in a flat matter of fact tone which conveyed to Walt he was being insubordinate.

There were similar expressions on the faces of the rest of the group, but no one argued it, they knew what William had said had been the truth. They slowly turned and moved back into the forest, doubling around.

Walt turned back around and faced them, "West! Make sure you get them pouring out of that base!" he then galloped off into the forest.

Roost who was the last to leave, tipped his hat. "See you on the other side, Will."

William, Bulloch and King Owen found themselves in the middle of the Piazza; they were in sight of several cameras but had not drawn any attention that they could see. William pulled out his anti-materiel rifle from its sheath on Slingshot's side; he carefully took aim at one of the many satyrs, and squeezed the trigger. The head on the statue exploded, leaving nothing more than a cloud of dust where the head had been.

William smiled broadly "Knock, Knock", he said as he took aim at another one of the satyrs.

William looked at King Owen and Bulloch who were puzzled by his behavior.

"Hey look I know it's stupid, but I want to shoot up some stuff!"

Bulloch laughed and followed suit, shooting at the streetlights.

William stopped for a moment, his mind seeming to be a thousand miles away, "If we live through this, and I don't spend the rest of my life in prison, I hope that if I have children, this will help them not to be ashamed of me," he confided in King Owen. The King smiled and placed his hand on William's shoulder.

"You are very brave, you are selfless and deep down I know you have always had a noble heart. I am proud to call you my friend."

William nodded his appreciation at the kind words as they shook hands. King Owen then turned and joined Bulloch in shooting at windows and streetlights. Even with the streetlights being extinguished, the glow from the approaching dawn grew brighter and the stars dimmer. The trio continued to shoot up the empty town; although it had been no more than a minute, they began to wonder if the base and town was a decoy, when they finally heard the rumble of approaching armor. They started moving into position for the four mile gauntlet they were going to run, when they heard something they had not expected, the roar of tripod motorcycles, they stared in horror at the sight of six centurions speeding in their direction. The noise grew louder and two more centurions emerged from below the hillside they were on, that the Romans had another weapon was something they had not considered. The tripods were armed with standard machine guns, which the remaining horsemen discovered were subject to the restrictor chips as well. But the centurions did not need a weapon to defeat an opponent, their armor made them unbeatable in hand to hand combat, unless the opponent knew that the joint in the neck was the vulnerable part of the suit. William and Bulloch slapped the reigns of their horses and broke into full gallop, King Owen, however, turned and galloped towards the centurions. Like a modern day joust he pulled his sword from its sheath on his back and held it blade down in his hand. He picked the closest centurion to target, and held the sword steady as he closed in; at the last second when the centurion lurched at him, he thrust it into the neck. Owen removed the sword in one continuous motion, a skill acquired through years of swordplay, and the centurion fell back, his tripod speeding off with his body dangling backwards, his hideous face pointed at the sky.

William looked back to see King Owen charging for the next centurion.

"Aw come on! What are you doing?" he said to himself as he watched the ill- advised attack.

William pivoted Slingshot and galloped back in the King's direction. He looked up and noticed two drones bearing down on them; he quickly raised his rifle and shot one and then the other from the sky. Another centurion jumped King Owen from behind knocking him from his horse.

"That's just great!" William fussed to himself as he rode headlong into the battle.

The centurion on top of King Owen had a tight grip on his throat, choking him. King Owen struggled to get air into his lungs; he felt them begin to burn from the lack of oxygen. Panic began to set in and his judgment became less rational. He realized that if he panicked, he would undoubtedly die. He fought against the urge to grab the wrist of the centurion, and instead focused on his sword. He felt on the ground with his hand for the sword, his fingertips brushed the end of the handle, just out of reach. He struggled not to pass out as he watched the centurion raise his fist far behind his head, reading it for a blow that would crush his skull. He stretched with all his strength and grasped the handle, and with all he had left in him, drove the sword into the joint on the centurion's neck. The grasp was released and he drank the air into his lungs, and found the strength to scamper to his feet. King Owens's vision was still somewhat blurry, but he could see well enough to defend himself. His horse had galloped off back into New Pompeii, leaving him on foot. He turned to ready himself for the next attack. He saw another centurion just about to grab him with an outstretched arm, leaning far off the tripod. Suddenly there was a flash in front of him, a large white horse, its rider let out a blood curdling howl and dove into the chest of the centurion. When the horse moved aside, King Owen could clearly see Walt driving a knife into the neck of the centurion. There was a cry from the centurion through the speaker in his helmet and then he went limp. William rushed in and offered

King Owen his hand which he took. He swung King Owen up on the back of Slingshot and galloped off.

Walt had managed to remount his horse and immediately went after another Centurion. Then they saw Morrison come galloping out of the woods and use the same maneuver he had taught Walt. Another centurion sprang from his tripod and hurtled at Morrison's back he ducked and the centurion went headfirst into the rocky ground, knocking him unconscious. Morrison opted to take the empty tripod rather than try and get back on his horse. They could see the long line of tanks and screamers approaching at a rapid clip.

King Owen tapped William on his shoulder "They are definitely trying to kill us William!" he shouted.

William shook his head no, "They are trying to kill you", he said smiling "they don't realize who you are! They have not even taken a shot at me or Bulloch."

"I'm afraid I don't have any identification that says King of England on it!" he said as they watched Morrison and Walt subdue the remaining centurions.

Bulloch rode up next to Walt who was wild eyed, scanning for more centurions, "I thought I ordered you to the bridge."

Walt's eyes flashed around at Bulloch "You did Colonel; once you rode off, I was in charge. I opted we shadow you on the way to the bridge, in case assistance was needed."

"Major Smith, that was an ill- advised stunt worthy of William, but not you. We will have to have a discussion when we are through with the mission." Bulloch said with a stern voice and a stare that seemed to burn.

"Understood Colonel.........."

Walt was cut off as a sniper's bullet ripped through him, spraying blood everywhere, propelling him forward and sending his horse off at a full gallop. William caught a glimpse of Walt's limp body slumped over his horse, his arms dangling and a hole in his Emerson Suit. He started to go after him, but he was stopped as Bulloch grabbed his reins.

"There is nothing we can do for him now, you will be killed or captured if you try and retrieve him. We need to keep focused." Bulloch shouted to William over the din of the approaching armor.

William glanced behind them at the armor; he quickly counted thirty pieces of armor and five armored carriers racing towards them. He reluctantly turned around glancing behind him as he did. He had lost sight of Walt; the horse had carried him off somewhere east of their position. William promised himself that after the battle was over, he would return to retrieve Walt's body. Although he was his biggest rival, he had become a trusted ally, and the reason he had become an effective soldier. He felt the same feeling of helplessness that he experienced watching Drake fall to his death. William realized he had no time to mourn and shook off the feeling, focusing again on the mission. He had deduced the Romans had no intention of killing him so he turned Slingshot around and started shooting at drones; he shot one down as it swooped by, causing it to crash into the ground a few hundred feet in front of him. He missed the next one that swooped by, as he suspected, it did not fire on him. He turned to catch up with Bulloch and Morrison.

They raced towards the ambush, the sound of hooves hitting the dirt and the heavy breathing of horses was almost hypnotic. William realized he was becoming complacent, just like he had in Oklahoma City. He remembered Walt's words to him and focused. The bridge was in sight, the Rio Grande Gorge Bridge straddled the gorge it was named after, six hundred and fifty feet above the bottom. It had stood since it was constructed in September of 1965, on top of two mammoth concrete pylons. There was steel railing on either side of the bridge with respective narrow sidewalks, intended for tourists to peer into the chasm below; there was even a small platform in the middle of the bridge to take pictures of the depths below.

On the opposite side of the gorge, the Renegades had set up for the ambush, hidden in rock formations and behind rest stop buildings just on the other side of the bridge. Their horses had been hidden a few miles up the road from the bridge at an abandoned Ranch; the Renegades had marched back to the bridge where they lay in wait for the dawn ambush. Phoebe had set up nearly a mile away behind two orange sandstone boulders, her barrel wedged between a small space in-between. She had just enough room for her sight to peer through, like the rest; she sat silently anticipating the battle. The twilight had grown brighter, and the sun was not far from rising. William, King Owen, Morrison and Bulloch thundered past the Renegades, the horseshoes making a cracking noise as they hit the asphalt. They continued well past the bridge, drawing the armor onto the other side. They stopped a half-mile down the road from the end of the bridge. They turned to see the armor coming off the other side, lead by a screamer lifting its arm to unleash a sensory barrage on the prey it had been chasing. Suddenly Colonel Coulter's voice cried out "Fire" in his familiar gruff tone. An eruption of gunfire hit the Romans. The Roman personnel carriers' empted their passengers and charged to join the fight.

William was about to ride forward to join in the fight with the rest when he noticed Bulloch looking at the sky, and completely ignoring the skirmish in front of them. It struck him more than odd that Bulloch would be distracted, then he remembered the final cryptic message they received. William looked up to see what he was looking at, King Owen and Morrison followed suit. A moment passed and then there was a faint red glow coming from the southeast. William did not know what the glow was, but King Owen and Morrison immediately recognized it, it was the glow from an approaching scramjet missile, but at a much higher altitude than the ones that struck the Romans in Kansas City. The glow came directly over them and then made a vertical move, climbing straight up; they strained their necks to look at it when Bulloch yelled.

"Look away! Look down! LOOK DOWN!"

They all followed the instructions, unaware of why it was necessary, but trusting Bulloch. They looked down, seconds later a bright white flash lit the entire sky, everything became visible, as if it were noon, and not before sunrise. William shielded his eyes as he turned back to look at it, it was the brightest flash he had ever witnessed. The incandescent glow faded and they looked up to see an electric blue ball of energy crackling and surging forward, surrounded by an eerie red glow stretching in front of it. It lit the sky; all were staring at it, renegade and Roman alike, mesmerized by the balls unearthly glow. Then they noticed the silence, the Romans had stopped shooting and the engines on the armor had fallen silent no longer running. William jumped off Slingshot and walked over to Bulloch whose toothy grin had returned.

"What was that? You know what that was! What the hell was that? You know, don't you?" William thought for a second and then spoke, "Was that a nuke? That was, wasn't it? You cagey old scoundrel, you knew this was coming all along! That's why we had to transmit the data from the field tablet wasn't it?"

Bulloch nodded, but did not speak; he held his tongue like a parent keeping a surprise from a child. The ball was a cloud of gamma ray energy from the nuclear warhead that had detonated fifty miles above them. It had released an electromagnetic pulse that had shorted out all of the Roman's weapons, paralyzing them and leaving them defenseless.

They stood silent, most were confused and frightened. The sun broke over the horizon and bathed the bridge in golden light. The Romans sought to find anything they could to defend themselves, but then stopped. They all heard it at once, a growing hum in the distance, echoing off the mountains and through the gorge. The sound was like a thousand saws combined with angry bees. The legionnaires held their hands up to block the sun, trying to determine where and what the noise was emanating from. The hum grew to a roar, clearly coming from the sound of engines, their pistons racing. The roar grew to a deafening pitch, and then finally they all saw it. Emerging from over a peak to the shock of all who saw it, save Bulloch, was the source of the sound. A squadron of P-51 mustangs, put together as part of a top secret program was barreling above the gorge, and coming straight at the Romans.

The plan was born at George Vernon's farm that day when Bulloch, Vernon, Wright and Hardin had held their secret meeting. The brainchild of Alex Wright, it was a plan the Romans had not expected, nor could have ever imagined. The unconventional plan that the United States had been willing to set off a nuclear weapon, and darken thousands of their own cities, in order to defeat them. William suddenly remembered when he was racing Walt in the Ocala National Forest; he saw the Air Racer Planes practicing a bombing run. At the time William had thought it was a basic training exercise for new pilots, but now he realized it was part of a greater plan.

The planes were streaking toward a large number of Roman troops, whose leaders' arrogance had put them in harm's way. Bulloch looked over at the Bridge and saw General Kravchenko walking down the front, an enraged expression on his face.

"Look, it's General Kravchenko!" Bulloch exclaimed.

Kravchenko broke into a sprint, anticipating what was coming, opting to save himself rather than instruct his cohorts. When the legionnaires saw him running, they all exited their vehicles in order to see what was happening.

The planes from a bygone era had been chosen because of their rudimentary technology, an EMP would not affect their systems- the radios worked on Vacuum tube technology. The Romans, who moments before thought they would finish the Renegades, were now trapped on the bridge, their weapons useless. They stood still, like a stunned boxer about to be knocked out, staring at the punch surging towards him. Suddenly, they realized the peril of their situation, and scrambled in terror. Some remembered their training and raised their disabled weapons in vain; others tried to hide under the screamers or clamber back into the armored personnel carriers, some in despair jumped off the bridge plunging eleven stories to the canyon floor. A panic that had not been seen in the Romans through the entire conflict had set in like a disease. The tool of fear, which Caprera had used so effectively against his enemies, was now being used against his forces. A din, made up of hysterical murmurs and terrified screams filled the air. The fall of the Roman invasion was at hand. William watched in both horror and fascination as a wave of acceptance swept over most of the Roman troops as they turned to face the instruments of their demise.

The first wave of P-51's descended, dropping from the sky, and then splitting into two separate formations, pitched and rolled to either side of the old steel bridge swooping in for the attack. The roar of the planes descending towards their prey grew more deafening with each foot they plummeted. They swept in and delivered their bombs, and rolled and ascended away from the bridge as if it were some kind of aerial ballet. A simultaneous thud and ball of orange flame erupted from both sides of the bridge as the bombs found their mark. Debris and soldiers were cast through the air with equal velocity. Bulloch and William could feel the concussion and scorching wind from the blast rush against them. Another group of planes followed behind the first and repeated the same deadly maneuver. William found he actually felt pity for the Legionnaires; he wondered what kind of horror they felt as they faced their final moments, knowing their death was imminent.

There was a low groan from the old steel girders underneath the bridge, like a great beast that had been mortally wounded and was crying out at its own demise. There was a jerk from the bridge and it dropped a few feet and stopped for a moment, and then a sharp ringing peal as the bridge cracked at both ends. They watched as the bridge sank straight down, Romans and their tanks floating inches above the bridge weightless. Then they disappeared into the gorge; it was silent for a split second and then another thump, louder than the first, shook the ground, followed by a plume of rust colored dust from the floor below. The Renegades cheered in unison. William, Bulloch, Morrison and King Owen hopped up and down cheering and hugging each other. Two more planes swooped in and opened fire on the rest of the Roman forces on the other side of the bridge, sending the survivors fleeing for their lives, running back to the Roman base that was also coming under fire. One of the Mustangs caught the rays from morning sun and its silver chasse reflected it, making it incandescent like the sun itself.

When William saw the plane he spoke to himself under his breath "It looks like an angel," in his mind it was as if the planes had been sent from heaven to hasten their victory.

In a single moment, all the Romans had worked for, all their soldiers had died for, all of Caprera's dreams of grandeur, all were wiped out in that one moment. They had underestimated both American ingenuity and American resolve, and it proved their undoing. The planes circled back over tilting their wings up and down in the universal sign for a wave. Then they saw hundreds more of them, planes from bygone eras filling the sky in all directions. There were saber jets, B-52's and F-105 Thunderchiefs, they filed the sky heading south, like birds migrating in the spring. They were on their way to attack the Romans across the rest of the occupied territories. The Romans would be helpless against the archaic plans without their Stacked Projectile Cannons.

There were countless hours, in secret locations, doing tedious work to resurrect the planes. The skill and innovation that went into planning, restoring, and training to bring the plan to life were unparalleled. Titanium was used in every possible replacement part including the propellers, landing gear and the .50 inch Browning machine guns loaded with armor piercing bullets that the P-51's carried. The lighter weight of titanium allowed the planes to fly farther without re-fueling. This was a secret kept by thousands, patriots who would give the ultimate sacrifice rather than divulge the plan to the enemy. Others endured sadistic torture, crippled for the remainder of their days, but still kept the secret. The Romans were unaware of the fist about to strike them; shadows of America's past glory, returning to restore her future. The planes had come from all over the country, and in fact the globe, rescued from scrap yards, museums and private enthusiasts. King Owen watched them fly off; he thought for the first time since he came to the United States, that his belief that Rome could be defeated was becoming a reality. He knelt down on one knee bowed his head and gave a silent prayer of gratitude. William could not help but to be moved by the sight, and he sincerely hoped that he could help King Owen sit on the throne again. He decided he would volunteer to help the King, if he did not go to prison for the rest of his life.

William jumped on Slingshot and rode to the edge of the gorge, still not believing what he had just seen. He tried to make out the wreckage below without getting too close to the drop-off. His focus changed when the crack of gunfire broke out again, the Renegades were shooting at the Legionnaires clinging to the rock face and some climbing up the hills.

Bulloch galloped up and shouted.

"Cease Fire! Those men are unarmed! Stop shooting!" He galloped right up to the men doing the shooting, "Do you hear me?" The shots died down. "Take them prisoner, we are the good guys, we are Americans! We don't shoot unarmed combatants. That's what they do!" Bulloch bellowed in a rare loss of temper.

Some were surprised by the outburst, but not William who knew how deeply principled Bulloch was. William saw Roost coming out from behind a rock formation where he had been entrenched; he galloped over to see his old friend. Roost and Quesada had taken a route around New Pompeii and straight across the bridge in time to join the ambush. Roost offered up his hand to William at the sight of him riding up. He smiled.

"Damn fine day, Will" as William shook his hand vigorously.

William smiled "Best one I think I ever had."

Roost looked around behind William "Morrison and Walt?" he said anxiously awaiting news of his new friends.

"Walt didn't make it", William's expression showed the bitter sweetness of the day.

Roost shook his head in disgust, "Damn! If it were not for him, we wouldn't be here right now. What happened?" He looked downward and kicked a rock into the gorge watching it skip to the bottom.

William squinted looking at the sun climbing higher and the remnants of the nuclear blast.

"Sniper, he never knew what hit him," William smiled to himself "I am sure he would have rather gone in battle than die of old age in his sleep."

Walt looked up at William, "Yeah, I guess you're right, it's still a lousy break though."

"Phoebe?" William said looking around for her in the crowd.

Roost pointed to the boulders where she had been hiding "Somewhere over there, I am sure she winged a few of them before the bridge ever went," he said with a chuckle, "Go get her, Will."

William rode over to find her clambering to get up the incline she had climbed down. Her eyes looked upward to see William and her face lit up. William jumped off Slingshot and ran down to her. There, just above the boulders she had been hiding behind, they stared at each other for a moment and said nothing, William walked forward and took her by the shoulders and they kissed.

"I can't believe it's over. I am so glad you're alive" Phoebe said still staring in his eyes.

William gave her his best smile "I was never worried for a second," he boasted.

Phoebe laughed and they rode Slingshot to where the rest of the Renegades were still busy celebrating. It had been a long journey for William, he was happy, even though prison was likely in his future; even the tinge of sadness over losing his friends had not taken away the joy he felt. He still wondered though, what was next?

William, Roost and Morrison sat inside the Pompeii Lodge on the brown leather couches brought over from Rome. They stared at the giant logs in the ceiling, the redwood pillars that stretched the entire five stories from the floor to the ceiling, the four giant inverted Tuscan style chandeliers that were designed to light the mustard yellow walls and the catwalks on each floor with redwood log railing. The row of windows on each floor on the east and west side of the building provided enough natural light to see without electricity. A fire had been lit in the giant river stone fireplace in the Throne Room. The lodge was nearly completed, and the weary Renegades had raided the kitchen and bar for anything they could get their hands on. Some of the Renegades had even opted to try and get the plumbing to function.

Everyone snapped to attention at the sight of General George Vernon who had arrived after the previous day's battle. They all watched as he strode into the Throne Room flanked by Generals Alex Wright and Henry Hardin. He walked all the way up to the pedestal that held Caprera's intricately carved throne. All eyes were on him; he did not speak, but instead took a seat in the throne and gave a wry smile. There was a boisterous cheer that followed. He stood up and saluted them and spoke in a loud clear voice:

"Never have I been more proud than I am today. Truly, you are a special group and the nation owes you a debt it will never be able to repay. Know that I am proud of each and every one of you!" William was applauding with the rest of the Renegades when he heard Phoebe behind him.

"Guess what I found" she said.

William turned around expecting to see some prize left by the Romans, but instead saw Walt. His arm was in a sling from his shoulder being shattered, and his head was bandaged from where the thrust of the bullet had sent his forehead into the horn of the saddle. He also had a concussion, but was otherwise unharmed.

"Walt!" he exclaimed.

Walt smiled "That's Major Smith to you!" he growled.

William saluted, "Wow, this is great! I thought you were toast for sure."

Phoebe looked at Walt and smiled "Will, Walt wanted to tell you something himself."

"Colonel Bulloch, Colonel Coulter General Wright and I spoke to the President. He is ready to give you a full pardon."

William smiled and shook his head "No, I can't accept it. I want to face any charges against me."

Walt stared at William for a moment "I respect your sense of Honor William. I will stand behind you."

Bulloch walked up overhearing William's words. He did not try and persuade him to change his mind, he just shook his hand. William was indebted to Bulloch; he took a chance on listening to William when he was still a fugitive. He knew Bulloch could have as easily turned him in and he would have been right to do so, but instead he gave him a chance. He had one question that had been bothering him and he asked Bulloch.

"Who are Mister White and Mister Long?" he said recalling the message on the field tablet.

Bulloch postured himself, taking a stance that he did when he gave serious speeches.

"Mr. White was the warhead that went off this morning; I am sure where the name originated from is clear enough. Mr. Long was a project to ready cities that would be darkened by the EMP to survive. We laid thousands of miles of copper wire so that old fashioned pulse telephones could be used for communications after the EMP went off;

it took thousands of miles of wire, hence the name: Mr. Long. We also started producing thousands of generators to be distributed from the east coast, so that power could be restored to hospitals and first responder facilities. We are of course going to be bringing in food and water. We informed some of the Mayors that we felt we could trust that the EMP was coming, but there were many more we did not dare tell. I'd venture to say the plan worked better than expected."

William was glad Bulloch had explained what the code names meant. William savored the moment, outside of his family; he was with the people he cared most about in the world. The moment may have been fleeting, but William would not have given it up for anything, even his freedom. William was ready to face his future; no matter, he thought, whatever it may be.

# CHAPTER XX

Four months had passed since the Romans had been defeated at Taos; the cleanup against the invaders was going well, there were still pockets of resistance, but they were poorly armed and usually surrendered after a little pressure. Already, towns were starting to be restored, new construction abounded, life, was not back to normal however. Hundreds of thousands of Americans had been sent either to the north part of England as forced laborers, or if they were attractive females, to Rome as personal slaves. America, however, was regaining its footing faster than anyone had expected. The cities that went dark after the EMP went off from Denver to Los Angeles, and Seattle to Dallas, had only minimal problems. Hospitals had to scramble to save patients, and some were lost, but nothing near the numbers that had been projected. Looting was not as widespread as feared and people pulled together when news reached them of the Roman defeat. The most challenging part was restoring the power grid, and providing clean water to the cities. There had been pockets of typhoid due to unsanitary conditions, but those were also quickly dealt with. All in all, life in America had begun to slowly return to normal.

President Braintree had asked Alex Wright to oversee the rebuilding of the occupied territories, which he gladly did on an advisory basis. He retired from the military the day he was asked by the President to take up the job. A return to practicing Law was his first act of civilian life- his second was to be hired as a columnist, as it was one of his true passions. Wright opted to work from his home in Weehawken, New Jersey rather than move to Washington in an official capacity. He wanted to spend more time with his wife and three children. His house overlooked the Hudson River, where he made the walk from the old Victorian home to the ferry that took him to Wall Street twice a week. He was returning from one such trip, the weather was crisp, but not too cold and he enjoyed making the trip.

Early December had not always been as mild, and Christmas lights were just beginning to be strung in the neighborhood. It was a tranquil, rustic scene that seemed to bring more hope since the Romans had been defeated. Still there were obstacles to be overcome and the inevitable confrontation in Europe with Rome, which were never far from his mind. He was still getting used to wearing a suit again after so long in uniform, he was constantly fidgeting with his collar. He was anxious to get home and take his two daughters and son to get a Christmas tree. He had promised his children they would go as soon as he returned. He followed the same path home as he did every night, but there was something different, amiss. He noticed a black sedan parked against the curb in front of his house, the door slowly opening. He saw General Kravchenko emerge, wearing a brown suit and trench coat. He had inserted colored contacts to hide his two different colored eyes. Both the clothes and contacts were part of an emergency kit he had put together in case he had to escape. He had buried the kit in the Santa-Fe National Forest, and had retrieved it as he fled. Now he stood in front of Alex Wright's home, his intent was clear before a word was spoken.

Wright looked at him and shook his head. "Have you come to kill me Yakiv?" he knew the answer to the question but still asked. "Nothing can come if it."

Kravchenko sneered and gave a smirk that took up the right half of his face.

"You have caused me nothing but misery," Kravchenko's English was broken, but understandable, "You write articles about me that cause my wife to leave me and take my children where I can never find them ever again. You defeat me in battle, and you tell me nothing can come of it? My satisfaction can come from it."

Wright did not move, staring straight into Kravchenko's eyes "If you kill me Yakiv, you will make me a cause to rally around. Emperor Caprera will not take you back in; he will despise you, that is, if you make it alive out of this country. The facial recognition software will catch you before you can get on a plane or boat."

"You destroyed me," Kravchenko produced a small revolver from his coat pocket, "and I will destroy you! You have brought me nothing, nothing you understand me, but misery and shame! "

Wright crosses his arms and defiantly stared back at Kravchenko, "I am surprised you are going to shoot me face to face, I expected you would shoot me in the back, which is more your style. I have always been perplexed by the dichotomy of someone who can show valor in battle, and then in the next moment show unparalleled self-absorbed cowardice."

Kravchenko took another step forward "Even now, when your death is imminent, even now you still have to mock me!" his hand shook as he held the gun out at arm's length.

Wright shook his head "I am not going to beg if that is what you want."

"I want you to acknowledge that I have done kind things; that I am a good father."

"I know about the orphans you helped in the Ukraine. I know about what a devoted father you were. What about the infants and toddlers who were slaughtered in this country because they could not be used as slaves? What about the elderly who were allowed to rot and die because they were too old to be useful? What about enemy POW's that were shot and buried in mass graves? What about all the atrocities that you ordered Yakiv? All of that erases any kindness on your part."

"It was war!" Kravchenko said, as he began to shake all over.

"No Yakiv, it was evil, it was disregard for human life. Now you are going to kill me in front of my own home, where my children will see me lying on the sidewalk. There is no valor in that Yakiv. At least have the decency to shoot me somewhere else."

Kravchenko looked at Wright for a moment without speaking, then raised the pistol and fired three shots in rapid succession into Wright's chest. He fell over landing flat on his back, and rolled over to his side before letting out a long breath, and then, with his last thought, he shut his eyes, not wanting his children to see his corpse staring blankly at them. He was dead within a few seconds. Kravchenko walked over and looked at Wright's lifeless body for a moment, before turning and walking quickly into the small park behind him. Joggers and people walking their dogs rushed past him to see where the gunfire had come from. Several more people rushed past him, and then he heard the wails of Wright's children, who had come out to see what the noise was. Kravchenko came to a park bench and sat, gazing at the New York skyline, Wright's words still echoing in his head. He stared out at the city for a few more moments, then raised the gun to his head and pulled the trigger without hesitation.

# CHAPTER XXI

T he Clay County Court House, which had jurisdiction over William's trial had been destroyed in the Roman's raid on western Missouri, the courts In Kansas City had been destroyed as well. All criminal cases that had taken place in Missouri, Kansas and New Mexico were being tried in St. Louis. William's trial was being held in courtroom number thirteen of the old St. Louis Court House, which until the Roman's defeat had been a museum. The venerable old building had been pressed back into service by the lack of usable courtrooms in the region. It was the goal of the President and Congress to clear as many cases related to the war off the docket as possible, with as much rapidity as could be generated during the reconstruction under way. The administration had pushed to get William's trial moved up in appreciation for what he had done for the country.

Power was still being restored and the old building was without electricity. It could have been mistaken for the same era of western expansion when the building was constructed, candles and lamps could be seen in windows at night. The room, which had been restored to its 1910 splendor, was lit by battery-powered lamps. Generators were being used for other parts of the city and the building afforded more use of natural light.

Courtroom thirteen was a combination of Romanesque and Victorian, an irony that did not escape William. The ceiling was a Romanesque dome; the floor was tan and brown marble checkers against white marble squares. A large antique bench sat as the focal point of the court room. Its dark brown wood marked with the nicks and scratches that it acquired in its duty over the decades. A banister with a swinging gate opened to a desk and cubby where the court reporter was shutting his holo-def tablet on and off with high frequency to keep the battery from draining. On either side of the cubby were two rectangular cabinet doors followed by two Corinthian style columns carved into the wood separated by two square cabinet doors. On top of each column was a round protrusion of the desktop, each one contained a Handel lamp topped with an opaque white domical lamp shade. The entire bench was literally and figuratively a museum piece. It was in this quaint, rustic setting, that the trial of the twenty-first century was taking place. The members of the press and the public who had been allowed in the courtroom were all wearing heavy coats and gloves since the heat was not working. Temps had been consistently frigid during the entirety of the trial, yet no one there would have been deterred by the weather. The room was packed with press and those who were there in a show of solidarity with William. Where seats were not filled, people stood shoulder to shoulder, waiting to hear what would happen.

William hands and feet were chained, attached to another chain around his waist. He was wearing a tangerine jumpsuit, and orange jacket; the prosecutor had persuaded the judge that his uniform would put him in too favorable a light. Stories of William's heroics and his transformation from outlaw to hero had become legend. Most of the stories were dispensed to the press by Bulloch on and off the record. William was fortunate to have a deft politician on his side; Bulloch was unparalleled in getting an issue into the public's collective conciseness. He knew where every camera was in a room, and could turn any mundane activity into a photo-op. Now Bulloch sat in the back of the room with William's family. William had not seen his Mother, his brothers or his sister for nearly a decade. When he first made eye contact with his little sister she mouthed the words "thank you."

Bulloch had managed to find William's family among the chaos of re-construction where many families were separated, and desperate to find out if their loved ones had been taken as slaves. William was appreciative of the efforts on his friend's part, and even though Bulloch had worked to clear his name; he wanted to be judged on the merits of the case, which he was. The prosecution had tried William on the charge of first-degree murder, but the jury felt that the charge of second-degree manslaughter was fair. The jury also made a recommendation that William serve no prison time, that he had not intended to kill his stepfather. William knew the truth that he had set out to kill his stepfather, but could not go through with murder, and instead wanted to maim him. The result of his actions was still death. He knew because of his actions during the war, if he had taken the stand and professed he intended to kill his stepfather, the jury would not believe it. In addition, Bulloch had arranged for an endless stream of character witnesses who came forth to testify to William's reformation. Among them was George Vernon, Colonel Coulter, Bulloch and the last column that Alex Wright had written before his murder, in which he extolled William's patriotism, faith and courage; that the war would not have been won without him.

William sat waiting for the judge to enter the courtroom. His eyes scanned the room for Bulloch and his family, but instead he saw Roost and

Cassidy. Cassidy was frail and drawn, because of the snake bites her liver eventually failed and she had undergone a transplant. He was shocked, not because of the operation, Bulloch had relayed information to William about her surgery, but she looked worse than he expected. When they noticed William looking at them they both gave beaming smiles to him. He was glad to see them, and then he saw just past Roost, obscured by the sea of onlookers, was Phoebe, her tiny figure lost in the crowd. William's heart skipped, he had not seen her out of uniform, or with makeup on. He wished for the first time through the entire trial that he would not be sent to prison. Phoebe pushed her way forward through the crowd to take a seat next to Bulloch. She wore a simple long sleeve white blouse and a long heather gray skirt, yet William thought he had never seen such a pleasing sight. Her eyes were cast down and she had a determined look on her face. When she looked up her eyes met William's, she nodded, displaying the quiet strength that made her inner beauty a match for her outer appearance. William was affected by the show of support; he had not realized he had forged such strong friendships. King Owen had visited him in jail just before he, Walt, and Morrison left for Europe. Walt sent word through the King that he admired William for who he had become. Walt had been given permission by General Vernon to assist King Owen in raising an army. All the thoughts William had about anything else became secondary when the judge entered the room. A bald, overweight man with a walrus like grey mustache, he conveyed authority in the way he carried himself. The call of "All rise" was given and he sat behind the antiquated desk. Everyone sat after he did. He then turned to William.

"Will the defendant please stand" he said with piercing eyes.

The murmur in the room went silent when the Judge spoke.

"William Parker West, the situation you present to this court is complex with many gray facets. That being said, the law does not deal in gray areas it deals in facts. The facts are that you have been one of the most notorious criminals in this nation's history, robbing and stealing with the same bravado as a ringmaster in a circus. You made no secret of your love for your own criminal acts, in fact you shared them every chance you got with whatever media outlet was willing to listen to you, and on the holo-def web. All of your public spectacles took place after the death of your stepfather, which occurred due directly to your action. You went at the very least with the intent to maim him, if not to kill him. The circumstances of your sister's rape by your stepfather were heinous, and your anger was not unreasonable, but Mr. West, it is not up to you to take the law into your own hands. You acted as the ultimate authority in deciding your stepfather's fate, which you are not. In doing so you deprived him of his constitutional rights and not in least, his life. The facts of this case are quite clear; you shot your stepfather with the intent of doing great bodily harm. That kind of law may work for the Vasekts Mr. West, but not in this country. The abject lack of respect for this country's law you displayed not only in shooting your stepfather, but also in the stealing and damage of property, speaks to your character. However this court is not blind to the actions of the past few years that you undertook. Those actions also speak to your character. The court is aware of your rescue of lost hikers as a teenager. Thanks to your many friends the court and the country are aware of your uncommon bravery and sacrifice in the service of defending the constitution. A little boy has reached his second birthday because you were willing to ride into heavy gunfire to save him, with no regard to your own safety. The court is also aware that your dedication to the cause of liberty, and the use of your unusual skills was a major factor in gaining intelligence that lead to the defeat of the Romans. These facts have been considered by the court. Mr. West, you are therefore sentenced, as the law allows in a war, to time served in the defense of our nation and a suspended one year probation period. The court, and even the family of your stepfather, finds no fault in your character and the transformation that you have undergone is a sincere and humble one." With that the judge dropped his gavel resulting in a boisterous cheer from those gathered in support of William.

The bailiff came forward, unlocked the handcuffs, and gave William a warm smile. William's family came rushing forward. He hugged his sister and his mother.

"I won't ever do that to you again, I promise." He whispered in his mother's ear.

His mother was a short wide eyed woman in her late fifties with shoulder length dark black hair in which were sparsely interspersed grey strands. Her face bore the lines that came with years of worry about her son, but now she was glowing. She wore a simple black dress that covered her shoulders down to the wrists, and a heavy grey pea coat. His sister was a younger version of his mother, except for her blonde hair and smooth skin;

she too was wearing a pea coat and a blue dress. His sister grasped his hand tightly, tears streaming down her face.

Phoebe came walking up and threw her arms around his neck and embraced him. William pivoted to face his mother.

"Mother this is Phoebe; I plan on making her my wife one day."

William's mother spread her arms wide and gave Phoebe an enthusiastic squeeze.   Bulloch came forward and shook his hand.

"We need to make you more presentable" Bulloch said. William's lawyer re-entered the room holding a bag containing his dress uniform.

Having changed, William stepped out into the crisp clear daylight, wearing his dress uniform. The hundreds of reporters and photographers gathered there lunged forward as a single mass when they spotted him. He was flanked on one side by his family and Phoebe; on the other were Bulloch, Cassidy, Roost and the Renegades. There was a loud din as questions were hurled at him at a rapid rate. William gave his best smile and waved his hands in a downward motion, indicating he could not hear the questions. He pointed at one reporter in front of him that was so bundled up from head to toe in a snow hat and parka that her face was the only flesh visible.

"William, now that you are a free man, what are your plans?"

William stood for a second, displaying his best serious expression, looked up at the sky then to those next to him. He smiled again, and then pushed up the brim of his hat.

"Well, I hear England is a nice place to visit this time of year."

Caprera sat staring at the holo-def screen in front of him, the image of William holding court with the press hovering over his desk. His nostrils flared and his face turned red with rage seeing the American's new face of victory. He leaned forward and barked Charles Fletcher's name at the screen. The next moment Charles image appeared

"What can I do for you Cesar?" Caprera snarled.

"Get me General Severi; we are going to prepare the United Kingdom for aggression. I am going to wipe that smug grin off of that insolent cowboy's face."